Come Rain or Shine

Books by Denise Grover Swank

Rose Gardner Investigations
Family Jewels
For the Birds
Hell in a Handbasket
Up Shute Creek
Come Rain or Shine

Neely Kate Mystery
Trailer Trash
In High Cotton
Dirty Money

Rose Gardner Mysteries
Twenty-Eight and a Half Wishes
Twenty-Nine and a Half Reasons
Thirty and a Half Excuses
Thirty-One and a Half Regrets
Thirty-Two and a Half Complications
Thirty-Three and a Half Shenanigans
Rose and Helena Save Christmas (novella)
Thirty-Four and a Half Predicaments
Thirty-Five and a Half Conspiracies
Thirty-Six and a Half Motives

Magnolia Steele Mystery
Center Stage
Act Two
Call Back
Curtain Call

The Wedding Pact Series
The Substitute
The Player
The Gambler
The Valentine (short story)

Discover Denise's other books at
denisegroverswank.com

Come Rain or Shine

Rose Gardner Investigations #5

Denise Grover Swank

Chapter One

"Today is a good day to die."

I threw back my bedroom curtains and glanced over my shoulder. "You stop talkin' nonsense right now, Violet Mae Beauregard."

"We all know it's comin'," she said with a sigh. "I should at least have a say about the kind of day I'm gonna go out on."

I spun at the waist to face her, lowering my hand to my hip. She'd spent the last two months under my roof, but I still wasn't used to seeing my previously healthy and robust sister looking like a concentration camp victim. I wasn't sure I could ever get used to that. But I held on to my irritation, because she much preferred it to pity. "You already had your say when you refused further treatment. You want to special-order the weather now?"

"Well, of course I do," she said, leaning back on her stack of pillows. "I'm the one dying; I should get to choose the weather."

I turned my attention to the next window. "Why don't I ask Jonah to come by and help you put in that special request."

Jonah Pruitt was the pastor at the New Living Hope Revival Church, and a good friend who had helped me in more ways than

I could count, including counseling me off and on for the past year.

"No need," she said in a smug tone. "Already taken care of."

"You talked to Jonah?" I asked in disbelief.

She gave me a look that suggested I was a fool. "I've got the same line to God as Jonah Pruitt." Then she held up her hands in front of her as though in prayer.

She had a point, and I was actually relieved my sister was still trying to manipulate the world to her liking. Death had her in its jaws, but she was still Violet. The past few days had been rough. Her pain had progressively worsened, and the only thing that seemed to help was a medicated sleep. She'd been on heavy doses of pain medication for the past week, and the hospice nurses had told me she'd need it from now up until the end.

They'd warned me that the end would be here much sooner than I would like.

But today seemed like a good day. Violet was sitting up and had a bit of color in her cheeks.

"Good mornin', Violet," a cheerful voice called out from behind me. "How are we feeling today?"

Carly. Violet had called her one of my "strays" when I'd first brought her to the nursery we co-owned, and there was no denying that my best friend Neely Kate and I had found her stranded on the side of the road next to her broken-down car. We'd known from the beginning that Carly was running from something that scared the crap out of her. I'd given her a job and a room in my four-bedroom home until she could figure out where to go next, but she'd paid me back a hundredfold. She was helping me care for Violet, which had turned into a nearly full-time job over the last week or two as Violet's health deteriorated.

"I've had better days," my sister said. "I was just telling Rose that today would be a good day to die."

"True," Carly said as she started to take Violet's blood pressure with a mechanical device hospice had loaned us. "The weather's perfect today. The sun's supposed to shine all day. But if you haven't keeled over by midafternoon, maybe we could get Joe to help carry you downstairs so you can sit on the front porch and watch the kids play with Muffy. Mike said he'd bring them out to the farm after he finished work."

Violet was silent for a second, then said in a softer voice, "I'd like that."

An eavesdropper would have been horrified by Carly's statement, but Violet loved the way she talked. Carly held her own, throwing back irreverent comments, and she didn't treat my sister like she was made of glass.

I was relieved to hear that Violet's kids were coming to visit, but it hurt knowing we'd gotten to this state with Mike. Up until now, I was the one who'd made the arrangements to get the kids to and from Violet's ex-husband, but he'd obviously gone around me. Mike had become more and more distant over the past few weeks, so while I was relieved the kids were coming, his attitude didn't bode well for my relationship with them after Violet was gone. At least he wasn't as confrontational as he had been before Violet had moved out to the farm. For that, I knew I had James "Skeeter" Malcolm to thank. The last time I'd seen James, he'd promised to see to it that Mike would be more cooperative. But that begged the question: how did my brother-in-law know the king of the Fenton County crime world?

The world may have known him as Skeeter, but he was James to me. We'd neither spoken to, nor seen, each other for two months, but he was never far from my thoughts. I tried to remind myself that I'd known from the beginning he would never be mine. Still, I lay awake at night thinking about him. Wondering where he was and what he was doing. Hoping, above all, he was safe.

The last words he'd spoken to me had implied that he was working undercover for someone. That he was attempting to protect me and clear the way for us to be together, although he hadn't explained what he'd meant. More than anything, I was confused—if he truly loved me, wouldn't he have found a way to reach out? Especially when he knew my sister was dying and I needed the people who loved me more than ever.

There wasn't much time to stew over it, all told. Violet deserved my full attention, and so she got it. The kids had been staying at the farmhouse with us at first, but they'd started spending more time with their father as Violet's illness progressed. While I knew Violet hated missing a single minute of what time she had left with them, I also knew she was relieved they didn't have to see her suffer.

It was a delicate balance between letting Violet be with her children yet sparing them the horror of her illness. I suspected two-year-old Mikey would only have hazy memories of Violet—a snatch of a song she'd sung him, the sense of being loved in the way only a momma could—but six-year-old Ashley…she'd remember everything. Violet always put on a show of cheerfulness whenever the kids were visiting, and then she'd fall into a deep, exhausted sleep after they left.

But Vi's sassiness this morning gave me hope. Maybe we'd have weeks or months rather than days.

"I think Joe has several meetings this afternoon," I said. "But I bet Jed would be more than happy to help."

Violet grinned. "I wouldn't mind Jed Carlisle carryin' me down the stairs like Rhett Butler carryin' Scarlett O'Hara on that grand staircase in *Gone with the Wind*."

"You have that silky robe your Aunt Bessie brought you last week," Carly said as she removed the cuff from Violet's arm and set it in the nightstand drawer. "We'll make sure you're wearing it."

I laughed. Violet was all about the drama, and Carly not only encouraged it but took it to the next level. "I'm pretty sure Rhett carried Scarlett *up* the stairs."

Violet rolled her eyes. "Details."

"You better be careful," Carly teased. "Neely Kate's pretty protective of her man."

"She won't mind," Violet assured her, then looked up at me. "In fact, this plan works perfectly. I invited Neely Kate and Jed for dinner."

That was news to me. "When did you invite them?"

"Yesterday afternoon. I guess I forgot to tell you." It was a perfectly reasonable explanation, but I knew my manipulative sister, and I could see she was up to something.

"Neely Kate's not cooking, is she?" Carly asked, scrunching her nose. "I love that girl, but I can't eat another one of her concoctions."

We all laughed, but Violet's laughter transitioned into a deep cough, a bitter reminder that she was living with me and sleeping in my bed while we waited for her to die. No amount of banter would change that. Nothing about our situation was normal. Violet slept in my bed, day and night, while I slept in a spare bedroom. Joe, Neely Kate's brother and my ex-boyfriend, had moved into the farmhouse to help keep us safe.

Carly picked up a cup from the bedside table and headed into the bathroom to refill it.

Violet's coughing episode settled down, and I forced cheerfulness into my voice as I said, "I'll cook. We haven't had a good dinner party in ages."

"I want lots of people," Violet said.

Carly emerged from the bathroom, handing the cup to Violet. "Sounds fun," Carly said. "I'd love to help. In fact, why don't you leave dinner to me, Rose?" She shot Violet a mock glare. "Any more surprise guests? I figure I'll take your head count and make twice as much food."

"Joe, of course," Violet said. "Now, that man *loves* your cookin'."

"*Violet*," Carly said in a warning tone as she turned to tidy up the room.

"What?" Violet said. "Joe's unattached. *You're* unattached. You should try to snag him. He's probably the best catch you can find around here."

"Second-best catch after that vet, Levi Romano," Carly teased. "Every married woman I've met since arriving in Henryetta has been quick to point that out the moment they find out I'm single." She lifted a brow and shot me a teasing grin. "And we've been over this before. The last thing I need is another man in my life. The last one was a lying asshole, but I would have married him none the wiser if I hadn't overheard him scheming with my father. Obviously, my judgment in men is *not* to be trusted."

Carly had run from her old life after discovering her fiancé had proposed to her as part of an arrangement with her father.

"Then trust *me*," Violet cooed. "I've known Joe for over a year, and they don't make men as good as him. You better snatch him up before someone else does."

"Even if I were interested in Joe," she said, "he's not interested in *me*. He's not interested in *anyone* right now. He's still getting over his last breakup."

Violet released a white-flag-waving sigh. "If you're not interested in Joe, you should take Muffy to the vet. I'm pretty sure I saw her limping."

Muffy, who had taken up residence under the bed, let out a whoof.

"See?" Violet said. "Even Muffy approves."

"Muffy doesn't have a limp," I said.

Violet gave me a look that said *shut up and go along*. She knew I wasn't interested in Levi in the slightest, and I'd told her until I was blue in the face that Joe and I were two entirely different people from the couple who'd fallen in love a year and a half ago. She must have figured it was Carly's turn since I'd passed on both Levi and Joe. She knew I'd been involved with someone, although I hadn't given her any details, and since I'd steadfastly refused her matchmaking attempts, she seemed determined to get at least one person in our household matched up.

I understood all that…so why did I feel a pinprick of jealousy over her trying to hook Carly up with Joe?

"I don't need a man, Violet," Carly said again as she pulled back the bedding, revealing Violet's emaciated frame. "I'm quite content at the moment."

"Content living in a house full of people you didn't even know two months ago, taking care of a dying woman?" Violet asked in disbelief.

Carly helped Violet sit up. "As a matter of fact, yes. I absolutely love it here."

"Don't you miss your family?" Violet asked. This wasn't a new line of questioning from her. Naturally nosy, she hated Carly's reticence about her mysterious past.

"I've already told you that I don't have any family to speak of. My mother died when I was a girl and I don't have any siblings."

"And you're not close to your father. I get it," Violet said as Carly wrapped an arm around her back and pulled her to a sitting position. "But what about friends? Aunts and uncles? Cousins? Who just takes off and leaves their life behind?"

Pain washed over Carly's face, but Violet's attention was on her legs, which she was attempting to swing over the side of the bed.

"Violet," I softly chastised. "Enough."

Violet's feet were now hanging over the edge of the bed, but the effort had cost her. Her breath was coming in pants. "I want to know your story before I die."

All hint of teasing was gone as she held Carly's gaze.

Carly stared at her for several seconds, then grasped her hand in a firm grip and nodded solemnly. "I'll tell you, but not until you're about to enter the pearly gates. You're too far from the end for me to be spilling my story now."

"Deal," Violet said, then slowly slid off the bed until her feet touched the wood floor. Her knees started to buckle, and Carly wrapped an arm around her back to hold her up.

My heart throbbed in my chest. Violet wasn't better. She wasn't going to get better either.

I rushed to her side, intent on helping Carly get her back in bed, but Violet resisted. "I still have to pee."

It took both of us to walk Violet to the toilet. When she finished and we got her back into bed, she said in a matter-of-fact tone, "Rose, will you call hospice and tell them Carly needs help?"

"I don't think we need to do that quite yet," Carly protested. "I just didn't have a good grip on you."

"I can't go to the bathroom without two of you holding me up," she said, her voice breaking. "It's time."

Carly gave me an apologetic look, as though she thought she'd let us down.

"Carly, we all know I'm getting weaker, and goodness knows you've gone above and beyond," Violet said. "You need help, and Rose and Neely Kate have to work."

"The landscaping business has slowed down," I lied. "I can spend more time at home or even work from home. Joe's been letting me use his large-screen laptop for my designs."

"Rose," my sister said in her know-it-all tone. "You know bringing in additional help was always part of the plan." She glanced between Carly and me. "Why are you two fighting this?"

Because bringing in a nurse for even part-time care would mean we were closer to the end than I was willing to admit.

"Just call them, okay?" Violet said, reaching for my hand.

Her bony fingers squeezed my hand, and I tried to blink away tears as I looked down at our joined hands.

"I'll do it," Carly said, her voice sounding strained. "You have a full day ahead of you, Rose. I'll call them."

"That wasn't so hard, now was it?" Violet said as she released me, her hand falling to her lap as though she'd used up all her strength. "I'm feeling tired again. I think I'll take a nap."

"Not yet," Carly said, tucking her in. "You've got some pills to take first."

"I'm going to go catch Joe before he heads out," I said, my eyes still burning with tears, "and let him know attendance is mandatory at our dinner party."

Out in the hall, I took several long seconds to get myself together before I headed downstairs. Muffy sat at my feet, offering her silent support. I squatted down next to her and rubbed her head. "You're a good girl, Muff, and I know you love comin' to work with me, but I need to ask you to do me a favor. I need you to stay with Violet today, okay?"

I knew it was silly, but I knew how much comfort Muffy gave me, and I knew that Violet secretly loved having her around.

Muffy jumped up and rested her chin on my bent knee, releasing a low whine. Then she licked my hand as though to say *you can count on me.*

"Let's go get you a special treat."

She ran down the stairs ahead of me, and I hurried after her, not surprised to find her sitting patiently in front of the counter that held her jar of treats.

Joe was in the kitchen nursing a cup of coffee, studying his laptop screen. When I walked in, he glanced up and nodded to

Muffy. "It's a wonder Muffy hasn't packed on the pounds with all the treats the people in this house give her."

"She deserves every one of them, and she runs it off in the yard," I said. She wolfed down the treat I gave her, then trotted over to the door.

"How's Vi today?" he asked as I walked past him to the back door to let Muffy out.

I headed for the coffee maker and poured myself a cup. "Ornery as ever. She's currently special-ordering the weather for the day she dies."

He chuckled. "That sounds like Vi. I wouldn't be surprised if she managed it somehow." He shook his head. "What's she goin' for? Bright and sunny, or the angst and somber mood of a rainy day?"

"Bright and sunny." Biting my lip, I turned to look at him. "It seems so wrong to joke about it."

"It's how Violet's dealing with it, and frankly, I respect the hell out of it," he said with a soft smile. "She wants to make her exit with grand flair. I wouldn't expect anything less from her."

"She's invited Neely Kate and Jed for dinner tonight, and she wants you here too."

He pushed his chair away from the table. "Is she up to a large dinner party?"

He must have been too thrown at the idea of a get-together to show his usual tension at the mention of Jed. Although he acknowledged that Neely Kate's boyfriend would do anything for her, and was grateful for it, he struggled with the knowledge that Jed had been his criminal adversary's right-hand man.

"Violet's request, or orders are more like it." I poured creamer into my cup, then moved to the table. "Carly said Mike's bringin' the kids over this afternoon."

His brows shot up. "I didn't know they were comin'. Are they spendin' the night?"

"He made the arrangements with Carly, so I don't know either. I suspect we'll have to take them home later. They haven't spent the night in nearly two weeks."

He rubbed the back of his neck. "I'd take them home, but I've got to be at the station later."

"That's all right. I'll get them back to Mike's. Will you be able to make it to dinner?"

"Sure, as long as it's at a reasonable time. The last time Neely Kate cooked, we didn't eat until nearly nine o'clock, and it wasn't even edible."

"Carly's cookin," I said with a grin. "And I expect we'll eat around six. It's a school night for Ashley, so we'll have to get her home by eight thirty." I paused, then said, "Violet wants me to bring in a nurse to help take care of her."

He set his coffee cup on the table. "What brought that on?"

"When Carly helped her get out of bed to pee, she nearly fell. It took the both of us to get her to the toilet and back."

He made a face. "I should probably come home at lunch to help get her out of bed…unless you plan to."

I shook my head. "I've got several appointments today. I won't be back until later this afternoon."

"Is Neely Kate goin' with you?" he asked in a stern tone.

"She's workin' at the nursery, Joe. I'll be fine."

"When was the last time you saw someone following you? The truth."

"I haven't seen any kind of threat for at least a few weeks."

"You sure?" he asked, holding my gaze.

"I wouldn't lie about Denny Carmichael or his men. I let you move in to protect me, Carly, Vi, and the kids, but it looks like we're fine for now."

Denny Carmichael, the biggest drug dealer in Fenton County, and likely all of southern Arkansas, had killed two Sugar Branch police officers who'd attempted to rape and kill me, and now he thought I owed him a favor. Joe didn't know about the favor—he only knew Denny had taken a special interest in me. He'd originally moved into the farmhouse in the hopes that the presence of a sheriff's deputy would dissuade Denny Carmichael from making a move on me. Besides which, it would hopefully throw off anyone who suspected I had a personal relationship with James. So far it had worked—the tongues in town were wagging, all right—and it wasn't such a stretch for people to believe Joe and I had a relationship. We had dated in the past, and he'd moved into my house immediately after breaking up with his girlfriend. The fact that I hadn't seen Denny's men in a while made me wonder if he believed the ruse and had given up.

Did James believe it too?

I'd worried the arrangement would be awkward, but Joe had insisted we could live together as friends, no more or less, and now that he lived with us, I was starting to believe it. I never got the feeling he wanted anything more from me, although I sometimes caught him sneaking glances at me when he thought I wasn't paying attention. It didn't seem like he was pining for me—more like he was having a hard time processing how much I'd changed. Before Joe had moved in, I'd told him about the interactions I'd had with Denny Carmichael—how I'd held my own with him and other criminals with my wits and my gun. Joe knew I wasn't the woman he'd met that chilly May night, and I suspected that was exactly the type of woman he wanted—soft, quiet, and wanting a simple life.

I'd wanted that life then; I had no idea what I wanted now.

I'd outgrown what Joe wanted in a wife. Maybe he was finally willing to let that dream go.

In the beginning, I'd wondered how Joe would fit into a household full of women, but he'd found his place just fine. He seemed to love living with us. Truth be told, I enjoyed his company more than I should, and it was a comfort knowing he was here at night to help watch over us. Neely Kate had moved in with Jed, and I missed her something fierce. While I was getting close to Carly, she'd been focusing more on Violet these past few weeks. Joe was a helping hand, a shoulder to cry on, and a great friend, but lately I couldn't help worrying that I was taking advantage of his kindness...and his singleness. While Carly wasn't interested in him in that way, I realized there were plenty of women who would be—and as long as they thought we were together, Joe would never get another chance at love.

Maybe it was time for him to go.

He studied me for a moment. "If you're tryin' to claim I can move because you're safe now, don't waste your breath. Even if you were, I wouldn't leave unless you kicked me out. I suspect things are about to go from bad to worse with Vi, and I'll feel better all the way around if I'm stayin' here."

"Plus you have nowhere else to go," I teased. The enormity of what he'd done struck me again—he'd given up his rental house so he could move into my first-floor office.

"There *is* that." He grinned, his lopsided boy-next-door grin that smoothed out the stress lines he'd accumulated over the past year.

"I'm grateful for your help," I said. "I don't know how I would have done this without you."

"That's what friends are for." He got to his feet and took his coffee cup to the sink. "I've come up with some plans for redoin' your kitchen. I can show them to you tonight."

"You know I can't afford a new kitchen."

"Just look at the plans, okay?" he asked. "I know I'm not the only one tired of hand-washing and drying dishes for a house full of people."

He had a point. "Yeah, I'll—"

I stopped when we heard someone pounding on the front door.

Joe instantly turned serious. "You expectin' anyone?"

"No."

His face hardened, and he picked up his gun, which was in its holster on the table.

"Stay in the kitchen," he grunted as he headed to the living room.

Like that was going to happen.

Worried that Muffy might attack whomever was on the front porch, I went to the back door and called her in. She instantly made a beeline through the house for the front door and I followed.

Joe had already opened the door, and my heart skipped a beat when I saw a state police officer standing on my front porch.

"I'm lookin' for Rose Gardner," the officer said, then lifted his gaze from Joe to me. "Are you Ms. Gardner?"

I hesitated, stopping a foot behind Joe. "Yes."

He lifted his hand, holding out a large manila envelope. "Ms. Gardner, you've been subpoenaed to appear before a grand jury tomorrow afternoon at two o'clock."

My worst nightmare had just come to pass.

Chapter Two

J oe must have seen how shaken I was at this news. He shut the door and turned to face me.

"We knew this was likely gonna happen," he said softly.

Only we'd expected it to happen weeks ago. When two months had passed without any word about a grand jury, I'd started to hope it wouldn't happen.

"It's going to be okay, Rose. You're not in any trouble. Just be honest."

Which sounded great in theory, but Joe didn't know the whole story.

He narrowed his eyes. "Is there something you didn't tell me about that night?"

By *that night*, he meant the night Denny Carmichael had killed those police officers. *That night* had effectively ended my relationship with James.

"I'm worried about facing Mason." My ex-boyfriend, the special prosecutor assigned by the attorney general, had come back to Fenton County with a mission—to clean out the corruption in the local government, but my relationship with

James had put me in his crosshairs. Neely Kate and I had discovered in our last investigation that the new police force in Sugar Branch wasn't doing any policing. The "officers" were paid by a third party, and they seemed to be paving the way for criminal activity rather than putting a stop to it. I'd reported the matter to Mason, hoping it would wrest his attention away from James. Little did I know, James himself had been fronting the salaries for the very men who had then tried to rape and kill me. They'd been killed instead, and now the whole mess would be spilled out in front of a grand jury.

I couldn't tell Joe everything. He only knew that the officers who'd been killed had attacked me. Like most people, he suspected Denny's involvement.

A grim look washed over Joe's face. "I didn't know they were formin' a grand jury or I would have warned you. In fact, sending a state police officer instead of having my department serve the papers is highly unusual."

"What does that mean?"

"It means he's trying to keep me out of this."

That didn't bode well for any of us. "Why?"

His eyes glittered with fierce determination. "I intend to find out."

This was all too much given everything else I was dealing with. "I need to finish gettin' ready. I need to prepare for my presentation."

"Is that the one with Sonder Tech?" he asked.

An internet-based business relocating to Henryetta had asked us to present them a proposal for their new office building. It was a big job that could help us finish out the year so that we could actually give the workers a holiday bonus in a couple of months. I hated that the grounds guys often went days without work during the slow season.

"Yeah. So I have to make sure I'm prepared. A lot is riding on this, but I also need to stop by the doctor's office to pick up a prescription for Violet."

Joe glanced at his watch and frowned. "It's already eight thirty. Do you want me to pick up the prescription for you?"

"It's pain medication," I said. "A controlled substance. I'm authorized to get it, but I don't think you are."

He laughed. "I think they'd release it to me if you want me to try."

"That's okay," I said. "Carly and I made cookies for the staff last night too. It won't take more than a minute. But thanks for the offer, Joe." I paused. "You've been more help than you know."

A soft look filled his eyes. "Glad to be here."

❧◃

A HALF HOUR LATER, I was in my truck, dressed up more than usual—makeup, hair curled, and wearing a dress for my presentation—heading to town and fretting over the subpoena. I considered calling James to get his opinion on how to handle it, but we hadn't talked since our last meeting at Sinclair Station, when he'd admitted to having hired those two police officers.

If I told the grand jury the truth, I'd implicate James, but the alternative was to commit perjury. I needed legal advice and there was only one person I could trust with all of this information.

Using my voice command, I told my phone to call Carter Hale.

"Rose Gardner," he said as soon as he answered. "Let me guess the reason you're calling."

"You know about the grand jury?" I asked in surprise.

"I make it my business to know everything and anything that has to do with my client."

My stomach churned and I felt like I was about to throw up. Carter seemed to be confirming my suspicion that Mason planned to use the grand jury to take down James. "Do you consider me calling you for advice a conflict of interest with your client?"

He paused. "Perhaps you should come in and pay me a visit."

"I have something I can't reschedule this morning, but I can come by later."

"I have court at ten. How about this afternoon?"

"Just tell me when and I'll clear my schedule."

"Let me get back to you in a little while. I've got several cases today."

"Just as long as I can see you before two tomorrow, I'm good." I would prefer to see him sooner rather than later to hopefully settle my anxiety.

"Do not discuss this with *anyone* until we speak," he said. Then his voice turned gruff. "If you talk, I'll know."

I paused, certain I'd heard him wrong.

"Are you threatening me?" I asked with plenty of attitude.

"My goal, as always, is to protect my client."

"And if you think I'd ever purposely hurt *your client*, then you don't know me at all."

"The legal system has a habit of making friends turn on each other."

"Call me when you have some free time, Carter." I hung up, madder than a wet hornet. How dare he threaten me, and how dare he accuse me of potentially hurting James? Even if we could no longer be together, I cared about him—I loved him. I was the last person who'd hurt him.

I was still fuming when I got to the doctor's office. I sat in my truck for a minute, forcing myself to calm down, then grabbed the plastic storage container of cookies and headed inside.

"Hey, Loretta," I said, stopping at the receptionist's desk. "I got a text that Violet's prescription is ready."

The young woman cringed and glanced over her shoulder toward the exam rooms. "About that"—she slowly turned back around to look at me—"Dr. Newton wants to talk to you first."

I shook my head in confusion. "Who's Dr. Newton?"

"She's replacing Dr. Arnold."

I couldn't hide my shock. "What happened to Dr. Arnold?"

Grimacing, she said, "Something about an extended trip… that's all I know."

That didn't sound good, and from the look on her face, she knew a whole lot more than she was saying.

"*Anyway*," she said with forced cheerfulness. "Dr. Newton read Violet's file and said she'd like to meet with you in person this afternoon if you're available."

I hoped to meet with Carter this afternoon, but Violet trumped all. "Sure, but is everything okay?"

"Dr. Newton's just tryin' to get to know her patients and such. It's a formality." Glancing down at her computer screen, she said, "I have an opening at three."

"Yeah," I said absently, my gaze drifting to the woman walking in the front door with a cat on a leash. She was young, probably about my age, but her long blonde hair was in need of a good brushing, and her clothes were mismatched and inappropriate for the weather—a pair of purple sweatpants and a brown halter top. Bruises covered her upper arms and I went on full alert. It looked like someone had been manhandling her.

Loretta stood and leaned over the chest-high counter. "Wendy, for heaven's sakes! You can't bring your cat in here. I've told you that before. This is a medical office for people."

"I need to see Dr. Arnold and thought he could look at Stinkerbell too. He's got a swollen foot," Wendy said, her eyes wide and wild.

"Dr. Arnold's not here anymore," Loretta said in a stern voice. "And you don't have an appointment."

The news about Dr. Arnold seemed to surprise Wendy as much as it had me, but her reaction time was a good two seconds off. "What happened to Dr. Arnold?"

Loretta pursed her lips and shook her head. "It's a long sordid tale, but the important part is that you don't have an appointment, and neither does Stinkerbell. Dr. Newton's no vet. She's a people doctor."

I was pretty sure the term was family medicine, but I wasn't about to correct her. Maybe that was all Wendy could comprehend just now.

"What am I gonna do about Stinkerbell?" Wendy asked, staring at me like she expected me to have the answer.

The cat tried to jump up onto a waiting room chair, but the leash held him back. He released a loud meow of protest.

"You could take your cat to Dr. Romano," I said in a hopeful tone. "He's a wonderful vet. My dog Muffy loves him." When she looked stumped, I added, "I can give you his number if you like."

"Yeah," she said, her gaze turning to the waiting room TV, which was tuned to a game show. The cat was stretching its leash again, this time trying to reach a potted plant, but she didn't seem to notice.

I put the container of cookies on the counter so I could dig a business card and pen out of my purse, then found Levi's office number on my phone . "He's a great vet," I said, scrawling down the number. "He really loves animals."

Wendy took the card and looked it over. "Rose Gardner. This says you're a private investigator."

"In training," I said, realizing I'd given her the wrong card. "I'm mostly a landscape designer."

"Huh." She dropped the card into her purse, then turned her attention back to the TV, muttering to herself, "Rose bushes have thorns. Rose bushes have thorns."

Loretta frowned at her. "You been drinkin' this morning, Wendy?"

Wendy's neck whipped around so fast I worried she'd hurt herself. "I have *not* been drinkin'. How can you ask me that?"

Loretta cast a glance my direction, then shifted her attention back to Loretta. "You seem...off."

"Why do you think I'm at the doctor's?" she snapped.

Loretta lifted her hands up in surrender and sat down in her seat.

Wendy's attention turned to the plastic container on the counter. "Are those cookies?"

"Uh...yeah," I stammered in surprise. "Chocolate chip."

"Can I have one?"

I hesitated, then gave Wendy a warm smile. "Actually, I made them for the office staff as a thank you for bein' so nice to my sister."

"So can I have one?" she demanded with an outstretched hand.

Wendy was either the bluntest woman I'd ever met or something really *was* wrong with her. Based on the size of her pupils, I was going with the latter. "Uh..."

Loretta snatched the box of cookies from the counter and put them on the desk next to her keyboard. "You need to get goin', Wendy Hartman. You don't have an appointment and neither does your cat."

"But I need more pills. Will the new doctor give them to me?"

Loretta gave her a pointed stare. "Wendy, I'm not in charge of patient care. I simply make appointments and take co-payments."

"I want a cookie," Wendy said, fixated on the cookie container.

"She's not right," I said to Loretta in an undertone. "Maybe someone should tell Dr. Newton and see if she can fit Wendy in."

"I want a cookie," Wendy shouted, banging her hand on the counter.

The cat let out a screech and made a dash for its owner.

Loretta gave her a patient look. "Wendy, why don't you take a seat. I'll see if Dr. Newton can get you an opening." When Wendy tried to reach over the counter, Loretta moved the plastic container to a counter behind her. "I don't think you should be havin' anything to eat or drink until you see Dr. Newton."

"But I want a cookie now!"

"Just give her a damn cookie and shut her up!" an older man shouted from the corner of the waiting room. "She's ruining the show!" From what I could tell, there wasn't much to be ruined. A woman had just won a lifetime supply of American cheese after successfully guessing how many slices were in a ten-foot-tall stack.

"Wendy," Loretta said, drawing out her name. "I think we need to just wait to see Dr. Newton, okay?"

While I really did need to get to the office to prepare for my presentation, I didn't feel comfortable leaving Wendy alone like this. Not when she so clearly wasn't well. I wrapped an arm around her shoulders and turned her toward the waiting room. "Why don't we go sit down? I'll wait with you."

She let me lead her to a seat perpendicular to the grumpy older man and his wife, and across from a woman with a school-aged boy. The man was once again riveted on the game show, and his wife had her nose buried in a large-print *Reader's Digest*. The mother tried to wrap her arm around her boy's back, but he shoved her off. With a harrumph, she glared at the cat.

"You can't have that cat in here," she snapped.

Wendy gave her a belligerent look and glanced around the room. "I don't see any signs sayin' I can't."

"It's just plain common sense," the mother said.

"Maybe I ain't got no common sense," Wendy drawled out in a slur, making me wonder if she *had* been drinking…or taking drugs.

I leaned closer to the woman next to me. "Wendy, we should probably take Stinkerbell out to the car."

Wendy's eyes widened. "Stinkerbell's here?"

"He's at your damn feet!" the older man shouted.

His wife startled and looked up from her reading. "Huh?"

The mother shot the older man a glare as she placed her hands over her son's ears. "Watch your language. Little pitchers have big ears."

"Oh, come on," the boy said, shoving her hands away. "That's bullshit. You and dad talk a hell of a lot worse than that."

Wendy burst out laughing, while the older woman returned to her reading, tuning all of us out again.

The mother shot Wendy a dark look. "Are you *laughing* at me?"

Wendy was laughing too hard to answer.

"What's so damn funny?" the older man asked me.

"Language!" the mother shouted.

As Wendy continued laughing, I started having second thoughts about getting involved. I had enough messes of my own without taking on anyone else's.

"You're completely off your rocker," the mother said, pointing her finger at Wendy. "You've got a one-way ticket to crazy town. I've seen you at Burger Shack before. You're lucky I don't report you to your boss."

Wendy stiffened. "I'm not crazy."

"And get your mangy cat out of here," the woman added, waving her finger at the cat, who was now scratching one of the waiting room chairs.

"What cat?" Wendy said.

"She's crazy!" the mother shouted at the front desk. I had started to back away, hoping to extricate myself from the situation, when the cat launched itself at the mother's bright red purse on the floor, attacking it like it was in a fight for its life.

It was no surprise, really—it was shaped like a dog.

The woman tried to kick the animal away, and Wendy released the cat's leash and grabbed the purse, holding it tight and rocking back and forth as she cooed, "There you are, Mr. Wiggles."

"I thought you said your cat's name is Stinkerbell," the old man said in confusion.

His wife looked up for a moment, lowering her magazine. "*What?*"

"She's stealing my purse!" the mother shouted.

Reluctantly, I inched closer to Wendy and leaned over. "Wendy, why don't you give this nice lady her purse back?"

"She ain't a lady."

I would have gone with she wasn't nice, but Wendy wasn't all there right now.

The mother leaned forward and grabbed the strap of her purse and tugged, but Wendy merely tightened her grip on it. "I'll die before I let you have my purse! It cost me $39.99 on Etsy and an additional $5 for the ears and tail!"

Sure enough, there were floppy ears sticking out above the dog's face...which Stinkerbell was now trying to rip off the bag. The woman gave a hard jerk and sent the cat flipping backward end over end.

The cat let out a screech loud enough to wake the dead and bolted for the potted plant, the leash trailing behind him.

"Everybody, calm down!" Loretta shouted as she leaned over the counter, but Wendy and the mother continued their tug-of-war, now getting to their feet. The contents of the bag flew all over the room, a tube of lipstick smacking the older woman in the forehead, but she absently brushed her head as she continued to read, paying no attention to the melee in front of her.

The boy grabbed his mother's phone from the seat and started videotaping the escapade with a huge smile.

The older man had abandoned the game show for the more interesting competition unfolding in front of him. "My money's on the crazy woman. She's scrappy."

There was no way in tarnation I was betting against Wendy.

The mother tilted sideways and both women tumbled into the chairs. Neither had tried to assault the other—the purse was taking all the damage. One of the ears now lay on the floor, and something long and skinny, which I presumed to be the tail I hadn't seen before, was whipping around between them.

I considered trying to separate them, but shrapnel was still flying out of the purse. Pennies. Loose gum. Half of a broken action figure. I turned to Loretta with a pleading look, but she was already on the phone. She glanced up at me, pointing to the receiver. "Don't you worry. The Henryetta police are on their way."

Great. My favorite people.

Chapter Three

Why hadn't I just left? Now I wouldn't have the time I needed to prepare for my meeting at ten. Instead, I'd be giving a statement to Henryetta's finest.

I pulled out my phone and called Joe, but it went to voice mail. Crap. Loretta was still standing by the door, watching the brawl. Several other office staff stood behind her in shock, but no one intervened. The two women were now rolling around on the carpeted floor, which I supposed was the safest place for them. They still hadn't tried to hurt one another, although there was plenty of shouting. The police were on their way, so I supposed the safest thing for all concerned was to let them go at it.

"Loretta, I've really got to go," I pleaded, "especially if I'm gonna come back and meet Dr. Newton this afternoon."

She gave me a distracted wave. "You scoot along," she said. "I've got this covered."

I almost told her that I'd likely need to give a statement. God knew, I'd witnessed enough altercations to have learned that lesson. But the police could track me down to get it…heavens knew the sheriff's department had done it a time or two.

"Thanks," I said. "I owe you."

She leaned closer and grinned. "Hey, I had one of your cookies. I think I'm the one who owes *you*."

I hurried out the door and to my car. I'd just pulled out of the lot when I saw a Henryetta police car headed in my direction, and I was thankful I'd gotten out in time.

The downtown square wasn't very busy, so I found a parking spot right in front of RBW Landscaping. But I couldn't ignore the allure of the Daily Grind. Violet's illness had taken its toll on me, and I found myself exhausted more often than not lately. After the debacle at the doctor's office, caffeine was a must.

The usual morning crowd at the coffee shop had thinned out, and I was relieved to see only one person in line in front of me. It made me feel less guilty about wasting time I could have used to review my presentation.

Thankfully, the man in front of me just ordered a coffee with room for cream, so I placed my order of a mocha with an extra shot and a blueberry muffin within seconds of entering the shop.

As I finished paying, I heard a voice I recognized say, "What does he see in her? She's a pathetic mess. Look at her." A slight I was obviously meant to hear.

Sure enough, a slight turn of my head brought Dena Breene into view. She was cradling a cup of coffee. Margi Romano, Levi's sister, sat across from her with her own coffee, but her face was flushed.

"Dena!" Margi whispered in admonishment when she saw that I was facing them.

But Dena didn't back down, giving me a flat-out hateful glare. "You just couldn't stand it that someone else wanted a man you'd thrown away. You had to snatch him back."

I could understand why she saw it that way, and while I sympathized, I was confident that I wasn't to blame for her breakup with Joe...at least not entirely. Dena had been controlling, so much so Neely Kate had sat Joe down for a come-to-Jesus meeting over the way he was letting Dena interfere with their fledgling sibling relationship.

"Do you have a magic hoo-ha?" Dena asked, getting to her feet. "How many men have you been through in this town? Joe, Levi, Mason. Who else?"

I gasped in shock but didn't say a word. I had no beef with Dena, although she clearly still had one with me.

Dena propped a hand on her hip. "If I go after Mason Deveraux, will you drop Joe like a hot potato and go after him next?"

"Dena!" Tony, the barista, called out. "Watch your mouth. We won't stand by that kind of talk in here."

"Then maybe you shouldn't be servin' sluts," Dena said in a snide tone.

Tony handed me my order. "I'm sorry, Rose." Then he put both hands on the counter and leaned forward, shooting her a glare. "Dena, I'm gonna have to ask you to leave."

"Are you *kiddin'* me?" she demanded. "She's the man-stealin' whore, and you're kickin' *me* out?"

"That's okay," I said with a tight smile. "I'm leavin', so let her stay."

I hurried out the front door, clutching my coffee and the bag with my muffin. About a half minute later, I was in front of my office, fumbling to get my keys out of my purse, when I heard a woman say, "I'm really sorry about what happened back there."

I turned in surprise to see Margi.

She took the coffee cup and pastry bag from my hands. "Let me help."

I shook my head, focusing on inserting the key in the lock. "Thanks, but I'm sure Dena won't appreciate you helpin' *or* apologizin'."

"Dena's like a stubborn donkey who doesn't know when to let something go."

Her warm tone soothed my defensiveness, and I couldn't help but smile. "Are you callin' Dena an ass?"

She laughed, and it was so pure and genuine the rest of my wariness faded. "If the shoe fits."

I took a breath and pushed the door open. "I'm sorry. I shouldn't have said that. She's your friend."

"Only because I don't have many friends here in Henryetta yet," she said, sounding embarrassed. "You know, I think the way a person reacts to conflict says something about their character. I admire the way you dealt with that."

"Maybe I just recognize I'm guilty as charged," I said slyly, dropping my keys in my purse and turning to face her.

"Levi doesn't have a bad word to say about you." The earnest look in her bright blue eyes took me by surprise. "I was wrong to treat you so poorly when we met before. I didn't know the full story—I just knew that my brother was crazy about you and you dumped him. He explained the situation to me later. He said you weren't ready to date yet and he pursued you anyway. I'm sorry for how I acted."

I gave her a warm smile. "You were just bein' a good sister."

"You could have told me off, yet you didn't. Just like you didn't put Dena in her place. That says a lot about you."

I blushed and glanced down at the sidewalk before lifting my gaze. "I've had my fair share of public verbal confrontations," I admitted, "but truth be told, I realized you were standing up for your brother, and I respect that. Just like I realize that Dena really liked Joe and is lookin' for a scapegoat to blame for their breakup."

"She's a fool if she thinks Joe moved in with you because you two are back together."

My mouth parted in shock and I lifted a hand to brush a few stray hairs off my forehead. "What makes you say that?"

"You and Joe have never gone on a single date since he's moved in. And the few times I've seen you out together, I never once got the feeling that you two were a couple in love."

I wasn't sure what to say to that. Was it a bad thing if people figured out we weren't romantically linked?

She cringed. "I'm so sorry. I overstepped my bounds. I haven't told anyone my suspicions—it's just something I noticed." Her face pinkened. "What I'm trying to say—and doing a piss-poor job of—is that Dena's a fool to think you broke up her and Joe. She took care of that one all on her own. Joe's just helping out his friends."

"If you're friends with Dena, should you be sayin' all of that?"

Margi released a small laugh. "I told her pretty much the same thing before I ran after you, so don't go thinking I make a habit of talking about my friends behind their back." Then she turned serious. "This is all kinds of awkward, but would you consider meeting me for coffee sometime?"

My life was a hot mess, but I could see that Margi was lonely and I was a firm believer that you couldn't have too many friends. Especially after I'd gone so many years without any. Plus I knew she was dating my friend Randy Miller, a Fenton County deputy, and I considered him a good judge of character. "Yeah," I said softly. "I'd like that."

"Would it be okay if I asked Levi to give me your number so I could text you?"

I blinked. "Yeah…sure. Or I can give it to you now."

"That's okay," she said, taking a step backward. "I don't have my phone handy." She turned to leave, then spun back. "Hey. I heard you have an empty horse pasture."

How had she heard that? Had I told Levi? Or maybe Randy had mentioned it. "Uh…yeah. My birth mother had horses when she was growing up."

"I'm not sure if you know, but I'm working with horses—boarding and such—and we're currently full. Occasionally we'll get word about a horse needing rescue, and I hate turning them down."

I made a face. "I don't know the first thing about takin' care of horses."

"That's okay," she said. "You wouldn't have to. I'd come and take care of them, and they wouldn't be there long term. Maybe a few weeks at the most."

"I'm not sure my barn can house horses. There aren't any stalls."

"Can I come out and look around anyway?" she asked. "You can always tell me it won't work, but at least let me see if you've got adequate facilities."

It was hard to turn down an animal in need. Muffy had been a rescue, but she'd been the one to rescue me, both physically and emotionally. "I guess it wouldn't hurt for you to check it out."

"Great!" she said with a bright smile. "Let me know when would be convenient for you."

"Tonight won't work," I said. "We're havin' a big family dinner, but I might be free tomorrow morning."

"Thank you, Rose," she said with a warm smile.

I walked into the office, grateful Margi had helped me calm down after my encounter with Dena, but I still felt bad about the whole thing. I hated that Dena couldn't move on, but I reminded myself that was up to her, not me.

I turned on my computer as I took a bite of my muffin. The proposal was ready. I just needed to print off a few copies, then run through everything I planned to say. I'd intended to go over everything the previous afternoon, but I'd had to leave early to pick up a prescription dietary supplement drink for Violet. Over the last few weeks, she'd been feeling nauseous and hadn't been eating much, so her doctor—well, her previous doctor—had suggested she start drinking the high-calorie supplement.

After a few bites, my muffin churned in my stomach. I chalked it up to a side effect of the anxiety that had wreaked havoc on my own digestive system over the last month or so, causing me to lose six pounds. But my body was finally adjusting to the stress, because I'd started feeling better over the last week, enough so to eat entire meals. Nevertheless, I gave up on the muffin and focused on preparing the proposal copies.

I was sitting at my desk, clipping the printed copies together, when the back door opened.

I whipped around to face my intruder, but it was only Bruce Wayne.

Placing a hand on my chest, I sank into my chair. "You scared me half to death. What are you doin' sneakin' in through the back?"

He cringed. "Sorry. I didn't mean to scare you. The last time I came in through the front, a woman pulled me aside and asked me half a dozen questions about gardening, so I figured I'd…"

I chuckled. "Get out of dealing with people by slippin' in through the back."

He nodded, offering no further explanation. Bruce Wayne had come a long way since we'd first started working together a year ago, but he would never be an extrovert. He still felt uncomfortable around strangers. After years of being beaten down by everyone around him, he had trouble believing he was worthy of other people's time and attention. Those of us who loved him tried to show him otherwise, but I'd been beaten down too, so I understood how hard it was to break free from those chains.

"I'm surprised to see you at all," I said. While Bruce Wayne had his own desk and computer, he was rarely in the office.

"I need to pick up the updated plant list for the job we're workin'."

I groaned. "Bruce Wayne, I'm so sorry! I plum forgot."

"No worries, Rose. Violet's more important, and besides, I was happy for the chance to see you," he said with a soft smile. He rested his butt on the edge of his desk and studied me. "How's she doin'?"

I sucked in a breath, willing myself not to cry. "Not so great. We're askin' for a day nurse to come in and help Carly." I gave him a sad smile. "Part of me feels guilty for not bein' there. I should be the one helpin' her." I'd stayed home for several days over the last few weeks, but work had been steadily piling up at the office. It seemed awful to think about a thing like paperwork when Violet was so ill, yet someone had to pay the bills. She wasn't the only one relying on me.

"Rose," he said, leaning forward. "You can take more time off. We can move Neely Kate back here. I'm sure Anna and Maeve won't mind workin' extra."

I shook my head with a bitter laugh. "Violet wouldn't allow it anyway. She said having me there all the time was like havin' a vulture circling over a dying animal. She made me come back to work."

Bruce Wayne burst out laughing. "Your sister is somethin' else."

I grinned. "That she is." Then I turned serious. "I have that presentation with Sonder Tech this morning. Do you mind if I run through it with you? Do you have time?"

"This is a huge job. I'll make time."

I had him sit at his desk, and then I laid out the plans and ran through my presentation, showing him one of the copies of my proposal. When I finished, he made a few suggestions, all of which would make for a better pitch.

"You should do this with me," I said as I rolled up the plans. "We're partners."

He shook his head, looking adamant. *"No, thank you.* I like workin' outside and lettin' you deal with all the business aspects."

"You're smarter about business than you give yourself credit for, Bruce Wayne. We wouldn't be doin' nearly as well if you hadn't had the foresight to purchase some of our equipment at that auction last year."

"Nevertheless," he said. "You're the perfect face for RBW. I'll stick with the grunt work."

"You've got just as much to lose as I do if I screw this up," I protested.

He beamed at me. "You've got this, Rose. Just do your best, and if they say no…" He shrugged. "No big deal. It's not like we're losin' money if we don't get the job. We only stand to gain."

"Still…"

"There will be plenty of other jobs, Rose. Don't sweat it." His phone buzzed in the holder on his belt, and he pulled it off and looked at the screen. He declined the call but got to his feet. "I've gotta get back to the job site, but I'm not worried in the least. You're gonna wow 'em. No doubt about it. If we don't get it, it won't be because you messed up."

"Thanks, Bruce Wayne. I'm glad you have faith in me."

He laughed. "And I'm glad you have faith in me." He headed for the back door, but he turned back once more before leaving. "Just remember, if you need more time off, we'll make it work, okay?"

"Yeah. Thanks."

Bruce Wayne left and I slipped the rolled-up plans into a cardboard tube and slid the copies of the proposal into a folder. I was reaching for my purse, ready to get up and go, when the bell on the office door clanged.

"I'm sorry," I said, without looking up. "I'm about to leave, but I'll be back this afternoon if you want to make an appointment to discuss your landscapin'."

"Good thing I ain't interested in any landscapin'," a man said in a gruff voice, and my heart kickstarted as I glanced up at a man I didn't recognize. From the look on his face, he probably wasn't someone I *wanted* to recognize. He wore a dark T-shirt and jeans. A scruffy beard covered most of his face and hung down to his chest. His dark beady eyes were so cold a chill went down my spine.

He turned to lock the front door.

I took advantage of his distraction to grab my gun out of my purse and set it on my lap. I suspected I knew who had sent him, but I needed to find out for certain.

"Since you seem determined to stay," I said in a firm voice, "what can I do for you, Mr....?"

"You don't need to know my name," he said as he took several steps toward me. "You just need to keep your mouth shut."

I knew I should be scared, and I was, but it had been one heck of a morning already and it wasn't even ten a.m. If this man made me late for the most important meeting I'd had in months... I was ticked.

"If you don't want to hear me talk," I said in a flippant tone, "then maybe you should turn around and march on out of here." I waved my free hand toward the door.

His jaw worked and his eyes hardened as he slipped a large hunting knife out of its sheath. "You've got a smart mouth."

I was done with being threatened. I stood and pointed my gun at his chest. "And a smart brain to go along with it. If you've got a message to deliver, spit it out, then get the heck out of here."

A look of pure hatred filled his eyes and his fingers tightened around the hilt of his blade. "You're one lucky bitch. If I had my way, you'd be dead, but the boss says he's got plans for you."

"And who might your boss be?" He didn't need to tell me. Denny might as well give out uniforms, because all his guys had the same rough look. I shouldn't be surprised he'd sent one of his men to check up on me. The subpoena had shaken everything up. Skeeter Malcolm wasn't the only man who could be hung out to dry by my testimony.

"Someone with a vested interest in what you have to say tomorrow afternoon. This is your friendly reminder to keep your mouth shut."

"Friendly?" I asked. "I'd sure hate to see *unfriendly*."

"Trust me, you will if you say the wrong thing."

I gave him a withering glare. "You've said your piece, now get out."

He pointed his knife toward me. "You're a little too uppity for my likin'. I'd love nothin' more than to put you in your place."

"Then lucky me that your boss would string you up for messin' with the merchandise before he's used it. Now *get out*."

If Denny Carmichael hadn't put this guy on a short leash, I suspected he would have tried to give me a scar to remember him by, gun or no gun. His face turned bright red and he picked up one of the chairs in front of my desk and threw it out the front window. The entire pane of glass shattered into pieces, some scattering across the wood floor but most ending up on the sidewalk.

"That was incredibly stupid," I said, my heart racing. "Now I have to explain that mess to a whole lot of people, and they're gonna want to know who's been threatenin' me."

He released a loud roar of frustration, likely realizing he'd screwed up, climbed out through the busted window, and stomped off in the opposite direction of the courthouse.

With shaking hands, I set the gun on my desk and took a second to calm down. I still had a presentation to do, and I couldn't let Denny's threat put a damper on that. We needed this job too much.

But what was I going to do about the busted window and the chair?

Not a damn thing.

I returned the gun to my purse, put the reports in my tote, then grabbed the tube and walked out through the busted window.

A passerby stood on the sidewalk, staring gape-mouthed at the broken glass and chair, then lifted his gaze to me in shock.

"Have a good day," I said, walking over to the truck. Moments later, I was on the road, using my voice command to call Jed as I headed out toward my appointment.

"Hey, Rose. What's up?"

"I need you to text me Denny Carmichael's number." I was proud of myself for the level tone of my voice.

He was quiet for so long I was sure he'd hung up. Finally, he choked out, "Why?"

"It doesn't matter why," I said, still sounding reasonable. "Just give me the number."

"Has he made contact?"

I debated whether to tell him about Carmichael's goon showing up, but I didn't want to deal with the fallout right now. I needed to be centered and focused for my presentation. "Just give me the number, Jed," I insisted, "or I'll drive to his property on my own. I know where to find him, remember?"

"Where are you?" His voice sounded strangled.

"I'm on my way to the Sonder Tech presentation, but I need Carmichael's number like two seconds ago."

"I'll give it to you after you tell me what this is all about."

"I'll tell you tonight." When he didn't respond, I said, "I'm not gonna do anything stupid, Jed. I need you to trust me."

I was certain he was going to say no, but he said, "I'm gonna trust that you know what you're doin', Rose. Call me if you run into any trouble." He hung up, and my phone's text alert went off seconds later.

Although the last thing I wanted to do was talk to Denny, I knew the longer I went without contacting him, the weaker I'd appear.

But who said I had to call him? I pulled over to the side of the road and sent him a text. *Your buddy left a heck of a mess on the sidewalk outside of my office. Too bad it's directly across from the county courthouse and the special prosecutor will be sure to ask me about it tomorrow.*

I pulled back onto the road, knowing that a response was coming, so I wasn't surprised when my phone rang seconds later from the same number. I put him on speaker phone.

"Are you threatening me, Rose Gardner?" Denny Carmichael asked in a low growl.

"Threatening *you?*" I demanded. "What about your guy who showed up in my office, brandished a knife, then threw a hissy fit before tossing my office chair out the window?"

He hesitated before he said, "That was just a friendly reminder."

His tone was slightly off, which suggested he hadn't known about his goon's fit.

"A reminder to keep your name out of my grand jury testimony," I said dryly. "Consider this to be *my* friendly suggestion for you to get someone to clean up the mess, because I refuse to take responsibility for it. I don't even know how to explain it."

"You'll think of something," he said.

"The hell I will. I've got enough malarkey to deal with without adding this nonsense to the mess." I took a breath. "You best figure out how to deal with this before someone shows up askin' questions."

"You think you can just call me up and threaten me?" he asked, his voice rising. "I know where you live. And don't think that sheriff deputy livin' with you can protect you. Just remember that when you're testifying tomorrow."

My breath stuck in my lungs but only for a moment. The helplessness I'd felt this last month, watching my sister step closer and closer to death, knowing the man I loved was out there risking himself in ways I didn't understand, erupted into a powerful anger. "Don't forget that goes both ways, Denny Carmichael. I know where *you* live and work. I took Daniel Crocker down, and I can take you down too."

I could hear him breathing on the other side of the phone before he said, "Be careful what you threaten, Lady."

"Likewise, Mr. Carmichael." Then I hung up.

Well, crap. I was pretty sure I'd just declared war on the drug czar of southern Arkansas.

Chapter
Four

I felt amazingly calm by the time I pulled into the parking lot of the office for Sonder Tech. I was five minutes early, and I considered taking a few moments to cleanse my thoughts of Denny, but I figured I was better off walking in a few minutes early to make a good impression.

Sonder Tech was taking over an old building that had once been an insurance office, and they were in the process of giving it a face-lift. As part of the redesign, they wanted a new landscape design, which was really a misnomer considering the building didn't have much landscaping other than a few dead bushes and a patch of dandelions on the west side. It reminded me of the big job that had first launched us into the landscaping business—the revitalization of Jonah's church.

When I walked in the front door, a young woman behind a sleek receptionist desk looked up from her computer screen and greeted me with a huge smile. "Rose?"

I smiled back. "Yes."

"I'm Rebecca, your contact up to now. Stewart and Chris are already in the conference room waiting for you."

My nerves rose up again, and a wave of nausea hit me, but I took a breath and kept my smile plastered on my face. "Lead the way. I'm eager to show you what I came up with."

I followed Rebecca down a short hall and into a conference room with a new whiteboard on the wall and windows overlooking the parking lot. Two men in polo shirts were sitting at the table, talking about some type of installation, but they stopped their conversation and stood when we walked in.

"Hi," I said. "I'm Rose Gardner with RBW Landscaping. Thank you for inviting me to create a design for your property."

They all settled in their chairs, and we made small talk about how much they loved the quaintness of Henryetta and the charming downtown—which was how they'd found me—and by the time we'd talked for nearly five minutes, I was relieved to discover I'd calmed down again.

"I'm so thrilled you love Henryetta," I said, wondering if they'd experienced the same town I had, but then to an outsider, I was sure it looked lovely. "I hope you love my plans for your property just as much."

I spent the next ten minutes showing them my designs. When I finished, I handed out the proposals and we went through the numbers. They wanted clarification on a couple of areas, and when I was satisfied they understood everything, I said, "We'd love to work on this project with you, and we can definitely fit your install into our schedule. Just let me know when you've made your decision."

Stewart, a gentleman in his forties, stood and said, "I, for one, love what I see here. We'll discuss it and get back to you within a few days. Thank you, Rose."

"If you have any questions after I leave, feel free to call," I said as I moved toward the door.

"I'll walk you out." Stewart followed me out of the conference room and down the hall.

Nerves had gotten the better of me earlier, so I hadn't noticed the changes they'd made to the building. For the most part, it appeared the updates were done, and they were setting up offices.

I gestured toward a room decorated in mid-century modern style. "This looks so great. I came here as a girl when my mother paid a visit to her insurance agent, and it's completely different."

"Thanks," he said. "We got the property for a steal, which gave us a higher budget for renovations."

"And landscaping," I said. "You'd be amazed at how many people underestimate the curb appeal good landscaping can provide."

"Maybe things are different here in Henryetta," he said, "but in Dallas we understand the importance of curb appeal."

My heart stuttered. "You're moving here from Dallas?"

"Yeah," he said. "I thought Rebecca told you that we're in the process of opening a new branch here."

If Rebecca had told me, I would have remembered. The crime syndicate that was interested in Neely Kate was based in Dallas. It seemed like a strange coincidence, but coincidences did happen. Carly was from Dallas, after all, and although we'd initially worried she might have some connection to the Hardshaw Group, that worry had quickly faded. Besides, surely they wouldn't uproot an entire business on account of my best friend.

"No," I said. "I only knew that y'all were relocating from somewhere else. In fact, she never told me what y'all do exactly. She said it was an internet-based business."

He smiled at me as we came to a stop at the front door. "That's right."

"What brought y'all to Henryetta?" I said, trying to sound light and breezy. "Most people move out not in."

He laughed. "I suspect it's a case of the grass being greener someplace else. There's a lot less overhead here in Henryetta. Plus many companies are moving out of the cities and into rural areas. Properties are cheaper, taxes are less, and there's often an eager underemployed workforce."

"How many people do you think you'll employ?" I asked. I wasn't sure about the first two points on his list, but Fenton County surely fit the last one.

"We'll bring some of our employees with us, but we'll need at least two or three." His grin turned teasing. "You happen to be lookin' for a side job, Rose? I know landscaping slows down in the winter."

"No, but I know plenty of people who are," I fudged. "What kind of qualifications are you lookin' for?"

"We'll need some office staff and probably a computer programmer. We're not entirely sure yet. Know anyone who might be interested in either position?"

"Perhaps for the office staff," I said. "Even if we don't get the landscaping job, I'd appreciate it if y'all would let me know when you're hiring so I can tell my friend."

He leaned closer, his eyes lighting up. "Between you and me, you've got the job. The discussion is only a formality."

I beamed up at him. "Thanks for taking me into your confidence. I look forward to hearing from you."

On the way back to the office, I took a detour to the nursery Violet and I co-owned with Joe. Neely Kate was filling in for Violet since they were busy with all the fall plants sales and pumpkins, but I hoped Maeve, the nursery's manager, would be able to give her an early lunch break.

Neely Kate was outside stacking a pile of pumpkins when I pulled into the parking lot. She had on a pair of jeans with a pink sequined heart on the thigh and a pink button-down shirt that was only buttoned to the bottom of her cleavage, revealing a tight white T-shirt with a hint of the Gardner Sisters Nursery logo visible. Her long, wavy blonde hair was pulled back at the sides and the rest hung down her back. When she glanced up, she beamed at me and set the pumpkin in her hands onto the pile. She pulled me into a huge hug as soon as I reached her.

"Rose. I've missed you!"

"We saw each other three days ago," I teased, but I'd missed her something fierce. Up until recently, we'd lived together and worked together at both the landscaping office and on our investigations. I was used to her being a daily presence in my life.

"You know that's too long." She grabbed my shoulders and leaned back, turning serious as she studied my face. "Jed called me. Why'd you want Denny Carmichael's number?"

Somehow I'd momentarily forgotten about the mess I'd left at the office. "I'm surprised you haven't heard by now. In fact, I'm surprised *I* haven't heard anything by now." I pulled my phone out of my pocket and checked the screen. "Oops."

I had several missed calls and texts. One of them, from Joe, read: *CALL ME.*

I knew why he was desperate to reach me, but I hadn't decided yet if I was going to rat Denny out. Texting seemed safer.

Don't worry. I'm fine. I'm at the nursery dealing with something. I'll explain everything later.

"What happened?" Neely Kate asked.

I glanced around to make sure we were alone, then leaned closer. "Denny Carmichael sent a friend to drop by the landscaping office."

Her eyes flew wide. "You're kiddin'."

"I wish I were. He wanted to warn me to mind my Ps and Qs tomorrow when I testify before the grand jury."

She gave a quick shake of her head. "Wait. What? What grand jury?"

Three days clearly *had* been too long. I told her about the Arkansas State Police officer showing up on my front porch that morning. "Joe had warned me from the very beginning that

Mason was likely to call one, but so much time had passed, I'd started thinkin' I might get out of it."

She frowned, her brows knitting together. "What are you gonna do?"

"I don't know," I admitted. "I'm supposed to meet with Carter this afternoon. I'm waiting to hear when."

Worry filled her eyes. "Are you sure it's a good idea to meet with Skeeter's lawyer?"

"He's my attorney too," I said. "And it's not like we're at cross-purposes here."

Her brow lifted as though to ask, *Are you sure?*

"Carter Hale helped me more than I expected when I was arrested for Momma's murder."

"At Skeeter's request."

"And James will want him to help me now."

She didn't look convinced. "Carter's gonna have Skeeter's best interest in mind, not yours. Maybe it's time to find a new lawyer."

She had a point, but the last time I saw James he'd admitted that he loved me, words that didn't come lightly for him. He wouldn't let Carter throw me to the wolves.

"What are you goin' to do tomorrow?" she asked. She and Jed were the only ones who knew the full story of what had happened to me that night. They knew the truth about James— that he'd financed the salaries of those Sugar Branch police officers and summoned Denny Carmichael to kill them rather than showing up himself.

"I'm hopin' Carter will advise me on that."

She scowled. "What did *Joe* say?"

"To tell the truth," I said. "If I don't, I'll be perjuring myself."

"Only if they find out you're lyin'."

Neely Kate had a good point, but what were the chances all of this would be kept quiet? Not to mention just a year ago, Mason and I had the same goal—clean up the corruption in the county. When had my goal changed? Keeping all of this to myself might be in my own best interest, but was it in the best interest of the county?

"There's something we need to look into," I said, hating the implications of what I was about to suggest. "Sonder Tech, the big landscaping job I just pitched—"

"Oh my word!" she exclaimed. "I completely forgot that was today! How'd it go?"

"Good. Great," I said. "One of the guys walked me to the exit and told me he was sure we got the job. We'll get the official word within the next couple of days."

"That's amazin'!" Neely Kate said. Then her excitement faded. "Why do I feel like there's a but in there?"

Grimacing, I said, "It's likely nothing."

"But it might be something," she prodded.

"I knew they had relocated here, but I didn't know much else. My contact had only told me they were an internet company."

"Oh mercy," she said with an ornery look. "They sell sex toys, don't they? Did you get a catalogue? Miss Mildred will keel over."

"*What?* I'm not sure what they do…" But I had to admit that would explain the secrecy surrounding their business. I could only imagine how the Henryetta Baptist Church would react to having a company like that in town. I shook my head to clear the mental image of Miss Mildred with sex toys. "I still don't know what they do, but I *did* find out that they're moving here from Dallas."

Her face lost color, and she took a moment before she said, "Dallas is an awfully big city."

"True, but first Carly and now them? And around the same time too," I said.

"No," Neely Kate said. "Sonder first started renovations on the property before Carly showed up, I think. Maybe a month or two earlier. I remember because Witt was still lookin' for a job and wondered if it might lead to something. But for some reason he thought they'd moved here from Oklahoma."

"We need to talk to Witt."

Her mouth scrunched to the side. "And Jed."

I quirked an eyebrow and gave her a sly look. "How convenient that they happen to work at the same place." I cast a glance at the pile of pumpkins. "Do you think you can get away to go ask them? I was plannin' on askin' you to lunch anyway."

"You don't want to wait until tonight?" she asked. "Jed and I are comin' for dinner."

"But Witt won't be there since it's a…" I saw the look on her face and realized he'd found out and invited himself. I laughed. "If there's food involved, Witt always finds a way to get a place at the table."

"Do you think Violet will mind?" she asked, looking worried. "When she called, she didn't make it sound like anything special. She said the kids like playin' with me and Jed."

"Don't be silly," I said. "Witt's family. And you know Vi loves him. He's an incorrigible flirt and she eats it up." I lowered my voice. "But I don't want to ask them about it tonight. We still don't know what the Hardshaw Group wants from you." I shook my head. "I'd rather put my mind at ease now than later, not to mention it would be better to keep it out of Violet's earshot."

"I'd rather deal with it now too," she confessed. "I still can't believe they sent goons to kidnap me and then *nothing* for nearly two months. The longer this goes on, the more nervous I get."

"Maybe that's the plan," I said. "Or maybe they're tryin' to make you complacent while they find another way to get to you."

She shrugged. "All I know is that I'm a nervous wreck, and Jed's even worse. He's gotten to the point that he's scared to let me out of his sight. In fact"—she waved to the pumpkin stack— "if he knew I was out here workin' alone, he'd throw an ever-lovin' fit."

Jed had a point—it would be easy for someone to drive up and snatch her—and I felt guilty that it hadn't occurred to me. "Then why are you out here?"

"Because it needs to be done. Maeve's workin' on the books and Anna threw her back out a couple of days ago." She paused, taking a deep breath, then said, "And because I don't want to live my life in fear, worried that the worst is gonna happen at any minute. I love bein' out in the sunshine and the warm weather and breathin' in the clean air."

"You don't like bein' caged," I said more to myself than her.

"After Branson locked me up for months, keepin' me on a short leash…" Her earnest eyes bored into mine. "I was rarely outside, Rose. I was in that godforsaken house or in his car goin' back and forth to the strip club, but I was hardly ever in the fresh air, feeling the sun on my face and the breeze in my hair." Her eyes glistened. "That was years ago, and I'd started to take my freedom for granted. But after I was almost kidnapped…" She paused, as though weighing her words. "I started appreciating what freedom means, and hiding in Jed's house and inside the nursery is only slightly better than bein' trapped in Branson's prison."

While being trafficked by her supposed boyfriend was a far cry from her current situation, I understood what she meant. Freedom was freedom.

"Then we need to try even harder to figure out what they want from you so you can stop lookin' over your shoulder."

She studied me for a long second. "Rose, maybe you should tell the grand jury everything you know so you can stop lookin' over *your* shoulder."

My mouth dropped open. "What?"

"No more secrets, Rose. Haven't you had enough of them? I'm sure weary of mine."

Out of the blue, I felt the tingling of a vision, and before I could process it, I was plunged into a field at night. Vision Neely Kate was face-to-face with Ronnie, whose expression was full of concern.

"What were you thinkin', Neely Kate?" he demanded.

"I need to be free of you, Ronnie! I need to live my life without you!" she shouted.

"If you keep this up, you won't have a life to live," he said, anger pinching the bridge of his nose. "You need to let this vendetta go."

"No!" I shouted, smacking his arm with my palm. "No! You did this, Ronnie Colson! You fix it!"

"No, *you* did it, Neely Kate!" he wailed, giving me a hard shove backward. "Why couldn't you just leave things alone?"

I stumbled on something but righted myself. Glancing down at the ground, I saw the body of a man, his eyes wide in shock. A bullet hole pocked his forehead.

The vision faded, and I was propelled back into my own body with a force more violent than usual.

"Why couldn't you leave things alone?" I whispered. Then my stomach heaved, and I leaned to the side, throwing up what little muffin I'd eaten.

"Rose," Neely Kate said in alarm. "Did you just have a vision?"

Had Neely Kate killed another man? I stared into her worried face, wondering if I should tell her or just tell Jed. It would kill her.

I spat to help clean the vomit out of my mouth. The bottle of water in my purse caught my eye, and I took a swig of it, swished out my mouth, then spat again. But when I stood, my head began to swim.

"Rose," Neely Kate said, grabbing my arm to keep me steady. "Maybe you should sit down."

Part of me wanted to protest, but she was right. I could feel a full-blown panic attack brewing in my chest, as though an elephant sat on my chest, sucking the air out of my lungs. I hadn't had one for nearly a year, but it was a feeling I could never forget. I needed to sit down and get ahold of myself. I stumbled to a low block wall and blindly reached backward to sit down.

Fear filled Neely Kate's eyes. "*Rose?*"

I sat, but I missed the wall, the blocks scraping my back as my butt landed on the concrete with a hard thud.

"Rose!" I heard Maeve shout, but her voice was faint—she was far away, and so was I.

I tried to lower my head between my legs, but then everything went black.

Chapter
Five

Rose, oh my God. *Rose.*"

I heard Neely Kate, but I felt like I was at the bottom of a well.

I blinked my eyes open and saw her worried face hovering over mine.

Relief filled her eyes and her shoulders sagged. "Oh, thank God."

"I'm okay," I said, trying to sit up, but a hand pushed me back down.

"Just lie still," Maeve said from my side. "Just take a moment."

I closed my eyes and took a deep breath. The memory of what had gotten me into this predicament came rushing back, and my eyes flew open. "How long was I out?"

"Not even a minute," Maeve said, picking up my hand and cradling it in hers.

I turned to look in her worried eyes. "Y'all didn't call an ambulance, did you?"

"Not yet," Anna said from behind me. I tilted my head back to look at her. When I saw the phone in her grip, I pushed

Maeve's hand off my shoulder and sat up, although I couldn't bring myself to release her other hand. "I'm fine. It was a panic attack, is all. I used to have them all the time before."

"Before what?" Anna asked.

"Before my real life began." Back when I was a meek, scared little girl in a woman's body. It shook me that I'd had one after so long. What did it mean about all the progress I'd made in my life?

I was sure Anna had questions, but Maeve spoke before she could ask any of them. "You've been burning the candles at both ends, Rose. You're not eating. You've looked exhausted and worn out for over a month. You're trying to run two businesses and take care of your sister at the same time. You're not Superwoman and your body is telling you to slow down and take a break."

It was the vision that had pushed me to this, but I didn't want to tell them what I'd seen. "I can't take a break," I said emphatically. "Too many people depend on me."

"And every single one of us is ready to pitch in." She gave me a warm smile. "Why don't you head up to Eldorado Springs tomorrow? Both you and Neely Kate. There's a new spa there and you girls can make the day of it. Just the two of you havin' a girls' day out."

I shook my head. "I can't. Violet's too sick. I don't dare leave for the entire day."

Maeve's body tensed. "She's gotten worse?"

"She won't let on to most people, but just this morning she couldn't get out of bed on her own." I took a breath to keep from crying. "I don't know how much time she has left."

"I didn't realize it had gotten that bad, although it stands to reason. She *is* dyin'." Her chin trembled and she looked close to tears. "I haven't seen her in nearly two weeks."

"Come to dinner tonight," I said. "Violet invited a bunch of people over."

"I'd hate to impose," Maeve said, her brow furrowing with a deep frown.

"Don't be silly," I said. "I'm surprised she didn't ask you already. You're family."

Maeve threw her arms around me and held on tight. While she hugged me often, this one felt more intense. "I was so worried you'd hold it against me."

"Hold what against you?" I asked, squeezing her back.

"Mason and his grand jury."

I tried to hide my surprise. "We all know that Mason's here for a noble cause," I said, truly believing what I said. He'd never wavered from seeking justice. I was the one who'd switched sides.

What did that say about *my* character?

If I were an outside observer, looking down on all of this, would I consider myself a hero or a villain?

"But he's hurting you in the process," Maeve whispered in my ear, and once again, I wondered if she knew about my relationship with James Malcolm.

I pulled back, looking deep into her eyes. "You're the mother Vi and I always wished we had. Violet loves you, but she also recognizes that you're Mason's mother, and as far as she's concerned, Mason is the enemy."

"She feels the way a good sister should," Maeve said.

"Yes," I said, tears rolling down my cheeks. So few people understood my complex sister, but Maeve had a rare ability to see people for who they were at their core. She had looked beneath Violet's bluster and had seen the sister I had always known—the woman who was desperate to be loved and needed. Her attempts to fulfill those needs were often suspect, but underneath it all, Violet was the same as me—one of two little girls huddling in the dark, clutching each other as their mother railed outside their door. And while I'd been the one to suffer most of the abuse, Violet had been powerless to stop it from happening. She could have turned her back on me—saved herself the heartache and the hopelessness—but she never once left my side. Never once left me alone.

Until now.

I could feel myself about to fall apart, but I couldn't afford myself the luxury of a breakdown. Not yet. I'd crumble after.

"All of that to say," I pushed out past the lump in my throat, "Violet would be thrilled if you came."

"Are you sure it's no imposition?"

"None at all," I said. "Carly's cookin' a big dinner, so I'll just let her know there's one more person comin'." I grinned up at Neely Kate. "Two more since Witt's comin'." And since we'd already invited most of our friends, I glanced back at Anna. "Would you and Bruce Wayne like to come?"

"It sounds fun," she said with regret in her eyes. "But we have plans."

"I'm sure we'll have more of these," I said, then wondered why we hadn't done this before now. Violet needed to be surrounded by people and laughter and love. "But Maeve, unless you have plans, I insist you come."

Maeve's mouth lifted into a wobbly smile, and the loneliness in her eyes caught me by surprise. Why hadn't I made sure she had people around her? "If you're sure it's okay," she said, "I'd love to be included."

"How much time are you spendin' with Mason?" Neely Kate asked, trying hard to keep the accusation out of her voice, but I could hear the hard edges of it. She must have seen her loneliness too.

Maeve's gaze shifted to my best friend, her shoulders stiffening. "He's very busy with his work."

"When *isn't* he busy with his work?" Neely Kate didn't hide her animosity this time. Her loyalty to me was as strong as Violet's.

"Mason has a very difficult job," I countered. "With very little budget."

"He's called you to testify in front of a grand jury," Neely Kate spat out with more venom than I would have expected from her given our conversation before I'd fainted. "How can you sit there and defend him?"

"Yes, he called a grand jury," I said in a level voice, "as he should. I was detained and nearly raped and killed by two officers of the law. I need to give an official statement so the state can determine if a further investigation needs to be done. I should welcome the opportunity to help stop corruption in this county. It's rife with it."

But that was only partly true. Grand juries were about filing charges…who was Mason wanting to file charges against?

Neely Kate started to say something else, but one look at Maeve clammed her up. She took a breath, then said in a more civil tone, "The timing is terrible. Violet is dyin'."

"Violet could be dyin' for months."

But we all knew different, even if they had the grace to not call me out on my delusion.

"I'm sorry," Maeve said. "I'm just so, so sorry about all of this."

I squeezed her hand. "You hush. You have absolutely nothin' to be sorry for. Now help me up."

Both Neely Kate and Maeve helped me to my feet, and I stood still as another wave of dizziness hit me.

"Maybe you should go to the doctor for a checkup," Maeve said, worry in her voice. "Obviously you're stressed to the point of it affecting your health."

I gave her a teasing grin. "That sounds more like a task for Jonah than my doctor."

Maeve brushed a leaf off my upper back. "Perhaps you should see both."

"A new doctor took over for Dr. Arnold, and I have an appointment to see her this afternoon," I said. "Apparently, Dr. Newton wants to meet with me before she'll let me pick up Violet's prescription."

"That's weird," Neely Kate said.

"That's what I thought," I said, turning to glance at her. "Does anyone know what happened to Dr. Arnold? I got the sense that it wasn't a simple matter of him retirin'."

"It all happened suddenly," Maeve said. "I'd say I was surprised you hadn't heard the gossip, but you've been preoccupied."

"He had an affair with one of his nurses," Neely Kate said. "Rumor has it that poor Mrs. Arnold didn't have a clue until the two of them ran off."

"How'd they replace him so quickly?" I asked.

"He's been plannin' it," Neely Kate said. "But no one in Henryetta knew until the new doctor showed up. He'd told his staff he was goin' to a medical conference and he had a doctor fillin' in, but he'd already sold his practice to Dr. Newton."

"That seems really fishy."

"Even fishier when you take into account the rumors that he was sellin' opiate prescriptions."

"Do you think that's why the new doctor wants to see you?" Anna asked. "Isn't Vi taking narcotics for pain?"

"Yeah," I said, now worried she'd cut Violet off.

"I wouldn't worry about it," Anna said. "If Dr. Arnold was prescribing opiates willy-nilly, it makes sense that Dr. Newton would crack down on the abuse. Vi obviously needs it."

Through this new lens, Wendy's situation this morning made a whole lot more sense. I glanced up at Neely Kate. "Has Jed heard anything about it?"

"I've never asked. He tries to keep that part of his previous life from me."

"I guess we should ask him about that too," I said. "Maeve, would you mind if I stole Neely Kate from you for the rest of the day? We'll finish the pumpkins first."

Maeve gave me a stern look. "She's your employee. You loaned her to me. And don't you dare think about moving those pumpkins around. You need rest. I hope you're planning on taking the rest of the day off."

Not likely. I had too much work to do, and half of it had nothing to do with landscaping. I wanted to know more about Dr. Arnold.

Chapter Six

Neely Kate finished stacking the pumpkins before we left. No one would hear of me helping, and to ensure I didn't try, Maeve dragged me inside under the pretext of showing me some of the seasonal merchandise that had just come in for the upcoming holidays.

When Neely Kate finished, we loaded up in her new baby—the new car Jed had bought in a junkyard and refurbished for her. I was exhausted after my morning from hell and leaned my head back on the seat.

"I know you had a vision of me," she said as soon as we pulled out of the parking lot. "What did you see?"

Well, crap. I'd hoped my panic attack would distract her.

I sat up straight. "Maybe we should pick up some lunch to take out to Jed and Witt."

"I packed Jed a lunch and sent one for Witt too. I tried out a new recipe for dinner last night, only Jed didn't seem to be very hungry and there were plenty of leftovers."

"Then how about you and I go to lunch?" I suggested. "That's why I swung by in the first place. If you'd like, I'll tell you all about my encounter with Dena and Margi this morning."

Her mouth parted and she turned to me in shock. "This morning? Good heavens. You *have* had a busy morning."

"You don't know the half of it. Wait until I tell you about the cat on a leash at the doctor's office." I launched into the story about Wendy, the purse, and the wrestling match.

Wearing a huge grin, Neely Kate shook her head. "Oh my word. I would have loved to see that."

"It was frightening."

"Speakin' of frightening, I want to know more about Denny Carmichael's guy tearing up the office."

"He didn't tear up the office. He got pissed and threw a chair out the window. I didn't have time to mess with it before the meeting. I texted Denny saying that he better take care of it, otherwise people would be asking questions."

"You just left?" she asked in disbelief. "If the window was broken, anyone could have gone in and stolen the computers."

She was right, of course. Leaving it like that had been beyond stupid, but in the moment, it had felt right, which made me question my own judgment. "I have no excuse," I said, my voice breaking. "All I knew was that we really needed that job and I had to get to the presentation."

"Why didn't you tell Jed when you called him? He could have run over and started cleanin' it up."

I turned to her, close to tears. "I couldn't talk about it until after the presentation. I know it was foolish. I'm sorry."

She reached over and grabbed my hand. "Rose. It's okay. We're all just worried about you."

"And you've been worried pretty much since you've met me. I'm so *tired* of people havin' to worry about me. I have to stand on my own two feet. I need to take care of my own problems."

"Where is this comin' from?" she asked, squeezing my hand.

"I don't know," I said, starting to cry. "I just need to learn how to be alone."

"Because Violet's dyin' and leavin' you alone? But we're here for you, Rose. Just like you've always been there for all of us." She made a face. "What are you gonna tell Joe? You know he's liable to be upset that you didn't tell him. He moved to the farm to protect you from Denny, and the first time something happened, you didn't call him."

"I know. You're right, but I need to figure out what I'm going to do tomorrow first." I looked up at her, my eyes burning with tears. "How many times can I hurt that man before he walks away from me completely?"

She squeezed my hand. "I don't know, Rose, but I know he cares about you."

"I know." I wasn't being fair to him, and once again, I wondered if I should encourage him to move out.

We were silent for a moment before Neely Kate said, "Let's go get some lunch. You still need to fill me in on what happened with Dena and Margi Romano."

I'd finished the story by the time we pulled into the drive-thru of the Chuck and Cluck, several cars back from the speaker. Neely Kate put the car in park and shook her head. "I still can't believe Dena was such a biatch to you."

"I'm not. She hates me. She still thinks I stole Joe from her."

"As if."

I shrugged. "That's what she believes, and we haven't exactly tried to dissuade people from thinkin' we're together."

A grin lit up her face. "Can you even imagine her with Mason?"

"It might work. He likes pie," I teased.

"I'm no fan of Mason, but I wouldn't wish Dena on him." She made a face. "What do you make of Margi bein' so nice?"

"She seems lonely, but I think her niceness has more to do with her needing a place to put emergency rescue horses and less to do with needin' a friend. That's okay. I understand."

"So are you gonna have coffee with her?"

"*We're* gonna have coffee with her. But I think she's comin' out to look at the pasture and barn tomorrow."

"But your grand jury testimony is tomorrow."

I grimaced. "Crap. You're right. Well, when she calls, I'll just tell her we'll have to postpone it."

"Unless you have Carly show her around."

"And let Margi hoodwink her into agreein' to something? No, thanks. Plus Carly's got her hands full with Vi."

"She really was a godsend," Neely Kate said.

"I couldn't agree with you more." And although I didn't like to think about what would happen after Violet died, I had to admit I was relieved to know I wouldn't be all alone at the house.

When we pulled up to the menu board, Neely Kate ordered a three-piece meal and I ordered a family bucket and a quart of mashed potatoes and gravy with a side of green beans.

Neely Kate narrowed her eyes. "You got something for Witt and Jed too. I told you they already had lunch."

"I know," I said, "but it didn't seem right eatin' fried chicken in front of them. Maybe we can all share like a potluck."

Her face lit up. "Good idea. Then you can try my lamb, turnip, and ketchup turnovers."

I tried hard not to show a reaction, especially when my stomach flip-flopped at the thought. "Can't wait."

We split the cost and headed out to the garage. I got Neely Kate to fill me in on what she'd been doing to the house Jed had recently purchased. He'd encouraged her to put her own stamp on it, and given the way he kept encouraging her to see what was his as hers, I couldn't help wondering if he wanted to marry her. Her marriage to Ronnie would put a damper on that, and while I knew Jed and Joe both were searching for him, neither of them had caught wind of him since Joe had seen him in New Orleans boarding a bus bound for Memphis with another woman and a wedding ring.

Except I knew Neely Kate would cross paths with him again, if my vision came to pass. I knew I had to tell her—she deserved to know—but I wanted Jed to be there when I shared the news. If anyone could keep my best friend safe, it was my former bodyguard.

Since the day was so nice for mid-October, the garage doors were up and all three bays had cars, one of them up on a lift. Considering the shop was pretty new and Witt and Jed didn't have any other employees, I took that as a good sign. Witt had worked in a garage south of town, and a few of his customers had followed him to their new establishment on the west side of town. He was a great mechanic, and although Jed needed more experience, he'd worked on cars in his youth and was a quick learner.

"Looks like they're busy," I said. "That's great!"

"Business has been pickin' up," she said as she pulled into a parking space. "In fact, they just hired a new mechanic in trainin'." Her eyes sparkled with mischief. "You might know him."

"Who?" I asked in confusion. Despite what I'd said to the Sonder Tech folk, I didn't know anyone currently looking for a job.

Her eyes twinkled. "You'll see."

We grabbed the takeout bags and Neely Kate headed straight for Jed, who had stopped working and stood waiting for us at the rear of the car in the middle bay.

"This is a surprise," he said, glancing from Neely Kate to me. "Or maybe not considering your phone call this morning and the fact someone busted the window of the landscaping office."

"You heard about that too, huh?" I asked, resisting the urge to squirm underneath his gaze.

"Yep. Surely you know I'm not the only person watchin' your comin's and goin's."

"I haven't seen any sign of James's guys watchin' me for over a month, but I didn't know you were watching me too."

"Not me," he said, tilting his head with a smug look. "There's plenty of others to feed the grapevine."

"Are you okay, Miss Rose?" a familiar male voice said. I gasped when I saw him walk around the car in the third bay, wiping his hands on a towel.

"Marshall." I turned to Neely Kate, my eyes wide in shock.

Marshall had sought out my help a few months ago, after he'd been shot. I'd declared my land neutral and he'd taken my word for it. I'd had to fend off Kip Wagner to protect him, which had caused a rift between James and I, but my word was the only thing I had going for me. That and the gun in my purse and the shotgun in my hall closet.

"What are you doin' here?" I asked in disbelief, then motioned to him. "Well, obviously you're workin' here, but how'd that come about?"

"Jed," he said with a bashful smile. "He told me if I ever needed help to let him know, so I did and now I'm workin' in their garage." He shot a nervous look at Jed. "I'm still in my training period, but I aim to prove I'm worth keepin'."

"He's green," I heard Witt call out from the back of the garage, "but he's showin' promise."

Marshall beamed with pride.

Witt walked around the cars to join us, his gaze homing in on the bags in our hands. "Whatcha got there?"

"We brought chicken and fixin's from Chuck and Cluck," I said, lifting the bag to show them. "I hope y'all haven't had lunch."

All three men stammered, and finally Jed spat out, "We haven't had time to take our lunch break yet."

"I'm starving!" Marshall said.

"Well, that's fortuitous," I said with a big smile. "I heard Neely Kate sent lunch for y'all, but I figured we could share. Sounds like I'll get to try out her lamb, spinach, and mustard turnovers."

Witt held my gaze. "That would be *lamb, turnip, and ketchup* turnovers."

I could feel him telegraph, *God bless you.*

My smile wobbled. "Even better."

Marshall snorted, and Jed jabbed him in the gut with an elbow. Marshall bent over clutching his stomach.

"Are you okay?" Neely Kate asked, sounding concerned.

"Yep," he wheezed out. "Just the thought of those turnovers is making my stomach rumble with hunger."

A huge smile spread across her face. "I'll go in and start heating them up."

She gathered the two bags I was carrying and headed into the office.

As soon as she walked inside, Witt said, "Someone is gonna have to tell her that her cooking sucks. And soon. I swear to God, I nearly went to the ER with gas a couple of nights ago after eating her jalapeño and tuna poppers."

Jed shot him a glare. "She loves creatin' recipes."

"That's all fine and good," Witt said, "but why do the rest of us have to suffer with you?"

Jed rammed his right elbow into Witt's gut, even harder than he had with Marshall.

"Jesus Christ, man," Witt grunted, doubling over. "Lay off at the gym."

I had to wonder if Witt had a point. "You know, at some point she's gonna figure out we hate her creations," I said quietly, watching the door to make sure Neely Kate didn't overhear. "It's so bad that even Carly mentioned it this morning."

"It should be somebody she loves and trusts," Witt said, rubbing his stomach as he straightened. "Someone who's known her for a while."

"So, you?" I said sarcastically. We all knew Witt had the tact of a razorback.

He rubbed his chin, looking skyward in a dramatic fashion. "I was thinkin' someone who can be gentle."

"Oh, heck no," I said, lifting my hands in surrender. "I've been dealing with her recipes for far longer than either of you. I've been eatin' them since last January. You've only just started eatin' them."

"All the more reason for it to be you," Witt said with a huge grin. "You've suffered the longest."

"No. Way." I shook my head. "I'm not saying a word. I love her to pieces, which means I'll choke my lamb and ketchup turnover down with a smile."

Witt chuckled. "Don't forget the turnips. Undercooked turnips. I'll be sure to give you my helpin' since you're lookin' forward to it."

The door opened, and Neely Kate gave us a confused look. "What are y'all waiting for?"

"That's right," Witt said, grinning ear to ear. "Whatcha waitin' for, Rose? Those turnovers are callin' your name."

Chapter Seven

The break room smelled like something had curled up and died behind the fridge, but the scent became more pronounced the moment Neely Kate opened the microwave door.

Witt started coughing and gagging while Marshall took two steps backward toward the door to the shop and said, "I'm not very hungry."

Neely Kate's face popped up with a confused look. "You just said you were starving."

Marshall's face turned red. "I...uh..." Then he turned and ran out of the room.

Neely Kate turned to me with a baffled look, which deepened when she saw my contorted face.

"Why is everyone acting so weird?" she demanded.

"Can you seriously not smell that?" Witt choked out.

I put my hand on my stomach, trying to breathe through my mouth. "Neely Kate, are you sure they didn't go bad?"

She lifted the plate to her nose and took a whiff, and her forehead wrinkled. "Huh."

"Oh my God!" Witt moaned, watching her in horror. "Has something happened to your sense of smell? How can you put your nose right next to it?"

She studied us with narrowed eyes, taking in our reactions.

"Good thing we brought plenty of chicken," I said with forced cheerfulness, even though I wasn't sure I could stomach anything at this point.

"They were just fine last night," Neely Kate said with a perplexed expression as she studied the plate.

If I didn't leave soon, I was going to vomit. "You know, it's a beautiful day. How about we take advantage of it and eat the chicken outside? And since your turnovers are suspect, why don't we play it safe and toss them out."

"In the Dumpster out back," Witt murmured. "Or the field *way* out back."

Jed elbowed him hard in the stomach again. Witt leaned over with a groan and hightailed it out the door.

"Can you really not smell that?" I asked, starting to worry about her.

"Well, yeah, but I thought it was supposed to be that way."

"Always trust your nose," I said, taking the plate from her. I slid the turnovers back into the open storage container and slapped on the lid. Maybe this was a good time to bring up the elephant in the room. "You know what I've been craving? Your candied sweet potatoes."

Her head tilted to the side. "But those are my great-granny's recipe."

"I know," I said brightly. "But they're *so* good."

"But I'm tryin' to make my own path," she said. "Make my own adventurous meals."

I pressed my mouth together as I fought an internal war. "I know," I said, lowering my voice in a conspiratorial tone. "But you know, not everyone is as adventurous as you." When she narrowed her eyes, I quickly added, "Or me."

Her lips twisted to the side as she considered it. "I think you might be right."

Relief washed through me. "It's Fenton County. People are used to good ol' Southern cookin'."

"I know," she said with a nod. "Which is why I'm considerin' openin' my own restaurant."

My mouth flapped open and it took me two full seconds to respond. "What?"

Her eyes lit up with excitement. "I know it's a surprise and all, but I've been thinkin'"—she leaned closer and lowered her voice—"maybe it's time Fenton County became more cultured."

"Neely Kate," I said, feeling a cold sweat break out on my forehead. "I don't think Fenton County is ready for culinary sophistication."

Her smile spread wider. "They're never gonna be ready. That's why I need to bring it to them."

"Does Jed know about your idea?" I asked, forcing a smile.

"Not yet. I wanted to tell you first."

"I...uh..."

"I know you need me at the office, but winter's coming and the landscaping business will slow down, which makes it a perfect time to get it all set up. What do you think?"

I couldn't encourage this, but I just couldn't find the strength to tell her that her food was inedible. "I think it's a lot to consider. Maybe you should make a business plan." A new thought hit me. "Or maybe set up one of those focus groups to taste-test your food." But the moment I suggested the focus group, I knew it was a terrible idea. They'd eat her alive. "I don't know, Neely Kate," I said in all seriousness. "I don't think you can force the simple folk of Fenton County to like highfalutin food. Besides, restaurants have high start-up costs, and who's to say the bank will give you a loan?"

She bit her bottom lip, lost in concentration. "You might be right." Then, just when I started to think I'd steered the Titanic away from the iceberg, she said, "I should get one of those food trucks. It would be cheaper. I bet Jed could find one in a junkyard and fix it up. Then I could take my food to them."

I was about to answer when Witt shouted from the garage, "Where's the food? I'm starvin'!"

"You're always starvin', Witt Rivers," Neely Kate grumbled.

The guys were waiting outside at a picnic table Jed had bought a few weeks back. Neely Kate brought out some paper plates she kept stocked in their break room, and the guys started divvying up the chicken. It was a good thing I wasn't very hungry because I hadn't accounted for the eighteen-year-old boy sitting across from me. Marshall's appetite was even heartier now that he wasn't recovering from a gunshot wound.

Jed noticed I had a small amount of mashed potatoes and a single scrawny little chicken leg on my plate and frowned.

"I'm good," I assured him. "All this mess with Vi has my stomach in knots."

I told them about Violet's dinner party, and I saw the wistful look on Marshall's face. "You're welcome to come if you like."

Excitement filled his eyes, but it quickly faded. "I wouldn't want to impose," he said, his face pink with embarrassment.

"I'm sure it's no imposition," I said, pulling out my phone to text Carly about the extra guests. Despite the fact she'd said she'd make extra food in case Violet invited more guests, Witt and Jed could put away a disarming amount of food, so I offered to come home early to help with the preparation. I figured I could head back after my appointment with Dr. Newton. "I think a houseful of people and laughter is just what Vi needs."

Carly texted back that Violet was thrilled to have the extra guests, but she insisted on handling everything herself. In fact, Violet had already called and invited Jonah and his girlfriend, so the more the merrier.

"I could always make something if Carly needs help," Neely Kate volunteered.

"Oh, that's okay," I said quickly. "Carly insists on makin' everything herself, and besides, I might need you to run out to a landscapin' appointment for me."

Her eyes lit up. "I'd love to. Just give me the details."

Jed was watching me closely. I knew he was dying to ask me questions, but he didn't dare do it in front of Marshall. Although he clearly trusted him to some degree, Jed was always careful of other people's secrets.

Once Marshall had wolfed down his plate of food and the sandwich he'd already packed for himself, Jed pinned his gaze on me and said, "Marshall, why don't you head on in to the garage and finish that oil change."

Marshall's eyes widened. "On my own?"

"Don't get all excited," Witt said with a laugh. "We're gonna be checkin' up on you."

Marshall nodded with an eager gleam in his eye. "Yes, sir."

Then he took off for the garage.

"Do I look like an old-fart *sir*?" Witt asked no one in particular.

Neely Kate laughed. "We all have to grow up sometime."

Witt made a face that suggested he was putting it off as long as possible.

Jed had kept his gaze on me the entire time, and I knew I was in for a grilling. He didn't disappoint. "What really happened this morning?"

I filled him in, then asked, "What's the scuttlebutt about it?"

He sat back on the bench. "People have noticed that Skeeter seems to have cooled down about you, and hardly anyone knows you've had an issue with Carmichael. The general consensus is that Skeeter sent someone to give you a warning."

I couldn't hide my shock. "James's own men believe that? Wouldn't they know if that had happened?"

"Dermot says Skeeter currently has most of his organization on a need-to-know basis. Most people have no idea what's going on in the inner circle. Me included."

I frowned. What was James up to? Everyone he'd previously trusted and relied on was no longer in his life. Although I knew he'd distanced himself to protect me, I had no idea who he was working for, or when the arrangement had started. And I had no way to ask. The powerlessness pressed into me. I lacked control over everything in my life.

"Well, it was definitely Carmichael," I said, losing my appetite again. "His goon didn't admit it, but Denny owned up to it when I talked to him."

Neely Kate had already heard this story, but she was still giving me her full, undivided attention.

"So you did call him." Jed sighed, and I couldn't tell if he was disappointed or proud. Perhaps a combination of both.

"It didn't go too well." I paused.

"Care to be a little more specific?" Jed asked. When I hesitated, he added, "Before I left Skeeter, I knew almost everything that was goin' on in his organization. Or at least I thought I did. But the point was that he confided in me. You need a confidant, Rose, and I think I've proven myself worthy enough to be yours."

I studied him, wondering if he was right. It would be a relief to unburden myself, and I trusted that he wouldn't lose his mind and charge off to defend my honor. "We exchanged some threats," I admitted. "Right before I hung up."

Jed kept his expressionless gaze on me, but Witt burst out laughing. "You are one crazy chick, Rose."

I was surprised he was so amused. He'd already told me that he worried about Neely Kate getting mixed up in the underworld of Fenton County and considered me a bad influence. This definitely fit into the bad influence category.

I continued to hold Jed's gaze. "I suppose you're pissed."

"Like I told you this morning, you're a grown woman."

"But...?"

"Denny Carmichael isn't prone to bluffing." He paused, then added, "Have you considered what questions you might be asked in the grand jury tomorrow?"

"Don't forget that she's talkin' to Carter Hale this afternoon," Neely Kate said in a tone that suggested she disapproved.

Jed shot Neely Kate a glance. "Are you concerned Hale will be biased?"

"Of course I am," she said in a huff.

Nodding, he looked back at me. "Would you like me to come with you?"

I hadn't considered that, and while I was tempted, I still felt a strong need to own my messes and handle them as independently as possible. Besides, Jed had enough to worry about with Neely Kate's safety still in question. "No. I think I should do this on my own. Especially if people are watchin'."

He gave me a grim look. "You go on your own and we'll discuss his advice tonight." Then he surprised me by adding, "And we'll include Joe in the conversation."

Neely Kate and I started to protest at once, but he held up his hand. "He's put his life on hold for the past couple of months. He has a right to know what's happening."

I couldn't find it in me to object to that. He was right, and although I wanted to protect Joe and keep him safe, he wasn't liable to thank me for it. Not when I'd lambasted him for his previous attempts to protect me. We'd come too far to go back to that.

We sat in silence for a moment before Neely Kate said, "He came around with Jed."

Or at least they could be in the same room without wanting to murder each other.

"Yeah," I said, "tonight."

He gave me a grim look. "Are you gonna call Skeeter?"

"He knows just as much or more than you do about all of this," I said. "If he wants to reach out to me, he knows how."

He nodded and was about to say something when my phone vibrated in my pocket. I pulled it out and answered, relieved to see it was Carter's number.

"My case has been postponed by an hour," he said without a hello. "How soon can you be here?"

I shot a quick glance to Neely Kate. "I could probably be there in twenty minutes tops."

"Give me a half hour," he said. "My assistant's gonna be out of the office, so let yourself in and head back to my office."

No witnesses. I wasn't sure whether to be worried or relieved.

"Okay," I said with a frown. "See you then."

I hung up and relayed our short conversation.

"I can drop you off at his office," Neely Kate said, starting to gather the dirty paper plates.

"Could you take me back to the nursery so I can get my truck?" I asked. "We should have time for that, and then I won't have to worry about getting to my appointment with Dr. Newton on time."

"Are you sick?" Witt asked, his usual glibness missing. "You look like you've lost weight."

His concern caught me by surprise. "I'm fine. It's about Violet. They won't give me her narcotics prescription for pain until I see the new doctor." I shot a look at Neely Kate, then leaned closer. "Did either one of you ever hear about Dr. Arnold selling prescription drugs?"

Neither of them answered.

"Okay…" I said. "Considering the fact I'm testifying before a grand jury tomorrow, I think I should refrain from askin' anything else."

"That's probably for the best," Jed said solemnly, and I wondered how much he knew. If Denny Carmichael was really the biggest drug dealer in the area, I couldn't imagine he'd let the doctor get away with undermining his business, which meant they had likely worked together. Had the doctor turned on Carmichael before he left town? Or had he perhaps caught wind that Mason was onto him? The timing of his abrupt yet well-planned departure was a little too coincidental for my liking.

Chapter Eight

When I walked up to Carter's office, the lights were off. An *Out of the Office* sign hung in the window, but the door was unlocked like he'd said it would be. I walked in and saw a note taped to the inside of the doorframe telling me to lock the door behind me.

A little more cloak-and-dagger than I'd expected, but I turned the lock before heading down the hall to his office. "Carter?"

The door was cracked open, but the lights were on in the windowless room. His office chair was spun around to face the wall of shelves full of law books behind the desk.

"Carter?"

The chair spun around, and I gasped in shock.

James Malcom sat in Carter's chair, staring at me with an intensity that stole my breath.

Tears stung my eyes. I backed up into the door I'd just closed behind me, but I had no intention of leaving. It felt like a pit I'd been carrying around for the last two months had suddenly been filled.

"How?" I finally asked. "Why?" I glanced around, realizing Carter was nowhere to be found. "Carter's in court, isn't he?"

"This seemed like the safest way for me to see you."

He wanted to see me. My skin flushed like I was some preteen with a crush, only what I felt for him was no crush. What I felt for him scared the crap out of me, especially since he'd practically abandoned me twice—the first time when he'd told me he was coming to save me and sent Denny instead, and the second time when he'd told me he loved me then drove away.

"Why haven't you reached out to me?" I asked, anger warring with my eagerness to see him.

He rose from his chair, but he was all quiet control, his face unreadable. His short brown hair was slightly longer than the last time I'd seen him. His face was covered in a couple of days' worth of stubble that my fingers ached to touch. His jeans hung low on his hips and his dark T-shirt clung to every muscle, giving me a reminder of the rippled body underneath.

Power radiated from him as he moved around the edge of the desk and advanced toward me. Had he always been this powerful? Or had his confidence and determination grown since I'd last seen him?

He stopped in front of me and studied me with wariness, the first sign that he wasn't in complete control of himself. "Do you want me to go?"

I started to ask him how he could say such a fool thing, but I realized my back was still pressed to the door. Maybe my intuition had better sense than my heart. The smart thing to do would be to turn around and walk away, but I'd already proven that it wasn't my day to make good choices. Besides, I was curious why he was suddenly here.

"No." I tried to make the word sound tough and decisive, but my emotions won out. His face became blurry through my unshed tears, and before I could stop myself, I lifted my hand to his cheek, my fingertips giving in to their need to feel his stubble. The familiar rasp of it comforted me—and then pissed me off. I pushed on his chest and he took a half step back as I blasted him. "Where the hell have you been, James?"

His face remained impassive. "I told you we couldn't have contact."

"You also told me that you love me."

"It's because I love you that I have to stay away. It's the only way I know to keep you safe in all of this."

I closed my eyes, trying to listen to the voice of reason, but my hormones were winning out. "I don't even understand what *all of this* is."

"It's safer that way," he said as his hand cupped my cheek.

I opened my eyes to see his face inches from mine, the longing in his eyes arresting my breath.

"God, I've missed you," he groaned as his mouth claimed mine. His hand sank into my hair as the other slipped around my waist, his fingers digging into my skin and holding me in place.

I kissed him back like a woman dying of thirst.

His lips became more demanding as he hauled me to his chest.

I slipped a hand under the edge of his shirt, my fingers seeking out his bare skin.

He sucked in a breath at my touch, then stilled. "You make me forget why I'm here." Pulling back slightly, he looked me over with closer scrutiny. "Are you okay?"

It took me two seconds before I realized he was talking about the incident in my office. "I'm fine."

His grip on me tightened, and his face hardened. "What did he want?"

I partially froze. "Carmichael?"

I almost asked him how he knew. I hadn't seen his men watching me for ages. Then again, Jed had already said people were attributing the attack to James. He, of course, knew better. Carmichael had plenty to worry about given that the grand jury had been called on account of those two dead police officers.

"Who else could it be?" His eyes widened slightly. "Was it someone else?"

"No. Carmichael sent one of his idiots to warn me about my testimony. The guy got pissed and tossed a chair out the window. I texted Carmichael and told him it was his responsibility to clean it up. He called me, and we threw around some threats."

His entire body became rigid. "What do you mean you threw around some threats?"

Exhaustion washed over me. I was tired of carrying so many burdens. I didn't want to think about Carmichael right now. All I wanted to do was soak James in. I leaned my cheek into his chest, the sound of his steady heartbeat filling me with reassurance.

He wrapped me up in his arms, holding me close.

"He told me he knew where I lived. I told him I could say the same thing. Then I reminded him that I took down Daniel Crocker and I could do the same to him."

His arms squeezed me tighter. "You threatened to *kill him*?"

"Look," I said, pulling back. "There was a lot of trash talk."

"Denny Carmichael doesn't trash-talk. He makes threats, then follows through."

Which was exactly what Jed had told me, but I could hardly change what had already happened.

"Do you really think he'd have me killed? He must know he'd be at the top of the suspect list." A new thought hit me. "You don't have anyone following me anymore. Did you think I was safe?" Then again, if he believed that, why had he chosen to stay away?

A dark looked crossed his eyes.

Even if one of James's men had been watching me, it wouldn't have kept Carmichael's man from smashing that chair into me rather than the window. I felt a throb of powerlessness again. I couldn't count on other people, even James and Joe, to keep me and my loved ones safe. I had to learn to do that myself.

Concern washed over his face. "You look tired, Rose. You've lost weight. Are you sick?"

"It's stress. Violet is getting closer to the end."

Before I realized what he was doing, he scooped me into his arms and walked over to a love seat against the wall opposite the door. He sat in the middle but kept me in his lap, my legs draped over his. "Tell me about your sister."

And so I did. He held me close, and I laid my head on his shoulder as I told him about our moments together over the last month. How hard it had been to watch her get weaker, how grateful I was that Carly had come into our lives.

"This Carly... you trust her?" he asked.

"You investigated her?" Something told me he'd done his own digging.

Irritation flickered in his eyes. "She appeared out of nowhere and she's livin' in your house. Of course I had her investigated."

I could have been pissed, but I'd felt so alone these past two months, and it felt good to know he'd been looking after me as best he could. That he hadn't completely walked out of my life.

"You're far too trusting, Rose."

"I'm not gonna ask if you found out anything threatenin' about her, because I already know who she really is and why she left home."

"What do you think you know?" he asked.

"I know there's a coincidence that ties her to Neely Kate, but that's all it is. Coincidence. She found out her fiancé had only proposed to her in exchange for a spot on the board of her father's company. Her daddy wanted her to come back to Texas, and rather than call her to talk about it, he tried to force the issue. When she overheard them talkin', she fled and spent the weekend with her friend. He gave her a beater car to take out of town, but it broke down on the highway into Henryetta."

His eyes narrowed. "No one just comes to Henryetta." He paused, then asked, "I suppose you know who her father is?"

"I know he's the sole owner of Blakely Oil."

"Randall Blakely is worth millions. Close to a billion. What the fuck is his daughter doing playing nursemaid to your sister?"

I rubbed my hand on his chest, trying to settle him down. "She's never been close to him. She says her mother died when she was little, and she was raised by nannies. She rarely saw her father until her fiancé encouraged her to make amends with him. When she found out the engagement was a ruse, she ran."

"You seriously believe that?" he asked, incredulous.

I leaned back to look at him. "It might not be the whole story, but yes, I believe her."

"Even if I told you I think her father's part of something shady?"

"Is he involved with Hardshaw?" Even if he had ties to the Dallas crime syndicate, I knew Carly wasn't part of it. I *knew* Carly.

"I don't know, but I've heard his name whispered in places." He gave me a sad look. "You always look for the good in people, but in this instance, you need to put some distance between yourself and that woman, Rose."

I slowly shook my head. "She's not part of her father's world. I trust her."

"You trust everyone." It wasn't a compliment.

"That's not true and you know it," I said softly. "I have great instincts with people."

He studied me for a moment. "You trust her with your defenseless sister?"

I chuckled. "First of all, Violet defenseless? Hardly. But yes. I even trust her with Mikey and Ashley." I paused. "Some people are born to be nurturers, and Carly is the walking definition of one."

He gave me a dark look.

"She spends all day takin' care of Vi, which isn't an easy chore. Especially since Vi is having trouble getting out of bed. Carly doesn't resent it—she likes feeling loved and needed. I can see it in her eyes," I said with a soft smile. "That's what she wants, what she *needs*. Not millions of dollars." I rubbed a nonexistent wrinkle from his shirt. "Money isn't everything, James Malcolm."

He was silent for a moment, then said, "Was that comment aimed at me?"

I could understand why he might see it that way. He had plenty of money—although I had no idea how much. But I knew that wasn't why he was embroiled in this mess. He'd taken over the crime world in Fenton County after it had been run by a maniac for years. He was trying to make the county a better place and worried who would fill the vacuum if he left.

"No," I said. "But you place too much value on it to see that it's not always a motivator."

"And you're naïve if you believe that's true."

I could have been pissed, but it wasn't a hateful statement, more an observation from his personal experience. Or maybe I just plain missed him too much to waste time on anger. I wrapped my arm around his neck and buried my face into his shoulder.

"Is your lack of money why you have a complete stranger workin' as your sister's nurse?" He frowned. "I should have thought of it sooner."

"No, I don't need your money, and that's not my independent streak talkin'. Violet has insurance. We're goin' to get more help, but for some reason it's hard for me to cave and bring in hospice nurses." My voice broke. "It's killin' me."

"Because it means accepting the inevitable," he said as he gently caressed my bare arm. I had a feeling he was referring to something else too. Whatever was going on in his life.

I lifted my head to look him in the eye. "What are you up to, James Malcolm? I know you've got something goin' on behind the scenes."

A grim look filled his eyes, but he tried to crack a smile. "It doesn't seem very prudent to share my secrets with you given your appointment with the grand jury tomorrow."

I frowned. While I savored every minute with him, his comment was a sharp reminder that I was supposed to be seeking counsel from my attorney. "I need to talk to Carter. Do you know if he'll be available later? I need to know what to do tomorrow."

He gathered both of my hands in one of his as he held my gaze. "You don't need Carter to know what to do tomorrow. You need to tell the truth."

I gasped in shock. "What?"

Slowly shaking his head, he placed a gentle kiss on my lips. "Don't worry about me. We need to worry about you. It's imperative you answer Deveraux's questions truthfully, otherwise he'll find out you perjured yourself."

"But…"

He kissed me again, more insistent this time. "Answer his questions but don't volunteer anything the jury doesn't ask." He lifted a hand to my cheek and stared into my eyes. "Hale would make you practice, but you're a smart woman. You'll figure it out."

"What if he asks me questions about you?"

"Answer what they ask with as little information as possible." He paused and his gaze bore into mine. "You can't lie, Rose."

"What if I implicate you?"

He gave me a reassuring smile. "I'll be okay."

But *how* would he be okay? Was Mason the person he was working with? Was that why he was so confident I wouldn't be asked any impossible-to-answer questions? I wanted to press him, but at this point I figured he was right—the less I knew the better. "Are you sure?"

"Nothing's a certainty, but I'm as sure as I can be. I'm too valuable."

His response only elicited more questions, but it seemed to confirm he was working with the authorities.

"What if he asks about how I became the Lady in Black last fall?"

"Leave out the visions, but tell him everything else."

Leaving out my visions made sense, but the rest? "And what about this summer? Buck Reynolds and Dermot? What about Merv kidnapping your brother?" I sucked in a breath. "What about you killing Kip Wagner? We told the sheriff's department I was the one who pulled the trigger."

His mouth drew into a tight line. "That too."

Panic swept through my head. "James, I'd be implicating myself."

He gave me a soft kiss. "It's okay. They won't do a thing to you. They know better than to touch you."

I stared at him, scared spitless. "I don't understand. What have you done?"

"I'm doin' what I have to do to protect you."

After everything he'd done in the criminal world—most of which I didn't even know about—I doubted he could get out of everything scot-free. If they *had* offered him immunity, he must have offered them something huge to earn it. But what? Why would the Feds care about a bunch of small-time criminals in Fenton County? "James…"

"Everything I do is for you, Rose. For us." He didn't give me a chance to ask more questions, because he kissed me senseless. His hand slipped under my shirt, stroking my back and pulling me closer.

I twisted and straddled his lap, facing him as I broke our kiss. "You'll go to prison."

He gave me a sad smile. "Things have been set in motion. It's too late to turn back now."

"*James.*"

He kissed me again, our lips parting only when he pulled my shirt over my head. "God, you're beautiful."

He quickly unhooked my bra and tugged it down my arms, leaving my chest exposed to him.

He trailed kisses down my collarbone to one breast, cupping the other in his hand. I leaned back my head and reveled in his touch.

"Rose," he groaned, "this is both heaven and torture."

I leveled my gaze to his and gave him a soft smile. "We'll take what we can get and focus on the present." Leaning forward, I captured his mouth in a fiery kiss.

He quickly caught up with me, sliding my skirt up my thighs. His hands slid underneath, slipping between my legs.

Gasping, I closed my eyes as my core tightened, making me ache for more.

"You feel so damn good," he grunted, his fingers sliding under the fabric.

I grabbed the bottom of his shirt and tugged it up, breaking our kiss to pull it over his head. "Carter—"

"Knows better than to walk in before I tell him he can come back," he growled, hooking his fingers around the top of my underwear and tugging down.

I rose up on my knees to help him while unbuttoning his jeans.

"You still on the pill?" He discarded my panties, then lifted his hips to slide his jeans down to his thighs.

"Yes," I said, but my answer was muffled by his kiss. Somehow we got his jeans off and my skirt removed.

His eyes narrowed and he paused. "Are you sure you want to do this in Hale's office?"

It was far from ideal, but I wasn't passing up the opportunity to be with him. "Why are you still talkin'?"

A slow, sexy grin spread across his face as his hand slid between my legs again. "I like the talking, and I'm pretty damn sure you do too."

My skin flushed at the memory of some of the things he'd said in bed before, and my whole body was soon aflame as he told me what he planned to do.

"*James.*"

He lifted my hips and entered me, filling me as I cried out. I didn't last long, he felt too good, and he came soon after me. I collapsed against his chest, resting my cheek on his shoulder.

"I want every day with you," I said, tears burning my eyes. "I know I should be grateful for what I can get, and I am, but I want you in my life."

His arms wrapped around me and held me close, his silence answer enough.

Even if he got out of this, how could our relationship work in the real world?

I'd worry about that tomorrow and be grateful for today.

Chapter
Nine

We cleaned up and dressed, then spent the next half hour talking, mostly about what had been going on in my life. After I told him about Violet's dinner party, I asked, "What did you say to Mike? I know you had something to do with him being more agreeable."

He swept a strand of hair from my face. "Don't you worry about that. But if he starts giving you a hard time again, just let me know through Carter. He has to be our go-between. You can't be contacting me after you leave." He paused. "And don't worry about seeing your niece and nephew after your sister dies. You'll still be a part of their life."

I narrowed my eyes, wondering again what he had on my brother-in-law. What had Mike done? I knew he'd bribed a building inspector when his career was taking off and Ashley was a baby, but as far as I knew, that was the only time he'd ventured into illegal activities. But what if there had been more?

I started to ask him, but he put a finger on my lips.

"Considering what you're doin' tomorrow, the less you know all of that, the better."

Worry burrowed into my gut, but James was right. The less I knew, the better. Vi and the kids had enough to worry about without the fear of Mike being arrested.

I stifled a yawn, only then realizing I'd been here for far longer than I'd intended. "What time is it?"

"Nearly three."

"What?" I jumped off the sofa. "I'm gonna be late for my appointment."

James stood and gently grabbed my arms. "Just call your client and tell them you're on your way."

Shaking my head as I picked up my purse, which I'd dropped by the door, I walked over to a mirror hanging on the wall to check my appearance. "It's a doctor's appointment."

"Are you sick?" he asked, his voice strained.

I started to finger-comb my disheveled hair. "It's not for me. It's so I can pick up Vi's pain medicine. A new doctor has bought Dr. Arnold's practice. The receptionist told me that she's meeting with all her new patients, but I suspect she's only checking on the ones who have narcotic prescriptions."

James stood behind me, watching my reflection.

I lifted my gaze to meet his. "I have my suspicions about what's goin' on there, but don't worry. I won't waste either of our time asking you questions you can't answer." I shot him an ornery grin and his face lit up with a genuine smile. I spun around to face him, grinning at him. "I love when you look like that."

"Like what?"

"Happy."

His smile fell and he lifted a hand to my face. "You need to know..." He swallowed, turning serious. "There may not be a happy ending here, Rose."

I already had my own suspicions about that, but I twisted my mouth into a wry grin. "You already told me that, James Malcolm.

You're not a forever guy, and certainly not a family man. I never expected anything more from you."

"But maybe my priorities have changed."

My heart skipped a beat. He'd alluded to this very thing the last time I saw him, but I couldn't let myself count on us having a future.

"I have to go," I whispered.

"I know," he whispered back, staring at me with a wistful expression.

We stood like that for several seconds before I said, "Take care of yourself, James. I don't know who's got your back now, but make sure you can trust them."

"I'm fine," he said, turning gruff. "I can take care of myself."

And he had. For years. Practically since he could walk. But over the last year and a half, I'd learned I couldn't do this on my own. In my heart, I believed the same was true of him. But telling him that was wasted breath. It didn't take a fool to see he was trying to steel himself for whatever was about to come.

Leaning over, he gave me a toe-curling kiss. "Go out the front and leave the door unlocked," he said, pulling back slightly. "Carter's assistant will be back soon enough to make sure the place doesn't get ransacked.

I nodded, close to tears.

"Don't worry about tomorrow," he said, his voice tight. "Just answer truthfully with one exception." He held my gaze. "Don't tell them you met with me this afternoon. If anyone asks you about this afternoon, tell them Carter left some papers for you to look over to prepare for your testimony. No one can ever know I was here, and it's important we keep it that way. Not even Jed or Neely Kate."

I started to argue with him, but only on impulse. If it helped keep James safe, this was a secret I'd keep. I nodded instead.

His hand cupped my cheek as he stared into my eyes. "I love you, Rose."

"I love you too."

I forced myself to turn and walk out of the office and out the front door. It wasn't until I'd climbed into the truck and started the engine that what had just happened fully hit me.

I'd just seen James.

But I didn't have time to dwell on it, because I was already late for my doctor's appointment, and I really needed that prescription for Violet.

I'd partially settled down by the time I pulled into the parking lot, but I needed to get myself together. This was no time for tears. I took three deep breaths, then got out of the truck and headed to the office.

The waiting room looked none the worse for wear when I walked in. Loretta was at the front desk with a phone pressed to her ear. She shot me a worried look, then said in a quiet tone, "I've gotta go," and hung up.

"Rose," she said. "I thought maybe you'd changed your mind."

"Sorry I'm running late," I said, glancing at the clock. 3:07. "Can I still meet with Dr. Newton?"

"Yeah, her next appointment isn't for another half hour," she said, getting out of her chair. "Come on through the back door."

I started to ask her about Wendy, but her phone rang. She ambled back to answer it, moving none too fast, and a nurse pushed open the door to the back. "Rose?"

I followed her into the short hallway.

She offered me a smile. "I would take you to the office, but Dr. Arnold left it a mess. Dr. Newton has been meeting with patients in the exam rooms."

"Sure," I said. "No problem." I'd meet her on the roof if that's what it took to get Violet's pain medication.

93

The nurse showed me to Exam Room Two, and I sat in a chair against the wall and settled in to wait for the doctor.

Less than a minute later, someone knocked lightly on the door, and a thirty-something woman in a lab coat walked in with an electronic tablet in her hand. She already struck me as more professional than Dr. Arnold, from her perfectly pulled-back light brown hair to the high shine on the stethoscope around her neck.

"Rose?" she asked, her gaze searching out mine.

"Yeah." I squirmed in my seat.

She held out her hand. "I'm Dr. Sylvia Newton. I'm sure you've heard that Dr. Arnold sold me his practice."

"Yes," I said, offering her a warm smile as I shook her hand. "I'm here for my sister, Violet Beauregard."

She sat on a stool and set her tablet on the counter beside her. "Yes, I was reading Violet's file this weekend." Her mouth twisted into a sad smile. "I'm so sorry that you've reached this point."

I swallowed the lump in my throat. "Thank you."

She leaned forward, clasping her hands in front of her. "Our goal is to make your sister's last days more comfortable, but I don't want to forget about her caregivers. How are you doing?"

I swiped a tear from the corner of my eye. "I'm still struggling to deal with all of this."

She sat back up. "I read in Violet's chart that she's living with you. That must be quite difficult."

My back stiffened, unsure of where she was going with her line of questioning.

"I have support. An old friend moved in to help and our cousin is also staying with us," I said, giving the official story we'd come up with to explain Carly's presence.

She gave me a warm smile. "That wasn't a judgment or criticism, Rose. It's a lot for one person to handle all alone. I was making sure you have a support system."

"Oh," I said. "Sorry."

"Don't be sorry." She shifted on her stool. "Part of the reason you're here is so I can check on you too. Caretakers often overlook their own needs while dealing with extraordinary stress. How are you handling everything?"

I tried to answer her, but the lump in my throat was too thick to make way for any words.

"Do you have someone to talk to? In larger cities there are support groups. I can check to see if there's something like that around here."

I shook my head again. "I doubt there is, but I talk to my friend Jonah sometimes. He's the pastor at the New Living Hope Revival Church."

"When was the last time you talked to him?"

I bit my lower lip, then released a small laugh. "Funny, I was just thinkin' about that this mornin'."

"Maybe you should fit a chat with him into your schedule," she said in an encouraging voice. "It might help relieve some of the pressure you're feeling." When I shot her a look of surprise— Dr. Arnold had never seemed fussed about my well-being—her eyes brimmed with sympathy and warmth. "You're taking care of your dying sister. You're both very young, and according to the gossiping office staff, your mother died last year." She cringed. "Don't worry. I've laid down the law about gossiping. I won't tolerate it in this office. I hesitated to mention anything, but I must admit it made me even more eager to check in with you."

The office staff was gossiping about me? I was used to being the topic of gossip, but given everything that was happening at the moment, it made the wheels in my head spin. "Can you tell me what else they're sayin' about me?" She looked horrified, and not a little embarrassed, so I quickly added, "Please, I've heard it all. I just need to know what's goin' around about me now. I'd rather be able to address it head-on rather than be left to wonder. My best friend usually knows, but people have clammed up around her lately."

She squirmed in her seat. "Rose…"

"Please. You won't offend me."

She paused a long moment, then said, "There was some talk about whether you killed your mother or not, but I've since learned that a criminal murdered her."

I nodded. "Anything more recent?"

Her cheeks flushed. "There was talk about your ex moving in with you."

"He's the old friend I mentioned. Do they think we're back together?"

Her face turned a deep rose color. "There was some disagreement about that."

I nodded, because Margi's comments earlier had indicated as much, although I still wasn't sure if that was good or bad.

"Rose," she said in a rush. "I don't condone gossip and the staff was reprimanded."

I gave her a reassuring look. "Trust me, I've been the source of gossip for longer than you know. Don't worry. I don't hold any of this against you."

She nodded, turning to her tablet as her embarrassment eased. "Back to you and your sister…are you having issues with anxiety or insomnia?"

"No more than I would expect," I said.

She gave me a weighing look. "Don't be a hero, Rose. There are things we can give you to help with the anxiety if it's overwhelming."

I shook my head. "I don't think I need anything. It's just stress."

"Tell me how it's been affecting your health."

I glanced down at my hands. "I've been very anxious. I haven't been sleeping well, yet I'm tired all the time. I haven't been eating because my stomach is in knots. I know I've lost about five or six pounds." I looked up at her. "But I don't want to go on anything. I'll be fine."

She pursed her lips and studied me for a moment. "When was the last time you had an exam?"

"Almost a year ago."

She turned back to her tablet and opened a new file. "Yes, I see that." Taking a breath, she turned back to me. "Would you be opposed to me doing a quick exam? I know you don't want to take anything now, but if you change your mind, I can write a prescription for you without seeing you again."

I hadn't planned on my own exam, but I saw no reason to refuse one. I needed to come in for one soon anyway, and this would save me time. "Uh…sure."

Dr. Newton stood, offering me a warm smile. "Just hop on the table."

After she'd listened to my heart and lungs, looked into every orifice in my head, and felt around on my neck and abdomen, she said, "Everything looks good, but I'd like to take some blood and do a urinalysis for a baseline. I'll also want to get your height and weight."

Carrying her tablet, she led me out to the hall and had me step on the scale. After she recorded my weight and height in her tablet, she sent me to the bathroom to pee in a cup. "When you're done, Anne will take your blood." She paused and held my gaze. "Rose, I'm here not just for Violet, but for you too. Please don't hesitate to reach out to me for help."

"Thank you, Dr. Newton," I said, overwhelmed by her kindness.

She walked into the next exam room, and I heard her greeting someone as I stepped into the restroom to pee in the cup. When I was done, I went into the hall and a nurse I recognized from my visits with Violet was waiting for me in the hall. The cold glint in her eyes indicated the animosity I'd felt from her in the past hadn't been in my imagination as Violet had suggested. I had a feeling I'd found the source of some of that office gossip.

She took the cup and gestured to a room down the hall. "Head down there."

I'd been to the lab room with Violet, so I knew where to go despite the nurse's vague directions. I sat in a blood draw chair and glanced around the room, reading the posters to stave off my nervousness about getting stuck with a needle.

Anne washed her hands, then pulled on a pair of gloves.

"Great weather we're having," I said, trying to clear some of the tension from the room. Anne didn't seem happy to be here with me, which only added to my anxiety.

"I guess," she said, taking a seat on a stool and rolling closer to me. She got everything ready to draw my blood, then wrapped the tourniquet around my arm, looking cross the entire time.

It didn't seem like a good idea to antagonize a woman who was about to stab me with a needle, but I couldn't help asking, "Have I done something to offend you?"

Her dark eyes lifted to mine. "I'm friends with Dena."

Well, crap.

Anne stabbed the needle in my arm with more force than necessary, and I cried out in surprise.

"Gonna snitch on me for that too?" she asked with a sneer. A hateful look filled her eyes. She looked down to change the tube in the syringe, making me realize what a precarious situation I was in.

"What on earth are you talkin' about?" I asked. "I've barely spoken to you. How could I have snitched on you?"

Surprise washed over her face, like she'd said something she hadn't meant to say, but she buried her head as she finished filling the tubes. She slapped a bandage on my arm hastily, as though worried she might catch the bubonic plague from me. "You're good to go."

I stood and the room began to spin, so I sat back down.

Anne gave me a funny look, then grudgingly asked, "Are you okay?"

"I guess I stood too quickly," I said, sucking in a deep breath. Instinctively, I put my head between my legs.

"Rose?" I heard Dr. Newton say from the doorway.

"I'm just feeling a little light-headed. Give me a minute." I took several more breaths, then sat up, still feeling light-headed but no longer close to passing out. "Sorry about that."

"Do you usually feel light-headed when you have your blood drawn?" she asked with concern on her face.

"No," I said. "But I've been feeling light-headed a lot lately." I figured she, at least, was on my side and I should tell her everything. "I passed out this morning at the nursery I own."

Her eyes widened as she turned to Anne, who was standing in the doorway, and added more tests to the blood work. It sounded like gibberish to me.

"I'm fine," I insisted. "It's just stress."

She squatted next to me. "Stress doesn't usually make people faint. I want you to take it easy for the next day or two until I get these results back."

My mouth twisted into a wry grin. "I'm testifyin' before a grand jury tomorrow. There's no gettin' out of that."

She studied me for a moment, not looking entirely surprised. "You knew?"

"Not that you, specifically, have been called to testify, but I'd heard about the grand jury."

Why would the state police tell the new doctor about the grand jury? It seemed to confirm my suspicions about Dr. Arnold's possible involvement with Denny, although there was no point in asking her about it. She wouldn't be able to tell me anything.

I stood. "I need to get goin'."

She placed a hand on my arm. "Rose, you're obviously under a great deal more stress than I realized. I suggest you take some time off from work and focus on yourself and your sister."

I started to protest that I couldn't stop working. I was the only person supporting three people—me, Violet, and Carly—but the words dried up. She was right, and besides, Maeve had reminded me earlier that help was at hand if I needed it. Bruce Wayne and his crew were carrying the load for all of us. He'd encouraged me multiple times to take a break, this morning included.

"Thanks, Dr. Newton. I'll see what I can do to rearrange my schedule."

I headed for the door, but she called out, "Wait. I forgot to give you Violet's prescription."

Embarrassment washed through me. How could I have forgotten?

"Thank you," I said, taking it from her outstretched hand and stuffing it into my purse.

"Don't forget to call your friend Jonah."

"Good idea." Since Violet had invited him to dinner, I could talk to him then.

Right now, I had some questions for Loretta.

I stopped at the checkout counter, and Loretta motioned that I could just leave.

"Actually," I said, leaning against the chest-high ledge, "I ended up having a checkup of my own. Do I need to give you my co-pay?"

She walked over and narrowed her eyes. "Are you okay?"

I waved my hand. "I'm fine. I was due for one, so Dr. Newton decided to go ahead and take care of it."

The look she gave me suggested she wasn't totally buying it, but she pulled my name up on the computer, and I handed her my debit card.

"Say," I said, trying to sound nonchalant. I was curious about Wendy but decided it would be best to inquire about her in a roundabout way. "I know you can't talk much about Dr. Arnold, but do you think there's another reason he left other than runnin' off with his nurse?"

Loretta paused mid-swipe, holding my card aloft. "What have you heard?"

"I think plenty of us have heard rumors that he was selling prescriptions," I said. "But frankly, I never believed it."

She rolled her eyes. "Of course he wasn't. I still can't believe what people are saying. Next thing you know, they'll be sayin' he took off in a spaceship."

I forced a chuckle. "Trust me, I know how groundless rumors can be. But then Wendy showed up this morning...and now I wonder if there might be some truth to it after all."

"Don't be silly," Loretta said, tearing off the receipt and handing it to me with my card. "Wendy is a hot mess."

"What happened to her?" I asked. "Did the police arrest her?"

"Nah," she said, flopping back down in her seat. "She took off before they got here, and Mrs. Preston decided not to press charges."

"Wendy never saw the doctor?" I asked.

"Of course not. Even if she hadn't run off, Dr. Newton didn't have time to fit her into the schedule. I just said that to appease her."

I was more curious than ever, and I knew where to go next.

I offered her a wide smile. "Thanks, Loretta."

"You go home and take care of your sister," she called after me.

I planned to. After I made a trip to the Burger Shack.

Chapter Ten

The mother in the waiting room had insinuated that Wendy worked at the Burger Shack, so it seemed like the logical place to look for her. It was worth a try, anyway, and I was actually a little hungry. On my way to the fast-food restaurant, I stopped by the pharmacy to fill Violet's prescription, telling them I'd be back later for it. I also sent a text to Neely Kate, telling her my appointment had gone fine, and that I'd see her at the farm later.

I was pretty sure there was probably a picture of Neely Kate behind the counter of Burger Shack, warning the staff not to mess around with her. She and I had once questioned a Burger Shack supervisor, a suspect in a case we'd worked on.

The place was empty when I walked in, but it was close to four, not exactly peak lunch or dinner times.

"Hi," I said when a teenage girl walked up to the counter to take my order. Her uniform was stained and her name tag read *Viv*. "I'd like a small burger with ketchup and lettuce."

She pushed out a bored sigh as she punched my order into the register. "You want cheese with that?"

"No."

She kept her eyes on the register as she asked, "Fries or a drink?"

"No," I said. "Just the burger."

"How about a cookie for a dollar?" she asked in a bored tone.

"Just the burger," I said in frustration.

"Gawd," the girl snapped. "No need to get huffy."

I stared at her in disbelief, then grumbled under my breath as I handed her a ten-dollar bill. No need getting worked up over this girl. Besides, I needed to get on her good side.

She handed me the change, and I glanced around the counter. "Do you have a tip jar?"

Her eyes widened. "Reggie won't let us have one."

"Can I just hand the tip to you?" I asked, trying to look innocent.

"Yeah. Sure." She grinned as she held out her hand.

I handed her a five-dollar bill and her eyes grew wider.

"Is Wendy workin' today?"

Her frown was back. "Whatcha want with Wendy?"

"I'm worried about her," I said. "I saw her this morning at Dr. Arnold's, and she wasn't in a good place."

She snorted. "Is that your way of sayin' she was high as a kite?"

I grimaced. "She *did* seem a little out of it."

She snorted again. "What the hell was she doin' at Dr. Arnold's?" She shook her head. "Stupid bitch."

"Why do you say that?" I asked, trying not to sound too curious. The last thing I wanted to do was scare her into silence.

The girl narrowed her eyes. "Why do you care?"

She was touchier than a bramble bush. "I'm a friend of hers. She asked me for advice on how to take care of her cat's swollen foot."

"Stinkerbell?" she asked with a laugh. "That's her neighbor's cat. Wendy gets obsessed with him when she's stoned. Weird-ass shit if you ask me."

I frowned. "Is she scheduled to work today?"

Her upper lip curled. "What's it to you?"

"Like I said, I'm worried about her. When I left the doctor's office, she was wrestling with a woman over her purse."

A huge grin spread across her face. "I sure would have loved to see that. Did you happen to get video?"

I chose not to tell her that Mrs. Preston's little boy had probably plastered it all over the internet. "No. Wendy was almost arrested."

"Like it would be the first time," the girl scoffed. "Wendy's fine."

"So she's not working today?"

"She opens tomorrow."

Deciding to take a chance, I said, "Do you happen to know where she lives?"

"I'm really not supposed to tell anyone," the girl said as she grabbed a burger from under the heat lamp behind her. As she stuffed it into the bag, she said, "Besides, Wendy's fine. She does this from time to time, although I heard Dr. Arnold left town, so maybe it's the end of the line for her."

"Dr. Arnold supplied her with drugs?"

"She worked for him."

My mouth dropped open. "What?"

"Yeah," she said with a shrug, then pursed her lips. "That's probably why she's so upset." She handed me the bag. "Have a nice day."

I took it from her, lost in thought. "Thanks."

I headed for the exit, my mind whirling. Was Wendy working with Denny Carmichael?

As soon as I got into the truck, I unwrapped my hamburger and took a bite, but my stomach turned when I got a mouthful of onions. Normally I liked them, but over the last month they'd turned my stomach every time I ate them. I tossed the sandwich back into the bag in disgust and grabbed my phone. I needed to talk to Joe. I wanted to tell him about Wendy, but I was more curious to hear if he'd found out anything about Mason. Not to mention I'd have to explain what had happened at the office. Better to do that *before* dinner tonight.

I sent him a text. *Are you busy right now? Can we meet for a quick chat?*

I'm at the courthouse. I can be at your office in a half hour.

I needed to check on the office anyway. *See you then.*

I stopped by the pharmacy and picked up Violet's prescription, then headed back downtown.

When I parked down the street, I was surprised to see particleboard had been nailed over the opening and the glass had been cleaned up off the sidewalk. There was no sign of the chair, and I hoped someone had put it back inside, although it was secondhand and would be no great loss.

Shame washed through me. How could I have left it like that? But I knew the answer, even if it wasn't much of an excuse—I was completely overwhelmed by all the upheaval in my life. It had been one thing too many, so I'd run from it and tried to pretend it wasn't there.

That was the old me, and I didn't like the implications.

Pushing out a sigh, I unlocked the front door and let myself in. The glass on the office floor had been cleaned up too, and the office chair was back in its original place, looking none the worse for wear.

I sat down at my desk and booted up my accounting program. I was in no frame of mind to design anything, but I could handle inputting receipts.

I was focused on my work when the bell on the front door sounded. My heart skipped a beat, but I reminded myself Joe was supposed to drop by. It surprised me to see Carter instead.

"Rose, I take it this afternoon went well."

"Uh…yeah." My face flushed with embarrassment, but I still gave him a grateful smile. "Thank you."

"Don't be thankin' me," he said in a dry tone as he sat in a client chair in front of my desk. "I told him it was an asinine idea, but since when does he listen to me?"

"I'm sorry if he's frustratin' you," I said, meaning it. While I was thankful we'd had that hour to ourselves, I knew James didn't always take the advice given to him, which meant he was making Carter's life ten times more stressful.

He leaned back and crossed his legs. "You and I still need to have a chat to discuss your testimony."

I wasn't surprised. Although James seemed to think there was nothing for Carter and me to discuss, Carter was our attorney. He wouldn't be doing his due diligence if he sent me off to testify without a chat.

"Okay." I clicked my mouse and put my computer screen to sleep. "I need to warn you that Joe Simmons will be showing up at any time."

He nodded. "I'm your attorney. We're having a professional meeting." A dark look filled his eyes. "But if he shows up before we finish, I suggest you send him on his way. I do hope you haven't shared sensitive details with the chief deputy sheriff."

I could have gotten angry, but I understood his loyalty to his client. In fact, I was grateful for it. "As I told you earlier, we share the same concerns. I've been loyal to your client, and he knows it."

He gave me a curt nod. "I take it he discussed your testimony."

"He told me to tell the truth."

Carter looked like he'd swallowed a cockroach. "Yes." The word sounded strangled.

"You disagree?"

"With telling the truth? Given the situation, and given that both of you are my clients, yes, it's what you should do."

I cocked my head as I studied him. "But it's not what you would have me do."

"We've moved past that point. He's made a decision and it's too late to turn back now."

Which was exactly what James had implied earlier. Icy fear settled into my belly. "What has he done, Carter?"

He gave me a wry grin. "So he still hasn't told you? He's adamant that no one know the details. Not even Jed." He shook his head, then narrowed his eyes on me. "He's a fool. A fool for *you*."

Fear snaked its way into my gut. My head. "He's working with the FBI, isn't he?"

He studied me. "He's made a risky move that I wholeheartedly advised him against. But rest assured, this has been in play for far longer than you think. It's only recently that the heat has been increased." He took a breath, then exhaustion covered his face. "Tell the truth. Keep your answers short. Don't volunteer information, but for God's sake, don't lie. Then I'll be havin' to haul *you* out of a mess."

"What about Denny Carmichael?"

"What about him?"

The bell on the door dinged and Joe walked in, freezing mid-step when he saw Carter.

"Hale," he said in a hard tone.

"Simmons." Carter sounded amused, but then he loved riling up law enforcement officers.

The two men shared a dark look, full of undercurrents, before Carter stood and said, "I need to be goin'. The special prosecutor is keeping me on my toes."

Joe's face lit up with an amused smirk. "I bet."

Carter ignored him and headed toward the door.

"Carter, will you be there tomorrow?" I asked.

He stopped at the door and turned to face me. "I'll likely be tied up, but they wouldn't let me in with you anyway. Just do what we talked about, and you'll be fine."

He gave Joe another cocky grin, then walked out and shut the door behind him.

I watched Carter through the window on the right side of the door as he crossed the street and headed back to his office.

Joe lowered into the chair in front of my desk, looking stiff and ready to do battle. I was sure it was over my irresponsible behavior after the window was broken.

"Joe," I said with a sigh. "I'm so sorry. I should have called you right away about the window. You've put your life on hold for me, and I was thoughtless and irresponsible. Can you please forgive me? I don't think I can handle the cold shoulder from you right now."

Surprise washed over his face once again, and his body relaxed. "Rose," he said, but this time with much more warmth, "I realize you've been running around the last year hoarding a closet full of secrets, but I'm here for you. You have to know that by now."

"I do," I said, suddenly feeling the weight of the world on my shoulders. I needed to change the subject. "Did you know about Dr. Arnold fleeing the county?"

He grimaced and sat back in his chair. "I learned about it this morning at my meetin'. Apparently, the FBI knew all about it but didn't feel obligated to tell any local law enforcement." Irritation flickered in his eyes, but he shifted in his seat and then it was gone. "Did you have trouble picking up Violet's medication? I wondered after I found out about Arnold. We can move her paperwork to a new doctor. I heard about a good one up in Magnolia."

"Nah," I said. "I met the new doctor, and she's very nice and supportive. I had to go in this afternoon to chat with her. I think she's meetin' all her patients who use narcotics, but I didn't have any trouble. She knows Vi needs it."

"Sounds like she's got her head on straight," he said in approval.

I hesitated, wondering if I should bring this up, but decided he had a right to know. "Did you know half the town thinks we're datin'?"

"That was the plan," he said, his voice firm as though preparing for an argument, "and I decided not to leave it to chance. I've gone out of my way to make people think we're a couple."

I blinked. "How did you do that?"

"I've dropped your name in conversations with people I knew were gossips," he said. "Saying you and I had watched a particular movie the night before and loved it, or that we'd gone to the new movie theater up in Magnolia."

All true, but he'd manipulated the information to make our time together sound romantic.

His jaw tightened. "Now, before you get mad—"

"I'm not mad," I said sincerely. "I'm grateful to have such a good friend."

He sat back, looking stunned.

"We really are growin' up, aren't we?" I teased.

We sat in a comfortable silence for a few seconds. I'd tried to push him away earlier, and he'd dug his heels in. I couldn't deny I was grateful for his support, and that he'd settle for friendship, whatever he might privately want. Maybe I wasn't ready to let him go just yet. Did that make me selfish?

My mind was still on my visit with Dr. Newton. "When I showed up at the doctor's office this morning, there was a woman who came lookin' for Dr. Arnold. She was stumbling around like she was drunk or high. She ended up gettin' into a scuffle with a woman in the waiting room, and the office staff had to call the police."

A grin lit up his eyes. "Sounds like you had an eventful morning."

"True," I said slowly. "But I found out from Wendy's coworker that she was workin' for Dr. Arnold."

His eyes narrowed and he shifted forward. "Doin' what exactly?"

"She didn't say."

Confusion washed over his face. "*Who* didn't say?"

"The cashier at the Burger Shack." When he gave me a look that suggested he didn't follow, I said, "That's where Wendy works. I take it her work with Dr. Arnold was a part-time gig."

He paused for a moment, his face going blank. "Did someone hire you and Neely Kate for a case?"

"No."

A familiar irritation filled his eyes. "So what were you doin' askin' around about Wendy?"

That was a great question, one I wasn't sure how to answer, especially given my upcoming grand jury testimony.

Pushing out a sigh, he shook his head. "You can't help yourself. You're like a cat with that damn curiosity."

He was right. All of the previous investigations I'd done had only encouraged my innate desire for answers. Especially when it involved the criminal world. And especially when it might affect James in some way.

"Rose," he said emphatically, "I'm beggin' you to let this one go. The FBI's all over it, and if they think you're messing in something you don't belong in, they'll bring the hammer down." His eyes held mine. "Promise me you'll stay out of it."

"I didn't mean to investigate anything, Joe," I said. "I was worried about Wendy because she was so out of it and wanted to check on her."

"And you just happened to know where she worked," he said, clearly not buying a word of it.

"Someone mentioned it at the doctor's office. Plus I was hungry for a burger, so I figured why not get one there and inquire about Wendy?"

His gaze narrowed. "Uh-huh…"

"And the cashier volunteered the information after I mentioned I was worried about Wendy. She said Wendy was probably at the office because she worked for Dr. Arnold." When he still looked unconvinced, I added, "I could have tried to press her about what Wendy did for Dr. Arnold, but I let it go."

His face softened. "Rose, with the grand jury and Violet…you really need to keep your nose clean right now. Especially with the FBI sniffin' around."

He was right and I knew it, and I had to admit he wasn't wrong about me. Part of me was interested in more than just Wendy's well-being. "I know. I'm sorry. I'll be more careful."

Sitting back, he turned serious. "Now, let's talk about why you didn't tell me about the window."

I should have expected this one, but it still made my stomach tumble. "I think you know why."

"Denny Carmichael sent someone to keep you quiet."

Raking my teeth over my lower lip, I nodded.

"Did he hurt you?"

"No." I told him about the entire exchange. He listened intently, and after I finished, he was silent for a moment.

"I wish you'd trusted me enough to tell me. To let me do the job you asked me to do."

He had a right to be hurt, so I didn't say a word, just stewed in my guilt.

He took my silence as an admission that he was right. "After everything, you still don't trust me."

The hurt on his face was my undoing. "That's not it at all, Joe. I'm tryin' to *protect* you."

"Protect me?" he asked, incredulous. "Need I remind you I'm the one wearin' a badge *and* a gun?"

I glanced down at the weapon holster at his hip and flashed him a tight smile. "I've got one too."

His mouth twisted, making it clear what he thought about that, yet he'd agreed weeks ago that I needed to carry it.

"I have the law on my side, Rose."

"And what kind of position would you be in if I told you everything? We already agreed that some things were better left unsaid," I reminded him.

He glanced over his shoulder at the particleboard covering the window and rubbed his chin. "I'm startin' to reconsider that decision."

"Joe…" I paused, waiting for him to meet my gaze. "I intend to tell them the full truth tomorrow."

His body tensed. "What exactly does that mean?"

"It means I'm telling them about Denny. And I'll answer whatever they ask me about James too. I'll answer whatever they ask."

Fear flashed in his eyes. "I'm gonna need to get a detail assigned to the farm. I also think it might be a good idea if you skip work for a few days."

I nodded. "Dr. Newton already recommended the same thing to me. At my physical, she suggested I take some time off and spend it with Violet."

He gave a slight shake of his head. "I thought you just went in to talk to her about Violet."

"I did," I assured him. "But when I told her how anxious I've been feeling, she decided to do a physical in case I need something to help with it."

"Like antidepressants?" he asked in surprise.

"I don't know exactly. I told her no, but she said I was due for another exam soon anyway, so I figured I might as well do it. If I change my mind about the pills, I can let her know." When I saw the concern in his eyes, I rushed to say, "Joe, I'm not depressed. The stress of everything has been gettin' to me, is all. I'm tired all the time and I've lost weight over my upset stomach. Normal reactions to stress."

Guilt washed over his face. "I should be helpin' more."

"Don't be silly. You're already helpin' more than you know. We have Carly helpin' too, for heaven's sake. But the end is approachin'…" A lump filled my throat. "I'm strugglin' to consider a world without my sister."

Tears filled Joe's eyes. "You won't be alone, Rose. I'll be here for you. So will Neely Kate." His throat bulged like he'd just swallowed a bug, but he added, "And so will Jed."

The fact that Joe had accepted Jed into his circle of trust, however reluctantly, wasn't lost on me. "I know y'all will be there. And you know how grateful I am for that."

"But she's still your sister," he said softly.

"Yeah," I said. "She's far from perfect, but she's my family."

"I get it," he said, glancing at the wall with a faraway look. "I feel that way about Kate."

Joe's younger sister had been locked up for being criminally insane, but a couple of months ago, she'd escaped and wreaked all kinds of havoc, including murdering a few people, all in the name of helping Neely Kate. But then she'd disappeared, and as far as I knew, neither one of them had heard from her since.

"Do you miss her?"

He gave me a half smile. "We haven't been close for years, but there's a part of me that wishes for something I can't have."

"I get that," I said, repeating his earlier response with a sympathetic smile.

His gaze held mine. "I think you're one of the few who does." Glancing away, he cleared his throat. A moment of silence passed, and then he said, "I hate to put a sheriff detail on you tonight for fear of clueing Malcolm and Carmichael in to the fact that you're a threat." His brow furrowed. "I might need to ask the state police for help."

"James won't come after me, Joe. And as for Carmichael…I'm sure he thinks I have too much to lose to testify against him and James."

His jaw tightened. "I know you think—"

"James is the one who encouraged me to tell the truth. About everything. Even the Lady in Black, if they ask about that."

He froze as he grasped my meaning. "You'll implicate yourself." He reached for his cell phone. "I'm gonna make a call and see about getting you a plea deal. If you have information they want, then we need to ensure you're given leniency." Anger washed over his face. "Why the hell isn't Hale asking them to work a deal for your testimony?"

"He told me I'd be safe."

His face reddened. "How the fuck does Carter Hale know that you'll be safe? Has he worked out a deal already?"

I pushed out a breath. "It wasn't Carter who told me I'd be safe."

Some of Joe's bluster deflated. "Malcolm." Once that sank in, he said, "He called you."

I didn't correct him, but I needed to tell him something. I was caught in a catch-22. I felt like I would be betraying James if I told Joe everything, but I didn't want to betray Joe either. Joe had put his life on hold to protect me. He deserved some answers.

"You can't tell anyone, Joe. This has to be between just you and me." I held his gaze. "I mean it. *No one.* If you think keeping this to yourself will compromise your job or your ethics, then you need to tell me now."

He studied me for several long seconds. "If I'm gonna help you, I need to know what's goin' on. What did he say to you?"

"Joe, while I appreciate everything you've done for us, I don't expect a single thing from you," I said in a tight voice. "If you decide this is too much, you're not gonna hurt my feelings if you pack up your stuff and move out tonight."

He reached across the desk and placed his hand over mine. "Rose. I'm here, and I'm not telling a soul. This is between you and me, but I have to know if Malcolm's playin' you."

I understood his suspicion. Joe knew Skeeter Malcolm only by reputation—which I reminded myself was likely well earned. It stood to reason he'd assume the worst.

"He said they'd know if I lied. When I reminded him that I could get in trouble, he told me they wouldn't risk everything to go after me."

Shock filled his eyes. "Malcolm really did make a deal."

My stomach somersaulted with anxiety over my possible betrayal. "I don't know for certain—he's never confirmed it—but…"

His face hardened. "You believe he'd risk his deal for you?"

Was I a fool to trust him? If I reviewed our history, maybe. And yet the answer came easily.

"Yes."

He got to his feet and began to pace. "I don't like it, Rose. There's too much at stake." He stopped and turned to face me. "You need your own lawyer. You need your own deal."

I couldn't help thinking he was right, but would I ruin whatever James was up to? He'd assured me that everything he'd done, and agreed to, was to see me safe. Could I stake my life on that?

Closing my eyes, I leaned over my desk and rested my forehead on my crossed arms. "I can't deal with this right now."

Seconds later, Joe's hand began to knead my stiff neck. "Let me make some calls. Given everything you're goin' through with Vi, maybe I can get you an extension for your testimony. I'm sure you're not the only witness they're callin'."

I lifted my head off my arms and glanced up at him, trying to temper my hope. "Do you think you can manage it?"

He gently tugged my hand, pulling me to my feet. "Go home, Rose, and I'll head over to the courthouse and see what I can do." He frowned as he searched my face. "You look exhausted, so maybe fit a nap in there, although it's highly unlikely given the fact Ashley and Mikey are there." He grinned, but it didn't quite reach his eyes. "They'll never let Aunt Rose slip past."

I wrapped my arms around his shoulders and pulled him in for a hug. "Thank you, Joe. You have no idea how much I appreciate you."

He kissed the top of my head and pulled away. "I'm just bein' a good friend. You'd do the same for me."

After everything he'd done for me, I'd walk through fire for him, but he and James were at cross-purposes. If I were forced to choose between being loyal to either of them, would I choose the man who'd stood by me the past two months, expecting nothing in return, or the man who claimed to love me yet made it very clear he never wanted to settle down?

I only hoped I was never forced to make that choice.

Chapter Eleven

It was shortly before five when I turned off the highway onto the farm, so I was surprised by the number of vehicles already parked to the right side of the house. Violet sat on a wicker chair on the front porch while Ashley and Mikey ran around in the front yard with Muffy. Witt was kicking a soccer ball to the kids, although Muffy thought she was playing too. Marshall stood to the side with his hands stuffed in the front pockets of his jeans, looking like he wanted to join them but was unsure of his place.

I parked my truck next to Neely Kate's car and got out just as Jed and Neely Kate were rounding the back corner of the house, carrying some folding chairs. Neely Kate had four of them slung over her arms.

"How did the doctor's appointment go?" Neely Kate asked, then blew a puff of air toward a strand of hair that had fallen into her eyes.

I hurried over to take a chair from her, but she turned to the side, keeping it out of my reach.

"Neely Kate's tryin' to prove to Witt that she's not a lightweight."

My brow furrowed in confusion.

Jed laughed. "Witt bet her she couldn't carry four chairs at once." His eyes lit up as he stared down at her. "I tried to convince her it was Witt's way of gettin' out of lendin' a hand, but she's bound and determined to prove him wrong."

They weren't heavy, but they sure looked awkward as she walked around the edge of the front porch.

"There!" she called out as she dropped all four chairs to the ground.

Witt cast Neely Kate a grin as he kicked a ball toward Mikey. "Well, I'll be daggum. You did it."

"Don't you ever call me weak again!" she shouted at him.

Witt's grin spread even wider—right before he turned back to Mikey and got a face full of the soccer ball.

Violet burst out laughing and I heard Carly giggle as she walked out the front door with a pitcher of lemonade and a handful of glasses.

"Looks like Mikey showed Witt," Carly said, setting the pitcher on the small table tucked between two chairs. "Proof that karma truly exists."

"Thanks for the sympathy, Carly," Witt grumbled, reaching his hand to his face to check for blood.

"Don't you worry," Violet called out. "You still have a pretty face, Witt Rivers."

He turned back to look at Carly, holding his hands up at his sides. "What do you think, Carly? Do you think I have a pretty face?"

Her brows lifted, mischief in her eyes. "I used to tell my kids that pretty is as pretty does."

Everyone stopped in their tracks and stared at her. Carly's previous life was pretty much a secret from everyone except me, Neely Kate, and Jed. She never let information slip, but here she was dropping a huge clue about her past career as an elementary school teacher.

Violet was glowing at the accidental slip, but Witt's eyes filled with horror.

"You have kids?"

A cocky grin lit up Carly's eyes. "Sure did. About eighteen of them."

Leaving him to stew on that, she turned around and went back into the house.

Neely Kate and I exchanged a glance. Carly was growing more comfortable with us, which came as a relief. I wanted her to feel at home here. I wanted her to stay.

Witt watched her walk away, his mouth hanging open. "She was jokin', right?"

Another soccer ball hit him in the back. He whirled around to glare at Mikey as Neely Kate, taking umbrage at Witt's tactlessness, stood scowling at him with hands on her hips, then laid into him the moment he turned back to face her. "You leave Carly alone, Witt Rivers!"

"I was just makin' small talk. Besides, how in the hell could she have eighteen kids?"

"I'm gonna let you figure that one out," Neely Kate said, heading up the porch steps and through the front door. "You need to set up the lawn chairs so I can help Carly."

"How many people did y'all invite?" he grumbled as he headed over to the mess of chairs.

Jed was setting his chairs up and shaking his head at the whole mess.

I walked up the steps and considered going inside to deflect Neely Kate from helping Carly in the kitchen, but Violet reached out and snagged my wrist. "Come sit with me."

Offering her a worried smile, I sat in the empty chair on the other side of her. "Are you warm enough? Do you need another blanket?"

She released a soft laugh. "I'm fine. Just sit."

I took my seat, but my stomach was a ball of stress. Although I felt I should be helping, I had to admit to myself that I needed a minute to unwind.

Worry filled Violet's eyes. "What happened?"

I blinked. "What are you talkin' about?"

"I heard Jed and Neely Kate talkin' about you and a grand jury. You should have told me, Rose. I'm not dead yet. I can still help."

I shot her a deep frown. "Stop talkin' like that, Vi."

"Why not? It's true. I take it Mason's asked you to testify."

"By sendin' a state trooper with a personal invite," I said sarcastically.

"Are you worried?"

I wondered how much to tell her, especially since other people were within hearing distance. "Let's just say I know things the grand jury will want to know."

"Things about the criminal world?" she asked. "I'm not stupid," she said in response to my look of surprise. "I know Joe's here to protect you."

"Vi…"

"It's okay." She gave me a smug look. "I know Mason came back to look into corruption in the county. And I know you were involved with Skeeter Malcolm last winter. You must have seen things." Worry washed over her face again. "Are you scared?"

"More nervous than scared. But Joe is planning on gettin' extra help to protect us until this is done. Denny Carmichael is our biggest threat." I wasn't sure why I had confided that, but she was living here, so she had a right to know the potential danger.

"I knew it couldn't be Skeeter Malcolm," she said with a sad look in her eyes.

Were we the worst-kept secret in Fenton County? "Why not?"

"From what little you told me about the entire nightmare last fall, you always spoke about him with respect."

I wondered if I should protest, but instead I asked her something I'd been stewing over. "Is that why Mike hates me now?"

She paused before responding, keeping her gaze on her kids. "Mike…" She pushed out a sigh. "Rose, there's something you should know."

I shot out of my seat when I heard the crunch of gravel toward the highway. Jed stood straight up, and Witt released the chair he'd been unfolding and stood at attention too.

"It's only Jonah," I said, pushing out a sigh of relief.

"You're expectin' trouble?" Violet asked, her voice firm.

I leaned down and patted her shoulder. "No. Denny Carmichael's not stupid. He'd be at the top of the suspect list if anything happened to me or my family."

"What do you know that Denny Carmichael wants you to keep quiet about, Rose?" she asked in a small voice.

"I'm more worried about what he knows about *me*."

Her eyes widened with fear. "Your visions," she whispered.

I nodded.

Jonah's sedan pulled up behind Witt's car. He and his girlfriend, Jessica, got out of the car, and I was overwhelmed with relief at the sight of him. Jonah had been my rock after my breakup with Joe. He'd taught me how to keep my momma's hateful voice out of my head.

The kids squealed with excitement that someone new had arrived, and Muffy ran over with them to join the welcoming party.

Jonah smiled at me and Vi, showing off his pearly white teeth. "Violet, thank you for inviting us tonight."

"You're important to Rose, so that makes you important to me," she called down to him.

Carly came out soon afterward and waved to Jonah and Jessica. They'd come by to visit with Violet a few times, so she'd met them, but she seemed more withdrawn with them. They were still mostly strangers. But Jonah being Jonah, he soon had her smiling and chatting as she started passing out glasses of lemonade.

"Carly," I said, "let me help. You've made dinner and helped with Violet all day. Why don't you sit and chat with the others?"

She hesitated, so I got up and took the pitcher from her, then nudged her toward the chair I'd vacated. Once I got close to her, I could see the exhaustion on her face. Guilt clogged my throat. While Carly was a nurturer, just like I'd told James, nurturers rarely asked for help or complained. How could I have forgotten that fact?

"Something sure smells good," Witt said.

"Carly made a pork loin roast," Neely Kate said. "Along with scalloped potatoes, asparagus she's about to roast, and homemade dinner rolls."

"How long did you say we had to wait for dinner?" Witt asked.

Carly laughed. "We never said."

"Then how long do we have to wait?" he pressed.

"The asparagus won't take long," Carly said. "We're just waiting on Joe and Maeve."

"Maeve will be here soon," Neely Kate said. "She was takin' off early."

"Joe might be a while," I said. "He had something to take care of at the courthouse."

"Is it about the grand jury?" Neely Kate asked.

I knew he was there on my behalf, another source of guilt, but I didn't want to share that information with everyone else. "I'm not sure."

Neely Kate pulled out her phone and sent a text. A few seconds later, she said, "He says he's on his way."

Carly got to her feet, having sat down for less than a minute. "I'm going to start the asparagus." She cast me a look. "Rose, can you come help?"

Her question caught me off guard, but I said, "Sure. I'd love to."

I expected Neely Kate to come in with us, but when I caught her eye, she gave a little shake of her head.

Oh. Carly wanted a moment alone with me, and I suspected I knew why.

I was nervous when we headed to the kitchen.

"Is this about callin' hospice for more help?" I asked quietly as we neared the kitchen.

She moved closer to the sink, which was farther away from the door. "They already came by to evaluate Violet. I wanted to call you so you could sit in on the meeting, but Violet forbade it."

"Why?" I gasped.

"She said there was nothing you could do, so what was the point?" She grabbed a small notebook off the counter. "I took lots of notes for you." Her mouth twisted. "I'm sorry, Rose."

"No," I said, taking the notebook. "That's okay. Why don't you give me the condensed version?"

"They're sending someone for a few hours a day to help with the physical things like bathing her and helping her move around. When the time comes, they'll send someone multiple times a day to help with her medication."

I shook my head in confusion. "Why would someone come by just to give her pills?"

Sympathy filled her eyes. "We'll need the help when she's on an IV and needs medicine in her line."

"Oh," I said, my heart sinking. "How's she doin' with all of this?" I asked, surprised I was dry-eyed.

"You know Violet. Ever the pragmatist, but I can't help wondering if that's her way of dealing with her fear, you know?"

"Yeah," I said, finally feeling the familiar burn in my eyes. "I know." I gave her a grateful smile. "Carly, you've been so much help...I don't know what I would have done without you."

"You would have managed," she said softly. "I've seen you in action. You would have made it work. But now you have me to help ease the load."

"If it's ever too much," I said. "If you want to go back to work at the nursery...or not at all..."

She reached out and grabbed my hand. "I'll tell you, okay? Don't worry about me. I know you both think it's strange that I want to be here and help, but I've spent most of my life alone, and I love being part of a big happy family."

"We're not a real family," I countered. "Well, besides Violet and me, I mean. We're just an assortment of friends."

"Don't let the fact they're not blood relations fool you," Carly insisted. "They're family, and they all love you and your sister."

I gave her a quick hug, then said, "Put me to work."

"Everything's ready," she said, walking over to the stove. "I just need to take the potatoes and the pork loin out of the oven and put in the asparagus and the bread."

"What can I do to help?"

"Finish setting up the dining room table?" she asked.

"On it."

Neely Kate had already set out the plates and silverware, and I was thankful the farmhouse had a huge dining room and a dining room table big enough to crowd all thirteen of us around—likely from when the original owners had hired farmhands to work the land.

I'd just set out glasses when I heard a commotion outside. The kids were shouting, "Uncle Joe!" and when I got to the front door, he'd scooped them both up into his arms and was swinging them around. Ashley had her arms around his neck and Mikey squealed with delight.

Maeve pulled in seconds later, and I told them all it was time to come into the house and eat.

Neely Kate and I helped Carly haul out the food while Joe and Jed carried Violet in and got her settled into the wingback chair Jed had set at the head of the table so she could sit comfortably during the meal.

Ashley stood back watching her mother, anxiety etched onto her face. She held her little brother's hand, and I realized Ashley had taken up her own cross—caring for her brother—and somehow I'd missed it. The ever-observant Maeve gently herded them to the half bath to wash their hands, keeping them from seeing Violet at her most feeble.

Finally, the food was laid out on the table and we were all in our seats. Everyone had been talking at once, but now that we were settled in, we hushed and turned to Violet in expectation.

I sat at Violet's right hand and Ashley sat at her left, with Mikey sandwiched between his sister and Joe. I knew he'd purposely situated himself next to the kids to help take care of them.

"Everyone got so quiet," Violet said with a smile. "I suppose you're wondering why I called this dinner, but I'm not gonna tell you yet. Let's eat first and we can discuss it over dessert."

Voices and laughter filled the air again as the multiple bowls and platters were passed around. We all ate, with the guys taking seconds and thirds, and everyone thanked Carly profusely for cooking such a delicious meal.

Violet mostly pushed food around on her plate, so I excused myself and fixed her a protein shake so she'd at least get some calories in her. She didn't drink much, but I felt better about her by the time we cleared off the table and Carly and I served dessert—apple crisp with vanilla ice cream.

When everyone was almost done with dessert, Violet shifted in her seat, cuing us in to the fact that she was ready to tell us the reason for our get-together.

"I'm sure you're wondering why you're all here," she said with a smug smile. "I could say it's because I love being able to get y'all to do what I want at the snap of my fingers, and we all know that's true." Her grin spread. "But that's only part of it."

Ashley looked up at her mother in confusion.

"I'm dyin'," Violet said matter-of-factly, but her voice broke the tiniest bit. "It's no secret, and once I accepted it, there was no runnin' from it. I decided I wanted to spend every moment I could with my family and friends. I know it was hard for some of you to accept that I didn't want any more treatment, and I'm sorry for that, but I don't regret my decision to give it up." Violet reached across the table for her daughter's hand.

I wondered if she should be discussing this in front of the kids, but she'd been very open with them that she was dying.

Violet smiled at her daughter, squeezing her hand, then looked up at her guests. "Once I'm gone, I want you to have a party."

"What the heck are you talkin' about, Violet?" Joe asked, sounding incredulous. Mikey, who had finished his ice cream, was getting restless, so Joe scooted his chair back and slid the toddler onto his lap.

"I expect there to be tears—there better be lots of 'em—but then I'd like you to celebrate my life rather than just mourn it. It's partly for Rose and Ashley," she said, squeezing Ashley's hand. "So they can see that there is life without me. You have to show my girls that as long as they have great friends and family, they can survive anything." She glanced around the table at all of our friends. "That's where all y'all come in. I need you to plan the party." She reached for my hand then and squeezed.

I swallowed the lump in my throat.

"We'll plan it," Neely Kate said, swiping at a tear on her cheek. "We'll have it here at the farm."

Violet gave Neely Kate a beaming smile. "I knew I could count on you, Neely Kate."

My sister started giving everyone directions about what she expected, and Ashley, not fully understanding what was going on, soon began throwing out suggestions too.

My phone vibrated in my pocket, and I pulled it out, surprised to see *Henryetta Medical Clinic* show up on my screen.

"I'll be right back," I said, heading for the front porch so I would be able to hear over all the voices. When I reached the door, I answered, trying not to worry that I'd received a phone call this late. "Hello?"

"Rose?" a familiar voice asked. "It's Doctor Newton."

I shut the door behind me, surprised I was speaking to the doctor herself. "Hi, Dr. Newton? Have you gotten the test results back already?"

"We won't hear back about the blood tests until tomorrow at the earliest, but I had our lab tech run an in-house test. Then, just a short while ago, I heard a nurse on the phone telling someone about the results." A hard edge crept into her voice. "I want you to know that I've already fired the nurse in question and have personally called all the other staff who had already left to remind them about HIPAA laws. I'm not treating this lightly, and I want you to know that I'll do my very best to make sure your privacy is protected, but I fear it might be too late to contain the breach."

I leaned against the porch railing as I tried to understand what she was saying. Why would she care if a lab tech gossiped about a test she ran unless there was something wrong with me?

"Am I sick?" My breath stuck in my chest. What if I was dying too? Now that I thought about it, I had a lot of the same symptoms Violet did. Was her type of cancer hereditary?

"No, Rose, you're not sick, and I'm so sorry you're finding out this way. It was just a standard test I give before prescribing certain medications. If I had thought it was a serious possibility, I would have mentioned it while you were in the office."

My heart was beating so hard I'd become breathless. "Dr. Newton, what's wrong with me?"

"Rose, you're pregnant."

Chapter Twelve

N o," I asserted in a strong tone. "That's not possible. I've been *very* faithful about taking my pills, and I've been spotting every fourth week. I *can't* be pregnant."

"I repeated the test myself to be sure. You're pregnant."

Feeling light-headed, I sat in one of the wicker chairs while she explained that it had likely happened in August, after I started taking my new pills, and that Dr. Arnold should have warned me to use backup contraception. She told me it was possible to have spotting during the placebo week, even though I was pregnant, and the soreness I'd felt in my breasts over a month ago, which I'd attributed to the new pills, was actually due to my pregnancy.

"How pregnant am I?"

"Given that the pills would have made ovulation erratic, I understand your confusion, but based on the date you changed your pills, I would guess you're anywhere from five to eleven weeks along, but it's hard to say because the usual gestation period is determined by your last period, not ovulation, which means we're dealing with quite a spread of time. It could have happened this month, which would mean you're still quite early," she said.

I did a quick estimate in my head. "I haven't had sex in nearly two months, Dr. Newton."

I figured this afternoon didn't count since I couldn't have gotten pregnant *that* quickly.

She hesitated, then said in a strained voice, "Oh."

"So I'm at least nine to ten weeks along," I said, surprised at how rational I sounded.

"Given that information, I'd say yes, *but* I'd like for you to come in so I can do a sonogram and narrow it down. There are certain tests we need to do to make sure you and the baby are healthy. We'll need to get you started on prenatal vitamins right away." She paused. "When you come in, feel free to bring your boyfriend so he can see the baby too."

Boyfriend? Then I remembered what she'd heard about Joe. "Uh…I need to get my head around this before I drag someone else into it."

"I realize that the timing stinks, but sometimes life's biggest surprises are our greatest blessings."

A baby? In this mess? What was I going to do?

"Or…" she said, sounding less sure of herself. "If this isn't something you want, finding out the due date is even more important, especially since we suspect you're farther along. If you're ten to eleven weeks, your window for changing course has greatly narrowed."

Changing course. An abortion.

I instinctively placed my hand on my belly. "No. That's not an issue."

"I still want to see you right away, Rose," she said, "especially since you haven't been feeling well. And I fear you might be the subject of some gossip. I'm sure that Anne told someone. I know this is a small town and you're not married…"

Anne.

My heart sank. I knew exactly who Anne had told—her good buddy Dena. Which meant half the county likely knew by now.

My heart seized. *Joe.*

Dr. Newton continued, oblivious to my distress. "I assure you that there are recourses for this. We'll file an official complaint to the state to have her license revoked."

I shook my head, too overwhelmed to think about that part.

"We'll discuss it more tomorrow," Dr. Newton said. "For now, why don't you take some time to process the news?"

"Thank you, Dr. Newton," I said, then hung up and cradled the phone in my lap, staring out at nothing, feeling nothing.

I was going to have a baby.

The front door opened and Joe walked out. "I should be back around ten or a little after," he said as he tromped down the steps. "Are you still good with taking the kids home?"

It struck me that the gossip might be thrown at him at whatever meeting he was about to attend. Dena wouldn't hold back.

When I didn't answer, he turned to look at me. Whatever he saw on my face must have alarmed him because he hurried back. "Rose, what's wrong?"

I looked up at him, still in shock. "I'm pregnant."

His eyes flew wide and he dropped to his knees in front of me. "Wait. What?" When I didn't answer, he said, "I…Are you sure?"

I swallowed, my mouth suddenly dry. "That was the doctor." I shook my head as it all began to sink in. "She said she runs a pregnancy test before she prescribes certain kinds medication, but she didn't seriously think I could be pregnant because I've been taking my pill." My chest began to heave. "I've been taking my pills, Joe. I haven't been careless, but she said Dr. Arnold should have told me to use a backup when I changed pills. He didn't, and now I'm pregnant." I ran a hand over my head as the implications of what this all meant hammered into me. "People are going to think it's *yours*, Joe." Tears flooded my eyes. "Dr. Newton caught a nurse in her office calling someone to tell them, and I'm sure she was callin' Dena, because that same nurse was ugly to me. She said she was Dena's friend."

Joe looked shell-shocked.

"I'm so sorry. *So sorry.* I keep trying to do the right thing, but I just keep diggin' a deeper hole and pullin' everyone in with me."

"Hey," he said with a gentle smile. "When did I ever care about what everyone else said?"

"But Dena…"

"I stopped carin' about what Dena thought about me the day I told her it was over." Some of the warmth left his eyes but not his voice when he said, "I'm presuming it's Skeeter Malcolm's."

Shame filled me, but I lowered my gaze and nodded.

"What do you plan to do about that?"

I sniffed, keeping my gaze down. "In a perfect world, I'd spend a few days—or weeks—figuring it all out myself. Then I'd tell him." My face lifted and I looked him in the eye. "I'm not sure how he'll respond. He's made no secret of the fact that he's not a family man."

But James kept his ear to the ground. If there was even a rustle of gossip about me, he'd hear about it, and he deserved to learn the truth from me first.

His eyes hardened. "Will he think you tricked him?"

I shook my head, my chin trembling. "No. He'll know better."

Given his profession of love and his assertion that he wanted a life with me, I wasn't sure how he'd take the news, but I had no delusions that he would be happy about this.

"What do you need me to do, Rose?" he asked, sounding firm yet encouraging.

I shook my head. "I don't know. I don't know what I'm going to say when Violet asks me who the father is, let alone the rest of the world."

He swallowed, then took my hand. "We'll figure it out. Just tell them it's none of their business." A sympathetic smile lifted his lips. "Unfortunately, you're well acquainted with gossip."

Sadly, he was right.

I felt a tingling in the back of my head, and I was plunged into a vision.

I was sitting in front of a desk I recognized all too well, along with the man behind it.

"Didn't waste any time getting her pregnant so you could lock it down, huh, Simmons?" Mason snapped.

"You've got no claim on her," I said in Joe's voice, sounding equally harsh. "She risked her life to save you, and you ran off with your tail between your legs because of what she resorted to doin' to save your ungrateful ass."

"She lied to me," Mason spat out. "She was working with Skeeter Malcolm."

"Savin' your sorry ass. Would you have preferred to die?"

"She should have come to me," Mason said heatedly. "She should have told me what was going on."

"Maybe so," I said. "But then you never really knew her, did you?" I stood. "I confess, I didn't either. I'd pigeonholed her, thinking she was innocent and naive, and she *was* when I met her. But she outgrew my perception of her, just like she outgrew your perception of her too." I leaned forward and rested my hand on his desk. "You didn't leave her because she lied to you. You left her because she grew up without you, and your damn ego couldn't take it."

Mason got to his feet. "Get out of my office, Simmons."

A huge grin spread across my face. "Gladly. I'd rather go home to Rose's warm bed than sit here with you any day."

Mason charged around the desk and threw a punch at me, clipping my chin. But I shoved him up against his bookcases, making the books shake on the shelves, and clenched his shirt in my fist.

"Careful, counselor," I said in a mock chipper tone. "I'd sure hate to be forced to file assault charges against the state's special prosecutor. I'm sure *that* would make headlines."

Mason's body shook under my hand, and then he shoved me off. "Get the hell out of my office."

"Gladly, Deveraux."

The vision faded and I blurted out, "Mason thinks the baby's yours."

He blinked and rocked back on his heels. "You had a vision?"

I nodded, wondering what it had all meant. Had Joe just made that comment about sleeping in my bed to provoke Mason?

"Is he gonna confront me tonight?" he asked, worry in his eyes.

I mentally reviewed the vision. "I don't know. I think you saw him at night because you mentioned going home...to bed." Better to leave the rest out of it. "I doubt he'd find out so quickly, but Dena said something about goin' after Mason."

"When the hell did she say that?" he asked with a hint of a growl.

"This morning." I waved him off. "I can deal with her."

"Where'd the confrontation with Mason happen?"

"His office."

Joe stood, his grin spreading. "Even better."

"Joe..."

"Don't you worry about a thing, darlin'. We'll sort this out when I get back. And my meetin' isn't even in the courthouse. It's at city hall." His smile faded and his gaze darted to the front door.

"If gossip's already spreadin', maybe you should go in and tell everyone. I'm sure they'd rather hear the news from you."

My stomach fell to my feet. "I found out like five minutes ago." I stared up into his face. "I had no idea, Joe. Not a clue." I took a breath. "I don't know if I can handle this."

Joe grasped my upper arms and gently tugged me to my feet. "Yes, you can. You're the damn Lady in Black. You stared my father down with eyes so cold you could have cut diamonds with 'em." He placed his hand under my chin to keep my gaze on him. "If you can do that, you can do and face anything. Go inside and take ownership of this before people start treatin' you like a victim, because you, Rose Gardner, are a victim no more." He pressed a quick kiss to my forehead and smiled. "I know this seems like the worst possible timing, but you'll be a great mother, Rose."

Then he headed down the steps, got into his car, and drove away.

Chapter Thirteen

Joe was right. I needed to face this head-on. If I was really ten weeks pregnant, I wouldn't be able to hide it too much longer. Besides, the news was likely already running rampant through Henryetta. Maybe it would be best to get ahead of the wagging tongues and tell all my friends at once. Part of me felt it was wrong to tell them before I told James—he had a right to know first—but I had no idea when or how I could talk to him.

Taking a deep breath, I walked inside.

Jed was bouncing Mikey on his knee, and Neely Kate was braiding Ashley's hair, all while Violet watched with a soft smile on her face. Her gaze lifted to me when I walked into the room and my stomach churned.

At least I understood the reason my guts had been upset over the last two months or so and why I was always tired.

I forced a smile, ready to drop the bombshell, but I couldn't do it. Neely Kate wanted a baby so badly and I'd accidently made one. This would crush her. And Violet… I had no idea how she would react to the news, although I felt certain she'd insist on knowing who the father was. I needed to tell her the entire truth. I owed it to her.

"Everything okay?" Carly asked, looking up from her conversation with Jonah and Jessica.

"Yeah. Great." Telling everyone separately would be harder, and I'd still have to get to them all quickly—likely by tomorrow—but it felt like the right thing to do.

Jed glanced down at his watch. "We need to be gettin' the kids home."

"I'll do it," I said, harboring an ulterior motive. "You take Violet upstairs." If I put Jed to work, I could get some time alone with Neely Kate.

Jed frowned. "I'm not sure that's such a good idea given everything else goin' on."

Violet gave me a worried look.

"I'm fine," I said nonchalantly. "I don't expect to hear from anyone tonight. Besides, I think we're about to have a shadow watchin' over us." Courtesy of Joe, although I wasn't sure if that would be tonight or tomorrow. I had to believe we weren't at much of a risk from Carmichael. Surely he thought I had too much to risk by sharing anything about him.

Jed studied me for a moment, then nodded his approval.

I reached for my plate with my barely touched apple crisp and melted ice cream and gathered up a few others. "I'm goin' to start clearin' the table while Vi says goodbye to the kids. Carly, don't you dare touch a single dirty dish. Neely Kate, would you help?"

Eyeing me speculatively, she finished wrapping a hairband at the end of Ashley's braid. "You bet."

She hopped out of her chair and grabbed two plates, then followed me into the kitchen. "What's goin' on?" she said as soon as we were alone. "Who called you?"

I set my plates in the sink, one of them clattering loud enough to startle me.

"Rose, your hands are shakin'." She put her plates on top of mine and snatched up my hands. "What's goin' on?"

I couldn't drag this out. I needed to treat it like a Band-Aid.

"The doctor called me," I said in a tight voice.

Her eyes widened. "Is Violet okay?"

"It was about me. She did an exam while I was there."

She inhaled a sharp breath. "Are you sick? I *knew* something was wrong." When I didn't answer, she led me over to the kitchen table, pulled out a chair and turned it sideways. After pushing me down, she yanked out a chair for herself, and sat facing me. "What's goin' on?"

I started to quietly cry. "I'm so sorry."

This was going to hurt her so much, and I had no idea how to make it better.

"Sorry?" she asked, her voice rising as she clutched my hands. "What do you have to be sorry about? What do you have?" She lifted her chin. "No matter what it is, we can handle it."

Her pronouncement made me cry harder. I pulled one hand from hers and covered my mouth to stifle the sound of my sobs as I cast a worried glance at the kitchen door.

Realizing I was concerned about being overheard, she stood and pulled me up with her. "Let's take a walk."

Nodding, I followed her. She grabbed two flashlights from the small table against the wall and held the door open so we could go out. Turning on the first flashlight, she handed it to me.

"Jed won't like us bein' out here alone at night," I said as she switched on her own light. "And rightly so."

"Please," she drawled. "I have a gun strapped to my ankle."

I stared at her in surprise. Her favorite handgun was a big heavy revolver that had belonged to her grandfather.

"We'll head up to the barn," she said, leading the way. "Now tell me what's goin' on."

I wanted to see her face when I told her, so I grabbed her arm and pulled her to a stop, looking her straight in the eyes as the light from the kitchen windows cast shadows across her face. "Neely Kate, I'm pregnant."

She stared at me in shock. After a few seconds, she said, "I thought you hadn't seen Skeeter since right after you were almost killed by the Sugar Branch police."

"I haven't," I said. I'd seen him this afternoon, but he'd implored me not to tell anyone, and it didn't play into the circumstances of my pregnancy.

Her brow lowered in confusion. "But that was practically the middle of August. It's early October. That would mean you're…"

"At least ten weeks along."

"Oh."

"I'm so sorry, Neely Kate," I said, starting to cry again. "Please don't hate me."

Her brows shot up to her forehead. "Why on earth would I hate you?"

"Because you want a baby so bad."

Emotions vacillated in her eyes. The shock was fading into something rawer, something deep and fierce. "I'm sorry," she finally said. "I'm just takin' it in."

I shook my head. "You take as long as you need. I'm still dealing with the news myself."

That seemed to shake her out of her stupor. "Did you have any idea?"

"No. I've still been on the pill." I gasped. "Oh my word! What if I've hurt the baby?"

She gave me a sad smile. "Your baby will be fine. Just stop takin' them."

"I wasn't careless, Neely Kate. I swear it. Dr. Arnold changed my pills. Dr. Newton said he should have told me to use a backup, but I didn't know."

"Rose," she said, grabbing my upper arms and squeezing. "I know you didn't plan this. And I'm sorry I'm not being a better friend."

"I don't want to hurt you, Neely Kate. I'm so very sorry."

"Oh, honey." She pulled me into a tight hug. "It's gonna be okay. I promise. Jed and I are here for you, and we'll all deal with this together. I just need a few minutes to let this sink in." She dropped her arms and took a couple of steps back. "I love you, Rose. Please don't doubt that."

"I love you too." A tiny sob escaped me. "I know this is hurtin' you and I'm so, so sorry."

Tears filled her eyes. "I'll be better tomorrow. I just..."

She turned and ran into the house. I understood her pain, and I didn't fault her one bit for it.

Despite what Neely Kate had said, I suspected the situation might be too hard for her to handle. I wasn't sure I could count on her full support. Joe had said he'd help, but this was huge, and rumors would be running rampant. What if he decided he needed to distance himself from me so he could live his own life? And Violet would likely be gone before the baby was born. Which meant I'd have to do this on my own.

No, I wasn't on my own. I had my baby.

I placed my hand on my belly. "I'll be here for you, baby. I promise you'll never spend a single day of your life feeling unloved or unwanted."

I wished I could have had a few days or weeks to get used to this on my own, but Anne had stolen that from me. She and Dena could drag my name through the gutter all they wanted, but God help the person who dared to hurt my baby.

I wiped my tears. Joe was right. I was no victim. Not anymore. The only two people who deserved an apology from me had gotten one. Everyone else could kiss my lily-white behind.

When I went back inside, I could hear Violet's voice on the staircase, telling Jed what strong muscles he had as he carried her up the stairs. Witt and Marshall had taken over clearing the table, and Jonah and Jessica were rinsing the plates at the kitchen sink. Neely Kate was in the living room, helping the kids pack up their things.

"Neely Kate," I said in the doorway to the living room, "could you take the kids and help them into their car seats in my truck? The rest of you, could you gather in the living room for a moment? I have something to announce."

Neely Kate shot me a grateful look and mouthed, *I love you.*

I love you too, I mouthed back.

She reached out a hand to Mikey. "Come on, you two. Let's get you buckled."

The others all gathered around me as Neely Kate and the kids left. Carly was missing, but she was likely upstairs with Jed and Violet. It seemed like Violet had the right to know before everyone else did, but I wanted to tell her alone. This wasn't ideal, but I'd learned there were no storybook endings for me. I'd strived for normal for so long and had yet to come close. Maybe it was time to wholeheartedly embrace the craziness in my life.

As soon as the door clicked behind Neely Kate and the kids, I took a deep breath. "I know Violet called this dinner together for her own purposes, but I've decided to take advantage of the opportunity and share my good news." I paused, telling myself it wasn't a lie. I was taking advantage of them all being here, even if I'd only learned about the pregnancy twenty minutes ago. "I'm expecting a baby."

Witt narrowed his eyes and shot me an ornery grin. "A baby what?" He laughed. "I'm not falling for that one again. Are you gettin' a new puppy for Muffy?"

Muffy. I shot a glance down to my little dog, who was taking a nap on the sofa, likely worn out from my niece and nephew. How would she handle a baby?

Marshall whacked Witt on the arm. "I'm pretty sure she means a *baby* baby." He turned toward me. "Am I right, Miss Rose?"

"Yeah, Marshall," I said, fighting a laugh. "A human baby."

Witt stared at me in horror. "You've got to be shittin' me."

"Congratulations, Rose," Jonah said, trying not to look worried. He pulled me into a hug.

"I'm fine, Jonah," I said. "We'll talk more later." I suspected I might need a bunch of appointments with him over the next seven months.

"Congratulations," Jessica said with a warm smile that lacked any judgment.

It struck me that I'd been wrong. Again. I kept thinking I had to do things alone, but Carly was right—the family I'd built was bigger than the one I'd been born into, and they'd be there for me.

Emotion clogged my throat as my gaze landed on Maeve, who didn't look all that surprised. She was capable of premonitions. Had she guessed this would happen? She knew I was involved with someone, although I hadn't told her who.

She stepped forward and pulled me into a hug. "Rose, you'll make a wonderful mother. Your baby will be one lucky child."

"Thank you, Maeve," I said, squeezing her extra tight. "That means so much coming from you."

"I know your mother's no longer living"—she pulled back just enough to meet my eyes—"and I'm not sure when I'll ever have grandchildren, so I'd be honored to help you in any way I can."

I stared at her in disbelief. "But Mason..."

Resolve filled her eyes. "Mason is busy with his own life. You and I are friends. I want to be as involved as you'll let me."

"Thank you," I said with tears in my eyes.

"How's Neely Kate taking the news?" she asked in an undertone.

I took a breath. "She's totally supportive, but I know it hurts her."

Witt gave me a grim look, then followed up with a short nod. "I'm gonna go check on her."

"Good idea," I said.

He'd turned toward the door when Marshall asked, "So is Skeeter Malcolm the father?"

Everyone's eyes flew wide, and Witt smacked him in the back of the head. "Have you lost your ever-lovin' mind, boy?"

Confusion filled his eyes. "But—"

Witt grabbed Marshall by the earlobe and started to drag him toward the door.

"What did I do wrong?" Marshall whined.

"You've got no common sense, boy. That's what got you shot and damn near killed this summer."

"But that's how I knew about Skeeter hookin' up with Rose."

Witt whacked him upside the head with his free hand.

"Ow!" Marshall exclaimed.

"Rose should have let you bleed to death in her barn," Witt grumbled as they stumbled out the door.

Jonah, Jessica, and Maeve stared at me with their mouths dropped open.

Jed came down the stairs, glancing around with a confused look. "What's goin' on? Where's Neely Kate?"

I took a second to pull myself together, but my voice still shook when I said, "I asked her to put the kids in the car so I could tell everyone else my exciting news." I held his gaze as he approached. "I just shared it with Neely Kate a few minutes ago."

Maeve stepped forward and gave me another hug. "I'm going to give you some space and head home. Try to get some rest, and let us help you more, okay?"

"Okay."

She gave me a concerned smile. "And don't worry. Your secrets are safe with me. *All of them.*"

I flashed a quick glance at Jed and swallowed. "Thanks."

She headed for the door, and Jonah said, "We need to be goin' too. Same for us about secrets, Rose. If you need to talk about this or anything else, I'm just a phone call away."

"Thanks, Jonah...and you too, Jessica."

"We won't tell a soul, Rose," Jessica said with a warm smile. "And we've heard much more controversial things."

Nice of her to say so. Surely Jonah had talked to an unwed mother or two in his capacity as a pastor, but how many of those babies had been fathered by the king of the criminal world?

They headed out the front door, leaving just me and Jed in the living room. Muffy was still asleep on the sofa, blissfully unaware that her world was about to change too.

"Rose, what's goin' on?"

I was half tempted to tell him to ask Neely Kate, but that wouldn't be fair to either of them. "Jed, that was the doctor's office on the phone call I took on the porch." I forced myself to look him in the eye. "I'm pregnant."

His eyes flew wide, then filled with concern. "Neely Kate."

"I know. She took it better than I expected, not that I'd expect her to get upset with me, but I know this has hurt her and will continue to do so."

A grim look washed over his face. "Yeah." He stared at the wall for several seconds, and I could see the wheels turning in his head. "When are you due?"

"I'm not sure. I'm at least ten weeks. Maybe more."

He was silent for a moment, then gave a sharp nod. "You told Skeeter yet?"

"No. I literally just found out. It wasn't even on my radar. I only had a physical in case I decided to let the doctor put me on anxiety medication. I...I would have kept it to myself awhile longer, but Dena knows and she's likely telling anyone who'll listen."

"How did *she* find out?"

I told him about Anne and Dr. Newton's call, his eyes growing darker by the second.

"We'll sue."

"That's not gonna put the horse back in the barn, Jed."

"No, but it'll give me some satisfaction."

I pushed out a sigh. "We'll decide on that later." I suspected it would likely hurt Dr. Newton and not Anne.

"How are you handlin' the news? You seem to be doin' pretty well considerin' you just found out."

"I was in complete shock, but then I thought about Dena draggin' my name through the mud and decided not to give her the satisfaction of makin' me feel bad."

"Does anyone know it's Skeeter's baby?"

"Marshall just said so in front of everyone," I said. "He knew I was connected to James and put two and two together."

"That stupid kid," he grumbled. "I'll have a talk with him." He glanced toward the door. "Can you count on them to keep quiet?"

"Jonah and Jessica are used to keeping parishioners' secrets, and Maeve..."

"Is Mason's mother."

"Won't tell a soul. She has her own premonitions, and I suspect she already knew James and I were involved. She gets feelings, not visions."

Jed frowned, clearly not appeased.

"She promised my secret is safe, Jed. She's none too happy with what Mason is up to."

"I still don't like it, Rose."

"Then get Marshall in line," I said in a firmer tone than I'd intended.

He looked surprised, but then he nodded. "I intend to."

"I'll walk you out," I said. "I need to get the kids back to Mike's."

His concern was evident, but he didn't try to stop me as we walked to the front door together. Carly stood on the staircase landing, cringing.

"I wasn't eavesdropping, I swear. I was just comin' down and overheard you."

"Don't worry," I said. "This is all very much a part of your life, so you have a right to know. What part did you overhear?"

"Most of it, I think." Her cheeks were pink and she wouldn't meet my eyes. "I heard you announce you're expectin' a baby." Her gaze lifted. "I'll be here, Rose, unless you want me to move on. After Violet—" Her voice broke. "After Violet passes, I plan on gettin' a job—whether at the nursery or someplace else—and contributing to the rent."

"Carly, you're welcome to stay as long as you want. Truth be told, I've never really lived here alone and I'm not eager to start. If you still feel comfortable here, I'd love for you to stay, and we'll work out the details later."

A warm smile spread across her face. "Thanks, Rose. You go take the kids home. Don't worry about anything else."

The front door opened, and Neely Kate appeared, her hand extended palm up. "I came in to get the truck keys. I loaded up the kids in their car seats in your truck, so I figured we'd just swap cars until tomorrow."

"I'll take them home, Neely Kate."

"You need to stay home and deal with everything. It's really no bother."

Since I could tell she meant it, and I still needed to talk to Violet and James, I grabbed the keys out of my purse and handed them to her. "I'm not goin' into the office tomorrow, so I won't need it in the morning. I may not go into town until the deposition."

"We'll sort it out," Jed said, taking the keys. "If nothing else, I'll send Marshall to pick you up and take you to your truck. You stay home and rest. You have a big day tomorrow."

I felt nauseous at the thought of it. If I told the truth, I still wasn't convinced I would get off scot-free. What would happen if they charged me? Would I have to have the baby in jail? I'd never asked Joe what had come of his fact-finding trip to the courthouse, although if he'd managed to get me an extension, surely he would have said so.

"Thanks," I said. "I owe you."

I walked out with them to tell the kids goodbye, making sure they were handling everything okay. Mikey was already falling asleep and Ashley was singing a song she'd learned at school for an upcoming school program.

I gave her a kiss on the cheek. "Did you have fun tonight?"

She nodded with serious eyes. "What's gonna happen after Mommy dies?"

I took a breath, caught off guard by her question, mostly because she seemed so aware regarding the entire situation. "Well…we're gonna have a party, only I guess you and I don't have to plan it."

"No," she said quietly. "After that."

"You'll live with your daddy all the time," I said softly. "Just like when your momma was in the hospital in Texas."

"Will we still get to see you?"

"Of course," I said with a smile. "Don't be silly."

"We didn't see you before."

She was right, and despite James's assurances, I feared Mike would try to keep them from me again. But I sure wasn't going to throw their father under the bus. That would only hurt Ashley. "That was different. I'm going to try to see you lots and lots."

"Will you come to my program? We're singin' Halloween songs."

"I wouldn't miss it," I said, vowing to find out when it was.

"Mommy won't be able to come, will she?"

I started to answer, then stopped. "The truth is I don't know," I admitted. "I know your momma loves nothin' more than spendin' time with you, but she may be too sick to go."

She nodded. "You could video it on your phone and show it to her."

"Of course," I said, fighting tears as I leaned forward and kissed her forehead. "Your momma would love that."

"I love you, Aunt Rose."

"I love you too, sweet girl." I kissed her again, then backed out the open door, realizing that Jed and Neely Kate had taken a few steps back to give us privacy.

Neely Kate surged forward and wrapped me into a huge hug. "I'm sorry I reacted so badly earlier, Rose. I'll be here for you. I promise."

"I know," I said as I pulled away, and I meant it. The question was how hard would it be for her? "And I love you for it."

"Get some rest," Jed said. "Leave the dishes until tomorrow."

I reached up on my tiptoes and kissed his cheek. "I love you, Jed."

He wrapped an arm around my back and held me close. "I love you too, Rose. We're here for you. Tomorrow we'll discuss beefing up security. Joe will be back in an hour or two, so y'all should be fine tonight. I would have thought Skeeter would have his men watchin' out for you, especially after what happened this morning at your office, but we can't count on that."

I started to ask him why we couldn't count on it, then decided it didn't matter. If I was having a baby, I needed to make sure he or she was protected all the time, regardless of who was watching over me.

But I'd deal with that tomorrow. Tonight I needed to tell James   he   was   going   to   be   a   father.

Chapter Fourteen

After I waved goodbye to Jed and Neely Kate, I pulled my phone out of my pocket and sent James a text.

I really need to speak to you in person.

An error message showed up immediately.

Undeliverable

Had James changed his phone number and not told me? I tried to call him and immediately got a message that his number was no longer in service.

A feeling of deep betrayal sucked the breath from me. James had always been there for me, even after our fight about Buck Reynolds' necklace. I'd called him when I'd been kidnapped, and he'd dropped everything to help me. I hadn't called or texted in eight weeks. Had he changed numbers to purposely avoid me, or had he done it later and decided it didn't matter since I hadn't reached out?

I wrapped my arms around myself and shivered. What did it mean?

I half considered calling Jed, but it would only piss him off, and he was already upset with James. No need to add fuel to the fire. Still, I needed to talk to him. I had to be the one to tell him the news. I placed a call to Carter Hale, not surprised when it went to voice mail. I hung up and sent him a text.

Call me.

Pocketing my phone, I stood at the base of my porch steps, scanning the trees for signs of James's men. He'd *always* watched over me when I was in trouble. Even before we were together. He loved me now, so wouldn't he go to extraordinary lengths to make sure I was protected? Especially with Denny Carmichael sniffing around?

Unease crawled down my back as I entered the house and headed upstairs to talk to Violet, but she was already asleep. I made my way to the kitchen instead, and Carly was already in there washing dishes.

I reached for the dishrag. "I told you not to do this, Carly. I'll take care of it. You've worked yourself silly today."

"I'd rather stay and help, if it's all the same to you," she said, continuing to wash a plate. "I like the company." Then she looked stricken. "Of course, if you'd rather be alone, feel free to watch TV or read or whatever you like. You may need a moment or ten to get used to the idea of having a baby."

"I'd like the company too," I said, picking up a plate from the dish rack and starting to dry it. "How'd you know I just found out? Maybe I've been sittin' on the news for a while."

Carly laughed. "I don't think so, otherwise you probably wouldn't have had those two and a half cups of coffee yesterday morning."

My eyes flew wide. "I've been drinkin' coffee the whole time."

"How far along are you?" she asked as she rinsed off a plate. "If it's early enough, it might not matter."

"At least ten weeks." How much caffeine had I consumed over the past two months? Given how tired I was, gallons.

"Ten?" She stopped rinsing and studied me as she set the plate in the rack. "I'm sure you're fine. I bet our own mothers drank coffee and tea like there was no tomorrow." A soft smile lit up her face. "My momma loved coffee. One of my favorite memories of her is waking up to the smell of coffee and finding her in the kitchen."

"I'm sorry you lost her so young."

Her smile tightened. "I've spent more years without her than with her, so how is it possible to miss her so much?"

I reached out and touched her upper arm. "She was your momma, and you'll love her until the day you die. There will always be a hole where she fit. I already know there'll be one for Vi."

"But not your own mother?"

I tried not to frown. "Our mother was not a good mother. Violet protected me as best she could, but she was only two years old than me. She was a child herself." I looked into her eyes. "People think the worst of Violet, and she's done some horrible things, I'll grant you that. But she's always loved me. Always. Even if her methods of proving it were suspect." I tilted my head. "She stuck with me when no one else would. Not even our father. She was more of a mother to me than our momma ever was."

"I'm sorry your mother was such a bitch," Carly said, turning back to the sink. "But I can see how much Violet loves you. She didn't have a role model for how to show love. She figured it out as she went along, but there's no doubt she cares about you." Her voice broke. "What I wouldn't have given to have someone like her in my life when I was a kid."

I leaned in and wrapped an arm around her upper back. "You have us now. We love having you in our lives, Carly. You're like a piece of the puzzle we didn't know we were missing. I'm glad you're here. And not just because of Vi."

Carly leaned her head into mine as we both stared at the wall over the sink. "Thanks, Rose. You have no idea how much that means to me."

Dropping my arm, I took a step back and placed the now-dry plate in the cabinet. "Tell me more about the hospice visit."

We spent the next half hour cleaning up the kitchen and then headed out to the front porch with cups of tea and fuzzy afghans, enjoying the cool fall evening.

"We should have a bonfire at your sister's party," Carly said, sounding like she was lost in thought. "The kids would love it."

"That's presuming she dies this fall or winter," I said.

Carly reached over and squeezed my hand, and I heard her wordless message. It would happen soon, and I needed to prepare myself for it. Wishing it weren't so wouldn't change things.

She released a long yawn, and I gave her a tender smile. "Go to bed, Carly. And sleep in if you'd like. I'm stickin' around here in the morning until I head into Henryetta for my grand jury testimony."

"Thanks, Rose. I think I just might, but if you change your mind, you let me know." She got to her feet, draping the blanket over her arm, and picked up her teacup.

I'd figured I was stuck out here since Neely Kate hadn't left me the keys to her car, but the sight of Carly's clunker next to the house reminded me I had options. "Carly, would you mind if I borrowed your car?"

She blinked in surprise. "Of course not. Did you change your mind about tomorrow morning?"

"No, I was wanting to borrow it tonight."

Her brows shot up, and then she quickly glanced down to my stomach and an empathetic smile spread across her face. "Of course, Rose. The keys are on the entry table. Just be careful."

"Thanks, Carly. I will."

I watched her go inside, then pulled out my phone again and sent Carter another text.

Carter Hale. Call me now. It's important.

I knew it was close to ten o'clock, but Carter didn't strike me as the early-to-bed type. After five minutes, I decided to take a riskier course.

I called the pool hall.

The background was noisy with music and the sounds of clinking pool balls, loud enough the bartender had to shout. "Eight Ballers Billiards."

"Is Skeeter Malcolm there?"

The bartender, whose voice I didn't recognize, hesitated, then said, "Nope. Want me to give him a message?"

He was lying. I was sure of it. James was having him screen his calls. "I'll give it to him myself. Just give me his cell number."

"No can do, sweetheart," he said with an amused chuckle. "Give me the message, and I'll be sure he gets it."

"He's gonna want to talk to me," I said, my tone firm. "If you'd like, you can put me on hold while you tell him that if he doesn't take my call, I'll march up there and take care of his family jewels."

The bartender chuckled. "Okay, hold on a minute." He put me on hold, and I listened to two full country songs before he came back. "He says if you're Tabby that he gave you your fifty dollars and he's not givin' you a penny more." Then he hung up.

I stared at my phone in disbelief. What the hell was that about?

I needed to talk to him and I had no idea where he planned to go after he got done at the pool hall. He might go to his house south of town—where the two of us used to meet—but somehow I doubted it. I considered marching into the pool hall and following through on my threat, but that didn't seem prudent considering half the county would be buzzing about my pregnancy, and if I was seen stomping into Skeeter Malcolm's office the night I found out… But waiting wasn't an option. We had to talk, and I knew another way.

I walked inside to grab my purse and Carly's keys. Muffy followed me in. I considered leaving her behind, but where I planned to go, it might not be a bad idea to have some backup. "Okay, Muff. You can be my bodyguard."

She trotted after me and jumped in the car after I opened the driver's door. Carly's car was a hunk of junk, but Jed had it up to its top potential. On the positive side, no one would notice me driving it. Stealth was what I needed, and this car fit the bill.

I had plenty of time to think as I drove into town. I was surprised at how quickly I was acclimating to the idea of having a baby. It scared the snot out of me—could I even afford a baby? Could I handle raising a baby on my own? But mostly I tried to imagine James's reaction when I told him. While he knew me well enough not to believe I'd trapped or tricked him, in no scenario did I picture him welcoming the news. I had to prepare for the worst.

Thankfully, his car was still parked out back of the pool hall when I got there. I parked several spots away, and after looking around to make sure no one was out in the lot, I walked over to the car with Muffy on my heels and sat on the hood. She jumped into my lap, and we waited together.

I'd considered banging on the back door, but this felt more dignified somehow. *Was* there a dignified way to tell the man you'd slept with that you were pregnant?

Would he think I wanted money from him?

What did it say about our relationship that I had to ask myself that question?

The pool hall had security cameras, so it wouldn't be long before somebody came out to investigate. I was surprised that it took ten minutes for James to come marching out the back door.

"What the hell do you think you're doin'?" he demanded, his face hard. "You can't be here, especially the night before your testimony."

"Then maybe you should take my damn call next time."

He stopped several feet in front of me. "That was you?"

"I figured the family jewels would give me away."

He shook his head. "He told me you said you'd cut off my balls and shove them down my throat." A slight smile tipped up the corners of his mouth. "That didn't sound like you at all."

"You changed your number."

His smile fell. "I needed to put distance between us, and I told you to call Jed if you needed help. So why are you here?"

My brows shot up to my hairline. "Excuse me?"

"You can't be talkin' to me, Rose. In person *or* over the phone. You need to go. *Now.*"

He took a step toward me and Muffy let out a low growl.

That stopped James in his tracks and his menacing glare softened. "You can't be here, Rose. *You have to go.*"

"This is important, and I needed to see you tonight. I texted Carter several times and told him to call me back right away, but I'm still waiting for his call." My voice took on a hard edge. "That doesn't make me feel all that warm and cozy about havin' him as my attorney. What if I needed him for somethin' urgent?" When he didn't answer, I urged Muffy to hop down and then slid off the hood. "I think it just became very clear that I need to find a new attorney."

"How are you gonna find a new attorney before tomorrow afternoon?"

I took a step forward and glared up at him. "Carter wasn't even plannin' on bein' there tomorrow afternoon."

He shook his head in frustration. "You don't need a new attorney. Hale's tied up in something right now. We both are. You need to go."

I shot a glance to the back door. "He's here now?"

James reached for my arm, but I took a step back as Muffy rushed in front of me and growled louder.

"Call off your dog, Rose," he said through gritted teeth.

Anger burned in my chest. "My dog has a name, and you know her from all the times she's come to your house."

"Then why the fuck is she growling at me now?"

"Because she clearly doesn't trust you." And she wanted to protect me from him—a thought that settled about as well as a bowling ball in a canoe. Although I knew James would never hurt me, I wasn't about to admonish her for having my back.

He took a step back, dropping his hand to his side in frustration. "You can't be here, Rose. How many fucking times do I have to say it? *Go!*" He half-shouted the last word, then looked pissed that he'd lost control. "Why are you here?"

I put my hand on my hip, even madder. "You're just now askin' me that?"

"Goddammit, Rose!"

I shook my head in disgust. "After everything we've been through, you're treating me like one of your booty calls showin' up and beggin' for more."

"What the hell are you talkin' about?" he asked, confusion swimming in his eyes.

"Who's Tabby?" I demanded, not even knowing why I was wasting what little time he had deigned to give me to discuss some random woman.

"Tabby?" His gaze shot up to the starry sky, then narrowed back on me. "That's why you're here? *You're jealous?*"

"No, you moron! I'm here because I've got something important to tell you and you changed your number, Carter wouldn't call me back, and you wouldn't take my call to the pool hall."

"Fine," he said with exasperation, holding his hands out at his sides. "You've got me. *What the fuck do you want?*"

My mouth dropped open. "Why in the hell are you acting like this, James? What if I'm in trouble? What if I need your help?"

"I told you to call Jed if you need help. What. Do. You. Need? I'm in an important meeting, and each second I'm out here is putting everything at risk."

I shook my head in disgust. "So why not lead with that, James Malcolm? Why not say, 'I'm sure you must have a *very important* reason for being here, because you know what's at stake, but I'm in the middle of something important. Can we table this for later?'"

Some of his irritation faded.

"Yeah," I said, my anger building. "The possibility never occurred to you because you have the emotional IQ of a toddler." I shook my head. "Fine. You don't have time to talk to me—I'll just let you hear about it from the town rumor mill." I flung a hand toward the back door. "Go on. Get back to your meeting."

I turned to stomp back to my car, but he reached out and grabbed my arm, hauling me back.

"*Get your hand off me*," I said under my breath, in no mood to be manhandled.

He dropped his hand as though my arm were a white-hot poker. Surprise filled his eyes.

I took two jerky steps away from him. "This isn't love, James. Treating me like I'm an annoying gnat isn't love."

He closed the distance between us, his anger fading. "I know. I'm sorry, Rose. I'm in a very tense meeting, but I shouldn't be takin' it out on you. I'm sorry."

My heart softened slightly. James Malcolm had never been in love before. It was like Carly had said about Violet—he'd never had a role model to teach him *how* to love. His world was full of violence, and his emotions reverted to anger whenever he was challenged.

A sudden gust blew across the parking lot, and I wrapped my arms across my chest to hold my chunky sweater in place. "I'm sorry I interrupted you, but this is important, and I'm insulted that you would treat it as anything other than that."

His eyes flashed with anger again. "Can we have this discussion about *feelings* later? Just tell me what you need to say so I can get back to my meeting."

While some part of me knew he was likely in the middle of something dire, another part of me was pissed at the way he'd reacted—and the impossible situation it had put us in. How could I drop a bombshell on him and send him back to his meeting?

Shaking my head, I shot him a glare, then said, "It can wait. Come on, Muff."

Muffy was still standing at attention, ready to attack, but she reluctantly turned and fell in beside me, casting a suspicious glance back at him.

I opened my car door and he shouted after me, "Are you fucking kidding me? We went through all that for you to just stomp off without tellin' me why you're here?"

Standing next to the open door, I said, "Maybe you should have started with that question."

"We've been over that," he said as I climbed in. "I fucked up."

I got inside and closed the door, but he marched over and pounded on the window. "Rose. Open the goddamn window."

I cranked the window down about six inches.

"Why the fuck did you come here?" His anger was back and in full force.

My mouth dropped open. Was this the real James Malcolm? Was the man I'd come to love a lie? No, I knew it was much more complicated than that. All of these many parts were him. The good…and the bad. And yet, I'd needed something else from him just now. I'd needed to see his soft side, and I'd gotten Skeeter Malcolm instead. My temper got the best of me. "How dare you?" I said through gritted teeth. "How dare you talk to me that way! You want to know why I'm here? Fine!" I got out of the car and slammed the car door shut. "I'm pregnant!"

His eyes flew open and he rocked back a step, pure terror washing over his face.

He blinked and started to say something, but I held up my hand and snarled, "I swear to God, James Malcolm, if you ask me if you're the father, I'll run you over with this car then back up and run you over again."

His mouth snapped shut. Confusion and some of the softness I'd hoped to see washed over his face for barely a second before his eyes turned hard. "Jed can deal with this. Go to him. See? You didn't need me after all." Then he turned and started to head back inside.

I gaped at him in shock. "What the hell is that supposed to mean?"

He turned back to face me, his jaw tense. "Jed knows a doctor in Little Rock. He's called her before for a couple of the girls at the Bunny Ranch."

My eyes about popped out of my head. "You're tellin' me to get an abortion."

"You sure as hell can't keep it." He nearly snarled the words.

Tears stung my eyes and I swallowed the lump in my throat as he stomped back inside without even a goodbye.

Numb, I got back inside and sat behind the steering wheel, trying to sort out what had just happened. James had reacted badly to seeing me, and I'd met him at his level, handling it just as badly, and then…

He wanted me to get an abortion.

You sure as hell can't keep it.

No, he *expected* me to get an abortion. No discussion. No asking what I wanted. Just an expectation that I'd bow to his wishes.

My anger rose anew.

So he wanted nothing to do with the baby. I was doing this alone.

A wave of sadness quickly followed as I stared at the metal door he'd disappeared behind. When it came to the two of us, I'd always been doing this alone. I'd just been too stupid to realize it.

Chapter Fifteen

As I drove through town, I passed the only twenty-four-hour pharmacy in Fenton County and decided to stop and get prenatal vitamins. I was worried about all the caffeine I'd consumed and figured some vitamins ASAP might help counterbalance it—although to be fair, a good portion of those cups of coffee had been left untouched due to my upset stomach.

Though there was less chance of me being seen at ten thirty at night, I scanned the parking lot to see if anyone was around, and then decided it didn't matter anyway. People were going to find out.

I told Muffy to wait in the car, and she sat in my passenger seat at full attention as I walked inside.

Sure enough, the pharmacy was empty except for a woman who was restocking the candy shelves and a middle-aged man behind the pharmacy counter.

The woman looked up as I walked in.

"Welcome to Beacon's. Can I help you find what you're lookin' for?" She was a lot more cheerful than I'd expect of someone working so late.

"I'm lookin' for vitamins."

"Aisle twelve. If you need help choosing what to get, Harvey can help."

"Harvey?"

"The pharmacist."

"Okay," I said. "Thanks."

I wandered toward the back and found aisle twelve, searching for prenatal vitamins.

"Do you need any help?" the pharmacist asked, leaning over the counter. The vitamin display was toward the front of the row, only ten feet away from him.

I flashed him a warm smile. "I'm looking for prenatal vitamins. I suppose they're all the same?"

"Actually, they're not," he said, then opened the door and walked toward me. "We carry some without omega-3 fatty acids, but you'd be better off getting these." He plucked a bottle off the shelf. "This has a good dose of omega-3 for your baby's brain development, along with folic acid, calcium, and vitamin D. Those are important for the first trimester."

I swallowed hard, fighting my panic. "What happens if you don't take them the first trimester?"

His eyes widened and he leaned back. "Ohh…you don't want to skip them." He shook his head, wearing a look of doom. "You run the risk of birth defects."

I took the bottle, very close to a panic attack. Had I screwed up my baby already? "Thank you."

"No problem." He started humming as he walked over to the blood pressure machine and stuck his arm through the cuff.

"Checkin' your blood pressure again, Harvey?" the woman called out.

"Yep," he said, pressing a button and turning it on. It seemed like an odd form of entertainment, but they clearly didn't get much business at this time of night, so I supposed they had to pass the time somehow.

I started toward the checkout, but an endcap display of diapers caught my eye, and I found myself wandering over to them. Studying the display, I bit my lip when I saw the price. I remembered Ashley and Mikey going through mountains of them when they were tiny. I walked down the aisle to look at the baby bottles and pacifiers, bibs and teething toys. I started to add up the price tags and grew more anxious by the second. I would need to find more landscaping jobs to pay for all of this.

The front door to the pharmacy dinged and the woman stocking shelves said, "Welcome to Beacon's Pharmacy." But her cheerfulness had faded by the last word.

The hair on the back of my neck stood on end, and instinct told me to duck behind the shelves just before a man said, "Where's the pills, Harvey?"

A wheezing sound came from the blood pressure machine and Harvey forced out, "Dr. Arnold left town. I don't have anything for you."

I carefully set the bottle of vitamins on the floor, trying to keep them from rattling, then pulled my gun out of my purse and clicked off the safety.

The deep male voice said, "I know for a fact that Arnold wrote a bunch of new scripts before he left. So where are they?"

"Wendy..." the pharmacist said, his voice high-pitched in his panic.

"We can't find the bitch."

"I don't know where she is either," Harvey said. "I haven't seen her since last week."

"The boss'll be none too happy about this," another man snarled. He sounded younger than the first, although I couldn't see either of them from my vantage point.

"I can't fill prescriptions I don't have," Harvey said, his voice shaking. "The authorities will catch on. The FBI already came around askin' questions."

"You have until tomorrow night," the first guy said. "Because we'll be back."

I heard a loud crash, followed by heavy footsteps and the dinging of the bell.

I stayed squatted for several seconds, waiting to make sure the coast was clear, then ran to the end of the aisle to the back of the store. I'd just rounded the endcap when the bell dinged again.

"Someone else is in here," the booming voice said at the entrance to the store.

How had he known I was here?

Terror squeezed my heart. *Muffy.* She was probably barking her head off. Had they hurt her?

I was in serious trouble. I suspected they didn't want some random witness left behind.

I quickly pulled my phone out of my back pocket and sent a text to Joe.

Trouble at Beacon pharm. Dangerous men. Need help.

After I pocketed my phone, I took a deep breath to calm my racing heart, not that it did much good.

"Who's in here?" the burly voice demanded.

The woman clerk stuttered. "I...I..."

"I know you saw them walk in," the man said. "Tell me now or I'll blow your head off."

The woman started to sob uncontrollably.

The man grunted, and then I heard heavy footfalls heading toward the pharmacy counter. "Who's in here?"

"No one," Harvey said. His voice still shook, but he sounded more confident.

"There's a car out there with a dog in it. Someone's in here." When Harvey didn't answer, the man shouted, "Come out now or we'll kill your dog."

Terror squeezed my throat. These guys might think twice about killing a person, but a dog? I suspected they would do it in the blink of an eye.

What should I do? I couldn't let them shoot Muffy, but I had no doubt they planned to kill me too. Why else would they have come back?

Squatting next to an endcap for hemorrhoid cream, I glanced at the back wall for an emergency exit. They'd still follow me outside, but at least I'd have the dark night on my side.

There was an exit in the back corner, opposite of the entrance. Perfect. Saying a quick prayer, I grabbed a can of athlete's foot medication, rose slightly, then threw it toward the front of the store in the hopes it would redirect the bad guys' attention. Only I threw it with my left hand, and my aim was off. It hit the top of the shelves in the aisle I was in, then bounced off and hit something else that made a loud crashing sound.

Deciding this might be a better distraction, I ran for the back door, keeping my head down, hoping they couldn't see me over the five-foot-tall shelves. I shoved the bar across the door, and nearly cried with relief when it swung open, even though an alarm announced what I'd done.

Once I got outside, I ran around the corner to the front of the store, glancing back for the pursuer I knew was coming.

I'd made it to the car when a man with long, scraggly hair and dressed in dark clothes came out the front door with his gun drawn and pointed right at me.

Muffy barked like a crazed beast, trying to get out of the car.

I held my gun up at the man. "Put your gun down, and I'll let you get away."

The man's eyes widened slightly. Then he belly laughed. "You'll let *me* get away?"

"And what about me?" the deep-voiced man asked from the corner of the building. "Will you let me get away too?"

I snuck a quick glance at him out of the corner of my eye. He was holding a gun on me too.

Crappy doodles.

I was in serious trouble and there was no way Joe would get here in time to help.

A gunshot rang out and the deep-voiced guy fell to the ground as I dropped to a squat next to my car. The man who'd followed me out of the back started shooting, and I squatted lower, wondering who had fired the shot and if I was in the line of fire.

Another shot rang out behind me, and then the shooting stopped as I heard a dull thud against the other side of the car.

"Put your gun down, Rose," a familiar male voice called out. "I need to make sure you won't shoot me."

"Who are you?" I asked, tightening my grip. I was a sitting duck. Whoever had just shot those men could take me out in a heartbeat. "Why should I trust you enough to put my gun down?"

"I just saved your life," the man said.

"Thank you," I said, trying to catch my breath. "I very much appreciate that, but how about we go our separate ways?"

"No can do, Rose. I need to stay with you until the sheriff arrives. But first I need to make sure you don't shoot me. So put *your gun down.*"

The voice was coming from behind the trees. Although I'd heard it before, I couldn't put a face to it. I was fairly certain it wasn't one of James's men, but the turnover had been so great lately that I was sure I didn't know most of them. And this man had called me Rose, not Lady. Most of James's men referred to me by my alter ego.

"If the sheriff deputies show up and you're here with two dead men, clutchin' a gun, you're likely to be a prime suspect. And that's if they don't shoot first and ask questions later. So drop the gun. Now."

Sirens wailed in the distance, and for all I knew, they were Henryetta police. They would make my life an ever-loving hell just for the fun of it. This man could have killed me by now if that had been his purpose, and I was still squatted here, still breathing. I set my gun on the ground.

"Good. Now stand and kick it away from you."

The hair on the back of my neck stood on end. "Why?"

A shadow appeared from the trees with a gun aimed right at me. "You so much as reach for that gun, I'll be forced to shoot you, Miss Rose. I won't kill you, but it'll hurt like hell."

I stood, facing Brox, the son of a prepper who lived in the hills with his sons. On our last encounter, Brox had brought me to his family's land for questioning on the orders of his father, Gerard. James had shown up, a bunch of guns had been drawn but not shot, and we'd driven away unharmed. James and Gerard Collard had parted enemies.

Gerard had thought I had inside information about what had brought Mason back to Fenton County, and I'd had a devil of a time convincing him I didn't know. What did they want with me now?

Brox marched closer, his gun still trained on me as he reached out his left hand. "I need you to leave your cell phone here."

He roughly patted my hips and butt, obviously feeling for the phone but making a show of not feeling me up.

Leave your phone here. He was taking me somewhere. Probably not to shoot me in a field somewhere. He would have already done it. No. He planned to take me to his father.

When he pulled my phone out of my back pocket and dropped it to the ground, I knew I'd jumped from the frying pan and into a roaring bonfire.

He grabbed my arm and started to tug me across the parking lot toward the trees, but I dragged my feet, trying to get away. The sirens were growing louder, so Brox scooped me into his arms. He took off in a sprint, crashing through the undergrowth, and turned sideways to take the brunt of a low-hanging branch instead of letting it hit me. I tried to squirm out of his arms, but he had a firm grip on me. When he emerged from the woods, I saw a lone pickup truck parked behind a strip mall.

He stopped at the driver's side of the truck, then opened the door and set me down on the ground. "I'm sorry, Miss Rose, but he says I have to do this."

My heart slammed into my rib cage. What had his father told him to do? "Do what?"

He grabbed a small bag from the floor in the back and pulled out a roll of duct tape.

I shook my head, my eyes wide. "You don't have to do this, Brox. I'll come with you willingly." It was a lie, but I was sure I sounded convincing.

A sad expression shadowed his face. "Even without his order, I'd still do this. I think you'll run first chance you get."

He was right, and I demonstrated how right he was by scraping my heel down the inside of his leg and stomping hard on his foot. He leapt back a step and I bolted toward the road, screaming, "Help!"

The sirens were louder now, and I hoped someone would hear me.

Brox caught up to me in five seconds, wrapping his arm around my stomach and lifting me off the ground. His free hand covered my mouth to muffle my screams.

"I don't want to hurt you, Rose. But I have to take you."

I viciously kicked his legs and bit his hand. He cursed loudly but didn't flinch away as I had hoped. "If you don't settle down, I'll be forced to chloroform you," he said as he walked back to his truck. "You'll wake up with a nasty headache."

I went stock-still. Would chloroform hurt my baby? I couldn't take the risk.

"That's a good girl," Brox said as he pressed my chest against the truck, his hand still covering my mouth. His hand only lifted so he could secure a length of duct tape over my mouth—and then he spun me around to face him.

I stared up at his face and he frowned as he started to tape my hands together in front of me.

"Don't look at me like that, Rose. We just have to be careful."

He ripped the tape with his bare hands, then hefted me into the back seat and grabbed my legs.

I started to panic, flooded with memories of the Sugar Branch police officer who'd nearly raped me in his car. Then I was hyperventilating, and the tape over my mouth made it so much worse.

Brox tried to ignore me as he wrapped tape around my ankles, but he kept sneaking glances at my face. When he finished, he gave me a worried look. "Rose, take deep breaths."

What was I doing? Panicking wasn't going to solve anything. I needed to get myself together. The Sugar Branch police had been evil; Brox was basically a good man in his core. The way he'd carried me through the trees proved it. I needed to ride this out and keep my wits about me.

When he finished with the tape, he pushed me to the floor of the back seat and leaned in. "I need you to stay down. If you try to get up, I'll have to chloroform ya." He held my gaze. "Do you understand?"

I nodded.

Regret filled his eyes. "I don't wanna do it, Miss Rose, but if you break the rules, I'll be forced to."

The sirens were even louder now, which seemed to spur Brox into action. He pushed the driver's seat back into place, then climbed in. I could feel the truck start to move. I tried to pay attention to the various turns and the conditions of the roads, but I began to suspect Brox was driving in circles like James often did when he was going to his house south of town.

James. I tried to keep my mind occupied with thoughts of escape, but memories of our encounter kept filtering in. His eyes had looked so cold when he'd told me to go to Jed to *take care of it*. I'd known better than to think he'd be happy, but I'd expected *some* type of support from him. Some softness. At least after he got over his initial shock. Would he come to his senses and check on me? What would I do if he did?

I didn't have time to think about it any longer, because the truck had pulled off the smooth road onto bumpy terrain and was slowing down. It was hard to see much out the windows since it was nighttime, but it didn't look like he was taking me to their property. So where were we going?

We came to a stop, and Brox remained silent as he opened the door and climbed out. Moments later, he tipped the front seat forward and grabbed my ankles.

"Just answer his questions and you'll be okay," he said softly, gently pulling me forward.

After he carefully pried the tape off my mouth, refusing to look me in the eyes, he pulled out a pocketknife and cut through the tape around my ankles. He set me on my feet, then grabbed my upper arm—my hands still bound together—and led me to a small, well-kept, one-story house.

The property was surrounded by trees, and a quick glance behind me revealed even more trees with a narrow road winding through them. The windows in the house glowed with a warm yellow, giving it an inviting look, but all I felt was dread. The last time I'd seen Gerard Collard, Brox's father and leader of their band of lost boys, I'd pointed a gun at him. I was pretty sure he was going to hold that against me.

The front door opened and one of Brox's brothers stood in the opening—Carey, if I remembered correctly from our previous encounter. He'd been none too fond of me *before* I'd held a gun on his father. Heaven only knew how he'd treat me now.

Brox steered me through the opening, but Carey barely moved out of the way to let me pass. He looked me up and down as though I was a plate of fried chicken with mashed potatoes and gravy—one that had been left on the counter to congeal all day, but his hunger was such that he'd still devour it in one sitting.

Brox sent him a dark glare, and Carey took a step back as his brother shut the door.

Gerard sat at a small table, only he didn't ask me to sit like he had last time. He narrowed his gaze on Brox, none too pleased. "There was trouble."

It wasn't a question.

Brox gave a slight nod. "I followed her from the pool hall to the pharmacy. I planned to get her when she came out, but two armed men went in soon after she did. I considered going in to get her, but she came out the back door. The men approached her from either side, and I took them out."

Gerard's thin lips pursed together. "I suppose the authorities could blame their deaths on Malcolm's overexuberance to protect her."

Brox shot me a quick glance, then turned back to his father. "They were Malcolm's men."

Chapter Sixteen

The blood rushed from my head and I gaped up at Brox.

"Malcolm's men were going to kill her?" Gerard asked, his surprise evident in his voice.

"Yeah, I remember one of them from our last deal," Brox said. "They were definitely his guys."

I turned back to face Gerard. He had his gaze on my face, studying me. "Based on your color, you didn't realize Malcolm had turned on you, not that I blame him after you were so quick to move the chief deputy sheriff into your bed," he said without a hint of gloating. "Brox, help her to a seat."

So he knew about Joe, not that I was surprised. He'd clearly been keeping tabs on me, but I didn't have time to process that. My mind was still caught on what Brox had said. James's men had been prepared to kill me. Had he known? No. He would never condone my murder.

They hadn't known it was me. They'd only known there was a witness.

Still, did that mean James condoned his men killing the innocent?

Brox pulled out a chair and tried to help me sit, but I managed it on my own. It irked me that I'd obeyed Gerard, but I figured I'd lose *all* respect if I passed out.

I leveled my gaze on Gerard. "Skeeter Malcolm wouldn't betray me, and I didn't recognize either of those men. They were there for prescriptions Dr. Arnold had written for the pharmacist to fill." I paused a beat, thankful my equilibrium was better and my confidence was returning. "They had to be working for Denny Carmichael."

A hint of a smile appeared on Gerard's face as he steepled his fingers under his chin. "What makes you think so?"

He acted like a man who knew something I didn't, but I tried to hide my fading confidence. "Everyone knows Carmichael is the drug lord of Fenton County. Likely all of southern Arkansas. His cook is very good and he's protective of him."

Gerard's brow lifted as amusement filled his eyes. "True. So why would Carmichael be interested in prescription drugs?"

I opened my mouth to answer, then quickly closed it. Gerard wasn't making assumptions. He had solid intel.

"You're tellin' me that Skeeter Malcolm is starting to branch out to prescription drugs?" I asked, sounding incredulous. James had told me he had nothing to do with drugs. The only reason he didn't stop Carmichael was because he believed people who were miserable would find a way to get drugs one way or another. Still, James was in the process of working with a manufacturer to bring a canning industry into town to give people well-paid jobs, reasoning people who weren't scraping by would be happier and much less likely to resort to drugs.

"Startin' to?" Gerard laughed. "This ain't recent, Lady. It's been goin' on for at least three years."

I slowly shook my head. "I don't believe you."

He shrugged. "Believe me or don't, but here's what I know: Carmichael has a guy putting out first-class, high-quality meth.

He's selling to big organizations in bigger cities and bringing in top dollar. Why would he waste his time nickel-and-diming with prescription drugs?"

My heart stuttered. I refused to believe that James was behind the prescription drug ring. "If Denny Carmichael is too successful to mess with prescription drugs, why is he living in squalor?"

Gerard laughed. "You been to his place, have ya?" His eyes narrowed slightly. "You've been to *our* place. We live in a humble abode, but that's not indicative of how much money we have." He shook his head slightly. "Not all men want to live in fancy houses, Lady. Your Malcolm doesn't."

Which meant he didn't know about James's secret house. If James had a secret house, I supposed Carmichael could have one too. But that was beside the point. What mattered was that Gerard's story had a ring of truth to it.

I took a deep breath, needing to get control of this situation. Holding out my still-bound hands, I said, "Cut me loose. I take it we're here for some type of discussion, and I refuse to participate if I'm bound like a prisoner."

Gerard grinned. "How do you know we don't plan to kill you?"

I pulled on my Lady persona like a pair of fireman's coveralls, my shoulders flexing back and my chin lifting. "If you wanted me dead, Brox would have let Malcolm's men take me out in the parking lot. Seems like a lot less trouble."

"Unless we wanted something from you first," he said with a glint in his eye.

"I can't think of a single thing you'd want from me. If you were hopin' to ransom me to Malcolm, the confrontation in the parking lot proves I mean nothing to him anymore." My heart twisted as I said the words, refusing to believe they were true. James might be upset with me, but he'd never condone my murder. In fact, I couldn't believe he'd condone the cold-blooded murder of any innocent. If those had been his men, they must have gone rogue. It had happened before, but it was alarming it was happening again. Whatever the case, I would deal with that later. Right now I had to placate Gerard. "Which means we're here for a chat, and the more hospitable you are, the more open I'll be."

Carey stood to the left, by the kitchen sink, and the snarl he released didn't sound very accommodating.

"The last time we offered our hospitality, you snubbed us and pulled a gun on me," Gerard said in a low growl.

"That's because I felt threatened. Up until that time, we were engaged in an active discussion."

"Not entirely true," Gerard said. "I wanted information you refused to give me."

"You wanted to know what Mason Deveraux was up to, and I told you the truth. I didn't know. He and I were no longer speaking, and that remains the case, not that it's any of your business."

"Why are you livin' with Joe Simmons?"

"That's not any of your business either."

"It's my business if they're both out to get me."

"That's between you and them. I haven't spoken to Mason in months, and Joe keeps his sheriff business to himself, just like I keep my business to myself. Joe has no idea what I'm doin' or who I'm talkin' to. I haven't betrayed a single person to him, nor do I plan to." I took a breath, wondering if I'd said too much. Presenting Joe as my backup could work in my favor, but it could just as easily backfire and get me killed. No, I'd played it right.

"Besides," I continued, "you're accusin' me of keepin' secrets from you. Seems to me that you ought to be glad I'm capable of keepin' secrets." When his eyes turned hard, I lifted my mouth into a partial smile. "Sounds like what you really want is for me to share my secrets about everyone but you."

His jaw tightened. "You know secrets about Malcolm. He just tried to have you killed. We'll help protect you if you tell us what he's up to with Carmichael."

As if I knew. Did he suspect James was handling the prescription drug end of the business while Denny cooked? "That information is not for barter *or* for sale."

"You'll scoff at our offer of help and let that man kill you?"

It struck me that Gerard hadn't brought me here to get me to speak out against James. Brox's news had surprised him, but he'd seen an opportunity and pounced on it. He had another purpose.

"I swore to keep his secrets. My word means something to me, Gerard. So let's cut to the chase. I know exactly why I'm here. You know about the grand jury and you're afraid of what I'm gonna say." I held out my hands again. "If you'd like to have a real discussion, I suggest you treat me with respect, and I'll do the same." I nearly issued a threat, but I bit it back. I was in a house in the woods with three armed men and no weapon of my own, with my hands bound. Fortune was not on my side. I needed to make sure any threats I issued had teeth.

"Or," Gerard said matter-of-factly, "since you refuse to provide us with useful information, we could just kill you and have nothin' to worry about." He lifted his shoulder into a half shrug. "No grand jury. No slipped secrets."

I pursed my lips, trying to hide my fear, because I doubted he was bluffing. "True, and Denny Carmichael could have done the same when he sent his man to see me this morning, but he was smart enough to realize he'd be high on the suspect list if something happened to me."

"We have the fact that no one knows you have a connection to us in our favor. We'll never fall on the sheriff's radar," Gerard said.

"Not entirely true," I countered. "Skeeter Malcolm knows you and I have had dealin's."

He raised an eyebrow. "And I thought we'd established that Malcolm's cut you loose."

"True," I said in a dry tone, "but with his men dead in a parking lot, he's gonna be lookin' for whoever killed them."

"It seems like *you'd* be at the head of that suspect list," Gerard said.

"Maybe so, but Joe's gonna come lookin' for me and Malcolm's not gonna cop to tryin' to snatch me from that parking lot. After your fallin' out with him, I wouldn't be surprised if he offered your name on a silver platter, especially since Malcolm and Carmichael seem to be gettin' pretty cozy." If Gerard thought the two of them were working together, I might as well use that to my advantage.

Gerard's jaw worked. "So Carmichael and Malcolm *are* workin' together?"

Oh. So his question had been a fishing expedition. Mercy, I was off my game, but I could still use this to my advantage. "I take my secrets seriously. I do not betray confidences." He continued staring at me. "But I will only give you this warning once: Carmichael has a future project he wants *me* to work on. He'll be pissed if you kill me before I can fulfill it."

Gerard scowled.

I held out my hands and offered him a saccharine smile.

Gerard flicked his eyes to Brox, and then the younger man pulled out his pocketknife. A quick slice through the tape cut me loose. He started to gently peel it from my skin, but I jerked my hands back and ripped the tape off, refusing to cringe from the pain it caused.

Carey shot me a hateful glare, obviously disapproving of Gerard's decision to free my hands. I could handle his glares. I was the damn Lady in Black.

"Now," I said, scooting my chair back and resting a hand on the table. "Let's get to it. You're concerned about my grand jury testimony."

"You think you're so fucking smart," Carey snipped.

I turned slightly to face him. Carey was a hothead and I'd be smart to keep him in my line of sight. "So there's something else you wish to discuss, then?"

"You fu—"

"Enough!" Gerard shouted. "She's no fool, Carey, and we're negotiatin'. We'll treat her with the respect she currently deserves."

Carey's lips clamped together even though it was clear he had plenty more to add to the subject.

"So what do you plan to say?" Gerard asked, his shoulder tensing. He didn't like that I'd taken control, but I didn't care. My life might depend on my taking charge of their forced interrogation. The fact I'd gotten them to free my hands was in my favor.

"My testimony's supposed to be a secret, Gerard. That's how a grand jury works."

His hand on the table stiffened into a fist. "I don't tolerate impertinence."

"And I don't tolerate bein' manhandled, but here we are, both of us unhappy, so let's get this discussion over with so I can go home and go to bed."

Carey took a step toward me and Brox's body vibrated with anger.

"We don't hurt women," Brox said.

"We do if they're disrespectful," Carey said, his hands balling at his side.

"Only if they're our wives. We aren't allowed to physically reprimand other women."

Were these guys for real? Sadly, I believed they were.

Carey groaned in disgust. "Malcolm doesn't want her anymore, and whatever purpose Carmichael might have for her, I doubt he'll care if she shows up with a few bruises."

"No," Brox snarled.

"She's disrespectful and uppity. She needs to learn her place." Carey stood inches from his brother, only a fraction shorter than Brox, though not as heavily muscled. I had no doubt that Brox could take him, but would he fight his brother over me?

"That's for her husband to decide," Brox said. "Not you. Not me."

"She ain't got a husband, you damn fool," Carey snapped. "So we'll teach her the lesson she badly needs, and her future husband will thank us for it."

"Hey," I shouted. "How about we don't talk about me like I'm not here. I'm a person, not someone's damn property."

Carey pointed his finger at me, anger twisting his features. "You're too arrogant for a woman."

"And you're a sorry excuse for a man. We're certainly not meant for each other, so I guess you'd better keep your grimy hands off me." I knew I'd gone too far, but I was sick to death of being a pawn in these stupid games. I turned back to Gerard. "I was told you're a smart, self-sufficient man who has a strong sense of right and wrong. And yet, I haven't wronged you in any way, Gerard Collard, and both times I've seen you, you've snatched me at gunpoint. Even so, I've sat at your table and participated in civil conversations instead of spitting in your face for insulting me." I got to my feet. "Maybe that was my first mistake."

"I have *not* insulted you," he snapped.

"Allowing your son to threaten me with physical harm is an insult. Sending your other son to fetch me not once but twice is an insult." I took a breath and told myself to hold my temper. I couldn't count on James anymore. I needed to be able to protect our baby on my own, and if that meant getting on the good side of every criminal in this county, so be it.

I held my hands up in semi-surrender. "It's late. Tempers are short. I understand your concern, Gerard, but I think we can come to some kind of agreement."

He narrowed his eyes with suspicion.

"You want something, and I want something. Let's work out a deal to ensure everyone walks away happy."

"What do you want?" Carey demanded in a hateful tone.

I leveled my gaze on Gerard. "Are *you* runnin' this meetin' or is he? Because I need to know who to address."

Anger flashed in Gerard's eyes, but he turned to his son and said, "Keep your mouth shut or leave."

Carey's hands fisted at his sides, and he looked like he wanted to lunge for me. I was sure I'd cemented his hatred and made a new enemy. He was just one more asshole I'd have to watch for behind my back.

One bad guy at a time, precious baby. We'll take care of them one at a time.

"What do you want?" Gerard barked.

"I want you to acknowledge my neutrality in the criminal world."

He looked suspicious. "That's all you want?"

He was right. I needed to think bigger. My mind shot to Denny Carmichael, and the favor I owed him. Two could play that game. "No. The second part is that I want a favor from you in case I ever need one."

"What kind of favor?"

"I don't know," I said. "But there may come a time I need help, and I want to know I can call on you."

Gerard burst out laughing. When he settled down, he said, "I make it a practice to ensure that I don't owe anyone anything."

"And that's a good philosophy to have. Keeps moochers from takin' advantage of you." It took all my willpower to keep from casting an accusatory glance at Carey. "But *you* want something that is very valuable. I can give you that if you give me insurance."

Gerard's face reddened. "You were plannin' on testifying against me."

"I never said any such thing," I said. "Do you even know why I've been asked to testify?" When he didn't respond, I said, "I was attacked and nearly killed by two Sugar Branch police officers, and they're bringing me in to question me about *that* incident. But I've been told the jury can and likely *will* ask me other questions. I have no plan to bring up your name, Gerard, but should it come up, I've been known to have tunnel vision and a poor memory when need be."

Part of me was horrified by what I'd just implied. He was a criminal, and I'd essentially offered him protection, but I knew too much about too many things to walk into that grand jury, spill all, and expect to live a long, peaceful life. Especially if I wanted to raise my baby on the farm. I had to make sure we were safe.

I continued. "Here's what I suspect I'll remember: You sent your son to issue an invitation to your land to discuss my investigation into who killed Carol Ann Nelson. You'd heard I'd stumbled on some files Kip Wagner had put together on important people in the county and you wanted to know if I'd found a file on you or your sons."

"You'd lie?" he asked, incredulous.

"Lie? You coerced me to your property because of a file—mine—so it's not a huge stretch." I paused, then added, "I want no trouble with you or your sons, Gerard. I just want to live my life in peace. Granted, I've gotten involved in multiple criminal endeavors, but I never butted into them. My involvement has usually come about from my work with my PI clients. I've never personally benefited from any of these encounters. I consider myself a mediator. I've saved quite a few lives and cooled many a temper. But doing so means earning men's trust, which means I'm the Fort Knox of secrets. I'd like to earn *your* trust."

When he still looked unconvinced, I began to wonder if I'd calculated wrong, but then his posture changed and respect filled his eyes. "I've heard that whatever confrontations you've been involved in, you've handled fairly."

I tried to hide my relief and play it cool. "I'd like to think so. I've ruled against Skeeter Malcolm before, and I'm sure I will again."

Gerard pushed out a long breath, suddenly sounding weary. "We won't kill people unless provoked. So if you're lookin' for a hit man, you're barkin' up the wrong tree."

It took me a second to realize he was negotiating the terms of our agreement. "I would never ask you to do such a thing," I said. "Violence should be a last resort and never committed in cold blood. I'm tryin' to make the county safer, not de-civilize it."

He nodded sharply.

"I have no idea what I'd ask for, but there are times I need support. Tim Dermot has offered me that support before, and so has Malcolm—although, as you pointed out, his support is now uncertain. If I ask you for help, and you provide no ethical reason to refuse, I'll expect you to follow through."

He cast a glance back to Brox. "What do you think?"

Carey's eyes narrowed with rage.

"I think we should accept," Brox said. "She's right. She doesn't take sides. She favors whatever is best for the county. I heard Malcolm was none too happy when she picked Reynolds over him in a dispute, but he stood by her decision."

Gerard pursed his lips.

Brox took his silence as encouragement. Sounding more emphatic, he added, "We both know there are selfish men out there who think nothing of ripping people off or even murdering them. She stands up to them. She tries to set things to right. We should support that. Especially now."

Gerard studied me again. "How do you justify lyin' to the court if you're all about followin' the rules?"

"I never said I was a rule-follower," I said. "I believe in standin' up for what's right. Sometimes the two don't go hand in hand."

He gave another nod and was silent for a moment. "There will be no mention of illegal activities in regard to me or mine?"

I lifted an eyebrow. "What criminal activity? I was an invited guest to your home. There were guns, but I'm sure all y'all have permits to carry guns. I don't know how you came about acquirin' them, nor do I care. We had our discussion and I left with Skeeter Malcolm, who kindly offered me a ride." I gave him a sweet smile. "But again, I have no plans to mention you at all. I'll only offer information on what I'm asked."

"And what about tonight?" he asked. "They'll think you shot those men and ran off. How do you propose to explain yourself?"

"Frankly," I said, "I haven't had time to consider it, but they'll know soon enough that those men were shot with bullets that didn't come from my gun."

Brox spoke up. "Someone else shot them, and she ran. A stranger forced her into his truck at gunpoint. He drove her out of town, but she got away."

I went over his story in my mind. It was simple and plausible.

"That could have been what happened," I said in a conspiratorial tone.

"You're willin' to commit perjury for us?" Carey barked, taking a step forward. "What's in it for you? And I'm not buyin' your story about needin' a favor."

"I'll tell you why," I said, spinning to face him and putting my hands on my hips. "I don't want to worry about sleepin' with one eye open. As for keepin' my mouth shut? I've made promises. I've garnered trust. I'm not reneging on that now. I stand for nothin' if people can't trust my word."

Gerard stood and moved toward me, slowly as though working out some kinks in his back. When he reached me, he extended his hand. "Lady, it's hard to find people of integrity these days. I'll grant you your request, but you only have a year to ask for your favor."

I sure hoped this was all resolved by the end of a year. I'd have a baby by then.

Oh, Lordy. I was having a baby.

But I'd deal with the second round of shock later. I still needed to wrap up this deal. I took his hand and shook it.

He held on and leaned closer. "Are you lookin' for a husband?"

I opened my mouth to say something, then closed it before saying, "I'm not currently in the market."

"I have four sons." He gestured toward the other two men in the room. "Brox is the eldest and is destined to take charge when I'm gone. He'd make a fine husband."

My face flushed. "Thank you for your generous offer, Gerard," I said, feeling flustered, "but I've got my hands full with my businesses and my dyin' sister. I don't have time for a relationship."

"See?" Gerard said, pointing to me while turning to look at Carey. "Integrity. A hard worker." He glanced down at me. "And good childbearing hips. You can't do much better."

Carey looked like he begged to differ, and Brox looked like he wanted to crawl under the house and die.

Gerard dropped my hand and nodded. "We have a deal, Rose Gardner. As long as you keep your end of the bargain, we'll keep ours."

"Thank you," I said. "I'm countin' on it." I gave him a nod of my own, then turned to leave before he could change his mind.

I walked around to the passenger door of the truck and climbed in the front seat, not wanting to give Brox any ideas about tying me up. He didn't comment when he followed me out—he just climbed into the driver's side and started the car. Moments later, we were heading toward the road.

We were silent until we reached a two-lane county road I didn't recognize and turned right. Once we were a minute or so out, the tension in Brox's shoulders seemed to ease.

"I can't drop you off very close to town, but I can drop you off a short bit from a convenience store. You can go inside and ask to use the phone." He paused. "You got someone to call?"

Who would I call? I used to call James in these situations, but even if I could get ahold of him, I doubted he'd help. Especially since the danger had passed. Jed was with Neely Kate. I needed to call the person who was most worried about me right now, and I could only hope I wouldn't put him in an even more awkward position. "Yeah."

He gave a sharp nod, keeping his gaze on the road. "Gerard... he's old-fashioned, ya know? He was serious about that marriage offer, but it was meant as a compliment. So far, he's only found one other woman he considered worthy of joinin' our family, and she had buckteeth and a lazy eye." He cleared his throat, clearly uncomfortable with this conversation yet pursuing it anyway. "You're much prettier."

I tried not to cringe with embarrassment. "Thank you...?"

"I..." He hesitated, then shifted in his seat. "I know you're expectin' a baby and that Malcolm expects you to murder it."

My heart fell to my stomach. How did he know? But then I remembered he'd told his father he'd followed me from the pool hall. "Were you watchin' me?"

"No," he said in a rough voice. "I was watchin' Malcolm. We *did* want to talk to you, though, so I called Gerard and we set things into motion. I was excited when I saw you stop at the pharmacy. Seemed like it would be less trouble than forcing you off the road." He paused and shook his head. Then his hand tightened on the steering wheel. "I tolerated Skeeter Malcolm before and semi-respected him because he seemed to have a sense of honor. But after what he said to you tonight…"

Shame washed through me. "I…" I swallowed, unsure what to say. "Why didn't you tell your father? Seems like he could have used that against me."

He paused. "That's why I didn't tell him. He just might have."

I turned to him in surprise.

"Gerard had it right when he said you have integrity. As long as we're safe, we need to let you be and support you." He shot me a glance. "We don't get involved with other people's shit. For him to offer you help if you need it… that's pretty rare."

I'd gathered as much.

"His other option was to kill you, and you didn't deserve that."

I let that sink in. "Are you tellin' me he would have killed me tonight if he'd decided I was a threat?"

"He couldn't risk you hurtin' the family. He wouldn't want to do it, but…"

No further explanation needed.

"Can you memorize a phone number?" he asked.

"Ordinarily, I'd say yes, but I'm exhausted and stressed and…"

"You've been through a lot tonight. You need to take care of yourself and your baby." He shot me another look. "You're not gonna kill it, are you?"

I leaned my head back against the seat, overcome with exhaustion. It seemed wrong that the son of the county's most notorious prepper would find this out before James Malcolm, but so be it. "No. I'm not havin' an abortion."

"Good."

I wasn't surprised he was pro-life, but it surprised me he cared so much. That was a discussion I had no urge to jump into.

I could see lights up ahead, and he slowed down and pulled over to the shoulder.

"There's a gas station about a quarter mile up the road. I know the guy workin' the counter. He'll let you make a call, but be sure to leave my name out of it."

"I never saw you tonight," I said, reaching for the door handle, eager to get out in case he changed his mind. Once I was outside, he rolled down the window and leaned out, looking at me.

"I'll let you know how to contact us when you need to collect your favor." Then he pulled into the street, made a wide U-turn, and drove away.

Chapter
Seventeen

I was sitting on the curb outside the convenience store when Joe pulled up twenty minutes later, lights flashing on his unmarked car. He screeched to a halt next to me, shut off the lights, and jumped out the instant the car stopped moving.

"Why are you out here alone? I told you to wait indoors," he said, glancing around for signs of a threat.

"I was getting claustrophobic in there." I wrapped my sweater tighter around me. The evening had turned chilly, but I preferred the cold air to the guy watching me from behind the counter.

"Are you okay?" he asked, worry in his eyes. I hadn't told him much when I'd called his cell phone. Just that I was in a gas station outside of Pickle Junction and I needed him to come get me.

I got to my feet, brushing the dirt off my butt. "I'm fine. A little shaken, but fine."

"A *little* shaken?" he demanded. "From the looks of it, you disappeared after killing two men in the parking lot of Beacon's Pharmacy."

"I didn't kill them," I said. "Someone else did, then I ran away."

He studied me closely. "Is that your official story or the real version?"

I hesitated. I felt like he and I were on a precipice, and if we jumped off, there was no going back. Was it fair to ask him to keep my secrets? Was it fair to exclude him after everything he'd done for me? "That part is true, but after that…which version do you want to hear?"

His gaze held mine. "Right now, the official version."

The absence of accusation in his tone caught me off guard.

I told him the real story, up until the point where someone had shot the two men. The lie picked up where the truth had left off, and I said I'd run off, only to be picked up by a man who held me at gunpoint and drove me south of town.

"I told him that I was about to barf in his truck, so he grudgingly pulled over. When I opened the door, I jumped out and took off running into the trees. He seemed spooked when he couldn't find me, so he left. I waited a little bit to make sure the coast was clear and walked to the convenience store."

He studied me for a few moments. "Your story raises a few questions. One, why did you leave Muffy behind? Two, if you were hanging out in the woods, why do your legs look relatively clean? Three, did you recognize the guy who kidnapped you, and could you pick him out of a lineup? Four, what kind of truck did he drive? Five, did he shoot at you? Six, did he tell you why he forced you into his truck at gunpoint?"

Well, crap. I hadn't thought of any of that.

His gaze held mine. "How much do you want to sell this story?"

I swallowed, feeling like I was about to throw up. "I'm stickin' with it."

He nodded. "Then we need to provide proof." He started for the driver's door of his car. "Get in."

I wasn't sure what he was up to, but I decided to trust him. He pulled out of the parking lot and headed south—away from town.

"Where are you goin'?" I asked.

"You need to show me where he pulled over," he said, keeping his eyes on the road, then pointed up ahead. "That looks like a good place over yonder. The shoulder is asphalt, so there wouldn't be any tire tracks and the woods are close enough for you to have made a run for them." He pulled over and stopped the car.

I gaped at him. He was staging my story.

"Why don't you show me where you ran and hid?" He got out of the car and waited for me to do the same. Turning on a small flashlight, he pointed it at the ground. "Seems to me, you'd go in that direction." The beam traveled from me toward the trees. "You'd run deeper into the woods, but likely not too far." He cut the flashlight off and the trees went dark. "If you were hiding back there, I doubt he would have found you. Especially since he didn't have a flashlight, right?"

I stared at him, dumbfounded, then nodded.

He walked over to me, shining his light on the ground. "Walk on out there and show me how far you went."

Tears filled my eyes. "Why are you doin' this, Joe?"

"You're gonna share what really happened with me later, but right now, you're gonna show me the official version, and we're gonna make sure it's airtight. Got it?"

I nodded, swiping at a tear.

"Good." He flicked on the flashlight and pointed it at the ground. "Now start walkin'."

I headed into the woods until he told me I was deep enough. Then he turned off his light to be sure.

"Hide behind a tree," he called out.

I did as he said, trying not to panic when it reminded me of that awful night in Sugar Branch.

Joe moved to the edge of the trees, stomping around and pretending to look for me, then walked back to the side of the road.

"Now come on out but stay on the shoulder." He turned the light back on so I could see where I was going. "And from here you walked to the convenience store, right?"

I nodded. "Yeah."

"Why did you leave Muffy?" he asked.

"I didn't have time to get her out, and I figured she'd be safer in the car."

He nodded, then shone the flashlight on my legs. "We took care of the scratches."

I glanced down at the marks on my bare legs.

"Did you recognize the guy?" Joe asked.

I shook my head. "No. He wore a hooded sweatshirt. I never saw his face in the dark, and he barely spoke, so I doubt I'd recognize his face."

He gave me a short nod. "What kind of truck did he drive?"

"An old red pickup. I don't remember the make or model, but it had ripped-up, dark vinyl seats."

He winked at me. "That accounts for about a third of the pickups in Fenton County. Now, did he tell you why he forced you into his truck at gunpoint?"

"No. Like I said, he barely spoke other than to tell me to get in, but I did wonder if he was the one who'd killed those men in the parking lot. He didn't call out to me after I ran off, but I could hear him searchin' for me at the edge of the woods, and it scared the bejesus out of me."

Joe nodded. "You've got at least an hour ahead of you givin' statements. Are you feelin' up to it?"

That surprised me. "Do I have a choice?" He hesitated and I realized what he wasn't saying. "I'm pregnant, Joe, not sick."

"I disagree, Rose. You forget I live with you. I've been worried for weeks. You don't look well, and you've lost weight instead of gaining it. How far along are you?"

"At least ten weeks."

His eyes widened. "You're almost out of the first trimester."

I gave him a watery smile, remembering again that he'd been through this with Hilary. "You probably know more about pregnancy than I do."

"Hey," he said, walking over to me and pulling me into a hug. "It's gonna be okay."

"I haven't been taking prenatal vitamins, Joe," I said, starting to cry into his shirt. "What if my baby is messed up because I wasn't taking vitamins?"

"It won't be," he said with a smile in his voice.

"I've been drinking caffeine. And taking ibuprofen. And I've lost weight. What if I've hurt my baby and I didn't even know it was happening?"

"Hey," he said, rubbing my back. "You didn't."

"You don't know that."

"Then we'll love him or her anyway."

That made me cry harder. This baby wasn't even Joe's and he was already including it in his life, while James… "He wants me to have an abortion."

His arms tightened before loosening again. "Malcolm?"

I nodded against his chest.

He was silent for a beat. "What do *you* want to do?"

"I want to keep it," I said without hesitation. "It's the worst possible time, and this grand jury is making every criminal in the county crazy." I shook my head, my cheek brushing against his uniform shirt. "I'm doin' what I need to do to make things safe for him or her. I need to make sure no one is gonna come after us."

He hesitated, then said, "You're not gonna tell them everything."

No, I wasn't, which went against what James and Carter Hale had told me to do. "Joe, do you happen to know a good attorney I can hire?"

He grabbed my upper arms and leaned back to examine me, shock on his face.

"I can't count on Carter Hale. I need my own attorney, but I have no idea how I can get a good one with such short notice."

A hard look filled his eyes. "I already found one."

"An attorney?"

He nodded. "I don't trust Hale, so I made some inquiries after I left your office this afternoon. Don't be mad. I would have mentioned it earlier, but I didn't have a chance."

"I'm not mad. I'm grateful."

Relief filled his eyes. "His name is Gary Hardisty and he's from Little Rock. He's comin' down first thing in the morning."

"How'd you make that happen so quickly?"

"A lot of money and the chance for Gary to stick it to Mason Deveraux." When I gave him a look of confusion, he said, "There's no love lost between Gary Hardisty and Deveraux, and he thinks it's a miscarriage of justice for Deveraux to go toe to toe with his ex. Gary's eager for the chance to one-up him."

"I thought my attorney couldn't go before the grand jury with me."

"He can't, but I doubt this will be the last time you'll be dealin' with Mason Deveraux." He pushed out a long breath. "Gary's coming to the farm at nine a.m., and seeing how it's now after eleven, I say we head to the station to get your official statement so we can get you home. You've got a busy day tomorrow."

I started to get in the car, then stopped, watching him over the roof of his car. "Wait. You said it took a lot of money. I don't have a lot of money, Joe."

"I know, but I do."

I shook my head. "I can't take your money."

"I'm livin' at your house, rent-free. It's the least I can do."

"I suspect what little you might pay in rent equals five minutes of his time, and not only that, you're sleepin' in the study. I should be payin' *you* to be puttin' up with such poor accommodations, especially since you moved in to protect us."

His face softened. "Rose, you're havin' a baby you didn't plan and its father wants you to get rid of it. Your sister's dyin'. You're about to face a grand jury, which I suspect is Mason's attempt to use you to nail Malcolm to the wall. We can't mess around with this. You need expert legal advice that is one hundred percent on your side. *Please.* Let me do this. Your baby needs you outside of prison so *you* can raise him or her, not Neely Kate and Jed."

My breath caught in my throat.

"Yeah," he said softly. "Prison."

I nodded, and he placed a call to a deputy to come out to survey the area where I'd supposedly escaped my abductor.

Chapter Eighteen

Joe drove me home around one in the morning, and on the way, I told him what had really happened that evening. While I admitted Brox had forced me to pay a visit to his father, I left out the part about the duct tape.

"You made a deal with Gerard Collard?" he asked in disbelief.

"I'm not givin' you any details of the meeting, and rest assured, the deal wasn't much of one, but I'm confident they'll leave me alone as long as I keep my mouth shut."

"You know about some criminal doin's with the Collards?" He sounded a little too eager to suit me.

"I know you and Mason were working together to build a case against them. But I'm not tellin' you anything I might know. Not even in confidence."

"Rose."

"Not happenin', Joe."

"We should bust them for kidnappin', Rose. They could have killed you."

"But they didn't. Because I promised to keep their secrets. And I plan to do just that. You know as well as I do that I don't need any more trouble."

Deputy Randy Miller had brought Muffy back to the farm, and he planned on staying the rest of the night to keep watch. Once Joe was assured that I was comfortable with the arrangement, he headed back to the crime scene at the pharmacy. I headed up to bed and fell asleep within seconds of my head hitting the pillow. Muffy slept next to me, watching the bedroom door.

The next time my eyes opened, soft daylight was streaming through the thin curtains, and Muffy wasn't on the bed. I grabbed my phone and checked the time, bolting upright when I saw it was nearly eight thirty. Not only had I told Carly that I'd take care of Violet this morning, but Joe's attorney was coming in a little over a half hour. But as I climbed out of bed, I realized how soundly I'd slept, for the first time in ages. I was still exhausted, but that seemed to be a continual state for me. I'd deal with it.

I hurried to Violet's room, worried that she had been left so long unattended, but when I reached her door, I heard Joe's voice on the other side.

I rapped on the door and pushed it open. "Good morning."

Joe was sitting on the edge of the bed, while Violet was propped up on pillows, beaming at him. She had more color on her face than she'd had the day before.

"Looks like I'm interrupting something," I said with a grin.

"You most definitely are," Joe said. "You're supposed to be sleepin' in."

"I did," I countered. "I slept until after eight."

Joe rolled his eyes. "That's pathetic. Besides, you need your sleep. Especially now."

As soon as the words left his mouth, he froze, realizing his faux pas.

But Violet ignored his slip and turned to me. "I thought last night was a huge success."

So much had happened the previous night that I had to stop and consider what she might be talking about. "Oh, the dinner party," I said. "Yes. We should definitely do it again soon."

"Of course the dinner party," she said. "What did I miss after I went to bed?"

Joe slid off the mattress. "I'll finish the story about my youth in the Simmons household later."

She gave him a soft smile. "I'm gonna hold you to it."

Joe leaned over and gave her a kiss on the cheek. "I'm countin' on it." He walked around the edge of the bed, and said to me, "Gary Hardisty sent a text that he's runnin' late. He won't be here until closer to ten. He's actually in the process of tryin' to get your appearance postponed."

While part of me wanted to put it off, the rest of me wanted to get it over with. Stalling wouldn't change much of anything.

"I need to run into town and check on the investigation," he said, purposefully keeping it vague, "but I plan on bein' back by the time he gets here."

"Thanks, Joe."

He lifted a hand in acknowledgment as he walked out the door.

"Who's Gary Hardisty, and why's he dropping by at ten?" Violet asked.

"My attorney," I said as I sat on the bed and situated myself. "Joe and I decided I needed a new one."

"For the grand jury?" she asked with a frown. "Are you in some kind of trouble?"

"Of course not," I said, trying to settle my own anxiety. "But I'm about to face Mason, and you know he's holdin' a grudge against me. Joe and I talked last night and decided Carter Hale was just a little too close to home for this, so Joe called Gary, and he agreed to help out." I was making it sound a lot less fraught than it felt, but the last thing she needed was more stress. "Joe says he's the best of the best."

Worry lines deepened on her forehead. "How can you afford the best of the best?"

I cringed, refusing to look up at her. "Joe's paying for his time."

When she didn't answer, I looked up and met her gaze. Her expression was grim. Neither of us had to say anything more about that—she of all people knew how hard it was for me to accept charity. "Tell me about the grand jury."

I reached over and grabbed her hand then squeezed. "The grand jury is likely nothin'. Joe says they'll be askin' about my incident with the Sugar Branch police. Hiring Gary Hardisty is like havin' insurance. Just in case."

"Just in case of what?"

I tried not to squirm. "In case Mason starts askin' about my involvement with Skeeter Malcolm last winter."

Her eyes narrowed. "You mean when you risked your life to save Mason's sorry ass by takin' on a role in the criminal world?"

I couldn't help grinning. My sister sure had a way with words. "Yeah. That."

She shook her head. "I have half a mind to go down to the courthouse and shake some sense into him myself."

My grin spread. "While I don't doubt that you could, I think he's basically doin' the right thing. There *is* corruption in the county. It *does* need cleanin' out. And who knows? Maybe he won't let his personal bias get in the way of questionin' me in front of the jury, but Joe and I feel like I need to be prepared."

She was quiet for a moment. "You know things about those criminals."

Her voice was so soft I barely heard her, but I held her gaze and gave a slight nod.

"That's not all," she whispered, squeezing my hand. "I can tell there's something else you're not tellin' me."

Tears stung my eyes, and I tried to swallow the lump in my throat. "There's a lot I'm not tellin' you."

"So tell me. There's no time like the present, and it might be all we have." When I glanced at our joined hands, she gave them a little shake. "I'm not that broken, Rose. I can handle more than you think."

I looked up at her teary eyes.

"Do you realize how much I like bein' your big sister? I want to help you with your troubles. You used to come to me for help all the time before."

Before.

Before Momma died. When Violet was all I'd had. As I'd grown as a person, I'd distanced myself from her, realizing our co-dependent relationship wasn't healthy, but after twenty-five years of being my everything, she'd struggled to accept that I had other friends. Other relationships. A life without her. That she was no longer the center of my small world. But it occurred to me that maybe I'd pulled back too far. Maybe I'd squandered time with my sister in the quest for independence. Time I'd never get back now.

Pushing out a long breath, I squeezed her hand and held her gaze. "I'm pregnant."

Her eyes flew wide in shock. "Oh."

"I just found out last night," I said in a rush. "I went to the doctor yesterday to pick up your prescription, and the new doctor said I had to make an appointment with her to get them. While I was there, she asked how I was doin' and suggested I might consider anxiety medication—since I've lost weight and had stomach issues over the last couple of months. They took blood and made me pee in a cup. A pregnancy test was standard procedure before prescribing pills like that." I paused. "It came back positive."

She still looked shell-shocked. "You didn't know?"

I shook my head, glancing down at the bed. "No. I'm on the pill. I've been faithful about taking them, but Dr. Arnold changed my pills back in August, and Dr. Newton said I should have been on another type of protection for the first month.

"August?" she asked in surprise. "How far along are you?"

"I don't know for certain," I said, still looking down. "But at least ten weeks."

"*Ten weeks?*" When I didn't say anything, she said, "Your mystery man is the father, isn't he? The one you wouldn't introduce to me. Who is he, Rose? You can tell me the truth. No judgment. I won't tell a soul."

I lifted my gaze to hers again. "Skeeter Malcolm."

Her mouth dropped open and her eyes flew wide. "What? You were carrying on with Skeeter Malcolm and you didn't say a word?"

Pushing out a sigh, I said, "You know I was the Lady in Black last winter, but I've still been actin' as her this summer. Some of our PI cases have involved the criminal element. Neely Kate and I stopped a couple of potential turf wars, but in the process, things between James and me…"

"James?"

My mouth quirked into a half smile. "That's his real name. James." I shifted my leg. "We stayed friends after that mess last winter." I told her everything about our relationship, from the way we'd saved each other, more than once, to the friendship we'd struck up and the Tuesday night meetings that had led to something stronger and deeper. I told her about the way our relationship had fallen apart over the incident with the Sugar Branch police and my suspicion that James was now working with the FBI, although he wouldn't tell me anything and had all but cut me out of his life.

When I finished, she remained silent for a good five seconds before she asked, "Does he know about the baby yet?"

"When Dr. Newton called to tell me last night—that was the call I took at the end of dinner—she said she caught one of the nurses sharing the test results with someone over the phone. That's why she called me right away." I paused, then said, "I'm pretty sure the nurse was calling Dena, so there's a good chance half the town already knows. I told Joe and everyone who was here for dinner last night, to get ahead of the gossip. I would have told you then, too, but you were asleep when I came upstairs and I didn't want to wake you."

"Oh," she said, her brow furrowing. "That's why Joe wanted you to sleep in."

I nodded. "Yeah."

"Does Skeeter Malcolm know?" she asked, repeating her earlier question.

"He does now," I said. "I went to the pool hall to talk to him last night."

"And?"

A burning lump filled my throat.

"Oh, Rose," she said, squeezing my hand again. "I'm so sorry."

"I didn't expect him to be excited. He told me from the very beginning that he never wanted a family. But he also said he loved me." I sniffed. "So I didn't expect him to be so…cold." I released a shaky breath. "He told me to take care of it. He wants me to get an abortion, Vi."

"Do you want an abortion?"

"No. I want to keep the baby. I've known for less twenty-four hours, and I'm already attached to it."

A soft smile spread across her face. "Of course you are. You were always destined to be a mother, Rose. You're such a nurturer. I only wish I could meet your baby."

"Vi…"

She shook her head. "No. None of that. We take what we can get and accept the rest. I know I won't meet your baby, but I'm here to help you through this part. You can do this, Rose. You can raise this baby without help from the daddy, but you won't be on your own, because you have Neely Kate and Jed, Joe, Carly, Maeve—Maeve will be thrilled to help you since I doubt Mason will give her the grandbabies she so desperately craves. You'll have plenty of help. You won't need me."

"That's not true," I said. "I'll always need you."

She settled back into her pillows. "I won't pretend I know what dyin's like. I don't think you can know until it happens, but I promise you this, Rose—I'll always be watchin' over you, doin' my very best to make things easier for you." She reached out her hand, and I lay down next to her as she wrapped an arm around my back. "You're gonna have a beautiful baby," she whispered. "And that baby will be the luckiest child in the whole world, because I've seen you love and defend your friends. I can't even imagine what you'll do for the sake of your own child."

I started to cry.

"Shh," she whispered in my ear. "You get your sorrow out now, and when you leave this room, allow only joy, because this baby will bring you so much joy. I promise."

"I don't want to do this without you, Vi."

"You hush," she soothed. "If you want to know the truth, I'm glad you're havin' a baby, because now I don't have to worry about leavin' you."

I turned to look up at her.

She gave me a soft smile, sweeping a strand of hair from my cheek. "There's no love like the love of a mother for her child, Rose. No one will ever take your child's place. Not even Skeeter Malcolm."

That was what I was worried about.

"I know things about the criminals in this county," I whispered. "And they're worried about what I'll say in front of the grand jury."

Her body stiffened. "They're worried you'll snitch on them."

"Like I said, I'm sure James made some kind of deal. He said they'll know I'm lyin' if I don't answer their questions truthfully. Carter Hale told me to do the same, although he didn't seem happy about it."

She shook her head. "I don't understand."

The worries that had been brewing in my head since last night came spilling out. "If I do what James asked me to do, I'll make more enemies than I can count. I'll have to move away or risk retaliation. I'll be forced to leave the farm, and Ashley and Mikey and everyone I love. But now I have a baby to think about, and I have to do everything in my power to protect him or her. I have to keep my secrets."

She studied me for several long seconds. "You're gonna lie."

"I don't want to lie, but if I tell the truth and all those men get arrested, they won't *all* be put away. I'll be a sitting duck." I sat up and turned to look at her. "I've worked hard to garner those criminals' trust and gain a neutral status. If I can maintain it, not only do I continue to have their trust, but also their loyalty."

She was silent for a moment. "I won't pretend to like that you're workin' with criminals, but Skeeter Malcolm dragged you into it, Rose. You're only doin' what you need to do to survive."

"But I suspect I'm betrayin' James if I cover for them."

"You do what you need to do to protect your baby," she said, her tone firm. "From here on out, your baby always comes first, and definitely before some man who doesn't even want it."

When she put it that way, it seemed so simple. Yet I knew it was anything but.

Chapter Nineteen

I'd worn Violet out, so I made sure she took her medication, then went to take a shower and get ready.

Carly was sitting at the kitchen table when I went downstairs, staring at something on my old laptop. When she saw me, she looked startled and pushed down the cover. "Hey, Rose. Can I get you something for breakfast?"

"No," I said, moving to the cabinet to get a coffee mug. "I'm not hungry."

A sudden wave of grief caught me by surprise. I loved having Carly here, but I missed Neely Kate something fierce. She'd said she only needed a little time, but would she distance herself from me now that I was pregnant?

"Did you sleep in?" I asked her as I started to reach for the coffee pot, then stopped. How was I going to give up coffee?

I put the mug back in the cabinet.

"I did," she said, "but I'm used to getting up early, so I got up at eight and went for a run."

I grabbed a glass of water and sat at the table. "Were there any cars out there other than Neely Kate's?"

"No, should there have been?"

"No," I said. "Definitely not. If you do, let Joe know immediately." If James had sent men to watch over me, I wasn't sure I wanted them hanging around after the way he'd acted last night. They'd proven they weren't of much use, so if we saw them, we should send them on their way. They might be spying on us.

"Okay."

"You probably noticed your car wasn't parked out front," I said, cringing. "It was involved in an incident."

She half shrugged and walked over to the end of the table. "I know. Joe told me."

"I'm so sorry."

"Don't. It's a piece of junk. I was thinking that I'll save up for a better one once I get a job, but I won't be able to apply for a loan. I don't even know how I'll get a job. I'm worried my father will trace my social security number."

"Don't you worry about any of that right now," I said. "We'll sort everything out as it comes."

"Thanks, Rose."

I hesitated, then said, "You know you can share things with me. I won't tell anyone."

She grinned. "I think I'll take you up on your offer when things die down." Her smile fell away as she glanced back at the closed laptop. "There's been a new development that worries me."

I leaned toward her. "Are you in danger?"

"Oh, no. There've been some changes in my father's company, is all. It's nothing. Seriously. I'm just paranoid."

"If you ever feel unsafe, please don't hesitate to tell us. No matter what's goin' on."

Worry filled her eyes. "I would never put you or Violet in danger, Rose."

"It's not us I'm worried about. It's *you*. Now promise me. None of my worries are too big for me to care about yours."

Gratitude washed over her face. "I have no idea how I got so lucky findin' you and Neely Kate, but I'll be forever thankful."

"Technically, we found you. And we're the lucky ones, so hush."

"Are you sure you're not hungry? Joe said to make sure you eat."

"Joe's a worrywart."

She laughed. "True, but he has a point."

"Okay," I said, getting up and walking over to the fridge. "I suppose you both have a point."

"I was gonna fix it, Rose," she protested, starting to get out of her chair.

"I'm not an invalid. I'm perfectly capable of fixin' my own breakfast." I grabbed some prewashed strawberries from the fridge and carried the container to the table.

"Are you getting used to the idea yet?" she asked softly. "I mean, I know it was a huge shock."

I popped the top off the container, screwing my mouth to the side. "I'm gettin' acclimated quicker than I'd expected. But when I stop to think about what it means, I'm shocked all over again. Still, this grand jury nonsense is hangin' over my head, obscurin' everything else."

She took a sip of her coffee. "Are you nervous about testifying this afternoon?"

"Yes," I said. "In fact, Joe arranged for an attorney from Little Rock to come down and talk to me beforehand. Joe said he's trying to get my testimony postponed."

"Do you think you're in trouble?" she asked.

Carly deserved to know the truth. "Maybe."

"I know you and Neely Kate get into situations that seem a bit… unethical, but you have a strong sense of right and wrong," she said. "I trust your instincts, Rose. You should too."

I heard a knock on the door. Then Jed called out, "Rose? Carly?"

"Back here," I said. He must have brought my truck back. Had he heard about the night before?

Seconds later, Jed appeared in the kitchen doorway. "Your truck's parked out front. The keys are in the bowl by the door."

He started to turn around, but I shifted in my chair and said, "Not so fast. You knew James was workin' with Dr. Arnold, didn't you? You let me look like a fool yesterday."

He slowly turned to face me, a sheepish look on his face. "How did you find out?"

I ignored his question. "How long has it been goin' on?"

Jed watched me, looking torn.

"Gerard Collard told me it had been goin' on at least three years. Is he right?"

His eyes darkened. "When did you talk to Collard?"

"Last night, when he sent his son to kidnap me and haul me off to a secret location so he could determine if he was gonna kill me."

Carly sat down in her chair, her face paling Apparently, Joe hadn't told her *everything*. To be fair, he hadn't known that part.

"What the hell are you talkin' about?" he demanded. "Collard sent one of his boys here?"

"You're losin' your touch, Jed," I said dryly. "Skeeter Malcolm's men showed up at Beacon's Pharmacy and nearly killed me. Brox Collard came out of nowhere and dragged me to his father, where I discovered that James had been workin' with Dr. Arnold for years."

"Rose, you're testifyin' at a grand jury today. I don't think we should be talkin' about this."

"He lied to me," I said in a cold tone. "He told me he didn't have a hand in drugs, and he lied."

"I didn't know he told you that," Jed said, sounding defeated.

"It doesn't matter anymore. He and I are done. For good."

He didn't look convinced.

"I'm surprised you haven't heard from him," I said, my tone turning sharp. "I went to the pool hall last night to tell him I'm pregnant, and he said he didn't know why I was bothering him with it when you could easily take care of it with your connection to a doctor in Little Rock. I figured he would have asked you to get that set up. Pronto."

His face blanched.

"I will not be requiring that service," I spat.

Jed took a step closer, looking contrite. "Rose. I'm sorry."

I shook my head. "I want no sympathy from you, Jed Carlisle. He already cut you at the knees, why should we be surprised he'd do the same to me?"

He stood next to me. "He cares about you."

"Maybe so, and I never expected him to be excited that he's gonna be a daddy, but I didn't expect him to be so ugly either." I shook my head. "Our baby deserves better than that."

"I'm sure you caught him off guard, Rose," Carly said, looking sheepish at butting in. "Sometimes people react badly to unexpected news, but then they change their tune once they've had some time to think things through."

She had a point, but I was still too hurt to consider it. "The baby aside, he still lied to me about Dr. Arnold, and he didn't even reach out to check on me after what happened at the pharmacy. He's told me one lie after the other." I took a breath. "I want to trust him, but I can't. He's lied and betrayed me one too many times."

But my fool heart still ached for him. Part of me was scared he'd come back to me. That I'd accept his apology and overlook all the times he'd hurt and betrayed me. The rest of me was scared that I wouldn't and I'd lose him forever.

Betrayal, lies, hatred. He'd heaped them all on me, and yet I still missed him.

How messed up was that?

"Carly's right," Jed said. "You know that's how he always reacts. He loses his temper, then calms down. He'll probably come around."

"He didn't lose his temper, Jed. He was so cold and ugly it was like he was made of ice. I've *never* seen him like that except when he was talkin' to his enemies, only this time he was talkin' to *me.*"

Jed's shoulders sagged. "I won't pretend to know what's goin' through his head right now," he said with a sigh. "But he's in the middle of somethin' tense, otherwise why would he have pushed us both away? I can't believe I'm sayin' this, but I think we need to cut him some slack."

I started to protest when the doorbell rang.

"That's probably my new attorney." I started to walk past Jed, but he blocked my path.

"What happened to Hale?"

"Joe and I think I need a new one." When I saw Jed put up his defenses, I said, "I called Carter Hale multiple times for over a half hour last night, trying to get ahold of James. Did you know James changed his number? But Carter still hasn't reached out to me. What if that had been an emergency?" I shook my head. "He's *James's* attorney. His loyalty will always lie there. I can't trust him to prioritize my interests."

I started to walk past him again, but Jed planted his arm on the doorframe. "What are you gonna do, Rose?"

"Ironically, I'm plannin' to do the opposite of what you're probably thinkin', so let me go, Jed."

He dropped his arm, but the dark look in his eyes told me that he wasn't happy about it. I couldn't blame him. We'd gotten ourselves into a right fix.

Jed stayed on my heels as I went to answer the door. A man who looked like he was in his late thirties stood on my front porch, wearing gray dress pants, a white shirt, and blue tie. His dark brown hair was styled, and it was obvious from a single glance that he wasn't from around here. The expensive leather computer case in his left hand only confirmed it.

"Mr. Hardisty?" I asked.

He held out his hand. "Gary Hardisty. Rose?"

I shook his extended hand. "Yeah. Thanks for comin' on such short notice, Mr. Hardisty." I took a step back and gestured to the living room. "Come in."

"Call me Gary." He walked in and took a look at Jed, lifting his brow. He held out a hand. "Gary Hardisty."

Jed hesitated before taking his hand. "Jed Carlisle. Close friend to Rose."

He dropped Gary's hand but gave him an intimidating glare.

"Ahh," Gary said with a knowing look. "Boyfriend?"

"No," I said, putting a hand on Jed's arm. "Just a very worried friend."

Gary appraised him, then nodded. "We have a lot to cover in case we don't get the stay to your appearance as I've requested. Do you have a table where we can sit?"

I nearly took him to the dining room, but we hardly used that room and I needed comfort. I loved the morning light in the kitchen, so I led him in there. Carly was at the sink, washing the few dirty dishes, and she gave us a startled look.

"Carly, we're gonna work in here, if that's all right," I said.

"Of course!" She shot a glance at the coffee maker. "Do you drink coffee, Mr. Hardisty?"

So she'd heard us in the other room.

"I think I'm gonna need plenty of coffee to get through everything we need to tackle," he said with a warm smile.

"How about I start a fresh pot, then check on Violet? Hospice said they were coming by later to assess the logistics of getting a hospital bed installed upstairs."

Gary gave her a curious glance but remained quiet.

The thought of switching Vi to a hospital bed made my heart sink. "I don't think we're quite there yet."

"No," Carly said carefully, "but they warned me that we're closer than we'd like."

Suddenly I wondered if I should be spending all my time upstairs. Maybe Mason would listen if I called him and told him he needed to get his priorities straight. But Violet was sleeping, and she wanted me to get this mess cleaned up. I suspected she wouldn't be at peace until she knew my baby and I were safe.

"Thanks, Carly," I said, swallowing the lump in my throat.

Gary crossed to the table and started to unpack his things.

Carly shot him a worried glance as she prepared a fresh pot of coffee. Jed stood in the doorway, watching Gary with a foreboding look. We weren't doing much to offer him a warm welcome.

"Would you like to stay, Jed?" I asked.

Gary's face shot up. "Is there any chance that Jed will be called as a witness?"

"It depends on how this goes," I said.

Gary gave a sharp nod. "Then Jed likely shouldn't be present during our conference. I'd suggest he consider consulting with an attorney of his own."

I drew in a sharp breath. "I'm not turnin' on Jed."

"That doesn't matter, Rose," Gary said in a kind tone that reminded me of a grandfather, despite his young age. "You should both have your own attorneys." He paused and a dark look filled his eyes. "The fact that you were sharing an attorney with the man you may be called to testify against is alarming. Mr. Hale should have told you to seek out your own counsel, just as I'm suggesting to your friend." He turned to Jed. "I have a list of associates I can recommend."

Jed stood still for a second, then nodded.

"I'm gonna walk Jed out," I said, trying to swallow my apprehension. This was becoming all too real and scary.

We walked to the front door. Then I followed Jed onto the porch and closed the door behind me.

"I don't like this, Rose."

"I don't like it either, but I'm thinkin' he has a point. I need a different attorney and you definitely need a new one. Carter Hale's gonna side with whoever's givin' him his fat paycheck."

Jed stared out into the empty hay field. "Skeeter would never turn on us."

"He told me to answer all the questions truthfully, Jed," I said softly. "He said to tell them everything they want to know."

His eyes widened in shock.

"I think he's made some kind of deal with the FBI, and something big is goin' down. That's why he's distanced himself from us. I agree that he's tryin' to protect us. But if I do as he asked, I may be implicatin' most of the big players in this county. They may even ask me to implicate you." I took a breath. "I can't do that. I *won't* do that. I convinced those men to trust me. If I snitch on them now, I can say goodbye to living here in Henryetta. Heck, I'd need to go into hiding."

His eyes turned hard. "So you lie?"

"Right or wrong, I'd lie through my teeth if that's what I need to do to protect my baby. James won't tell me what deal he made, but I can't believe I'll get out of this unscathed if I spill things about all the criminals in this county."

He remained silent.

"But here's another problem: I was told if I don't tell the truth, they'll know I'm lyin'."

Jed's gaze flicked to mine, surprise in his eyes. "Skeeter really did squeal to the authorities."

I swallowed, my dread making me dizzy. "How else would they know? I was told they can't touch James and they'll leave me alone as long as I tell the truth."

Jed looked like he was about to be sick.

"We might be borrowin' trouble," I said. "The grand jury might just ask about my incident with the Sugar Branch police and that's it."

He nodded slowly, but I could tell he didn't believe it for a minute.

"I'm not incriminatin' you, Jed. I'd never do that." I felt close to tears, but I pushed on. "But if they really know things, I could get arrested for perjury. I need you to promise me somethin'."

I could see the wheels were spinning in his head as he tried to come up with a plan, but he gave me his full attention. "What?"

"If I'm in jail when I have my baby, I need you and Neely Kate to take care of him or her for me." Joe had given me the idea, and I knew it was the right thing to do.

His eyes flew wide in alarm. "Rose."

I put my hand on his upper arm and patted. "Listen to me, Jed. How long can they put me away for perjury? A few months? A few years?" I swallowed the lump in my throat. "I know the baby will be safe with you, and when I get out, I know no one will come after us because I kept my mouth shut." My chin trembled. "I can't spend the rest of my life worried someone's gonna hurt us for testifyin' against them. Not to mention my word has to mean something."

"Rose—" Jed's voice broke. "I'm not gonna let any of this happen."

I shook my head. "You stop right there. You don't do a doggone thing to stop this. You hear me? If something goes wrong, I need you to be safe so you can take care of my baby and

Neely Kate." I shook my head, narrowing my gaze. "She needs you something fierce, Jed."

"And she needs you too. Don't you forget it."

I gave him a sad smile. "But you feed a part of her soul I never will. And that's okay." I paused. "She needs something good in her life. She deserves it."

Jed pulled me into a hug. "We'll find a way to keep it from gettin' that far. I'll talk to Skeeter—"

Pulling back, I looked up at him with a hard stare. "You'll do no such thing," I said, injecting plenty of bite into my words. "You'll stay as far from him as possible."

"Rose."

"*No.* This is my decision, and I need to know my insurance plan for my baby is in place. I need to know you'll be around to take care of the people I love. Will you do that for me, Jed?"

His eyes turned glassy. "Yes."

I pushed out a breath and nearly burst into tears. "Thank you."

"But we'll hope to God it never gets that far."

"Agreed." I reached for the doorknob. "Now I need to get back inside." I scanned the horizon. "Joe said he was gonna be here. I hope things are goin' okay with the investigation."

"Skeeter's men were really gonna kill you?"

Giving him a grim look, I nodded. "But I don't think they knew it was me. They only knew I'd overheard them asking the pharmacist for the prescriptions Dr. Arnold had written before he left town. But they were gonna kill an innocent bystander. Would James condone that kind of behavior?"

Jed's eyes widened slightly, and it was clear he was uncomfortable.

"I take it that's a yes?" I asked, trying to hide my horror. "Did *you* condone killing innocent people?"

"No," he said in a harsh tone. "I don't believe in killin' at all, but occasionally there's no way around it. Hurting an innocent bystander is something different. That's a line I would never cross."

"So James *would* condone it," I pressed.

Jed seemed to give it some thought. "Before I left, no. But now...I'm not sure."

I couldn't imagine the man I loved would kill someone who'd been unlucky enough to be caught in the wrong place at the wrong time. It didn't fit with what I knew of James, but Jed had been with him longer. He had seen the ugly parts James had hidden from me. And that wasn't the only thing.

I looked up at him, heartbroken all over again. "Why would he lie to me about the drugs?"

"I don't know, but he refused to let me be part of it. I wonder if he knew back then that something like this might happen and he was tryin' to protect me."

"Three years ago?" I asked.

"I don't know, Rose," he said, sounding defeated. "Obviously there's a whole lot I don't know."

He headed down the steps toward Neely Kate's car, and I went back inside, feeling more anxious than ever.

Carly had left the kitchen and Gary had his laptop, a legal pad, and pen arrayed in front of him, along with a huge cup of coffee.

He glanced up at me with a determined look. "Let's get started."

Chapter Twenty

I refreshed my glass of water and sat at the table. "Okay."

"First," Gary said, folding his hands atop his legal pad and holding my gaze, "whatever you say to me is bound by a confidentiality agreement. I can't tell anyone what you tell me. That's very important, because according to my call with Joe last night, you've been privy to a large amount of implicating information."

I nodded. "Yes."

"Since you're protected by that confidentiality agreement, I need you to tell me *everything*. I can't get blindsided in court or a deposition, should it come to that. I need to know all the potential issues we're facing so I can come up with a plan of attack. But I can only do that if you're honest with me, even if it's embarrassing. I should warn you, though, that you can't perjure yourself and keep me as your attorney."

My cheeks flushed.

"Trust me, Rose. I've heard it all. You won't shock me." He paused and took a sterner tone. "But I hate nothing worse than to be caught off guard. Especially if I'm facing that arrogant prick

Mason Deveraux. So if I find out you lied to me, I will cut you loose in a hot minute." He leaned forward. "Is that clear?"

"Yes," I said, nearly in a whisper. "I'll tell you everything."

He pushed out a slow breath. "Okay." Picking up his pen, he said, "Joe told me he thinks the grand jury is looking into the corruption of the Sugar Branch Police Department, but that the prosecutor will likely branch off and ask questions about Skeeter Malcolm. How did you come to know this person?"

I told him the same story I'd told Violet, only I focused more on logistics than feelings, starting with meeting James at the pool hall.

"James?" Gary asked, glancing up.

I flushed. "That's his given name. That's what I call him."

Understanding filled his eyes, and I continued my story, bringing him through my Lady in Black adventures, the progression of my relationship with James, and the investigations that had submerged Neely Kate and me deeper into the criminal world. I left out only my visions. When I got to the standoff with Wagner, where James had shot Wagner and I'd taken the blame—which seemed to catch Gary off guard despite his insistence that he'd heard it all—I stopped when I heard the front door open.

"I'm here," Joe called out.

My eyes widened, but Gary took in my expression and nodded slightly.

"Joe," Gary said good-naturedly as Joe walked in. "Good to see you, my friend." He got to his feet to greet him. "Looks like country life agrees with you."

Joe grinned as he and Gary embraced in a bro hug then stepped apart. "Call me crazy, but I like it here. Thanks for makin' the drive down."

"Of course," Gary said, leaning over to flip his notebook upside down as he noticed Joe's gaze drift to the table.

Joe ran a hand over his head, then glanced down at me. "Sorry I'm late. The FBI's gettin' involved, so I had some extra paperwork to deal with."

"FBI?" Gary asked in surprise.

Joe cringed. "Rose witnessed an incident last night at a pharmacy in Henryetta. She was nearly killed. The pharmacist has admitted to taking part in a drug ring involving prescription medication, and the FBI had been interested in the doctor who was writin' the prescriptions."

Gary narrowed his eyes as he studied me, then looked back up at Joe. "I take it that happened after we talked?"

"About ten thirty last night," Joe confirmed.

"Trouble seems to follow you around, Rose," Gary said with a half smile.

"Seems like it," I half-heartedly agreed.

"What did I miss?" Joe asked.

He started toward a chair, but Gary held up a hand and blocked Joe's path. "Hold up there, my friend. I think it's best if you weren't part of this."

Joe's mouth opened then closed. "What are you talkin' about? I was the one who called you."

"I know," Gary said, "but you also made it very clear that Rose is my client. And considering the fact that you were concerned she might be caught up in something illegal, I think it's best we continue this interview with just the two of us."

"I don't want to prosecute her, Gary," Joe said, his voice turning hard. "I want to protect her."

"I know, which is why I think it's best you don't sit in on our interview." Gary shifted his feet, then said, "Look, Joe. First of all, if you sit here and hear about some sort of criminal activity, you'll be forced to report it."

"I wouldn't—"

"Then you'd be breaking the law," Gary said matter-of-factly. "And if someone found out, you'd be in the very seat Rose is in, facing the same damn situation. Trying to judge how much to tell to keep from committing perjury and how much to keep to yourself to protect the people you care about. I think we can all agree that the less you know, the better protected you *both* will be."

Joe started to protest, then closed his mouth.

"Second," Gary continued, "Rose is far more likely to sugarcoat things or tone them down if you're here." He lifted his hands when Joe started to speak. "She'd do it to protect you, Joe, and we both know it. If you're truly friends, some of this would be difficult for her to admit in front of you, and I need to know every damn thing that happened."

Joe took a breath and looked close to letting loose.

Gary's tone softened. "You called me because you trust me, right? Then trust me in this. I'll fight tooth and nail to protect her. But I need you to let me do my job, which means kicking you out."

Joe turned to face me, indecision on his face. "Rose?"

"I'm fine, Joe," I assured him. "And Gary's right. If you're here, I'll be too embarrassed to answer some of his questions. And I don't want to get you in trouble. We've both been skirtin' that issue for months."

Frustration filled his eyes. "How can I protect you if I have no idea where the threat's comin' from?"

"How about this?" Gary said in a warm tone. "If I see an immediate threat, I'll encourage Rose to tell you."

Joe didn't look pleased, but he nodded. "Fine."

"Good," Gary said. "Now get the hell out, because it's nearly noon and I still haven't heard if they've postponed her appearance."

Joe frowned and looked at my half-full glass of water. "Have you eaten anything today?"

"Not yet. I was about to, but I didn't have time."

He turned to the fridge. "You need to eat, Rose."

A confused look washed over Gary's face.

"She's pregnant," Joe said, sounding short, as he pulled out a plastic container with leftovers from the night before. "And she's lost weight. She needs to eat."

Gary's eyebrows shot up to his forehead.

"I wasn't keepin' it from you," I said. "I just hadn't gotten to that part yet."

He nodded, and his eyes clouded over, lost in thought.

"She can't go to jail for her involvement," Joe said, scooping potatoes and pork onto a plate, then popping it in the microwave. "We have to keep her out."

"We need to cut her a deal," Gary said, reaching for his phone.

"You mean rat people out for protection?" I asked, starting to panic. "I'm not gonna do that."

Joe whipped around to face me. "What do you mean you're not gonna do that?"

I knew my life was riding on the line—no matter what I decided. I'd spent most of the last year counting on James's umbrella of protection, but I wasn't sure that was still a safe bet, which meant it was time to create my own umbrella. Maybe I'd already started. "I promised people I'd keep their secrets, Joe. I'm not breakin' that promise."

Joe's eyes widened in exasperation as his nostrils flared. "Carter Hale told you to tell the truth. I'm certain they already know, whether you tell them or not!"

"I won't be corroborating it," I said. "All I have is my word. I have to protect my baby."

His face blanched. "You're worried about blowback."

"Of course I am. But it's more than that. I encouraged those men to trust me. I declared myself neutral, and it's a position I've used to help keep the county safe more than once." I shook my head. "I didn't set out to play a role in the criminal underworld, but there's no denying I have. I can use that position for good. Which means I can't be spillin' any tales about the criminal misdeeds in this county."

"And that might get you sent to jail, Rose!" Joe shouted.

I stood and slowly nodded, hoping he was reassured even though I was terrified. "I'm well aware of that fact, and I've already made a contingency plan should that come to pass."

"What the hell are you talkin' about?"

I gave him a soft smile. "You're the one who gave me the idea. I asked Jed if he and Neely Kate would raise my baby until I get out."

Tears filled his eyes. "Rose, this is fucked up."

"Maybe so," I said, "but it's what I need to do. It's the only thing that will keep us safe once I get out."

"Tempers and emotions are flaring," Gary said, holding up his hands, "and if I do my job, Rose will never see the inside of a jail cell." He set his phone down. "But there's obviously a lot more to this story that I need to hear." He paused. "Who's the father?"

My face burned, but Joe spat out, "Skeeter Malcolm."

He seemed to reflect on that answer for a few seconds, then asked, "And does he know?"

"I told him last night," I said. "That's why I was out so late. I went to see him, then stopped by the pharmacy."

"And how did he take the news?"

I shook my head and took a breath to keep from crying. "He made clear he expected me to terminate the pregnancy."

"I see."

The microwave dinged, and Gary walked toward it. "Joe, get out. I know you care about her, but I need you to leave." He pulled the plate out of the microwave. "I'll make sure she eats while I question her. I need to decide how to use this piece of information." He turned to me. "How many people have you told?"

"Only a handful. I just found out last night, but half the county likely knows I'm pregnant by now." I launched into the story of what had happened at the doctor's office.

"Well, that's a potential malpractice case we'll put on the back burner. If necessary, we can hinge our defense on your fragility—your dying sister, your unexpected pregnancy, and the father's desertion."

"No one can know that James is the father," I protested. "I'm sure people think it's Joe's."

Joe stood by the kitchen counter, looking like he'd hoped he might escape Gary's notice.

Gary glanced back at him. "How do you feel about that?"

"I've encouraged it," he said, squaring his shoulders. "Two people already asked me this morning. I didn't tell them the baby was mine, but I didn't deny it either."

So the word *was* out. My stomach felt like it was sinking down to my shoes.

Gary nodded. "So we've staved off *that* potential disaster for now. Don't confirm it but don't deny." He gave me a sympathetic look. "Of course, you'll have to make up your mind by the time the baby's born for the birth certificate."

Oh, Lordy. The birth certificate.

I glanced up at Joe with a look of complete terror.

He walked over and knelt next to me. "Just deal with one problem at a time. You have seven months to figure it out."

I nodded. "Okay."

Joe stood, and then his voice grew hard. "I'm countin' on you, Gary. I need you to protect her."

"You know I'll do the best I can," Gary said in a grave tone.

Joe nodded. "I'm goin' back to town, but I'm only a phone call away."

He left the room without another protest. It didn't escape me that Joe, who'd once gone to unreasonable measures to protect me the way he saw fit, was trusting me to deal with this situation.

I told Gary the rest of it—taking the blame for Wagner's death, deepening my relationship with James, facing off with the Sugar Branch police, and meeting James one last time at Sinclair. I even told Gary what James had said about trying to figure out a way for us to be together, and how he'd taken off for Little Rock afterward.

Gary continued writing for several seconds. Finally, he looked up and said, "I think you're right. I think Malcolm's taken some kind of deal so he can break free to be with you. It sounds like he needs you to corroborate what he's told the Feds." He frowned. "But that doesn't make sense. Grand jury testimonies are sealed. The Feds will never know what you say." He tilted his head. "He said they would know if you lied. Which indicates the prosecutor will know, and the FBI doesn't usually share information with state prosecutors when they're in the middle of an investigation. Does Deveraux know about your relationship with Malcolm?"

I twisted my hands together on my lap. "Mason suspects, but I never confirmed it. When he came back to town, he told me to get my house in order because he was bringin' it all down."

"Which was one of the reasons I cited when requesting your continuance. Mason Deveraux is your ex-boyfriend. I officially protested and requested a new prosecutor. That should buy us a few weeks."

I looked down. "I'm not so sure that's a good idea. I'll be weeks deeper into my pregnancy. Which means I'll be in prison even longer without my baby."

Gary leaned closer and held my gaze. "You're not goin' to prison. Not if I can help it, but I need to know one thing. You don't want to risk testifying against the other criminals in the county, but are you willing to throw Malcolm under the bus to protect your baby?"

Tears stung my eyes. "That's not fair."

"No, Rose. It's not, but it's an option you need to consider." He took a breath. "He told you to tell the truth, but his deal is likely with the FBI, not the state, and you'd be surprised how little the two communicate. We can get you a deal with the state to give them information about Malcolm. Malcolm will be safe due to his deal with the Feds, but the state will be none the wiser. Once we accept, they can't take it back. Win/win."

"But if I spill what I know about James, then I might have to drag Jed into it, and out of the lot of them, Jed is the one who deserves my loyalty the most. He's *always* had my back, since the very beginning. He and my best friend will be my baby's godparents. I refuse to incriminate him in any way, shape, or form. I'll spend the rest of my life in prison before I let that happen." I rubbed the back of my neck, where I could feel a tension headache blossoming. "And if word gets out I made any kind of deal at all, I'll lose all credibility. I can't risk it."

Even more than that, I couldn't betray James. It didn't matter if it ultimately wouldn't get him into trouble. The love I felt for him didn't bend in the wind.

Even if his did.

Gary frowned. "You're making my job a whole lot harder, Rose."

"Loyalty isn't meant to be easy," I said. "Otherwise, there'd be a whole lot more of it."

He sighed. "I hope these criminals know what you're doing for them."

"I hope so too."

My whole future depended on it.

Chapter
Twenty-One

As we were wrapping up, Gary got a call from the courthouse. It was hard to determine what was being said on the other end based on Gary's one-syllable answers, but when he hung up, he looked relieved. "Well, at least they haven't taken leave of their senses entirely. Your appearance has been moved to tomorrow. For now. This afternoon I have a meeting in the judge's chambers to discuss removing Deveraux."

"Will it work?"

"Honestly? With the corruption down here, our chances are fifty-fifty." He gathered his things and stood. "Looks like you have the afternoon off. I suggest you lie low for the rest of the day."

"I'm not goin' anywhere," I said as I walked him to the door. "Thank you so much for helpin' me."

He grinned. "Honestly, I haven't had a case this intriguing in years. But I don't say that to make light of your situation. I swear, I'll do everything in my power to make sure you walk out of this a free and safe woman."

"Thank you, Gary."

When I shut the door behind him, I pressed my back to the door and closed my eyes, reminding myself that I'd put myself in this situation. I needed to accept the consequences.

Pushing out a sigh, I dug my phone out of my jeans pocket and texted Joe.

We're done. My appearance has been postponed until tomorrow.

He texted back immediately. *I have meetings all afternoon. I'll be home for dinner. Are you doing okay?*

I'm fine, I sent back. *Just tired.*

Take a nap.

Joe was going to baby the snot out of me.

But I had to admit a nap sounded good, so I walked over to the sofa and lay down, closing my eyes for just a moment. Muffy jumped up next to me and curled into my side. I absently rubbed her back, her presence relaxing me, and the next thing I knew, the living room was brighter from the afternoon sun and someone was banging on the front door.

Carly hurried out of the kitchen and cast me a worried look. "I'm sorry, Rose. Hospice got postponed, so I was watching for them, but I got caught up in the kitchen. I was trying not to disturb you."

"That's okay," I said, sitting up, my head feeling foggy from sleeping so long. "I needed to get up anyway."

She opened the front door, and I heard a familiar female voice say, "Hi, I'm looking for Rose."

Margi Romano.

Carly's back stiffened. "She's busy right now. You'll have to come back."

While I didn't feel like seeing Margi, especially not if Dena had been talking her ear off, I wanted to get this over with and off my plate.

"That's okay, Carly," I said, swinging my legs over the edge of the sofa. "I'll talk to her."

Carly stepped back but looked none too pleased as Margi walk in. Carly's protectiveness caught me by surprise.

"Oh, you look like you've been sleeping," Margi said with a guilty look. "Sorry to disturb you."

"That's okay," I said. "I needed to get up anyway. Do you want me to take you back to the barn and the pasture?"

"I can go back there on my own if you point the way," she said with a warm smile.

I was tempted to let her, but I'd been lying around or sitting most of the day. "That's okay. I could use the walk."

"Do you want me to come with you?" Carly asked with a worried look.

Joe must have put her in charge of my personal safety as well as my food consumption. "You stay and wait for hospice to show up. If I see them pull in, I'll walk back to the house so we can talk to them together."

Carly nodded and headed back into the kitchen, casting one final glance over her shoulder as if she expected to catch Margi up to no good.

I got up and grabbed a sweater. "We can head back out through the front."

Margi headed out onto the front porch, and Muffy and I followed.

"I love your farm," Margi said as she descended the steps. "It's so picturesque."

"I love it too," I said as I followed her.

"I heard you haven't lived here long."

I cast her a surprised glance, but she didn't look fazed.

"It's a small town. People talk."

"What else have they been sayin' about me?" I asked as we walked side by side along the fence separating the pasture from the deep yard up to the barn. I had a feeling I knew what she was about to say, and my stomach turned at the thought of having this conversation, but I figured we might as well get it out in the open.

"Dena called me last night," Margi said unapologetically. "She told me that you're pregnant."

"Oh," I said, pissed even though I'd expected it, "do you know she was told confidential medical information by a nurse at my doctor's office?"

"I never said she got the information in an ethical manner, but it hasn't stopped her from tellin' everyone she knows. She's livid."

"What's goin' on with my body is none of Dena Breene's business. Frankly, I don't care if she's livid. She'll be lucky if I don't sue her and the nurse who broke the law to tell her."

Margi's eyebrows shot up.

"She's spreadin' rumors about my baby," I spat. "God help the person who tries to hurt him or her in any way."

She grinned. "You're gonna make an amazin' mother."

"We'll see about that," I said, still pissed. "But my job is to love this baby and keep it safe, and I'll be takin' that job seriously." I'd let a lot of people run roughshod over me in the past. That would *not* be happening to my baby.

"I told Dena to mind her own business, for what it's worth. Not that it slowed her down any. But I *do* know she made a special trip to the courthouse with a fresh-baked pie to go see Mason Deveraux this morning."

My stomach sank to my feet. Mason was going to find out sooner or later, but I'd hoped he'd find out after my grand jury appearance.

I pushed out a heavy sigh.

"Joe's gonna make an amazing father," she said as we continued to walk toward the barn.

Was she fishing for confirmation that Joe was the father? Part of me thought I'd do best to keep quiet, but I found myself saying, "He definitely loves my niece and nephew. He's a natural."

"Do you know when you're due?"

Yep. She was here for information. "I'm not really sure yet," I said with a forced smile. "Anne, the nurse at the clinic, stole my opportunity to revel in the news before sharing it with the world. Dr. Newton wants me to come in and have an ultrasound so we can determine how far along I am."

"Dena's saying you tricked Joe by getting pregnant so he won't leave you."

I stopped and put my hands on my hips. "Is that so? Seems to me that Joe's ecstatic over the news, and he's free to come or go as he pleases."

She stopped and turned back to face me. "I'm just repeating what I've heard."

"Does it give you a strange satisfaction?"

Confusion flickered in her eyes. "What?"

"Droppin' by my house unannounced and sharin' all the awful things people are sayin'?"

Her brow lowered as she studied me. "I took you as a woman who likes to confront things head-on."

"What in the heck are you talkin' about?"

She took a step closer, a fire burning in her eyes. "How in the hell can you stand up to these narrow-minded, judgmental people if you don't even know what they're saying?"

"I ignore them."

"Well, fuck that," she said with a smug shake of her head. "Don't let them get away with that shit. Take what you know and use it against them."

I pushed out a sigh, exhausted by whatever game she was playing. "I don't have time for this nonsense. I've got bigger problems to deal with."

"The grand jury."

I tilted my head and narrowed my eyes. "Do you make it your business to know *everything* about me?"

Her brow shot up. "I don't know everything, but I intend to."

"Excuse me?"

Margi made a face. "I want to be your friend, but I'm not exactly great with people. It's one of the reasons I've stayed friends with Dena for so long. She doesn't have any friends because she's too bitter. I don't have any because I seem to lack social skills."

I shook my head in amazement. "Well, you obviously weren't raised in the South." I stared walking again. "Come on."

I led her to the corral to show her the broken fencing, then took her into the barn. "If there were stalls before," I said, "they're gone now."

"They'd be easy to put back in. And the fencing too," she said absently as she studied the floor and the walls. "I'd pay for it all, of course."

"I don't know the first thing about takin' care of horses," I said. "And to be honest, the thought of it is too overwhelmin' given everything else that's happenin'. I don't think this is gonna work."

"Now hold up," she said, lifting her hands, palms out. "You won't have to do a thing. I'll pay to mend the fence and build the stalls. And I'll be the one taking care of the horse, or horses. Or my helper, Jimbo."

I shook my head, dread skating down my back. "No. No strangers. I've got enough to worry about."

I sure didn't need to give any strangers access to my land and barn.

She studied me for a moment. "Okay, I'll take care of the horse, but it won't even be all the time. Just when we're overflowing and there's an emergency situation with a rescue horse."

Meaning a horse that had been mistreated and removed from deplorable conditions.

A grimace twisted her mouth. "I'll need to bring some guys out here to do the repairs, but you can have Joe vet them if you want."

I was sympathetic to her cause, but with everything else going on, this felt like one thing too many. "I want to help, Margi, really I do, but—"

"You stop right there," she said, holding up her hand. "I don't need an answer right now. Why don't you think about it?"

I nodded. What would it hurt to tell her no in a few days versus now?

We started walking back to the house and Margi said, "Randy thinks the world of you."

I found it hard to reconcile this brash woman as soft-spoken Randy Miller's girlfriend. "That has to be interestin', datin' Randy and listening to Dena."

"Let's just say Dena has been the source of more than one argument."

I walked her to her truck and told her goodbye just as another car was pulling in. I sucked in a breath, wondering what new hell was arriving at my doorstep, only to realize it was the hospice nurse.

Fresh hell indeed.

Chapter
Twenty-Two

The hospice nurse was nice but direct. When Violet got sicker, we'd need to move her downstairs. Violet, in all her stubbornness, insisted we didn't need a hospital bed—my bed would do just fine. Then, as if to prove that she was *dying just fine on her own, thank you,* she proceeded to get out of the chair she was sitting in and go down the stairs of her own accord (with me walking in front of her to break her fall should she collapse).

As Violet settled in on the front porch, looking over the front yard, she said, "Rose, would you call Mike and tell him I want to see the kids?"

"Sure." Part of me was worried about bringing them here with the potential threats, but I'd spotted a sheriff's car parked on the side of the road. The person surveilling us definitely wasn't hiding, more like he or she was making it clear that we were being watched. Besides, Vi needed to see her kids. "Let me tell Carly that we're adding more to the dinner roster."

As I went inside, I texted Joe to tell him about Violet's request—and my fear that Mike might refuse.

Let me handle it.

Part of me wanted to protest that I could do it. I'd fought tooth and nail to stand on my own two feet over the last year and a half, but then I realized two things.

One, this wasn't my fight. This was between Mike and Violet, and for whatever reason, Joe and Carly had become mediators between the two of them. I needed to welcome that, not feel insulted. And two, accepting help from my friends didn't mean I was weak. Nevertheless, Joe and I had history. I knew he could be controlling without meaning to, and he'd definitely taken on a self-appointed protector role since finding out I was pregnant. I needed to tread lightly.

Joe texted back a few minutes later.

Mike says we can pick them up from daycare, but I can't get away for another hour.

One hour Violet could be spending with her kids. *I'll get them.*

I'm not sure that's a good idea, Rose.

He had a point, but then it struck me that I'd heard from every major player I'd had contact with other than Tim Dermot, and if he planned to threaten me, I was sure he would have done so by now. *I think the threats are over. But I can pick up Neely Kate from the nursery and have her ride with me to get the kids. And I'll bring Muffy.*

The little bubble showed up in the text field, blinking on and off for nearly twenty seconds before his message popped up.

Okay.

Carly was in the kitchen absorbed in something on the laptop again.

"Mike's lettin' Vi have the kids tonight," I said, "so I'm gonna go pick them up from daycare."

She looked up in surprise. "Is it safe?"

"I think so. But if you're concerned, there's a sheriff's car watching the driveway from the road."

"I'm not worried about me," she said pointedly.

"I think I'll be fine. I'm gonna steal Neely Kate from the nursery to ride with me."

She got to her feet. "I'll go sit with Vi."

As I followed her out, I sent Neely Kate a text, telling her I was picking up the kids but I wanted to get her first. A minute later, she sent back:

That's good. We need to talk.

I froze, my heart kicking into overdrive. What if she needed a break from our friendship? I wasn't sure I could take it, but it was her right to take time for herself if she needed it.

I grabbed my purse and the keys to the truck, but I also grabbed a burner phone I'd purchased a month ago in case I needed to contact someone with an untraceable line. I realized now that I should have used it the night before to call James, but I obviously hadn't been thinking clearly.

I was thinking clearly now.

As I drove into town, I tried to set aside my worry about Neely Kate and deal with something I could control.

I called Dermot.

After three rings, I didn't think he was going to answer. I didn't want to leave a message, but he surprised me with an abrupt "Who is this?"

"Dermot?" I asked to be sure. "It's Lady."

There was a long pause before he said, "I didn't recognize your number."

"I know. I'm usin' a burner."

"Smart."

"I'm tryin'," I said.

"I heard about your grand jury testimony."

"That's why I'm callin'," I said. "I want you to know you don't have anything to worry about."

He paused again, and I was surprised at the warmth in his voice when he said, "I know."

I released a nervous chuckle. "Try tellin' that to the other people in the county."

"I figured Carmichael was responsible for the broken window in your office. You prepared to answer that question, which will undoubtedly come up?"

"I have no idea what happened," I said. "Some random man came in and threw a chair out the window, then left."

"You think Deveraux's gonna believe that?"

"Probably not," I said, "but he can't prove otherwise."

"It might make him dig deeper."

"Then I'll just keep on keepin' my nose clean," I said. "I haven't been involved in anything since the incident with the Sugar Branch police."

"What about last night?"

Of course he knew about last night. "That was a fluke of fate."

"And Malcolm's men?" he asked. "Has Malcolm turned on you?"

"No," I said, hoping to God it was true. "That was an unfortunate misunderstandin'."

"He told you so?" Dermot asked, sounding suspicious.

I could have lied, but if James really had turned on me, Dermot deserved to know. And a small part of me couldn't squash the hurt that he hadn't bothered to check on me. He'd claimed he couldn't contact me in any way, but he could have had Carter call for him. "No. I haven't spoken to him."

"When *was* the last time you spoke to him?" The wariness in his voice made me nervous.

"Recent enough to know he hasn't turned on me." I took a breath. "I happened to be in the pharmacy when his men showed up. They only knew I was a witness. One they likely decided to eliminate." Which, again, begged the question of whether James would condone such a thing. The man I knew would never consent to the murder of an innocent witness.

"This is bad, Lady."

"I know."

He was silent for a moment before he asked, "Who's the father of your baby?"

So he knew. I wasn't surprised, yet I hadn't expected him to confront me with it. "Does it matter?"

"If it's Simmons, that explains Malcolm's sudden change of heart."

"James and I are done," I said, hoping I sounded convincing. "He broke things off after the Sugar Branch incident, but we ended our friendship amicably."

"Like hell I believe any of that," he sneered.

"What do you want me to say, Dermot?" I shot back. "I never took you for a gossip."

"I want you to tell me the truth. I need to know if Malcolm has a beef with you or not."

"So you know to turn your back on me?" I demanded, my temper rising.

"No," he snapped. "So I know whether we need to take a side. Your side."

My mouth dropped open, and I was in so much shock, I slowed down and pulled over to the side of the road. "What?"

"Things are changin', Lady. The winds are turnin'. I can feel it. I'm sure everyone else can feel it too, and they're gettin' antsy."

"Because of my grand jury testimony?"

"No. This has been comin' before that even popped up on our radar. Somethin's afoot and Malcolm is losin' support." He paused. "But if you broke it off with him, that might explain some of his recent erratic behavior."

My heart leapt into my throat. "What erratic behavior?"

"He's meaner than usual, and it's causin' dissension in his immediate ranks."

"You mean they're turnin' on him?"

"Some are jumpin' ship, but the men he's replacin' them with are more volatile."

"Like the men who almost shot me last night." The ones who'd been willing to murder a potential witness without a second thought.

"Exactly. Now, who's the father of your baby?" he asked.

"James knows about my pregnancy," I said. "I told him last night."

"Before or after his men tried to kill you?"

"James wouldn't kill me," I protested. "He wouldn't."

"Did you tell him he was gonna be a daddy or that Simmons was?"

I felt like I was going to throw up. "Honestly, Dermot, he wouldn't have been happy with the news regardless."

"That doesn't answer my question, does it?"

"That information is confidential," I barked.

"You have confidential information about me. I'll keep confidential information about you. But I need to know your answer before I declare myself on your side. You owe me that, Lady."

My heart sank. He was right. "I may never openly admit who the father is," I said, my voice tight. "Are you prepared to take this secret to your grave?"

"That one and plenty more."

"James. It's James's baby."

He was silent for several seconds and I began to grow nervous. Finally, he said, "Simmons is lettin' people think it's his."

"He's tryin' to protect me."

"But Simmons knows it's not?"

I'd already shared my big secret with him. Why hold back now? "There's absolutely no way the baby could be his. Joe and I aren't sleepin' together. He's there to protect us from Carmichael and help with my dyin' sister."

"I heard about Carmichael buyin' the police department in Sugar Branch, and we all figured Malcolm killed them for darin' to touch you. But then things cooled off between you, so now I'm not sure what to believe."

"That's not my secret to tell," I said, my exhaustion bleeding through. But it was interesting to know the criminal world thought Carmichael had purchased the police, not James. What I couldn't figure out was why Carmichael hadn't set people straight. Did it have something to do with Collard's assumption that the two were working together? "Joe's not confirming he's the father, but he's not denyin' it either. When I was confronted this afternoon, I reacted the same way."

"And does Malcolm know this is goin' on?" he asked. "Those of us who suspected or outright knew there was something between you two might think he's a cuck, which honestly won't reflect well on him."

Well, crap. I hadn't thought of that.

I let out a sigh and rubbed my forehead. "I'm tryin' to protect my baby the best way I know how, Dermot," I said. "If I admit James is the father, my baby will become a potential target to every criminal who holds a grudge against him."

He was quiet for a moment. "You're certain he wouldn't kill you?"

I thought about the cold, hard look in his eyes when he'd insisted that I get an abortion, and for a moment I almost believed he was capable of it. But only for a moment. Call me a fool, but I knew beyond a shadow of a doubt that James would never hurt a hair on my head. "Positive."

"Maybe he sent those guys after you last night knowin' they'd get taken down. That way, at least it would look like he'd tried to kill you."

My heart skipped a beat. "That would be a risky move. Me against two hardened criminals? No, I don't think it went down that way. They were surprised to see me in the store, and besides, they almost *did* kill me."

"Obviously you took care of them."

"I didn't shoot them, Dermot. Someone else did."

"Who?"

"Let's just say Carmichael wasn't the only man to send someone with a message for me."

"Who?" he demanded, his voice rising.

"It doesn't matter, and it's confidential to boot. Rest assured, I put their worries to rest and made an ally."

"An ally?"

"Let's just say I can call upon this person one time to help me."

"Do you have their loyalty, or was it a grudging agreement?"

I considered his question. "It started off grudgin', but I think I worked them around to loyal."

He was silent for a moment. "Damn. You're doin' what Malcolm couldn't."

My heart skipped a beat at his implication. "What are you talkin' about?"

"Malcolm's spent the better part of a year tryin' to pull these men into his fold, and you're spinning your web, drawin' them in one by one without even tryin'."

I sucked in a breath of panic. "It's not like that, Dermot. They all came to me, not vice versa."

"Nevertheless, how many big players do you have now? Countin' Carlisle?"

"Only three."

"Only three loyal men, who likely come with men of their own," he said quietly. "One of them is Malcolm's onetime right-hand man. That's three more than he has right now. Think on that."

"I don't understand," I said in barely a whisper.

"Yeah, you do. You're a smart woman. Just watch your back. And let me know if you need help." Leaving me with that to chew on, he hung up.

I sat on the side of the road as a light drizzle began to hit the windshield, contemplating our conversation and trying to process it all as my horror began to grow.

Had I made James my enemy?

Chapter
Twenty-Three

Before I pulled back onto the road, I placed a call to Jed with my real phone.

"Rose, everything all right?"

I hoped someday people would stop asking me that the second they answered their phone, although I doubted it would happen anytime soon. "How many people are loyal to James?"

He was silent, and for a moment I wondered if he'd heard me over the roar behind him. From the sound of it, he was at the shop. Finally, he said, "We need to talk about this later."

Was he saying that because I'd called him on our real phones or because he didn't want to be overheard?

"I'm goin' to pick up Neely Kate from the nursery," I said. "We're goin' to get the kids from the daycare and take them to see Violet. I'll swing by the shop afterward so we can talk."

"How about this?" he said, the sounds behind him becoming quieter. "I'll call Neely Kate and tell her to drive over here. That way it will be easier to reunite her with her car later."

"Good idea," I said. "I should have thought about that."

"You've got a lot on your mind, and besides, we have plenty of other things to discuss."

I tried to ignore the tightening pit in my stomach. He was right. I hadn't told Neely Kate yet about my plan to have her and Jed take care of the baby should anything happen to me.

"Thanks, Jed. I'll see you in a bit."

When I hung up, I saw I'd gotten a text from my new attorney.

We got a new prosecutor, but they brought someone in immediately. Your testimony is still scheduled for tomorrow. I'll be at your farm first thing in the morning to prep.

I pushed out a sigh of relief. I'd bought myself a little bit of time to sort this out. Besides which, if Mason had really stepped down as the prosecutor, the interrogation might be a whole lot more manageable than I'd worried it would be.

I headed to the shop instead of into town and found all three guys working on cars in each of the bays and an older gentleman in the waiting room, drinking coffee from what looked like a Dixie cup. I had a serious case of coffee envy, Dixie cup and all. Neely Kate hadn't arrived yet.

Jed poked his head around the hood of a car, and he called out, "Let me finish this up and we'll talk in my office."

"Okay."

I didn't feel like sitting in the waiting room, especially since I hadn't had much luck with those recently. It was drizzling, which meant standing outside wasn't an option, but I didn't feel like sitting in my truck, so I started to walk toward the picnic table, which looked protected under the large canopy of several trees. Just as I started to sit down on the still-dry seat, my phone rang with a number I didn't recognize.

"RBW Landscaping," I said since it during business hours.

"I need to speak to Rose Gardner." The desperation in the woman's voice caught me off guard.

I sat up straighter. "This is her."

"I need help," she said, her voice tight. "You said you could help."

"Who is this?"

"Wendy. Wendy Hartman. I think I met you yesterday mornin'."

"Wendy."

"Rumor's going 'round that you help people in trouble. That you're neutral and don't take sides. Is that true?"

I took a breath, trying to process what she was saying and keep a level head. "It's not like I'm base in a game of freeze tag, but yes, I consider my farm to be neutral and several other people of importance do as well."

What was I getting myself into? If she was seeking sanctuary, I knew well and good who she was hiding from. Should I really be courting more trouble with James? Why was I fretting? I hadn't agreed to anything yet.

"I heard you were at my work lookin' for me," Wendy said, her voice shaking. "So I need to know if you were really checkin' up on me or if *he* sent you."

"He?" The fear in her voice struck a nerve. I'd always told myself James did bad things for a good reason, but if that were so, why would Wendy fear him? Was her life genuinely at risk?

No, surely I was wrong to think so. Wendy was merely uncomfortable with his new men, the new and less controllable ones.

"Skeeter Malcolm," she confirmed. "He has his men out lookin' for me too, but then I heard you'd killed 'em last night, so I thought maybe you were safe after all."

I wasn't sure her believing I'd killed James's men was a good thing, but I decided not to correct her for now. "Why did you call, Wendy? What are you lookin' for from me?"

She paused, and I wondered if my direct question had scared her off, but she said in a tiny voice, "I need you to hide me."

"You could go to the police." Even as I said the words, part of me wanted to reel them back in. Going to the police would mean naming names, and Skeeter Malcolm would be at the top of her list. But if her life was really in danger, I couldn't help wondering if that was in her best interest.

"No," she said. "No police. Not after I heard the Sugar Branch police had been bought."

"Okay," I said, trying to hide my relief. "No police, but I can't bring you to my farm. Not right now. My sister and her kids are there, and I refuse to put them at risk. Give me a second to think of someplace else." The answer hit me like a bolt of lightning. "I know a place. I'll pick you up and take you there. Where are you?"

"Are you comin' alone?"

"No, my friend Neely Kate will be with me." No way was I doing this alone. What if it was a trap?

"No," she protested. "I don't trust anyone else."

"I'm settin' the terms here, and I'm not pickin' you up and takin' you somewhere without backup," I said, not mincing words. "So if you want my help, tell me where I can pick you up."

She hesitated for several long seconds, then finally said in a defeated tone, "The strip mall on Third Street. I'm at Wash and Suds laundromat."

"Stay put and I'll text you when I'm almost there."

As soon as I hung up, I started questioning my decision. I was in a big enough mess, so why was I throwing myself into Wendy's problem? Especially since she was hiding from James. If we were really at odds, this was bound to make things worse, yet I couldn't tell her no. She might be guilty as sin, but I couldn't let him or any of his people kill or hurt her.

I stopped to consider the implications of that thought—I was saving a woman from the man I loved. The man who claimed to love me. The father of my baby.

Would he really kill her?

Before, I would have said no, but I had no idea what was going through Skeeter Malcolm's head right now. He'd dug himself into some stinking mess I couldn't unravel with what limited information he and others had revealed to me, and I wasn't sure what to think.

Neely Kate's car pulled into the parking lot, and I walked over to her as she got out.

"Why aren't you waitin' inside?" she asked with a frown as she popped open an umbrella. She'd curled her hair today and pulled the sides up and away from her face, letting it hang down her back in soft waves, even in this humidity. No wonder she'd put up an umbrella.

"I didn't want to be cooped up," I said as I walked up to her. "Something's come up that we need to deal with before we get the kids."

Her eyes narrowed. "Okay."

I stared at her for a moment. "You just agreed without askin' me what it is?"

"Well, yeah," she said in confusion, shifting the umbrella to cover us both. "If you need something, I'm there."

It struck me that the three underworld figures who'd offered me allegiance weren't the only powerhouses on my side. I had Neely Kate too. I'd been foolish to think she'd leave me.

I shook off my dread that something big was coming. "I just got a call from Wendy, the woman I saw in the doctor's office yesterday. She says she needs help and wants me to hide her."

"She called Lady?" she asked in disbelief.

"She called *Rose*," I said in a grave tone, "but she was sure I could help her. She heard I'm neutral."

"Sweet damnation," she said with a smile. "You've finally merged your alter ego with the real you."

I wasn't sure that was something to celebrate, but that was a discussion for another time. "She wants me to hide her from James."

Her face paled. "Oh, my stars and garters. That was one thing this summer with Marshall, but things are more tense now, and with Skeeter…"

"You don't have to help me do this," I said gravely. "I'm not sure where I stand with him right now. I'm not sure what Jed's told you, but James didn't react well when I told him I was pregnant. He wanted me to have Jed set up an abortion. He was deadly cold, and then not fifteen minutes later, two of his men nearly killed me. Now, the two incidents are very likely unrelated, and I don't for one second believe James would kill either of us, but that's my assessment to make. You need to make your own."

She squared her jaw and her eyes looked fierce. "I'm helpin'."

"You didn't even stop to think about it."

"I don't need to. I'm helpin'."

"But—"

"But nothing," she said dismissively. "We've been workin' toward this for months. We're not stoppin' now because Skeeter Malcolm has his undies twisted in a bunch."

I'd been angling to establish myself as a neutral entity since June, with Neely Kate as my second. It seemed that had finally gotten some traction. Sure, I'd given Wendy my card, but she'd heard about me and had taken the initiative to call.

Still, I paused to consider how this was unfolding. Given my grand jury testimony tomorrow, the timing stunk, but I wouldn't turn my back on her. Unless…

"What if this is a trap?" I asked.

Neely Kate frowned. "How could it be a trap?"

"I don't know," I said. "But the timin'…"

"Does it *feel* like a trap?"

I mulled over her question. "No. She sounded like a woman desperate for help. And she certainly didn't seem to be in a good state when I saw her yesterday."

"Then we help her. You and me," she said. "So where do you plan to hide her? I don't think the farm is a good idea. We need to put her where no one else would look."

"I already have an idea," I said, "and I doubt anyone will think to find her there."

"Where?"

"Momma's old house."

Chapter Twenty-Four

We decided to take Neely Kate's car to pick up Wendy since my truck had the RBW Landscaping logo emblazoned on the side. It also helped that her windows were tinted enough to hide Wendy's identity in the back seat.

I called Wendy and told her to be on the lookout for a dark sedan. The second we pulled up, she burst out of the laundromat as though her pants were on fire, then opened the back door and practically dove in.

Neely Kate gave me an amused grin but said nothing as she pulled out of the parking lot.

"Where are you takin' me?" Wendy asked as she got situated in her seat.

"To a safe house," Neely Kate said, looking pretty pleased about it. "We stopped to get you some necessities to tide you over for a few days. They're in the trunk."

"Where have you been hidin'?" I asked.

She shot me a nervous look. "Around."

"You said you're hidin' from Skeeter Malcolm?"

"He sent those guys after me. He wants the last round of prescriptions Dr. Arnold was supposed to give me. The doc didn't even tell me he was runnin' off, but Skeeter don't believe me. He thinks I stole the scripts for myself. He's ready to bash heads, and my name's at the top of his list."

I shot Neely Kate a nervous glance before I asked, "What list?"

"His list of people to eliminate."

"You truly believe he'd kill you?" I asked in disbelief, but deep in my gut, I already knew the answer. She wouldn't have called me if she didn't fear for her life. And considering the two men in the pharmacy had been willing to kill me for being a witness, it wasn't outside the realm of possibility.

What are you doing, James Malcolm? I pleaded in my head. What dangerous game was he involved in? What deal with the devil had he struck?

"He's already tried," Wendy said. "His men tore up my house and nearly killed Stinkerbell."

Neely Kate frowned. "Who's Stinkerbell?"

"Her cat," I said. Then I shook my head, scrunching my eyes as I tried to focus on the convoluted mess I'd landed myself in. "Her neighbor's cat."

"How'd you know that?" Wendy asked in confusion.

"Long story," I muttered, feeling sick to my stomach.

My old neighborhood wasn't far from the laundromat, so it was only a few minutes before Neely Kate turned down the street to Momma's house. It technically belonged to Violet, but she wasn't using it right now and she'd asked me to take charge of it after she died. My plan was to fix it up and either sell it or rent it out to bring in income for the kids.

Neely Kate took a few purposeful wrong turns to ensure we weren't being followed, then pulled into the driveway of the small, two-bedroom bungalow. When she stopped, I turned around to face Wendy. "You stay in the car until I get the door unlocked. Then we'll bring you in."

She stared at me with wide eyes. "Okay."

I grabbed my keys, thankful I still had the house key on my ring, and quickly unlocked the kitchen door on the side of the house. The interior smelled stale from being locked up for so long, but everything looked in order other than a thick layer of dust. I was pretty sure no one had been in here for a good two months, but the water, electricity and gas were still hooked up.

When I went back outside, Neely Kate and Wendy opened their car doors. I intercepted Wendy and escorted her inside as Neely Kate popped the trunk to get the two bags of necessities we'd picked up to tide her over for a few days.

I gave Wendy a short tour of the small house, and Neely Kate was setting the bags on the kitchen table when we returned to the kitchen.

My gaze landed on the table, and for some reason the memory of Joe breaking up with me at that very table slightly over a year ago rushed into my head. It had felt like my life, the one I'd only just reclaimed, was over. Little had I known what I would get myself into.

What would Rose of a year ago think of Rose now?

I rested my hand lightly on my belly. Did it matter? I was living in the here and now. Dwelling in the past was dangerous.

I realized Neely Kate had finished showing Wendy the supplies we'd purchased. She glanced up at me as though acknowledging I'd mentally checked out for a few seconds and had just rejoined them.

"I was tellin' Wendy she can't leave the house or answer the door," Neely Kate said, giving me a worried look. "Anything you want to add?"

I needed to pull myself together. I'd promised to keep this woman safe. I mentally put on my Lady hat. "I need to know how you got involved with Dr. Arnold and Skeeter Malcolm."

Wendy's mouth dropped open. She started to say something but cut herself off.

"You're here because you're scared that Skeeter will kill you if you don't give him those prescriptions, and you're worried you'll be in danger until that's resolved. So the only way out of this is a truce or compromise of some kind."

"Or I could run," Wendy said, wide-eyed, and I wondered if she was on something again. It likely wasn't wise to leave her here, but I didn't like any of my other options any better.

"You could run," I admitted, "but you didn't. You're still here. So that means you've got a reason to stay or you lack the means to get away. Which is it?"

"I need money and a car," she said. "I just need to get ahold of my sister in Memphis. Only she won't answer the phone."

Maybe she'd had enough of her drug-addicted sister. Neely Kate gave me a knowing look, confirming she was thinking the same thing. Also, Wendy could have taken a bus, but if she lacked money, she couldn't afford a ticket, let alone living expenses when she got to where she was going.

"You can't stay here indefinitely," I said, "which means you need to come up with some kind of truce with Skeeter Malcolm or run. If I'm gonna help you work out a truce, I need to know everything."

"You're gonna intercede with Skeeter Malcolm for me?" Wendy asked in disbelief.

The look in Neely Kate's eyes suggested she was just as shocked. "Rose…"

"I don't have time to get into this right now," I said. "But I'll come by in the mornin' to find out what you've decided. If it's a truce you want, then you need to be prepared to tell me *everything*."

Wendy gaped at me like I'd just told her she was about to become a colonist on Mars.

Neely Kate sucked in a deep breath, then said in a stern tone, "Lady is allowin' you to stay here out of the goodness of her heart. If you steal anything to sell it for drugs, I will hunt you down and make you hand over every last cent, and if you've spent any of it, I'll take it out in blood and flesh."

It was my turn to be shocked. Wendy's drug problem had occurred to me as a problem, but I hadn't been sure how to approach the subject.

"Two," Neely Kate continued in her stern tone. "No doin' drugs here. Three, no invitin' your friends over. If you have friends you trust that much, you should have gone and hidden with them. If you so much as let another person step foot in this house, we'll toss you out on your keister faster than you can blink. Four, this place better look just as neat and tidy when we come back tomorrow." Neely Kate ran a fingertip across the kitchen table, then looked at the dust on her finger. "Only you'll have nothin' but time on your hands, so you can dust. Any questions?"

Wendy stared from me to Neely Kate then back again, still in disbelief. "Do you really think you can work out a deal with Skeeter Malcolm?"

My heart sank a little. I'd been hoping she'd choose to run. "I can't promise anything, but I'm willin' to try."

"Rose," Neely Kate said more insistently.

"We've got to go," I said. "Obviously you have my number, so call me if there's trouble, otherwise stay hidden until we come back in the morning."

Neely Kate grabbed my arm and practically dragged me out the door.

"What are you doin', Rose?" she hissed as she continued to tug me to the car. "You can't be makin' deals with Skeeter."

"What else are we gonna do with her?" I shot back.

"I don't know," she said in exasperation as she dropped her hold and walked around to the driver's door. We got into her car and she continued where she'd left off. "Do you think you should be contactin' him at all? Let's forget the whole grand jury situation, the man is furious with you over this baby. Do you want to risk riling him even more?"

"What do you think he's gonna do, Neely Kate? He's no threat to me."

She shook her head, regret and sympathy on her face. "Oh, Rose. You've only seen the man you want to see. You don't see what everyone else does." She reached over and grabbed my hand. "I'm scared for you."

"James would never hurt me."

"Maybe not," she said solemnly, "but Skeeter Malcolm might. You need to give him a wide berth. Do not be bringin' Wendy's issues to his doorstep. I don't think you'll like the consequences."

I started to protest when a face appeared in Neely Kate's window simultaneously with a loud knock on the glass.

We both jumped, and while I released a shriek, Neely Kate already had her revolver out of her purse and pointed at the driver's window.

Miss Mildred shot me a glare, unaffected by the gun in her face, separated only by a plate of glass.

"What the Sam Hill are you doin'?" she shouted.

Neely Kate set her gun in her lap. "I'm gonna have to lower the window, aren't I?" she grumbled.

"Yeah," I conceded, none too happy. My cranky ex-neighbor was the last thing I wanted to deal with, but she could cause trouble if she got suspicious about the house. Better to appease her curiosity now.

Neely Kate rolled the window down halfway and said in a cheery voice, "Miss Mildred, this is an unexpected surprise."

The older woman's gaze landed directly on me. "What are you doin' here?"

How much had she seen? She considered herself the president of the neighborhood watch, so there was a chance she'd started watching the moment we'd pulled into the driveway. "Checkin' on Violet's house, of course. She's too sick to check on it herself."

Her expression immediately softened. "I've missed seein' her."

"I'm sure she's missed you too," I said, meaning it. While our neighbor had never cared for me because she considered my visions to be evil, she adored my older sister.

Miss Mildred paused, licking her upper lip as she considered us with nervous eyes. "Do you think I could drop by and see her?"

Her question caught me by surprise. My first reaction was to tell her heck no, but Violet loved her and vice versa, and I reminded myself this wasn't about me. It was about surrounding my sister with people who cared about her.

"Of course," I said, my tone softening.

"How's she doin'?" she asked in a shaking voice.

I started to answer, but unshed tears clogged my throat.

Neely Kate knew me well enough to understand I needed her help without my saying so. She turned to face the older woman. "Not well. They've called hospice in."

Miss Mildred pushed out a sigh. "It's not fair. It's not right. She's much too young."

I didn't respond. What could I say? She was right.

"Give Rose or me a call," Neely Kate said. "We'll let you know when it's a good time. Violet sleeps a lot now and we all try not to disturb her during her naps."

"Of course," Miss Mildred said, grabbing a wadded tissue from her housecoat pocket and dabbing her eyes. "She needs all the rest she can get."

She started to walk away, but I called out, "Miss Mildred?"

Turning back, she waited.

"I hope you find the time to come see her. It would mean the world to her."

She nodded and started to say something, but just then a man called out, "Millie! What's goin' on over there?"

An ear-to-ear grin spread across Neely Kate's face. "*Millie?*"

I twisted in my seat to look out the back, my mouth dropping open when I saw an elderly man I recognized standing in Miss Mildred's open doorway. He wore a worn blue bathrobe covered in white flowers, which he held closed over his gut with a fisted hand. A parrot sat on his shoulder.

"Dammit, Millie!" the parrot squawked.

"Is that Mr. Whipple?" I asked in shock. We'd found his lost parrot for him a few months back—in Miss Mildred's backyard. I'd thought there were sparks between the two of them, but I was still shocked to see such undeniable evidence.

"Where?" Neely Kate demanded, leaning out her open window. When she looked back up at Miss Mildred, her shoulders were shaking with suppressed laughter. "Miss Mildred, are you havin' a *nooner?*"

The older woman's face turned beet red. "It's well past noon, not that it's any of your business!"

She hurried across the street, and Mr. Whipple walked out the door to meet her. He stumbled on a crack in the sidewalk and lost the grip on his robe. The sides flapped open, revealing a pair of skintight, bright red boxers, before Miss Mildred reached him and pulled the robe closed.

"Hide yourself, Boomer!" Miss Mildred shouted.

"Dammit, Boomer!" the parrot squawked.

"What the heck just happened?" Neely Kate asked with a giggle.

I grinned at her. "I don't think we want to know the details. Hurry before Mr. Whipple shows his undies again."

Neely Kate pulled out and headed toward Jed and Witt's shop. I still needed to talk to Jed, but I could see him in the waiting room talking to a customer. Our interlude with Wendy had already eaten up half an hour. That was thirty minutes less time that Violet got to spend with her kids. My chat with Jed could wait.

I reached for the door handle of Neely Kate's car but didn't open it yet. "Do you want to ride in my truck to pick up the kids or follow me in your car?"

"Actually," she said, keeping her gaze on the steering wheel. "We still need to talk."

My heart started to race.

She turned to face me with an earnest look as tears filled her eyes. "I didn't react well to your news last night, and I owe you an apology so big you couldn't fit it in Witt's hollow leg."

My mouth dropped open, but I quickly recovered. "Neely Kate, *no*. You were entitled to your reaction and so much more. You have no idea how much it hurt me to hurt you. I'm *so sorry*."

She shook her head with a stern look. "Stop that right now. I had a night to revel in my pity party, but it's done." She grasped my hand. "I love you so much."

"Oh, Neely Kate," I choked out through my own tears.

Her hand tightened around mine. "I'm here for you. Every single step of the way, I'm here."

I started to cry harder. "I'm so scared, Neely Kate. My baby won't have a daddy."

"You can do this, Rose. And you won't be alone. I'll be here as much as you need me to be, and I know I'm not the only one who feels that way."

"James has never been so cold and ugly to me. Not even in the beginning."

Fear flickered in her eyes. "Jed won't let him hurt you. Joe won't either."

"I'm not scared he'll hurt me physically," I said through my tears. "He acted like he hated me. That I was nothing to him, and the baby was less than nothing." I started to sob harder, and she reached over and pulled me into an awkward hug over the center console.

When I settled down, she leaned back and gave me a watery smile. "Then Skeeter Malcolm is a fool to let the best thing that ever came into his life slip away."

"It's not that easy, Neely Kate. It's a whole big mess."

"I know, honey," she said, reaching up to wipe the tears from my face with her thumb. "But you knew from the beginning you and Skeeter were never meant to be." There was no attitude in her statement, only sympathy and love.

She was right, yet that didn't ease any of the pain.

"Jed and I will help you in every way we can," she continued, "and he told me about you askin' us to watch your baby if you go to prison." Her words choked off as fresh tears fell down her cheeks. "First of all, you never, *ever* have to worry about your baby. We will *always* be there for him or her." She took a breath, then said softly, as though worried she'd be overheard even though we were in the car with the windows rolled up, "But Jed and I will never let that happen. Your baby needs you, and no matter what, we'll find a way to make sure you don't get stuck in jail."

Something in her statement made my chest squeeze. "What are you talkin' about?"

"Jed and I talked over lunch. He has connections. I know you want to avoid leaving Henryetta, but we'll sneak you away if need be. He'll give you and your baby new identities."

"Go on the run?" I asked in shock.

"Hopefully, it will never come to that," she said. "And that's borrowed trouble for another day, but for now I need you to know I won't let my jealousy ruin this for you. I want to be part of this all the way, Rose. I want to share your pregnancy with you." She gave me a warm smile. "But I know some things are private, so to help you with that, I got you a gift."

I couldn't hide my surprise. "My first baby present?"

"No," she said, reaching under her seat and pulling out a rectangular gift box with a white bow. "It's for *you*. Open it now."

I took the gift, surprised at its heft. The wrapping paper was white to match the ribbon and bow, and she'd obviously spent so much time making it look pretty that I hated to rip into it. But I was eager to see what she'd gotten me, so I carefully tore the paper and slid off the ribbon, surprised to see a hardbound dark blue book.

"It's a journal," she said softly, and I lifted my gaze to hers. "Dora lived at your farm and journaled while she was pregnant with you. I thought it might help you feel closer to her as well as the baby."

A lump filled my throat as my eyes burned. How had I not connected the dots between my birth mother's experience and my own? Both single mothers, having a baby with a man we couldn't be with. Both living on the farm.

"Neely Kate…" I choked out. "This is the most thoughtful gift anyone has ever given me."

She swiped at a tear on her cheek. "Now don't go thinkin' you need to keep everything to yourself in that journal. I want to be very much a part of all of this." Her voice softened. "But I also know that no matter how much you love me, some things are just between you and your baby. Keep those moments in there, and maybe someday your baby will read them too." Then she quickly added, "But not because you're dead."

I hugged the journal to my chest. I was sure I'd fill this book with all kinds of doubts and fears about James, just like Dora had written about my father. But just because Daddy had eventually left Momma to be with Dora didn't mean I'd have a happy ending with James. Besides, Dora's happiness hadn't lasted very long. J.R. Simmons had had my birth mother killed while I was just an infant. If I stayed in James's world, I could end up suffering a similar fate. That was definitely a topic for my new journal.

"Thank you, Neely Kate. I love it and I love *you*. I'm so relieved you don't hate me."

"Hate you?" she scoffed. "That's plain crazy talk. I love you, Rose Gardner, and you have no idea how disappointed I am in myself for ruining your happy news."

"Happy news?" I choked out.

Her eyes shone as her gaze penetrated mine. "You're havin' a baby, and I can't think of anyone who will be a better mother than you. This is *happy* news. We need to celebrate it."

I smiled. No more sorrow over this sweet baby.

Violet was right. Only joy.

Chapter
Twenty-Five

We headed to the farm after we picked up the kids, and Violet seemed to get a second wind. They set up Candy Land on the coffee table and Neely Kate joined us for several rounds, all of us helping Mikey count out his spaces. Joe came home around dinnertime, and the kids nearly tackled him with their hugs around his legs, begging him to play with us.

Violet beamed and I did too—I hadn't seen her looking so content and healthy in weeks.

Jed and Witt showed up shortly thereafter, and Witt headed straight into the kitchen to pester Carly.

Neely Kate rolled her eyes and got up to go intervene.

"I should go set the dining room table," I said. The kids were crawling all over Joe, who'd just sat in a chair in the living room.

"Can we eat in the kitchen?" Violet asked with a hopeful look. "It's so much more homey in there. So much more *you.*"

Her request caught me by surprise, especially since she knew we'd all have to cram around the table.

"Can I get you anything?" I asked her. She still seemed to have more energy than usual, although I wasn't sure how long it would last. "Do you need to get up and go to the bathroom?"

"I'm good," she said with a contented smile. "Go set the table so we can eat. Whatever Carly's makin' for dinner smells good."

Maybe that meant she'd have a better appetite.

When I went into the kitchen, Witt was trying to help Carly cook, but she waved him off with a wooden spoon.

"I know what you're up to, and I'm *not* goin' out with you."

"Come on, Carly," Witt said, leaning his hip against the kitchen counter as she mashed a pot of potatoes with a hand masher. "It's just one date."

Leaving her hand on the masher in the pot, she put her other hand on her hip. "I've told you fifty million times I'm not ready to date." Her mouth twisted into a grin. "And besides, you're Neely Kate's cousin. How awkward will it be when I break your heart and we still have to deal with each other?"

"Very funny," Witt said sarcastically.

"No means no, Witt," Neely Kate said in a stern tone. "If you don't stop harassing her, Rose is going to stop letting you come to dinner."

I shot him a dark look, but he gave me his megawatt smile.

I didn't want to address Witt's antics right now. I suspected it was a game to him and he had no expectations that she'd concede, but I needed to find out if she was tired of it. The moment she felt uncomfortable I'd be sure to put an end to it.

Neely Kate and Carly carried food to the table as I finished setting out the plates and silverware. Jed and Witt carried in two extra chairs to accommodate all of us. Joe had insisted Mikey could sit on his knee to give us extra room, since we all knew Mikey would end up on someone's lap eventually anyway.

Dinner was loud and boisterous with lots of laughter. Everyone avoided the topics of the grand jury and my pregnancy and my sister's illness, and the kids added to our entertainment. I snuck a glance at Violet, relieved to see her looking relaxed and happy, and thrilled that she'd eaten her portion of mashed potatoes, a bit of her meatloaf, and even some green beans.

I couldn't help hoping that she might be getting better. Maybe all the love and good energy surrounding her had helped fight off some of the cancer in her body and we'd have her with us awhile longer.

After Mikey finished his dinner, he asked to sit on Violet's lap.

"Of course, baby," she said, holding out her arms. Joe helped set him on her lap, and I noticed he and I were both watching closely. Violet had lost so much weight, I was worried Mikey might hurt her if he got too rambunctious, and from the close eye Joe kept on them too, he must have been concerned about the same thing.

Witt was knee-deep in a story about some hunting expedition for opossums he'd ledwith his and Neely Kate's cousins, and we were totally entertained. I cast another glance at Mikey, who was now facing Violet, playing with her necklace. Violet was lightly stroking his back, only half listening to the story. Then, out of nowhere, Mikey sneezed in her face.

Everyone instantly stopped all conversation and stared at Violet in horror. Violet's immune system was compromised, and a secondary infection was our biggest fear.

Carly jumped out of her chair and ran into the living room. "I'll get the baby wipes."

Joe reached for Mikey and tried to lift him off her lap, but the sudden movement and the tension in the room scared him. He started to cry, wrapping his arms around Violet's neck and burying his face into her neck.

Violet lifted her gaze up to Joe, shaking her head. "Leave him."

"But Violet," I protested, my heart rate increasing. "He sneezed. In *your face*."

She gave me a pleading smile. "He wants his mother, Rose."

"But Vi," I insisted, my fear spiking. "He might get you sick."

"It was a sneeze, Rose," Violet said, her voice barely audible above Mikey's sobs.

"But it might be a cold."

Violet held Mikey closer. "The damage is already done. He stays."

I watched her in horror. If he got her sick, it might be a death sentence. As weak as she was, it probably would be.

The knowing look in her eyes told me she understood.

Mikey buried himself into her as she rubbed his back, whispering soothing sounds into his ear.

Carly came running back into the room with the wipes and stopped in the doorway, realizing everyone was frozen—all of us watching Violet comfort her son.

Violet looked up at Joe and said with a firm voice, "Can someone bring the rocking chair in my room down? I'd like to rock my baby."

I started to protest that she should hand Mikey off to someone else. We needed to wash her face and sequester her in her room and pray she didn't get sick. I wanted to beg her to think this through.

But then I saw the love and adoration on her face and held my tongue.

Violet had stopped treatment because she didn't want to waste any more time with her children than she already had. She'd spent months in Texas, hoping for a cure so she could spend decades more with them, but God had other plans. The bone marrow I'd donated to her hadn't helped, and she was back to square one. Instead of enduring more months away from her children for a cure that might not come, she had ended all treatment and came home to die surrounded by the people she loved. But the months away had disrupted her relationship with her children, and while Ashley had been quick to come around, Mikey had been much slower. Her little boy had begun to pull away, and the separation had been keener these last weeks, with the kids staying more and more at Mike's. But now he clung to her, sobbing into her chest as though he knew he didn't have her for much longer and was already mourning the loss.

"I'll go," Jed said in a gruff voice as he got to his feet. "I'll bring it down."

Ashley sat by me, her gaze locked on her mother and brother, but she turned back to look at me and whispered, "Is Mommy going to get sick again?"

"I don't know," I said softly as I started to rub her back. But as I watched Violet comfort her son, I heard him release a tiny cough. In my heart I knew she'd catch another cold. And this time it would likely kill her.

Neely Kate, Witt, and Joe stayed in their respective places, looking like they were staring danger in the eye and unsure how to react. Finally, Neely Kate said as she stood, "Come on, Muffy. Let's go outside."

Muffy was lying in her dog bed in the corner, but she jumped up and ran to the back door.

"Want to come, Ash?" Neely Kate asked.

She looked up at me with wide, frightened eyes, as though seeking permission.

I nodded and placed a kiss on her forehead. "Keep an eye on Muffy for me."

"Okay, Aunt Rose." She slid out of her chair and ran for the back door, as though she was racing Muffy to see who could get out first.

Neely Kate stood in the open doorway, watching Violet with horror-filled eyes, then she hurried out the door after them.

Witt scooted back his chair. "I'm gonna go out there and watch over 'em," he mumbled as he rushed out after the others.

I got to my feet, my thoughts racing. What could I do? I started to head for the living room to make room for the rocking chair, but the sound of furniture scraping along the floor in the living room told me Carly was already on it.

"Calm down, Rose," Violet said softly, clutching her son to her chest. "We all knew this was comin'."

"It might be allergies," Joe said as he eased onto his chair next to her. "No sense borrowin' trouble."

She gave him a sad smile.

"Got it," Jed called from the other room.

Joe tried to take Mikey from Violet so she could walk into the other room, but her arms locked around her little boy. So Joe and I got on either side of her and helped her walk into the living room with her son cradled in her arms.

Carly held the chair still while Jed took my place at Violet's side. Then both men practically carried Violet and Mikey's weight, easing her onto the chair as I stood to the side. Helpless.

As soon as she was settled, Carly let go and rushed over to the sofa, snatching up a throw to place over Violet's lap and legs and tucked it around her. Violet looked up into Carly's eyes as a warm smile spread across her face. She mouthed *thank you*.

"Do you need anything, Vi?" Carly asked.

"I have my baby," she said as Mikey sank into her, his eyes fluttering closed. "I'm good."

Carly grabbed a throw pillow and tucked it under Mikey's butt to help support his weight, then took several steps back. "I'm gonna clean up the kitchen."

The two men looked at a loss, so they followed Carly. I started to do the same, thinking she'd want time alone with Mikey, but Violet called out, "Rose? Can you sit with me for a moment?"

"Yeah," I pushed out as I perched on the edge of the coffee table.

"Being a mother means making choices—choices that people don't always agree with. Trust your gut and your heart—they won't steer you wrong."

I nodded slightly.

She watched me for several moments, her eyes glazed with unshed tears. "I wish I could stay long enough to see you hold your own baby."

I choked back a sob.

"I want to tell you a secret, something you must swear never to tell another soul," she whispered, then placed a soft kiss to Mikey's forehead. His eyes were closed, and his breathing had deepened.

"I'll keep your secret, Vi," I vowed solemnly.

"Until I had my babies, I loved you the most."

I blinked, unsure I'd heard her right. "What?"

"You have no idea how much I've loved you. You have no idea all the orchestrations I put into play to protect you. To punish the people who hurt you. I married Mike with the sole purpose of moving you out of Momma's house. I made Mike give up a job in Little Rock so I could stay in Henryetta and watch over you. For my whole life, my purpose was to love and protect you. I took it seriously, Rose." A sheepish look filled her eyes. "I admit, I devoted myself to it too seriously at times. I've made many mistakes, but loving you wasn't one of them."

"Vi..."

"You were my first love, Rose. My first responsibility, and while I feel like I've failed you by letting this cancer steal my life, when you told me that you were pregnant this morning, I realized my job was done. It's time to trust you to live your own life. And you'll be amazin'."

"Violet, I'm nowhere close to bein' ready to let you go."

"You'll be okay." She motioned her head toward the kitchen. "You'll be loved." She paused. "But I need you to make sure my own babies will be okay."

"I will, Vi," I vowed. "I swear it."

She leaned her head back, closing her eyes as she rocked. "I never once doubted it, but I had to hear you promise."

I could see she was dozing, her toddler sprawled across her chest, and I let her words soak in deeply. Had I been too hard on my sister? We were raised in an abusive family, and we both had our roles, roles that had been hard to break even after we were grown. Why hadn't I thought to cajole Violet to go to family counseling with me last fall when I started seeing Jonah for my own growth? Why had I squandered so much time?

I headed into the kitchen to help clean up, but they were almost done. Neely Kate and Witt were still outside with Ashley, but Carly, Jed and Joe eyed me anxiously.

"Do you think she'll get sick?" Carly asked.

"It's probably allergies," Joe insisted, drying his hand off with a towel.

I nodded, but it was forced, and I couldn't look into his eyes. I didn't think either of us really believed that.

"I'm tired," I said, turning to Joe. "Can you take the kids home? I don't think my heart can take it."

Joe walked over and pulled me into a hug. "Of course, Rose. You go to bed, and Jed and I will get Violet upstairs."

"I'll get her tucked in," Carly said. "I feel guilty that you've been working yourself to the bone this last month. You should have been getting to bed early."

I shook my head. "None of us knew why I was so tired, so no need for guilt." I pushed out a sigh. "But I still need to go back to the doctor for an ultrasound. I should have called to make an appointment."

Why hadn't I thought of that sooner?

"You should change to a different doctor," Joe said, his tone hard. "Your privacy was violated. Gary is adamant that we should consider a malpractice suit."

"I don't want to hurt Dr. Newton," I said wearily as I sat in a chair. "It wasn't her fault. In fact, I suspect she's cursing the day she agreed to buy Dr. Arnold's practice. And I don't feel like drivin' to Magnolia or El Dorado to the doctor either."

"You're gonna have the baby at Henryetta Hospital?" Joe asked in disbelief.

I momentarily froze in place as it hit me that I still needed to figure out where I was having my baby.

So many decisions... I was starting to feel overwhelmed.

"Most women don't figure that out until much later," Carly said in a soothing tone as she walked behind me and rested her hands on my shoulders. She started to knead my stiff muscles. I nearly cried out from the initial pain, then moaned when my muscle aches began to ease. "You've got time."

"Is there anything we should be doin'?" Jed asked, sounding unsure of himself.

Joe glanced back at him in surprise but remained silent. Those two had come a long way, all right.

"Nothin' that I know of," I said, then bolted to standing with a gasp. "My prenatal vitamins. I never got any prenatal vitamins." What kind of mother was I if I couldn't remember to get vitamins to keep my baby healthy?

"I picked some up for you," Joe said, getting to his feet. "I knew that's why you were at the pharmacy last night. I'll go get them now."

Tears flooded my eyes, which seemed stupid. They were just vitamins, but it was so thoughtful. Joe was dealing with Mason, the FBI, and the shooting the night before, yet he'd thought to get me prenatal vitamins.

"You got me vitamins?" My voice broke.

"It's no big deal."

"Did anyone say anything when they saw you with them?" Jed asked.

"I got some congratulations from people in the pharmacy," Joe said, giving me a sly grin. "I said I'd be sure to pass them on to you." He headed for the back door. "I'll let Neely Kate know I'm taking the kids home soon." He stopped on the threshold of the door, hesitating before he turned to Jed. "I don't want to leave Rose here alone very long while I'm gone. Will you stay until I get back?"

Jed's shoulders tightened as he stood straighter. "I would have stayed whether you asked or not."

"I figured," Joe said with his hand on the doorknob. "But I had to ask." He walked outside, closing the door behind him.

"Joe's right. You should go to bed," Carly said. "Get some sleep. We've got things covered down here."

I caught Jed's eye. "I need to talk to Jed first."

We had to finish the conversation we'd started earlier, the one we couldn't have in Joe's presence.

Joe brought me the bottle of vitamins, then headed into the living room to pick up Mikey, followed by Neely Kate and Ashley. Violet gave each child a long hug and a lingering kiss on the forehead. Mikey was too tired to deal with it, but Ashley clung to her mother.

"I love you," Violet told her. "To the moon and back. There is no end to my love for you."

"I love you too, Mommy," Ashley said into her neck.

Violet held her a few minutes longer, then glanced up at Joe to take her. I gave Ashley a long hug goodbye.

As soon as Joe left with the kids, Jed scooped Violet into his arms and easily carried her upstairs, with Carly going up ahead of him to make sure her bed was ready, and Neely Kate and I following behind. Muffy came too, pacing anxiously like she knew something was wrong.

We got Violet comfortable and made sure she took her meds. Everyone else left, but Violet reached for me with both arms, pulling me into a long hug. We sat like that for what seemed like forever, yet it felt like it hadn't been long enough when she finally pulled back.

"You go get some rest," she said with a smile. "You're cookin' my niece or nephew and you need rest to let him or her grow."

I kissed her cheek, then looked deep into her eyes. "I love you, Violet. I wouldn't trade you as a sister for anything in the world. You were the only one who loved me for so long." My voice caught. "I'll never, ever forget that."

Her mouth tipped up into a tight smile as she looked at me with a gaze full of love. "Go get some rest," she said, giving my chest a gentle push.

I kissed her forehead, then left the room, my chest aching. If it already hurt this much, how would I handle losing her?

Muffy refused to leave Violet's room, instead hopping up onto an overstuffed chair in the corner, so I left her to keep watch over my sister while I went downstairs. Jed and Neely Kate were waiting on the porch with steaming cups, but Carly was nowhere to be seen.

"Where's Carly?" I asked, seeing a third cup next to one of the empty chairs.

"She said she was going to bed early," Neely Kate said. "But she made us tea before she went up. She made you green tea—no caffeine."

I sat down, more weary than I cared to admit. "I honestly don't know what I would do without her. She knows more about taking care of Vi than I do."

"She loves it," Neely Kate said. "She needs to feel needed. This is her way of earning her keep."

I was lifting my cup to my lips but stopped midway. "She feels like she needs to earn her keep?"

"I doubt she thinks of it that way," Neely Kate said. "She just wants to belong."

"She's been opening up more about her past," I said, taking a sip of the tea, then cupping the mug with my hands as I turned to Jed. "Do you think she's still in danger?"

"Hard to say," he said with a thoughtful look. "I find it hard to believe that she's this worried about her father tracking her down if all she did was ditch her fiancé and leave the family fold. I think she saw something."

My eyes flew wide. "Like what?"

"Her daddy's hardly clean, but I can't help thinkin' there's something I don't know." He set his mug on the table. "I suspect he has ties to Hardshaw, but I don't have any concrete proof. Just a gut feelin'."

My defenses went up. "You think Carly's here to spy on us?"

He gave me an amused grin. "No. I'd bet my right eye she's clueless to the connection, but I think she ran from more than just a family squabble. Which means if Hardshaw is still snoopin' around, they're likely to discover her. Especially given her close proximity to you girls."

My heart skipped a beat. "We're putting her in danger."

"Possibly."

My mouth dropped open to respond, but I wasn't sure what to say.

"I've tried to get her to tell me what she saw," Jed said quietly, "but she refuses to discuss anything to do with her family. I've warned her that the Hardshaw Group is lookin' for Neely Kate." He paused. "I'll be honest, I think part of the reason she's holed up here at the house with Violet is to hide, though there's no doubt she loves Violet. It's been a win/win situation for everyone, you included, but she'll need to leave the house sooner or later. And I suspect we won't have the Hardshaw Group issue resolved by then."

"So what do we do?" I asked, starting to panic. "We have to protect her."

Jed leaned toward me, holding my gaze. "We will. And we'll have a backup plan, just in case they find her."

"What backup plan?" I asked.

"I'm creating a new identity for her," he said. "A new life."

The impact of what he was saying hit me full force. "We'll have to send her away."

"If she won't tell me what she saw so I can figure out a way to help her, it seems the next best solution."

I sat back as the horror of the situation washed through me.

"But it's only an option of last resort, Rose," Neely Kate said. "We don't want her to go, and it's clear she doesn't want to leave, but we need a plan to keep her safe."

I nodded slowly, but it felt like another blow. I didn't want to lose her too.

"I know you're bone-tired," Jed said softly, "but we need to discuss Skeeter."

I nodded, resting my head on the back of the chair.

"You need someone with you at all times," Jed said. "I mean it, Rose. You need someone guardin' you every time you go out your front door. When you go to the courthouse tomorrow, I want Joe to take you."

I sat up. "Joe?"

"And I'm gonna try to talk him into gettin' another sheriff's car as an escort."

"Doesn't that seem like overkill? I've worked out deals with just about every major player I've had a connection to over the last year. I seriously doubt any of them will touch me."

He was silent for a moment, and when he spoke, his voice was strained. "It's not them I'm worried about."

Neely Kate's gaze remained on her tea, and it was obvious she didn't want to look me in the eye. They'd talked about this, and she knew I wouldn't like it.

I realized what he was saying and set my mug on the table. "You said earlier you didn't think James would hurt me. Besides, he told me to tell the truth."

"Exactly, and we'll circle back to that crucial detail in a minute," Jed said. "But what if he caught word you're arrangin' deals?"

He was only asking me what I'd been asking myself.

"Do you really think he'd care? I've made deals with the players before. I don't need his permission for what Lady does. I tell him after the fact and he deals with it."

"This is different, and you know it, Rose," Jed insisted.

I stared at him in amazement. "You've changed your mind? You think he might hurt me?"

"I'd like to think he wouldn't…"

"But," I prodded.

"You don't know him like I do, Rose," Jed said emphatically. "Word's spreadin' like wildfire that you're pregnant with Simmons's baby. I've already fielded three calls of my own askin' for confirmation. I can only imagine the flack Skeeter's gettin'."

Which lined up with what Dermot had told me. People would think him weak.

"James and I never confirmed our relationship," I said. "And Joe's been livin' with me for almost two months. Why would anyone care now?"

"Whether you had a confirmed relationship or not, it was no secret that Skeeter had a thing for you. He considered you his and everyone else knew it, even if *you* were playin' the neutral card."

He paused, lowering his voice. "He's losin' face, Rose, at a time he can't afford to."

My chest tightened. "Is he in danger?"

"*Rose*," he said, leaning forward. "Listen to me. *You're* in danger."

"From *James*?" I asked. Something had changed. Earlier, Jed hadn't seemed to think it possible. "You spoke to him, didn't you?"

He held my gaze, his intent eyes urging me to take him seriously. "I reached out to him today, told him I needed to talk to him, that it was urgent, and he told me to fuck off. He said that I was dead to him."

My eyes narrowed in confusion. "No. He wouldn't do that."

"Rose, he *did*. And there's more I haven't told you yet."

I sat back in utter shock. Something clicked into place, stealing my breath. I took several long, slow breaths, fighting panic.

"He's done this before?" I finally asked. "Killed people who made him lose face?"

His answer was immediate. "Yes."

I knew he was capable of murder, but I'd always thought it was a last resort for him. Something he'd do in self-defense, certainly, but not in cold blood. And never to someone who was innocent of any wrongdoing.

It struck me again that those men he'd sent to the pharmacy had been willing to kill an innocent witness.

"But he told me he loved me," I insisted. Hoping he'd take it all back. "He told me just yesterday. I *know* he meant it."

"Did he tell you he loved you before or after you told him you were pregnant?" Jed asked.

"Before, but—"

"And he was cold and calculated when you saw him last night, right?" he asked. "Did he tell you that he loved you then?"

"No," I said, refusing to freak out. "But he was in shock."

"And then his men nearly killed you less than an hour later."

"It's not like that, Jed!" I protested. "You *know* him! He wouldn't do that!"

"I *knew* him," Jed said quietly. "But the things he's doin' lately." He shook his head. "Things like buyin' a police department… that's not the man I know. The men he's hiring from out of state… that's not him either. You need to keep the deals you've made with the criminal elements and leave Skeeter out of the equation. This is self-preservation, Rose, for you and your baby."

His words shook me, especially because I knew how close he and James had always been. Like brothers. His judgment of the man he'd known much longer than I had mattered. It counted. Although I still couldn't believe James would hurt me, he'd made it clear he was at best indifferent about our baby. I hoped he might come around, but I sure wouldn't bet my baby's life on it.

"For what it's worth, Dermot is worried too. He says he's cookin' something up."

"What?" I asked. This was all so surreal I felt like I was out of my body watching everything unfold.

"He wouldn't say, but he claims it'll protect you. Protect the county."

"Protect the county from what?" I asked. "James?"

Jed made a pained face. "He didn't elaborate, but I got the impression it included Hardshaw."

I pushed out a breath slowly, taking a second to wrap my head around all of this. "I know Hardshaw's after Neely Kate—and possibly Carly—but what are we looking at if they get a foothold in Fenton County?"

Jed held my gaze. "They've moved into several towns in Oklahoma. Violence increased at drastic rates—robbery, rape, murder—and not from the people livin' there. Outsiders."

"From Hardshaw?" I asked.

He nodded.

"What do you think Dermot's plan is?" Neely Kate asked.

"I have no idea," Jed admitted, "but I told him I'd hear him out." He paused, making sure he had my full attention. "But if it involves you, it's your call. I'm just your co-second."

That caught me by surprise. "What?"

"Neely Kate is your second, but I would prefer to take on the enforcer part of the role. So co-seconds."

I shuddered. "Let's hope it never comes to that." But truth be told, they'd both been backing me up for months. "Can we trust Dermot?"

Jed was silent for a moment. "You'd be in a better position to know that than me."

"You can trust him," Neely Kate said, sounding thoughtful. "He helped you with Marshall when he could have walked away."

She had a point, but still… "Why do I have a feeling that whatever Dermot's cookin' up will require me to betray James?"

"Rose," Jed said. "Skeeter's already betrayed *you*."

I shook my head. "He was upset last night. He'll come around, even if he doesn't want anything to do with the baby."

"Rose, that's not it." He paused, worry in his eyes. "You think he's workin' with someone to break free from this world, and he is, but it's not who you think."

I wasn't sure I could take any more shocks. "What are you talkin' about?"

"I've had my suspicions for a few weeks, and I had it all but confirmed this afternoon. Skeeter's workin' with someone all right, and it's not law enforcement. I'm worried that he wants you to tell the truth to incriminate yourself."

I shook my head, trying to clear it. "That makes absolutely no sense, Jed! I'd be incriminating him too."

"I have no idea how he plans to get out of that," Jed admitted, "but I know for a fact he's workin' with a bigger outside player, and he's pavin' the way for them to move into Fenton County. The Sugar Branch police force was part of it, although I'm not altogether sure why. But I *do* know part of the big plan is to take out Carmichael."

Terror filled my head. "Who's he workin' with?"

Jed held my gaze, looking more serious than I'd ever seen him. "Rose, Skeeter is workin' with Hardshaw."

Chapter
Twenty-Six

W hat?" I could hardly breathe. "No! He knows they're after Neely Kate. He would put a stop to it."

"Rose." Sympathy filled his eyes. "Skeeter's workin' with Hardshaw, and as far as I can tell, he's been workin' with them for three years."

"No," I insisted. "You would have known."

"Rose, he was workin' for J.R. Simmons, and I never had a clue."

"No. I can't believe he's in league with Hardshaw."

He looked at me with compassion, but in his eyes, I saw pain there too. I wasn't the only one James was betraying. "I didn't want to believe it either, but a few of his new men worked for Hardshaw. I found out this afternoon. But that's not all." He hesitated, as though determining if I could handle more.

"Go on."

"There's another link that makes me think Skeeter's cozying up to them—rumor has it the police force of the towns they've moved into have ended up in Hardshaw's back pocket."

I sucked in a breath. "Like the Sugar Branch police."

He gave me a grim nod. "Makes me think Skeeter's tryin' to ease their transition into the county."

So that was Jed's proof. I had to admit it didn't look good, but I struggled to believe it could be true. I couldn't reconcile the man I'd spent so much time with over the past year with this ruthless, lawless portrait Jed was painting, but I'd be foolish to completely ignore his warnings.

"He knows about Carly," I said, my heart sinking. "He's suspicious and doesn't like her livin' here." I turned to Jed. "Doesn't that mean he's not part of them? Wouldn't he have turned her in?"

"That doesn't mean shit," Jed said. "We don't know that he's been taken into the fold. I doubt they're telling all the men in their ranks to be on the lookout for her. If he knows there's a connection, he might think she's here to spy on *him*."

I started to protest, but headlights pulled into the driveway from the road, and Jed instantly threw himself between the car and me.

"Go inside, Rose."

"But—"

He reached back and grabbed my arm, pushing me backward as he stood facing the car.

"It's Joe," Neely Kate said in relief.

I pushed out a breath and nearly doubled over my legs.

"You can't tell Joe any of this," Jed said, spinning to face me.

"Of course I can't tell Joe. He's already put himself in enough danger for me."

"Listen to me, Rose." He sounded anxious, which perked up my attention. "Don't confirm or deny that Joe's the father. I'm not sure the best way to play this, so keep bein' elusive."

"Okay." I was in full agreement with him there. If James was really worried about losing face, he might decide to go after Joe instead of me. I couldn't let that happen.

"And don't worry about Wendy," he said. "Neely Kate and I will talk to her in the mornin', and I'll give you a report after you face the grand jury."

How had I already forgotten about Wendy? "Thanks."

Joe got out of his car, watching us with suspicion. "Did something happen while I was gone?"

"No," Jed called out, "but I'm not takin' any chances. In fact, I'm planning to stay the night."

Joe walked to the bottom of the steps and put his hands on his hips as he scanned the field next to the house. "Do you want the first or second shift?"

"First."

Neely Kate linked her arm with mine. "Looks like we're havin' a slumber party."

I wasn't complaining.

⇜⇝

VIOLET WAS ASLEEP WHEN I CHECKED on her, and her skin was cool to the touch, although it was much too early for her to come down with anything yet. Muffy kept her post on the chair in the corner.

When I walked out, Neely Kate stood in the doorway to the bedroom across from Vi's, the room where the kids usually slept when they stayed over.

"How's she doin'?" she whispered.

"She's asleep."

Neely Kate crossed over to me, gave me a big squeeze, then about-faced into the bedroom.

I headed to my own room, but I knew sleep was still far off. My head buzzed with thoughts and worries as I sat on the bed. A soft knock rapped on my door.

"Rose?" Joe called out softly.

"It's open."

He entered the room and shut the door behind him. "I know you must be tired, but do you have a moment?"

"Yeah."

He pulled over a chair from the corner, then sat down in front of me, leaning his forearms on his legs and clasping his hands together. "I need you to hear me out before you say anything, okay?"

I wasn't sure how many more shocks my system could take, but I nodded. "Okay."

He gave me a grateful smile, then took a long, slow breath as though settling his own nerves. "I got a few more inquiries about the baby tonight."

"When you took the kids home?" I asked in surprise. "Who?"

"Mike, for one," he said. "And then I went to the Stop and Go to fill up with gas and two people there mentioned it."

"Joe, I'm so sorry," I said in a rush.

"I'm not."

I frowned. "What are you talkin' about?"

"Everyone in this town thinks this baby is mine, Rose." He paused, then took another audible breath. "What if we told everyone they're right?"

"You mean until this all dies down?"

"No. For real. Permanently." He ran a hand over his head, then sat up straighter. "I want to be your baby's father."

I slumped back, feeling light-headed. "But James…"

"Doesn't want it. He made that very clear. You do. That hasn't changed, has it?"

Instinctively, I put my hand on my belly. "No. I'm more sure than ever that I want it."

"I've given this a lot of thought, Rose, so I don't want you to think this is rash, but I've already lost two babies, and we both know that I have terrible taste in women, present company excluded."

I couldn't help my grin.

"I want to be a dad. I think I'll be a good one. While I don't trust myself to choose the right woman, I *do* know you'll be the best mother. But you'll be raising this baby alone, and we both know you and the baby might not be safe if word gets out that Malcolm's the father." He leaned forward again, holding my gaze with an intensity that caught me by surprise. "I want to be a father. I want to be *your* baby's father."

"You want us to get back together?" I asked in shock.

His eyes flew wide as he abruptly sat up. "No. I'm sorry if I gave you that impression."

"No. You didn't. I just had to be sure."

"I have no idea how this would work," he said in a rush. "How we'd handle weekends and holidays. As far as I'm concerned, we could spend them together. Both of us had shitty childhoods. I think together we could give your baby the family we've both always wanted," he said, holding my gaze.

The intensity in his eyes told me that he really had thought this through. He'd come to me with his heart on his sleeve, although this time it wasn't his feelings for me that had put it there.

When I didn't say anything, he took my silence as encouragement. "Maybe I could build an apartment in the loft in the barn so I could be close but have my own place. That way I won't be crowding your personal space, but I'll be close. I want to be involved, Rose. I'd want to help with diapers and sleepless nights, and bottles. I don't know how it would all work, but I want to be part of it."

"Joe," I said, shaking my head in disbelief. "You need to give this more thought. This is a *huge* decision."

"I *have* given it thought. This feels right to me, Rose. This baby feels like the one good thing in this sea of shit we've been swimming in. But this is a bigger decision for you than it is for me. I hesitated to bring it up at all now, but Gary said they might ask you about your pregnancy when you're questioned by the grand jury. So if they ask about the father, feel free to tell them I'm the daddy, and as far as I'm concerned, that's not perjury. It's the truth."

Tears filled my eyes. "Joe."

"Don't cry, Rose. Please don't cry. Just give it some thought. That's all I ask."

I nodded, unable to speak past the lump in my throat.

He got up and moved next to me, wrapping an arm around my back. I rested my head on his shoulder, wiping my tears.

"You may decide to do this alone," he said, his voice clear. "And I have no doubt in my mind that you can. If you want to name me as the baby's father, birth certificate and all, yet want me to have no part in its life…" He paused, his voice cracking. "I'll agree to that too."

I turned to look at him. "Joe."

"And if you want to name me as the baby's father and sort out the rest later, then that's what we'll do. I'm makin' the offer, Rose. It's up to you to figure out how involved you want me to be." He kissed my forehead and stood to leave. "Try to get some sleep." He looked back once before leaving, a wry grin making his eyes twinkle in a way that reminded me of Joe McAllister, the man who'd moved in next door. "I know, easier said than done."

Chapter Twenty-Seven

I didn't sleep well, not that I was surprised. I had a lot to mull over. Aside from Joe's proposal, I couldn't wrap my head around the thought of James betraying me, but I intended to follow through on my promise to not incriminate anyone. Myself included. And somehow I'd do it without lying under oath.

Gary came over midmorning to prepare me for my testimony. When he heard I planned to keep what I knew to myself, he pursed his lips and said, "Then I hope to God you've had a recent head wound to blame on your memory loss."

"I was nearly strangled to death in August," I said. "I lost consciousness."

His eyes lit up. "Do you have a hospital report to prove it?"

"I can do one better," I said, sounding more enthusiastic with the plan than I felt. "I've got a sheriff's report sayin' Joe found me unconscious on the ground with my hands bound."

A hint of a smile crossed his face. "That'll do."

He ran me through a practice testimony, and I was so exhausted after answering all of his questions that I declared the need to take a nap.

Gary tapped his chin with the tip of his ink pen. "Maybe we really should use your pregnancy when you're testifying."

I pressed my lips together. "Seems like I'd be openin' a whole new can of worms. Especially since I'm not declarin' who the father is yet."

"Tell them you're not sure."

I snorted. "Henryetta's not that liberal. If I say that, I'll become the town trollop."

"Your testimony before the grand jury won't be a matter of public record."

I snorted again. "Like that's gonna keep it quiet."

He pushed out a groan and got to his feet. "I hate small towns. That means everything you tell them might be leaked."

"Yep."

He glanced down at his page full of notes and rubbed his forehead. "We'll table the whole pregnancy issue for now, although it might come up during your questioning. If push comes to shove, tell them Joe's the father. He's fully prepared to claim the baby. He already told me so."

That raised my ire. "He shouldn't have told you so. I haven't decided what to do about that yet."

Gary stuffed his legal pad in his leather case. "He's worried about you, Rose. Rightly so. We're movin' at light speed on something that usually takes weeks to put together."

He was right. I hadn't spoken to Joe since our talk the night before. He was already gone by the time I got up. But he'd sent a text telling me he would pick me up at one fifteen so I'd be plenty early for my two o'clock appearance.

I headed to my room for a nap and set an alarm, hoping a half hour would help me feel refreshed enough to handle the afternoon ahead. But when my alarm went off, my head felt heavy and it took me a good five minutes to feel halfway human.

Nevertheless, I was dressed and ready when Joe walked through the front door wearing a freshly pressed uniform.

Gary had told me to dress professionally but not to look too worldly. If it all went to hell in a handbasket, he was going to paint me as a naive soul too thick to understand what was going on around me, a plan that set my nerves on end but that might keep me out of jail.

My baby was more important than my pride.

I wore a soft pink A-line dress with a white Peter Pan collar and two-inch ivory slingback heels, both borrowed from Violet's wardrobe. My hair was long and loose, with a little bit of curl on the ends and natural-looking makeup.

Joe took in my appearance and stopped in his tracks.

My heart leapt into my throat. "Gary told me to go for professional but innocent." I put my hand on my belly. "Is it too much considering...?"

"No, Rose," he said with a soft smile. "You're beautiful."

I sucked in a breath. "I wasn't goin' for beautiful."

Releasing a chuckle, he walked closer and put his hands on my upper arms. "Rose, you'd be beautiful if you were wearin' a gunnysack."

I was too nervous to scoff. "But do I look okay for a grand jury testimony?"

"You look fine. Great. If Gary wants professional-meets-innocence, you've achieved it." His eyes twinkled. "You've always looked great in pink. You're practically glowing."

"Oh," I said as I realized what he meant. "Do I want to look pregnant?" I smoothed my hand over my belly, but it felt flat. "Gary was undecided."

"I say go with your gut," he said. "It's served you well up to now." He watched me as I picked up my purse off the coffee table. "Have you eaten anything?"

"I was too nervous to eat."

"You have to eat *somethin'*, Rose."

"I'm afraid I'll barf it up."

He walked past me into the kitchen and came out about a half minute later with a package of saltines and a bottle of water. "You're bound to be nervous during your testimony. You don't want your blood sugar to get too low. Can't have you faintin' on the stand."

As he ushered me out the door, I couldn't help thinking about the way I'd passed out in the jury box during Bruce Wayne's trial. Mason's face was the first thing I'd seen when I'd come to. I definitely didn't want a repeat of that performance.

Joe led me to the back of a sheriff's patrol car and held the door open. I was surprised to see Randy Miller sitting in the driver's seat.

"I thought you were takin' me," I said, hesitating at the open door.

"Randy's drivin'. I'm ridin' shotgun."

"Why?"

He patted the gun at his hip. "Just in case."

I almost asked him if he thought there would be trouble, but it struck me that I'd be more likely to know than he would. So I gave Randy a tight smile and climbed inside.

We were silent as Randy headed for the county road. When he took the turn, a sheriff's patrol car parked on the shoulder pulled out behind us.

"I hope they don't have high expectations for my testimony," I said, glancing out the back window at a deputy I didn't recognize. "I'm not sure I'm worth all the county's resources."

"You just do your best," Joe said, keeping his eyes on the road, but he sounded tense. "Don't be worryin' about disappointin' anyone."

Would the county and state be pissed after my testimony?

My mind wandered to James. He'd been adamant that I needed to tell the truth. He'd claimed it was the only way he could protect me. What would happen when I didn't admit to everything? Was I digging myself in deeper? Would I hurt whatever deal he'd worked out?

His only deal is with Hardshaw, I reminded myself.

Yet that didn't ring true to me. Even if Jed believed it, I couldn't. James wouldn't betray Neely Kate like that. Or Jed. Or me. Or *himself*. There was no way he was willingly working with them. I'd find a way to prove it to Jed before the criminals in the county lost their fool heads.

The ringing phone in my purse broke my reverie. I dug it out and checked the screen.

"Who is it?" Joe asked, glancing over his shoulder.

I almost told him it was none of his business, but then I realized it would be wrong.

"Uh," I said, starting to panic at the sight of Dallas, TX, on the readout until I realized it was the number for Stewart from Sonder Tech, the business I'd pitched to a couple of days ago. I'd forgotten to put the name and number into my contacts.

"Hello, Stewart," I said, forcing cheerfulness into my voice. "I wasn't expecting to hear from you until the end of the week."

"Well," he said in a friendly tone. "When you know what you want, you go for it."

"So I take it that's a yes?"

"Definitely."

"That's great to hear," I said. "I can come by tomorrow to discuss any changes you want to make to the plans, if you like."

"No need," he said. "Unless you want to pick up the signed contract and the deposit. Otherwise, I can just put it in the mail."

"No changes?" I asked in surprise. I'd put in more embellishments than they actually needed, expecting them to trim back. "That's great."

"Good. So when can you fit us into your schedule?"

I rubbed my forehead, trying to mentally switch gears. "Last time I checked, the middle of next week was lookin' good, but let me check with my partner and call you back."

"Sounds good," Stewart said. "I look forward to doin' business with you, Rose."

"Me too." I ended the call and held the phone in my lap. My life had been so crazy I'd completely forgotten I was waiting for his call.

"Everything okay?" Joe asked.

"Yeah," I said, coming to my senses and pulling up Bruce Wayne's number. "We got that big job I pitched the other day."

"That's great," Joe said. "Bruce Wayne's handlin' the install, right?"

"It's a big job and I don't have many consults for the next two weeks," I said as I typed a text to Bruce Wayne. "I might lend a hand."

"Do you think that's a good idea?"

"I'm pregnant, not ill."

"Still…"

I pushed out a sigh and lifted my gaze. "I'll ask Dr. Newton when I go see her."

"I still wish you'd go see someone else," he said. "I don't trust her staff."

He had a point, but I couldn't deal with finding a new doctor right now. Besides, Dr. Newton wasn't the problem.

"Congrats to you both," Randy said, clearly unsure if it was the right thing to say. I sympathized with him—saying nothing probably didn't seem like an option.

"Thanks," I said. "I'm sure you've caught an earful about it."

"Sorry," he said, keeping his eyes on the road. "It's just that Dena's been tellin'—"

"That's enough, Deputy Miller," Joe said. "This is none of her business."

"Yes, sir," Randy murmured, his ears turning pink. His gaze lifted to the rearview mirror. "Margi said she toured your barn and corral yesterday and it looks like a great place to board her rescue horses."

Joe's eyebrows shot up and he gave me a questioning look.

My phone vibrated with a text from Bruce Wayne, congratulating me on getting the job and confirming our schedule was clear.

"Margi boards horse and she's full. But she gets rescue horses from time to time, and she heard about my farm," I said as I sent Stewart a text saying we were free to start the next Wednesday. "She came and toured the barn yesterday afternoon, saying she'd pay to make the necessary changes and that she and her hired help would provide all the care."

"Do you think that's a good idea right now?" Joe asked. "With everything else goin' on?"

"I didn't ask her to come over, Joe," I said in exasperation. "She just showed up." Then I remembered her boyfriend was sitting in front of me. "I'd told her the day before that I'd show her around. I'd just forgotten."

"Margi would do all the work," Randy said, shooting a glance to Joe. "And I'd probably help with the construction. If you're worried about who'll be showin' up on her land, considerin' everything, they'll be vetted. I would never put Rose at risk. Especially now."

When Randy put it like that, I had to wonder why I was hesitating. "That was my biggest concern," I admitted, "and the possibility that I'll have to help take care of them. I don't know the first thing about horses."

"You have no business learnin' right now," Joe said in a stern voice. "One kick from a horse…"

"Joe," I groaned. "Enough with the overprotectiveness."

He turned to look at me, pain filling his eyes. "You forget I'm cursed when it comes to the pregnant women in my life. Neely Kate, Hilary. Savannah. Two of those women died, Rose, so I won't apologize for being overcautious."

My heart hitched. "Joe. I'm so sorry. I didn't think about that."

"My past isn't your problem," he said in a gruff voice. "But I hope you'll understand that this is only coming from a place of love. I can't let anything happen to you too."

If he hadn't included Neely Kate in his list—and if he hadn't already told me he didn't want us to get back together—I would have been concerned he meant he was *in love* with me. We were friends now, and I cherished his friendship. I loved him too—how could I not after everything he'd done for me?—I just didn't love him like I used to. "Thank you for your concern, and I promise not to take any unnecessary chances."

"Thank you." His voice was heavy as he turned around, refusing to meet my eyes.

After a couple of awkward moments, Randy said, "So what do you say about Margi's proposal?"

I suspected I'd never hear the end of it, and I couldn't think of a good reason to tell her no, even though I still wasn't enthusiastic about the prospect.

"Now is not the time, Deputy," Joe growled.

"It's okay, Joe," I said, then turned to Randy. "Tell Margi to give me a call next week so we can go over some specifics."

"Rose," Joe said in a low tone.

"It's my farm. My decision." But as soon as the words fell out of my mouth, I instantly regretted them. He was worried about me—with just cause—and I'd pretty much blown off his feelings and concerns. If it had been just the two of us in the car, I would have instantly apologized, but it felt awkward with Randy there. Especially since we weren't really a couple.

We rode in silence after that, and as we pulled up at the back of the courthouse, I was thankful the conversation had at least taken my mind off my upcoming testimony.

The other sheriff's car pulled up behind us, and the deputy got out and walked toward my door, his hand on his holstered weapon as he scanned the area around the building.

Joe got out and opened my car door, reaching in to help me out. As soon as I was on my feet, he wrapped his arm around my back and ushered me to the back door. When we got inside, I pulled him to a halt. "Joe. Wait."

"What's wrong?" he asked, looking me up and down as if making sure I was still in one piece.

"I'm sorry," I said, my voice tight with worry. "I shouldn't have been so short with you. You live on the farm. You've given up two months of your life to help us. I should have given your concerns more thought. I'm nervous about what's about to happen, but that's no excuse. I'm so sorry."

"Hey," he said softly, affection in his eyes as he lifted a hand to the back of my neck. "You're right. It's your farm. And it's your body. I have no say in any of it."

I closed my eyes. "I'm so confused right now, Joe."

His forehead touched mine, and I could barely hear him as he said, "I know, darlin', and I'm sorry for makin' it more difficult for you. I'll rein in my own issues. I promise. I just want you to be safe."

I opened my eyes and gave him a warm smile. "I know, and you have no idea how much I appreciate everything you're doin'."

"I do," he said. "Trust me, I do." He stood up straight. "You ready to go?"

I sucked in a breath, preparing myself for the performance of my life. I had to get this right. My baby's life might depend on it.

Chapter Twenty-Eight

We took the elevator up to the second floor. My new attorney was waiting for me, and to my surprise, so was my old one.

"Rose," Carter Hale said, walking toward me with a pinched mouth. "I believe there's been a miscommunication about who's representin' you."

"You think so?" I asked in a direct tone. "I decided I needed an attorney who has my best interest in mind," I said. "Not one who puts his other clients first."

His face reddened. "May we have a word in private?"

"No," Joe said, stepping between us. "You may not."

I shot a dark look up at Joe. "I'm perfectly capable of speakin' for myself."

He looked pissed, but my comment must have reminded him of the conversation we'd only just had because he took a step back.

"Yes," I said. "I will speak to you in private."

"I will be part of that meeting," Gary said in a stern voice as he stepped up next to me.

I met Carter's gaze. "No. We'll be havin' this meetin' alone."

"Rose," Joe protested.

I didn't look at either of the men on my team, instead holding Carter's gaze as though we were having a staring contest. I'd be damned if I was the first one to blink. "Where do you want to do this, Carter Hale? Because I'm only givin' you five minutes of my time."

He gestured down the hall, so I headed in that direction and he fell into step beside me. Halfway down, he reached for an unmarked door and pushed it open, revealing a small conference room. I walked inside and he followed, shutting the door behind him.

"What the fuck, Rose?" he half shouted as he turned to face me.

I crossed my arms over my chest and lifted my chin. "You'll have to be more specific."

"Good point," he said in a hateful tone. "Where do I start?"

"I'm only giving you five minutes, Carter Hale, and you've used about thirty seconds, so you better figure it out right quick."

"Why did you hire a new attorney?"

"Because I came to the conclusion it was unethical for you to represent us both."

Disgust washed over his face. "Who the hell told you that? Simmons? Your new high-dollar attorney?"

"Give it up, Carter. You know it's true, otherwise you'd be proving that you're right, not trying to gaslight me into thinkin' I'm wrong."

He pushed out a groan and plopped in a chair. "You obviously don't trust me. Why?"

"How about the fact you didn't prep me at all? Or that you told me to tell the truth without really telling me anything about what's goin' on? You left plenty of room for doubt, Carter, and it's not just my life on the line now."

He rolled his eyes as he leaned his arm on the table, tapping his pen. "Ah...the pregnancy. How convenient."

"*Convenient?* What the Sam Hill is that supposed to mean?"

"You expect me to believe you're pregnant and you *just* found out? I know for a fact you haven't slept with him since around the Sugar Branch incident, so if you're pregnant, it sure isn't Skeeter's."

James had discussed our sex life with him? Did he honestly believe the baby wasn't his? I tried to swallow my temper.

"First of all," I said, struggling to maintain my limited control, "my sexual history is none of your business. And second, this matter is between James and me."

"As his attorney, Mr. Malcolm has given me permission to deal with this on his behalf."

"*Deal* with it?" I said in disgust. "Let's get something straight. You and *Mr. Malcolm* don't need to deal with a damn thing. He made his position perfectly clear on Monday night."

He gave me a look of mock confusion. "What I don't understand is why you waited until Monday night to tell him. Why didn't you tell him when you saw him that afternoon?"

I opened my mouth, prepared to tell him that I'd informed James I had an appointment with a doctor that afternoon, but it was none of Carter's damn business. "I'm not having this discussion with you, Carter, whether James has given you his permission to be his proxy or not."

"Is it money you want?" he asked. "I have a check to give you right now, but this is a one-time offer."

I gasped. "Are you kiddin' me? What exactly are you buyin'? Are you askin' me to give up all claim to him or to get rid of the baby?"

His eyes turned cold. "If the baby is his, you need to abort it immediately."

I couldn't hide my momentary pain, but I said, "Does James know you're doin' this?"

"It was his idea."

I felt like the wind had been knocked out of me. After several seconds, I finally found the breath to say, "I want to talk to him."

"That's not gonna happen, Rose." He sounded embarrassed for me as he shifted in his seat. "You're not the first woman who's tried to trap him. He's ready to cut his losses and move on. He suggests you do the same." He pulled an envelope out of the inside of his jacket pocket. "We've made an appointment for you in Little Rock for tomorrow afternoon. It's discreet and the expenses have already been taken care of." He put the envelope on the table and slowly slid it toward me with his index finger as though it were contaminated. "When you've completed the task, feel free to cash this check."

I sucked in a breath. "How much is the life of my baby worth, Carter Hale?"

"The check is for twenty thousand, Rose. That money will help pay off the expenses you've incurred with your sister's illness, as well as replace the ancient furnace in your basement." He leaned forward and lowered his voice. "We both know you're not in a financial position to support a baby on your own. You're usually a rational woman, Rose. Do the smart thing."

Usually a rational woman?

I slowly picked up the envelope and ripped it in half, then ripped it again and tossed the pieces at him. "Tell your client that he can take the tattered remnants of this check and shove them up his ass."

Anger flashed in Carter's eyes. "He won't support this baby, Rose. If you try to get any child support from him, he'll—"

"He'll what?" I demanded. "Have me killed? He can try." I shook my head, my heart breaking, but I'd be damned if I let Carter see that. "Tell *your client* that as of this moment, I don't want a damned thing from him. In fact, I don't want him anywhere near me or this baby." I took a step closer and glared down at him. "Tell *your client* if he tries to lay claim to this baby, *he'll* be the one who needs to watch his back." I narrowed my eyes. "Your five minutes is up."

As I stomped toward the door, Carter called after me, "You better keep that appointment, Rose."

I opened the door and turned to face him. "Tell *your client* to go to hell. And you can follow him there."

I stormed out of the room, needing to find the bathroom before I burst into tears, but Joe was waiting for me about ten feet down the hall.

The minute he saw me, rage filled his eyes and he rushed over to intercept me. "What happened?"

I shook my head. If I tried to talk, I'd lose all control.

"What did he say?" When I didn't answer, his chest expanded, and his face went red. "I'm going to kill him."

"Don't say things like that, Joe. Not about him."

He paused. "You're not talkin' about Hale, are you?" Understanding filled his eyes, but it only made him look more furious. "Did he *threaten you?*"

Tears stung my eyes. "Let it go, Joe."

"*The hell I will.*"

I grabbed his arm. "Joe, please. He's not gonna hurt me." I took a breath, trying to calm down. "He was just tryin' to intimidate me into gettin' an abortion."

"What do you mean *intimidate?*"

"It's over. It's done. I need to settle down before I'm called in to testify."

Joe cursed under his breath. "If he was tryin' to shake you up, then it looks like he succeeded."

That caught me by surprise, but he had a point. Why ambush me with this before my testimony?

"But to what purpose?" I asked. "He already wanted me to spill what I knew about him."

Joe lowered his voice. "Maybe he caught wind that you were talkin' to his enemies. Maybe this was timed to make you pissed enough to rat him out."

"But why? It makes no sense."

"I don't know, Rose. None of it makes sense."

Gary walked toward us, looking pissed. "What did you discuss with him?"

"The baby," I said. "Or rather his twenty-thousand-dollar incentive for me to keep the appointment he made for me to have an abortion tomorrow."

"Please tell me you have that check," Gary pleaded.

"I ripped it up into tiny pieces and told Carter to tell his client to shove them up his ass."

A hint of a smile played on Gary's lips. "That's *almost* worth givin' up the leverage."

"If you're dreamin' up a paternity lawsuit, you can forget that nonsense right now," I spat. "I don't want a damn thing from that man."

A door opened down the hall and a woman walked out. "We're ready for Ms. Gardner."

Gary cursed under his breath and cast a dark glare back toward the room where I'd gone with Carter. "I'll ask them to give you a few minutes to get yourself together."

"No," I said. "I want to get this over with."

"Rose," Joe pleaded. "Just take ten or fifteen minutes to catch your breath."

"If I do even that, he wins." I inhaled and straightened my back. "I'm fine. I'm good." I looked Joe in the eye. "I'm the damned Lady in Black."

I walked into the courtroom and never once looked back.

Chapter
Twenty-Nine

Please state your name."

I kept my gaze on the man I'd been told was the foreman of the jury. "Rose Anne Gardner."

I sat at the witness stand in front of the grand jury, while Mason sat at one of the counsel tables with another man I didn't recognize. The new prosecutor, presumably.

"Ms. Gardner," the foreman said, looking at a paper in his hand. "We're here to talk about the incident on the evening of August 10th of this year."

I paused, wondering if he was going to give me more context, but he simply watched me, waiting for me to say something.

"Do you care to discuss it?" the foreman asked with a hint of attitude.

"I'm more than willing to discuss the incident on the evening of August 10th," I said agreeably, "but you'll need to be more specific."

"Why were you at Tiggy's Bar on County Road 22?" he asked.

"Yes. I was there for a case we were investigatin'," I said. "My best friend Neely Kate and I are workin' with a private investigator so we can take the PI exam. In any case, we were tryin' to find Sarah Freestone, a missing nineteen-year-old. Her mother approached Kermit Cooper, the PI we work with, and he passed the case along to us. She told us her daughter had been missing and the Sugar Branch Police Department refused to look into it. We agreed, but we hit a few dead ends, so I decided to go to Tiggy's, one of the places she'd frequented with her boyfriend Digger Malone, her best friend Nina Maxwell, and Nina's boyfriend Stewie Frasier, hoping to find more clues."

"Did you find any clues?" the foreman asked.

"Her mother was there, singing karaoke and drunk as a skunk. She'd found Sarah's journal, which indicated Marsha's live-in boyfriend had been molesting Sarah. She was convinced he'd killed her daughter. Marsha's friend and I were walking her out to the friend's car when Officer Johnnie Frasier approached us. He sent the other women home and made me stay."

"Officer Johnnie Frasier of the Sugar Branch Police Department?"

"Yes."

"Did he say why he was detaining you?"

The horror of that night was coming back full force. I remembered the sick gleam in his eye as he held me back. "He said he was arresting me for obstruction of justice." My voice shook and I took a deep breath to help settle my nerves. "He handcuffed me and put me in the back of his car."

"His police car?"

"Yes, only it looked like a regular car with a light bar. It didn't have the divider in the middle."

"So he put you in the back of his car, and then what happened?"

"He told me he was taking me to the police station, but I was certain they didn't have a jail cell, so I was worried that he intended to hurt me."

"What gave you that impression?"

I could feel the beginnings of a panic attack in my chest. "He made a call and told the person on the other line that he'd apprehended Rose Gardner. Then they discussed what to do with me."

"What did they say?"

"He said something like *they'll never know*, then told the person to come help him get rid of my truck."

"What happened next?"

"He didn't believe me when I said my keys were in my truck. So he patted me down, but his search was more than a standard pat-down."

"How so?"

I took a breath as tears stung my eyes. "He touched me inappropriately."

"Can you be more specific?"

Tears fell down my cheeks. "He fondled my breasts." I took a breath. "And touched inside my legs, under my skirt."

"Did you resist?"

"Yes," I said, wiping tears from my cheek. "The passenger door was open, so I tried to kick him in the chest to get him out, but he grabbed my ankles then lay on top of me, between my legs." I glanced up, surprised to see horror in some of the jurors' eyes. "I had a gun strapped to my leg, under my skirt. He asked if I had a permit, and I told him yes. Then he asked if I liked it rough. He said Sarah had liked it rough when he'd raped her. He insinuated he was the one who'd killed her too. He was about to rape me when we heard voices in the parking lot. He got out to make them go away. He said he'd kill me if I gave myself away, then took my truck keys—which he'd found during his search."

"Then what happened?"

"My cell phone had fallen out of my pocket. My hands were bound behind my back, but I groped around until I found it on the floorboard of the back seat of the car. Then I opened the car door and snuck out."

"Were you concerned that you would face charges for fleeing custody?" the foreman asked.

"Of course. That was part of the reason I took the time to find my phone. I knew it would be my word against his unless I got evidence of wrongdoing. I wasn't sure where to go. I figured if I went back into the bar, he'd haul me away and use his badge to get away with it. So I ran into the woods behind the building and got my hands in front of me. When he taunted me that he would come find me, I turned on my camera and videotaped what he was saying, especially after his friend showed up."

"And who was his friend?"

"Officer Flem Horton. The other Sugar Branch police officer."

"What were they sayin' to each other?"

"The other officer was angry that Officer Frasier had snatched me. Then Officer Horton said they'd need to hide my body."

My breath hitched as I struggled to hold back fresh tears.

"Do you need to take a moment?" the foreman asked. "Or a glass of water?"

"Water, please."

A woman brought me a bottle of water and a tissue box, and I grabbed the bottle and took a long swig. As I set it down, my eyes found Mason. His face looked paler than usual, but he refused to look at me.

"Then they discussed moving my truck," I said. "Where to hide it. They said they'd handle it just like they did with Sarah. They discussed having killed Emmitt Lincoln as well. They said no one had found either of the bodies in the junkyard, so it would be a good place for them to hide me. They said I was the only one looking for Sarah, so I needed to disappear." I took another drink of water, my hand shaking as I lifted it to my mouth. I'd left out their discussions about who had hired them and the likelihood that he wouldn't be happy about the turn of events, but I'd practiced this testimony with Gary. I was sure they wouldn't be able to tell.

"Then what happened?"

I lowered the bottle and screwed the cap back on, holding it in my lap with my left hand. "Officer Frasier said he wanted to rape me, but the other officer told him there wasn't time and they needed to kill me and be done with it."

"And you got this all on video with your phone?"

"Yes. They didn't know where I was, but my phone buzzed with a text, and they heard it. They caught me and Office Horton reminded Officer Frasier again he didn't have time to rape me. They realized people would hear the gunshots if they shot me, but they didn't want to haul me somewhere else to do it."

"Why was that?"

I released a bitter laugh. "They didn't say, but I can only presume it's because I wasn't the most cooperative hostage and they were afraid I'd run away again or cause some kind of trouble. So Officer Horton decided to strangle me with his hands right then and there. I tried to pry him off, but he was too strong, and I started to pass out. My body went limp and I heard gunshots that sounded quiet, like the gun was equipped with a silencer. I fell and thought I'd been shot, but Officer Horton fell with me, ending up on top of me. I lost consciousness, and the first thing I saw when I woke up was Joe."

"Joe?"

"Joe Simmons. The chief deputy sheriff of Fenton County. I'd called to tell him I was at the bar. He came because he was worried about me being there alone."

The foreman was silent for a moment, then said, "So both officers were shot. Do you know who shot them?"

"No. I never saw a gunman. I never saw anyone until I saw Joe." A lie, but only partially. I barely saw Denny Carmichael. I *heard* him tell me I owed him a favor for saving me.

"Why would the gunman shoot the officers and not you?"

"I don't know," I said. "Maybe it was a vigilante."

"Do you believe that?" he asked.

"I'm not sure what to believe. I only know they're dead and I'm alive."

"And you didn't see the gunman?"

"No."

"Do you have any suspicions who it might be?" he asked.

"None."

"Could it have been Skeeter Malcolm?"

I paused and said, "I couldn't say."

He looked surprised by my answer. Had he expected me to condemn him or exonerate him? "What happened to your phone?"

"It got knocked out of my hand when the officer caught me, but I couldn't find it after Joe helped me up. No one else found it either."

The foreman took a moment before he asked, "What is your relationship with Joe Simmons?"

His question caught me off guard. "I'm not sure what that has to do with the Sugar Branch police."

"Considering the fact that Chief Deputy Simmons found you and corroborated your story, it makes all the difference."

I hadn't expected this line of questioning. I shot a glance to Mason, but he refused to meet my eyes. "Joe is my ex-boyfriend, but we're friends now. If you're in need of corroboration, I expect the ER report speaks for itself. And the ambulance driver's report about the fact I was distraught and nearly hysterical. And I would suspect the autopsy report for Officer Horton likely shows that he had scratch marks on his hands from when I'd tried to pry his fingers off my throat."

"Simmons is living with you, correct?"

He wasn't going to let the issue of Joe go, and I knew exactly where that was coming from. Mason knew about the baby.

I almost answered with a retort but realized that wouldn't be helpful. I met his gaze, trying to hide my defiance. "Yes."

"And he moved in after the incident with the Sugar Branch police?"

"He was worried about my safety, not to mention my dying sister had just moved into my house. He's been a huge help."

"Why was he worried about your safety?"

"A gunman shot the two officers. He was worried the gunman would be back to finish me."

"Have there been any threats to your safety since Chief Deputy Simmons moved in for your protection?"

"If you're askin' if I've been in danger since, the answer would have been no until a few nights ago. I was at Beacon's Pharmacy when two men showed up asking the pharmacist for prescriptions from Dr. Arnold. I ran out the back and they followed. Someone shot them and I took off."

"So in August you were in an incident with the Sugar Branch police. *They* were shot, *you* escaped. Then, two nights ago, you were involved in another incident where two men were shot and you escaped."

Crap. When he put it that way, it didn't sound good. "That is correct."

"And where did you go after the men were shot in the pharmacy parking lot?"

"A man forced me into his truck at gunpoint, but after he'd gone a ways, I told him I had to throw up. He stopped his truck and let me out to vomit. Then I ran into the woods to hide."

"Another similarity to Sugar Branch."

"The strategy worked last time, so I decided to try it again."

"And again, you called Joe Simmons when you walked into the convenience store."

Double crap. "I had lost my phone in the parking lot and I knew his number. Not to mention I'd texted him when the men showed up threatening the pharmacist. I knew he was on his way and would be worried when he got there and found me missing."

"Did you do anything illegal, Ms. Gardner?"

His question caught me by surprise.

"Last time I checked, bein' in the wrong place at the wrong time wasn't an arrestable offense." I put some humor into it, and a couple of the jury members smiled and chuckled.

"I'd also like to point out," I added, "that before the incident on August 10th, I called one of the special prosecutors, Mason Deveraux, and told him that I was concerned the Sugar Branch Police Department had been bought. I'd heard rumors about it during my investigation. That was one of the reasons I'd called Joe when I went to the bar. I'd hinted to people that I didn't think the police had done a thorough job, so I was slightly concerned for my safety, and I asked Joe to come check on me if I didn't check in with him. But he decided to come right away."

"Do you think Joe Simmons shot and killed the Sugar Branch officers?"

I couldn't hide my surprise. "No. He's the chief deputy sheriff and he would have had grounds to apprehend them."

"You're certain it wasn't James Malcolm, who goes by Skeeter?"

I steeled my spine. *Here we go.* They might have brought in replacement for Mason, but these were his questions. His agenda. "Like I said, I don't know who it was."

"But you're acquainted with James Malcolm?"

I took a moment to think on that, then looked at the jury. "I met Mr. Malcolm last winter when we were both working toward a common goal: stop J.R. Simmons. I'd caught wind that J.R. was trying to kill my then-boyfriend, Mason Deveraux, who was the assistant DA for Fenton County. He's right over there." I pointed to him at the table. He glanced up briefly but had the good sense to look slightly embarrassed. "I needed contact with the criminal world to get to the sources I needed. Mr. Malcolm provided me with those contacts."

"Why would a notorious criminal help you? The girlfriend of the county's assistant DA? One who had sworn to take down James Malcolm?"

Thank goodness we'd prepared for this one. "I can't attest to the latter two questions, but I can answer the first. I provided a distraction," I said. "I wore a disguise of a black dress and a hat with a veil to cover my face." I paused and scanned the jury box, stopping when I saw a younger woman. "Powerful men often think women are weak. Objects. They loosen their tongues around them."

"And how did you get those men to loosen their tongues, Ms. Gardner?" the foreman asked in a condescending tone.

"If you're insinuatin' inappropriate things happened, then you're dead wrong. Some men try to impress women they hope to sleep with. They say things that maybe they shouldn't."

"So you lured them with the expectation of sex and tricked them into giving up secrets?"

I forced myself to remain cool and collected. "No. I didn't have to make any promises I didn't intend to keep. My hat and veil and mysterious persona were enough for them to try to woo me."

"And what did they tell you?"

I mentioned Mick Gentry's name and told the jury about his attempts to take over the underworld, and how I'd used him to set up a meeting with J.R. But I left out a whole lot of information.

"And what did James Malcolm get out of this arrangement?" the foreman asked.

"I helped him suss out who held a grudge against him."

"And who did?"

"Mick Gentry, of course." A safe answer. He was dead and tied to J.R.

"What other men did you tell Malcolm about?" the foreman asked.

I shifted my gaze to Mason. "I'll be honest, there were others, but their names are long forgotten. I had one purpose and one purpose only. To save Mason. I loved him with everything in me, and I was desperate to protect him. Mick Gentry was tryin' to kill Mason, and J.R. Simmons was behind it. I was willing to risk everything to save him and put Simmons behind bars."

Mason had the good sense to keep his gaze averted. The attorney next to him flushed red. He looked none too pleased as he furiously whispered into Mason's ear.

"But you're not with Mason Deveraux now," the foreman said, sounding confused, and I wondered if we'd just gone off-script. The other prosecutor might be here to make this all look proper, but there was no doubt that Mason had scripted the questions.

"No," I said, genuine tears filling my eyes as I continued to look at Mason. "My entire purpose last winter was to save him, but he couldn't live with what I'd done to accomplish it."

"He broke up with you because you talked to criminals to save him?" an older woman in the jury asked.

I turned to her in surprise, but Gary had warned me that any of the jurors could ask questions. "I'd embarrassed him."

"But you saved his life," the younger woman said, sounding angry. "And he broke up with you?"

Even after all these months, it still smarted, and if I was driving this dagger in, I figured I might as well angle it to kill. I held her gaze, a genuine tear slipping down my cheek as I said, "He proposed to me at Jaspers, but someone snatched me on my way to the bathroom. J.R. had arranged to have me kidnapped. If Skeeter Malcolm's men hadn't been watching the restaurant to keep an eye on me, I might have been killed. One of them followed me to the cabin where I was being held hostage and rescued me. After that, he took me to Skeeter."

I made some slight changes to the story, but they were mostly omissions. I considered it an acceptable version of the truth.

"J.R. had planned to kill Mason that night," I continued, "but I convinced Skeeter to save Mason, which he did. Then we cooked up the idea of setting a meeting with J.R. in which I'd try to get him to admit to criminal activities so we could capture it all with a wire. Mason was on board, but at the last minute he said he couldn't go through with it and left. So Jed Carlisle and I took a meeting with J.R. Simmons and Mick Gentry, while Skeeter listened in through a wire. J.R. killed Mick Gentry and then held me hostage. Joe Simmons and Mason both showed up with sheriff deputies, and I shot J.R. in the leg. That was when he was finally apprehended." I took a deep breath, casting a glance at Mason, then shifted my attention back to the jury. "Mason broke up with me a few days later. He said he couldn't trust me."

"You were nearly killed trying to protect him, and he *broke up with you?*" another woman asked, sounding outraged.

One of the male jurors leaned forward and turned sideways to face the woman. "She broke the law."

"To save him!" a third woman protested.

A quick glance told me that the women outnumbered the men, and they—along with a few men—sent looks of disgust to Mason.

They questioned me for another half hour, but the pall of Mason's betrayal hung over the rest of the questioning. None of the names of the men I'd made deals with popped up, and I gave Mason a long, dark look on my way out.

Go to hell, Mason Deveraux, I thought. *And Skeeter Malcolm can join you there.*

Chapter
Thirty

J oe and Gary were waiting for me outside the courtroom. Gary looked hungry for answers, while Joe wanted to comfort me, but I shook him off. Still, I let him join us when Gary led me to the same conference room where Carter had interrogated and insulted me. I told them everything, from what I'd been asked to the line of questioning that had skewed toward Joe for a time before things took a turn.

"And you're sure most of the jury was on your side?" Gary asked.

"All the women and most of the men. The foreman finally gave up."

"And Deveraux?" Joe asked.

"He looked properly humiliated."

Gary seemed relieved. "This grand jury was specifically set up to investigate the Sugar Branch police corruption. And while they could have broadened the scope of their investigation if they'd found anything worth digging into—which I'm certain he was hoping would happen—it sounds like the only thing they'll be digging is Mason Deveraux's grave." He gave me a wide grin and stood. "It's not entirely official, but I'm calling it. You're a free woman, Rose Gardner."

He held out his hand to shake, but I got up and wrapped my arms around his neck. "Thank you. I don't know what I would have done if I'd only had Carter Hale's say-so. I wish I'd known you a lot sooner."

He hugged me back, then said, "There's always the malpractice case and a potential extortion case against Malcolm for threatening you if you don't abort."

I pushed out a sigh. "He's bluffin'."

"Rose," Joe protested.

I gave him a sad smile. "He's bluffin'."

❧

WE HAD A CELEBRATORY DINNER THAT NIGHT—Neely Kate and Jed, Joe, Carly, me, and Vi. Violet looked more exhausted than usual, but she seemed relieved by our assurance that I was safe from the legal system. Although she hadn't shown any signs of coming down with a cold yet, I knew it was still too soon to tell.

Jed carried Violet upstairs, and Joe and Carly went with them, leaving Neely Kate and me in the living room. Neely Kate flicked on the TV to watch a cooking show.

"There's a great idea," she said as a chef started frying shrimp in a pan.

My eyebrows shot up in surprise. This wasn't *Chopped* and the chef was cooking Cajun food.

"You want to try Cajun food?" I asked in a hopeful tone.

"We're close enough to Cajun country that my food truck could sell a fusion of Cajun and German food."

"What?"

A huge grin lit up her face as she pulled out her phone to start dictating recipe ideas into her note app. I handled it okay until she mentioned sauerkraut and anchovies.

"I don't think anchovies are Cajun or German," I said, my stomach beginning to revolt.

Her eyes lit up. "Even better."

I was close to losing my dinner. "I'm gonna get a glass of water."

I'd just made it into the kitchen when my phone rang. I wasn't surprised to see Dermot's number.

"I heard things went in your favor," he said as soon as I answered.

I didn't bother asking him how he'd found out, but if he knew, then James did too. Had he expected me to say more than I had? Would he be pissed?

"Better than expected," I admitted.

"I heard you played Deveraux like a fiddle."

I couldn't help my small smile of satisfaction.

"You know grand jury testimonies are confidential, Dermot," I said, but I was sure he heard the grin in my voice.

"I've been thinkin' about your situation with Malcolm," he said in a solemn tone. "I have a proposition for you."

"Go on."

"I'd like to speak to you in person. Do you still have a sheriff detail watchin' the house?"

Joe would have preferred it, but there'd been no grounds to keep them now that I'd testified. "No. Joe's here, but I'll make him go upstairs or out to the barn."

"He'll do it?"

"If you truly have a way to help protect me from James, he'll do it."

"He won't have to go anywhere. I'll pull up in about ten minutes and text you when I get there. Come speak to me out front. If Carlisle and Neely Kate are there, bring them too."

"Okay." I hung up, my stomach in knots. After I grabbed my water, I headed back to the living room. Neely Kate had settled on a sitcom, and I nearly told her about my call, but I was still sorting it out in my head. I sat in a chair and nursed my water while absently watching the screen.

Why had I agreed to meet with Dermot? James loved me. Sure, he didn't want the baby—I was heartbroken and beyond pissed by how he'd reacted to the news—but I didn't believe he'd resort to hurting me. Ever.

Joe and Jed came downstairs not long afterward. Joe headed into the kitchen, saying he was going to work on a mountain of paperwork, and Jed turned to Neely Kate. "You ready to head home?"

I glanced up at him. "I think you should stick around for a bit."

He studied me with narrowed eyes. "What happened?"

"Dermot called. He's comin' by to see me." I paused. "He said he wants to talk to you too." I cast a sideways glance at Neely Kate. "The both of you."

Jed's brow furrowed. "He must be ready to talk about whatever he's been cookin' up."

I nodded.

"What about Joe?" Neely Kate asked in a half-whisper while glancing at the kitchen door.

"We need to do this without him for now." I gave her a sad smile. "We need to protect him."

She nodded.

My phone dinged with a message from Dermot telling me he was pulling up. I stood and grabbed my sweater off the coat hook. "He's out front."

Jed and Neely Kate followed me, with Neely Kate calling out to Joe, "We're gonna sit on the front porch."

I expected Joe to protest, but he must have decided it was okay since I was with Jed.

I went out the front door as Dermot pulled up in front of the house. I waited on the top step of the porch as his car pulled to a stop and he got out.

Wrapping my arms across my chest, I nodded as he walked toward me. "Dermot."

"Lady."

I tried not to read too much into his acknowledgment. He usually called me Lady, but this time the title seemed to carry more weight.

He looked up at Jed with a grim look. "Carlisle." Then he gave Neely Kate an ornery grin. "Neely Kate."

"We're eager to hear about this plan of yours," Neely Kate said.

Dermot nodded, his grin fading. "Don't worry. You play a part in it too." He turned his attention back to me. "You might want to take a seat for this."

He didn't look like he planned to join us on the porch, so I perched on the steps and Neely Kate sat next to me, while Jed stood behind us.

"Where's your dog?" Dermot asked.

"Upstairs with my sister. She won't leave her side."

"And Simmons?"

"Working in the kitchen," I said.

He nodded. "As I mentioned on the phone yesterday, I've noticed you've been collectin' allies, and that you currently have more than Malcolm does."

My back stiffened. "My goal isn't to best Skeeter Malcolm. My goal is to protect myself and my baby."

Dermot's eyes narrowed. "Not too long ago you claimed to be neutral. Have you changed your mind?"

"Well, no," I said reluctantly. "But that still doesn't mean my goal is to outwit Skeeter. I provide sanctuary to those who need it. Like I did with Marshall."

"But what about now?" he asked, motioning to my gut. "What about with a baby comin'?"

When I hesitated, Neely Kate said, "She's givin' sanctuary to someone even as we speak, so what do you think?"

I wasn't so certain we should have shared that information, but I could understand Neely Kate's motivation. She was trying to prove my word had weight. "Neely Kate's right. We're harboring someone." When I saw his gaze shift to the house, I said, "Not here. I have them in a safe house."

His brow rose. "You have a safe house?"

I didn't want to dwell on that. It wouldn't be too hard for someone to figure out where it might be. "That's neither here nor there," I said. "Now more than ever, I need to be seen as neutral ground in this Wild West." I shifted on the step. "Ever since the grand jury was announced, I've been doin' my best to soothe concerns that I might turn on people. I think it will come out soon enough that I didn't betray anyone in my testimony."

He studied me closely. "Not even Skeeter Malcolm?"

"Ratting out even one criminal would put me at risk. The men and women of this county have to trust that I'll hold their secrets, no matter which way the wind turns."

"Not even after Malcolm betrayed you? The men around the county know about it."

My breath caught in my chest. What did Dermot know that I didn't? "And exactly how do they think Skeeter Malcolm betrayed me?"

"By tryin' to have you killed at the pharmacy."

I lifted my chin. "I still believe that was a misunderstandin'."

"Has he called to apologize or inquire about your safety since the incident?"

The answer tanned my hide, but I bit out, "No."

"And would he have contacted you before?" When I didn't respond, he lowered his voice. "I saw him after the whole Merv mess. I saw how upset he was when he thought you were dead. That man would have moved heaven and earth to be certain of your safety."

"It's not that easy for him now, Dermot," I said, but part of me couldn't help thinking he had a point.

Dermot's gaze softened, and he took a step forward. "There are others, Rose."

"Other what?"

"Others who will pledge themselves to you. And others who only need to be convinced."

I shuddered, sure I'd misunderstood. "What are you talkin' about?"

He cast a glance to Jed before shifting his gaze back to me. "When Carlisle first started askin' around about Hardshaw, none of us saw them as a credible threat. But it caught our attention, and now we realize things aren't on the up and up and Skeeter Malcolm's mired in the thick of it."

"You think Skeeter's involved in Hardshaw," I said in a flat voice. "What's your proof?"

"Not just him. We think Malcolm and Carmichael are in it together."

"Because Denny Carmichael bought the Sugar Branch Police Department?" I asked, repeating the rumors. "Like Hardshaw has done in the past when they move into a town?"

"Yeah," he said, sounding surprised. Then respect filled his eyes. "You know."

"Not as much as you might think," I admitted, "but I want to know more."

"Knowin' more will only draw you deeper into this mess. Are you prepared for that?"

Part of me wanted to turn around and run into the house. Close my eyes and stick my fingers in my ears and pretend this wasn't happening. But I wasn't that woman anymore. In fact, it struck me that Rose and Lady hadn't just merged into one—Lady was taking over.

The thought bothered me, but right now, with an innocent baby in my belly and the county in trouble, I had to be strong. Maybe letting Lady out wasn't such a bad thing.

"Have you asked Carmichael about his involvement with the Sugar Branch police?" I asked.

"He denies it, but—"

"And what purpose would he have for denyin' it?" I asked with a hint of bite in my tone. "Fear that someone will rat him out? Seems like the only code of honor the criminals in this county have is not to rat each other out. So why would Carmichael bother keepin' this to himself?" When he didn't respond, I said, "Seems to me it would be a feather in his cap. Quite the coup. He'd earn the respect, if not the envy, of most of the men in this county. So why didn't he claim responsibility?"

He rested his hands on his hips, cocking his head as he studied me with a curious expression. "I'll be damned. Malcolm bought them."

My betrayal sank in deep, filling me with dread. "I never said any such thing. I only asked you to reason it through."

"And I did. Malcolm bought them."

What was I doing? But deep in my heart, I was facing a choice—protect James or protect my baby. I didn't want it to be an either-or situation, but James had made it clear that *he* saw it that way.

I couldn't pin my foolish hopes on James coming around, not with so much on the line. It was time to grow up and deal with the situation at hand. "So where does that leave Carmichael?"

Admiration filled Dermot's eyes. "That's a good question."

"Seems like an important one," I said with a firmness I usually reserved for when I interrogated suspects as Lady. "Especially if you're gatherin' men."

"You've figured out what I'm up to?" he asked.

"I'm capable of putting two and two together, but I'm still not clear on how I play into the picture."

"We're gonna ask the big players to take sides."

"Sides?" I asked, holding back my fear. I already knew what he meant, but I needed him to say it.

He stepped even closer. "They'll be asked to align with Skeeter Malcolm or the Lady in Black."

A bolt of adrenaline shot through my bloodstream. By asking those men to choose, I would be forced to choose. "The Lady in Black isn't real, Dermot," I said, although I'd just been thinking the very opposite.

"She's more real than you know," he countered. "She's become a symbol of fairness and neutrality. She's a potential leader, even more so after what I plan to propose."

"And what's that?" Jed asked, his voice flat.

Dermot turned to face him. "Lady will have no control over their enterprises and no share in their profits. Her sole role will be to act as an intermediary in disputes and to gather them in a united front when decisions need to be made."

"Like a court?" Neely Kate asked. "So when they get pissed at each other, they'll come to you to settle it instead of shooting it out between themselves?"

Dermot turned to face her. "Exactly."

"This is crazy!" I protested, starting to pace in the yard.

"No," Jed said as he descended the stairs. "It's what Skeeter's *supposed* to be doin', but he's never reined everyone in."

"Not only that," Dermot said, "but he's actin' like he's given up tryin'. Because he's sided with Hardshaw."

"You're dreaming if you think those men will listen to me," I scoffed. "Sure, I have you and Jed and I've got Gerard Collard in my pocket, but—"

"Wait. Gerard Collard is your third ally?" Dermot asked in disbelief.

"Well, yeah, but—"

"But nothin'." He shook his head. "Damn." His gaze lifted to Jed's. "Did you know about this?"

Jed gave a grim nod. "They snatched her from the pharmacy to make sure she wasn't snitchin' on them, and she maneuvered him into owing her a favor whenever she calls on it."

"It's just Gerard," I said.

Dermot's eyebrows shot to his hairline. "Just Gerard? He's never sided with *anyone*. Not once. *Ever*. He stays out on his land and sticks to his philosophy of live and let live." His brow furrowed. "What do you know about Collard for him to be concerned?"

"Never you mind about that," I said. "I shouldn't have told you anything about him. In fact, this whole thing is plum crazy."

"No," Dermot said, excitement filling his eyes. "This only convinces me it's the right idea."

"Dermot…what exactly do you think I'm gonna do?" I asked, incredulous. "I've addressed the few men who respect me one by one. Do you expect me to start makin' house calls to sway them?"

"No," he said. "I'm holding a summit."

"A summit? To get them to side with me?" I asked, raising my voice. "Are you insane?"

Dermot's expression remained unchanged. "You've gained more respect than you realize, Lady. The players in this world recognize that we need to get along in order to coexist. A war of any kind only brings unwanted attention. You can take control and keep peace in this county. Skeeter not only won't do that—he *can't.*"

I turned to face Jed. "Surely *you* think this is crazy." Then I added with more venom, "Traitorous."

Disgust filled Jed's eyes, though I knew it wasn't directed at me. "Any more traitorous than Skeeter telling me that I was dead to him? Any more traitorous than treatin' you like something he found in the gutter and insistin' you get an abortion? We won't even touch his possible assassination attempt."

I shot him a look of disbelief. "You're askin' me to become James's enemy. You think he's lost face because everyone thinks I'm pregnant with Joe Simmons's baby? What the heck do you think he's gonna do when he finds out I'm buildin' an alliance against him!"

Jed lifted his gaze to Dermot, his eyes hard. "Every member of the alliance will have to pledge to protect her."

Dermot nodded. "That's a given."

I had to put a stop to this. "Jed!"

"We're holdin' a summit tonight regardless of what you decide," Dermot said. "Hardshaw's comin' and we need a united front."

I turned to face Neely Kate, who had remained silent up to this point. "Neely Kate. Tell them this is crazy."

She gave me a soft smile. "You always said you were doin' this for the good of the county. The only crazy thing about it is that it doesn't seem crazy at all."

Dermot picked up where she left off. "Malcolm is reckless and out of control, and the players are skittish. Somethin's gotta give. You can be a solution or you can be collateral. The choice is yours."

"The term collateral is harsh," Jed protested.

"Is it?" Dermot asked. "If Hardshaw catches any wind about her and Malcolm...and their fallin' out, her reputation for neutrality won't protect her." He shook his head. "She'll be in even more danger than before. Especially if Hardshaw wants your girlfriend." He nodded to Neely Kate. "I think it's not harsh enough."

"You're implyin' I have no choice in the matter?" I said, my irritation growing.

"Of course you have a choice in the matter," Dermot countered, his voice rising. "But if you choose to do nothing..." He inhaled sharply then pushed out a breath. "Don't be surprised if you don't find the peace you're lookin' for."

I felt like I was going to be sick. I put my hand on my belly, surprised again by how attached I was becoming to the nameless baby I'd only known about for close to forty-eight hours. I couldn't imagine how attached I'd be when I could feel it move...or after it was born. What if someone came to hurt us...

James. What are you doing?

I'd hoped he'd soften his stance on my pregnancy, but Carter had made it very clear it wouldn't happen. The man I loved had offered me twenty thousand dollars to abort my baby.

Our baby. How could he so coldly want to throw that away? How could he think, even for a moment, that I would accept money for such a thing?

Tears stung my eyes, but I blinked them away. This wasn't only about me anymore. I had to think about our baby.

No. *My* baby.

James had chosen to remove himself from this. This baby was just mine.

I could mourn that fact later. Right now I needed to do everything in my power to make sure my baby was safe.

Even if that meant turning my back on the man I loved.

He'd already turned his back on me, but somehow that didn't make it any easier.

Chapter Thirty-One

O kay," I said. "I'll do it."

Neely Kate looked relieved for a second, then made a face. "What do we tell Joe?"

Joe. Before, I would have just snuck out and dealt with the consequences later. But I felt like I owed him so much more than that. Especially after his offer to be the baby's father. I hadn't even processed his proposal yet, but I wasn't ready to dismiss it either.

"I'll talk to him." When Dermot started to protest, I said, "I won't tell him what's goin' on, but I won't entirely hide it from him either. He needs to know I'm potentially walking into danger." I gave him a weary look. "How soon do we need to leave?"

He took a few backward steps toward his car. "You have an hour. I'll be back for all y'all then." He glanced at the yoga pants and T-shirt I'd changed into after I'd come home from the courthouse. "Dress for the part. You'll be selling yourself as the Lady in Black tonight."

As I watched him get into his car and drive off, one thought kept circling through my head.

What in tarnation had I just agreed to?

"Do you need help with Joe?" Neely Kate asked.

"No," I said quietly as I headed for the porch stairs. "I think I need to do this alone."

She placed her hand on my upper arm as I passed. "If you change your mind, just let me know. We'll be waitin' out here."

I gave her a smile as I covered her hand with my own. "Thanks."

Joe was in the living room, pacing the floor. He'd obviously known we were up to something, and he stopped his carrying-on as I walked in.

"Tim Dermot was here," he said. "Is there trouble?"

I gave him a half smile. "Isn't there always?" When he didn't return the smile, I headed to the sofa. "We need to talk."

His eyes widened slightly, and he swallowed before settling into an overstuffed chair. "What's goin' on, Rose?"

I took a breath. "I feel like you and I have come a long way. I'm over hidin' everything from you, but I don't want to get you in trouble by sayin' too much."

He leaned forward, resting his forearms on his legs. "Rose, if you're in trouble, I don't want you to hide anything."

"I'm not in immediate trouble," I said. "But Dermot thinks it's comin'. How soon, I can't say, but I'm guessin' sooner rather than later."

"Malcolm?" he asked in a tight voice.

"No. The Hardshaw Group."

His face lost all color. "How the hell did you get mixed up with them, Rose?"

"I didn't," I assured him. "But Dermot has reason to believe they'll come after me when they finally march into town."

"Why?"

"James."

His eyes darkened. "I'm gonna find a way to haul his ass to prison so he never sees the light of day again. And if that doesn't work, I'll flat-out kill him."

Fear squeezed my heart for both men—because despite all the evidence piling up against James, I still loved him.

"You hush," I said softly. "You'll do no such thing. This baby needs you."

He sat up, his eyes widening in surprise. "You've made a decision?"

I cringed, realizing what I'd said. "No, not yet. I'm sorry."

"No," he said, "don't be sorry. I didn't expect you to come to a decision yet, especially with everything else goin' on."

"No matter what my decision is, I want you to be part of this baby's life, Joe. Even if you're not the baby's daddy, I want you to be Uncle Joe."

A grim look filled his eyes. "You don't even owe me that, Rose."

"I know," I said, "but I've seen you with Ashley and Mikey. They love you, and I want my baby to have as much goodness as possible in his or her life. So no more talk about doin' things that could get you killed or incarcerated. Okay?"

He nodded. "Yeah. Okay."

I released a breath of relief. "I have to go to a meeting, and I can't tell you anything about it. It's not because I don't trust you—it's because I'm protecting you. Can you accept that?"

He studied me for a long moment. "Yeah. I can accept that."

I couldn't keep the shock from my face.

"I know," he said with a grin that faded just as quickly as it had appeared. "I guess we've both come a long way. Just promise me you'll be careful."

"I will."

"Then go do what you need to do to protect yourself and your baby."

❦

AN HOUR LATER, I climbed into the back seat of Tim Dermot's car. Jed sat in the front passenger seat and Neely Kate was in the back with me.

I lived on the northern end of the county, and everything of importance seemed to happen south of me, so I was confused when Dermot headed due west.

"Are we goin' to Lafayette County?" I asked.

"No," Dermot said, sounding grave. "We're goin' to my land."

"I didn't know you had land." I realized there was a lot I didn't know about him.

I suspected that was about to change.

Everything was about to change.

Fifteen minutes later, Dermot turned onto a private road leading into a tract of farmland. Two armed men were posted on either side of the road before a grove of trees. When they saw Dermot, they waved us through.

As we cleared the trees, light flared at us. Multiple metal trash cans had been spread around an open area, roaring fires burning in each one, but that wasn't the only source of light. Dozens of cars and trucks were parked around the edges of the circular clearing, their headlights pointed inward, and a large group of men stood in the middle.

Dermot slowed down and began to circle around the cars, toward the rear of the gathering.

I sucked in a breath, terrified out of my mind. "I can't do this," I said under my breath.

Neely Kate grabbed my hand and squeezed.

"Yes, you can," Jed said in a stern voice. "I've seen you do this more times than I can count."

"There's so many of them," I said. "There must be over fifty men and women here."

"Try seventy," Dermot said. "My men have been givin' me updates."

"Why'd they come?" I asked.

"I won't blow sunshine up your ass," Dermot said as he reached the back of the assemblage and came to a stop. "Not all of them are here to pledge themselves to you. Some are just curious. I'm sure a few are here to get a report to Skeeter. But this is your chance to win them all."

What in the world was I going to say? Did I even want this?

It might be my only way to live safely in Fenton County.

Both men got out of the car, and Dermot walked around the trunk while Jed opened my door.

It was showtime.

There was a chill in the air, but Jed had agreed with Dermot that it was important that I dress the part, especially tonight, so I'd worn a slinky black dress with long black sleeves and a plunging neckline that seemed to be rounded out with a little more cleavage than usual. Jed had insisted I wear the heels too, which would be a pain in the butt in the field after the recent rainfall. Thankfully, several pieces of particleboard had been set out for me to walk on.

I got out and the roar of conversation cut off, leaving dead silence as I walked to a small two-foot-tall platform that looked to have been constructed out of more particleboard. I was shorter than most of the men here, so it stood to reason I needed to be higher, not to mention I'd been Lady long enough to know small details mattered. They'd be forced to look up to me now. Not down.

Additional metal bins blazing with fire surrounded the platform, providing some heat and deep shadows, but I shivered for another reason. I was afraid, but if I allowed them to see that, this would be over before it started.

Dermot stepped up first, heading to the center of the approximately ten-foot-wide and six-foot-deep platform, while Jed gave me his hand to help me up with the ridiculous heels. Neely Kate stayed on the ground behind us, and to my surprise, several men stood in front of the stage, facing the crowd. I recognized some as Dermot's men, but I knew two of them personally—Witt and Marshall, both taking their sentry positions seriously.

My first thought was horror that so many men and about a dozen women considered themselves outside the law, but then I saw Gerard standing toward the back of the group along with his four sons, and I realized some of them weren't necessarily outright criminals. Instead, these were folk who skirted the law.

"There's a war on the horizon," Dermot called out, the only other sound the flicker of the flames surrounding us. "The Hardshaw Group from Dallas has been makin' a play for Fenton County right under our noses, and Malcolm's workin' right alongside 'em."

"Where's your proof?" a voice called out.

Jed stepped forward. "Y'all know that I was Skeeter's right-hand man."

"You turned traitor!" another voice shouted.

"Traitor?" Jed said, his voice booming in the night. "I worked with that man for fourteen years and he had more secrets than a spook. He worked with J.R. Simmons since the moment he came back to town over a decade ago, doin' the man's biddin', and never shared *a word* of it with me."

The raw pain in his voice sunk into me. I wasn't the only one James had hurt with his lies.

"That's his right!" another man called out.

"Yeah," Jed said in disgust. "It's his right to keep things from the men beneath him, but I was like a brother to him, or so I thought. He turned on me time and time again. He's been workin' with Hardshaw for three years! Under my nose! Under all y'all's noses too! What do you think's gonna happen when they get here?"

"You only care because they're after your girlfriend!" someone shouted.

"Y'all are gonna care when they move in," Dermot threw back. "I don't need to remind you of what they did in Henry County."

I had no idea what they'd done in Henry County, but if what Jed had warned me about was even close to true, I knew we had to stop them. The rumbling in the crowd suggested they agreed.

"Maybe Malcolm's workin' out a deal with 'em," a man said from the front of the crowd. I recognized him from the group Jonah had run for recently released cons—Lars Jenkins. He was not someone to mess with.

I reminded myself that this crowd was full of savage men. Some were guys like Witt and Bruce Wayne or even James's brother, Scooter, struggling to find their way in this world and doing illegal things to make ends meet. But others were like Lars Jenkins—self-centered and cruel. Men like that would never listen to me. They'd never assent to mediation with words instead of guns. Dermot and Jed were crazy to think this would work.

It struck me that we were going about this all wrong. Here I stood in the back, while the two of them worked the crowd. This wasn't a position of strength. If I didn't do something quick, things were about to head south.

"Skeeter Malcolm's not workin' out a deal with them for *you*," Jed said. "He's in this for himself."

"He's thinnin' out his inner circle," I said out loud before I could second-guess myself.

All eyes turned to me.

I took several steps forward. "How often does that happen? When a man steps into power, he pulls it closer. He doesn't clean his loyal people out. He's up to something."

"Did you find this out when he had you on your back?" a man I didn't recognize asked with an ugly laugh.

I searched out the crowd until I found the heckler. "You." I held his gaze. "What's your name?"

He gave me a defiant glare. "What's it to you? You lookin' for a new sugar daddy? 'Cause that's one job I'd be happy to apply for."

I felt Jed tense beside me, but he knew me well enough to let me handle it on my own.

I gave the heckler my deadliest stare, and asked no one in particular, "What's his name?"

"Tilmont," Brox called out, moving toward the middle of the crowd. "Andrew Tilmont."

I gave him a slight nod but kept my icy gaze on Tilmont. "Sugar daddy? From the looks of you, you haven't got two wooden nickels to rub together to make a fire."

Tilmont shot me a deadly glare.

"You don't have to like me, Mr. Tilmont, and I assure you the feelin' will be mutual, but if you're here at *this* meeting"—I jabbed my index finger toward the stage—"discussin' the future of *your dick* while the grownups are discussin' the future of our county, then perhaps you need to go back to the kiddie table." I pointed to the back corner where several teens had formed a cluster.

Several men chuckled, and while Tilmont looked furious, I noticed a growing number of men were now giving me their undivided attention.

"I haven't been in this world long, but one thing that has stood out to me from the beginning is the loyalty y'all show to one another." I shook my head. "But I was doubly surprised by the disloyalty. While all y'all have been running around the county switchin' sides and wreakin' havoc with little regard to what was goin' on around you, the enemy's been movin' in like an army of fire ants. Y'all need to stop foolin' around and take this seriously!"

"What do you expect us to do?" someone yelled.

"For one thing, start payin' attention to what's goin' on. Skeeter fired Jed Carlisle back in July—his right-hand man for half his life, if you count when they were kids. Why would he do that?"

Even as I asked the question of them, I asked it of myself. He claimed he was protecting us and I'd believed him, but what if he hadn't wanted the opposition?

From Jed. Or from me.

"Skeeter's been up to something for at least a year," Jed said. "More like two. He'd disappear for days at a time, and after the J.R. Simmons deal, I figured that was the reason why. But he's still doin' it, so where's he goin'?" Jed paused and scanned the crowd. "What man in charge shuts out his second? His *loyal* second? I'll tell you who—someone up to no good."

A few men began to voice their agreement.

"I know for a God-given fact that two of the men in his new inner circle worked with Hardshaw as recently as six months ago."

"You were his second," someone called out. "You're a traitor for turnin' on him."

"I didn't turn on him," Jed said in disgust. "He shut me out until he outright fired me. He won't even take my calls. I gave him my life, and he tossed me out like garbage," he said. "So which one of us is the traitor?"

More men murmured their agreement.

"Why's Lady here?" another man called out.

"Yeah!" someone shouted. "Why's she here?"

"Because she can unite us," Dermot said, stepping forward as Jed stepped back as though they were orchestrating a tag team wrestling match.

He let the men voice their protests before he lifted his hands. "How many of you met Lady last winter?"

A few men shouted that they had.

"How many have heard of her?"

A lot more men spoke up.

"And what did you hear?" Dermot asked.

"That she's a haughty bitch," a man called out, and I recognized him from one of James's meetings from last winter.

"Bear Stevens," I called out, surprised to see him. Not because he was turning against James, but because he'd been a problem for James—one James had told me he'd resolved. I was relieved to know Bear hadn't been killed. The sight of him added a niggle of doubt, but it was too late to turn back now. "Fancy meetin' you here."

"You're a liar," he spat with a look of disgust. "You pretended to be some highfalutin bitch from Louisiana, but you're no better than the rest of us."

"You're right," I agreed in a direct tone. "I misled you about who I really was, but I'm here now as myself, and I'm the same person you met at Skeeter's table and in his office."

"Pretendin' to be someone you're not. How do we know you're not tryin' to hoodwink us now?"

"I guess you can't," I said. "It was Skeeter's story about who I was, not mine, but I'm not sorry I played along. I was trying to protect the man I loved the only way I knew how." I scanned their faces. "How many of you would do the same for someone important to you?"

A murmur went through the crowd.

"I hear you're pregnant with Simmons's baby," a man shouted. "Does he know you're here?"

"No," I said. "He doesn't, but it doesn't matter because he doesn't own me. No man does."

"Not even Skeeter Malcolm?" someone called out.

My back stiffened. "Especially not him."

"Go back to the kitchen!" a man shouted, waving a beer can. He turned to the men next to him, as though waiting for an *atta boy*, but they wisely kept silent.

"You think my place is in the kitchen?" I demanded. "Where the hell were you when J.R. Simmons was tryin' to take over our county? Huh?" I glanced around the crowd and trained my gaze on the guy with the beer can. "I sure as hell wasn't in the kitchen. I was savin' your sorry ass."

A murmur went through the crowd. "I became the Lady in Black to save my boyfriend, and I won't lie to you now," I said, my temper rising. "My baby is a motivating factor. If I went to those lengths to save a man who cut me loose as soon as he found out I'd dirtied myself with the Fenton County underground, just imagine what I'll do to protect my baby. To protect *your* children. I will move heaven and earth to save them all, and I won't apologize for it either."

A soft rumbling reverberated through the crowed, and then someone asked, "And that makes you qualified to rule us?"

I didn't want it, not like that, and there was no doubt that I was far from qualified. Good thing I didn't want to rule them—I only wanted to help them police themselves.

"Answer me this. We live in a democracy, so why is someone rulin' you at all?"

Jed shot me a dark look. He was trying to make me the queen of the county, and this line of reasoning was counterproductive to his aim. But I had to help him, and everyone else, envision a different type of leadership.

"What are you talkin' about?" a man close to the front asked. "Everyone for themselves?"

"Has that worked for you before?" I asked.

"We've never done it before."

"And do you think it would work?" I asked. "You have your own territories. Your own turf. What happens when someone gets greedy and tries to take what someone else has claimed? Sounds like the Wild West to me."

"Then what do you propose?" Bear asked.

"I've acted as a mediator in the past, and I'd like to do the same in the future. I settled a dispute between Skeeter Malcolm and Buck Reynolds with a parley. I stopped an all-out war between them over the kidnapping of Skeeter's brother."

"You want to be like King Solomon," Gerard Collard said, moving forward.

I fixed my gaze on him, surprised he'd voice an opinion since he preferred to keep to himself. Come to think of it, I was surprised he was here at all. "I don't claim to be nearly as wise, but I'd like to listen to both sides and help reach a compromise. This county's seen too much upheaval. We need peace."

"What's in it for you?" someone asked.

"I want peace as well. I want to raise my baby without worryin' about its safety. I don't want to be watchin' over my shoulder, worried that someone's gonna hurt us."

"Just admit that you want a cut of our profits," Bear said.

"Your money is the last thing I want or need. The only currency I want from y'all is protection."

"From what?" Bear demanded.

"From Hardshaw. From Skeeter Malcolm. I don't expect you to stand guard, but I expect you to have my back." I paused, surprised they weren't protesting. "Hardshaw's comin' and you're a disjointed bunch. You can either try fightin' them in your own tiny skirmishes, or you can join forces and fight them together. If you do it that way, you just might have a chance."

Jed stepped forward. "But y'all squabble like a bunch of fishermen's wives. You need someone to mediate."

"Someone who has nothing to gain financially," Dermot said. "We need Lady."

Everyone was so silent that the only sound came from the flames whipping in the breeze until the sound of a slow clap in the back broke the silence and a lone man began walking out of the shadows. He continued forward, still clapping as he said, "Bravo. Great speech. Right up there with Winston Churchill."

He was tall and muscular, and his shaggy light brown hair was messy from the wind. Dark shadows clung to him, but I would have recognized him anywhere.

Denny Carmichael.

I had to wonder if he even knew who Winston Churchill was.

Jed and Dermot tensed and started to push me back behind them, but I held my ground. "Do you have a problem with this proposal, Mr. Carmichael?"

He gave me an amused grin. "You *do* realize that Malcolm still considers you his?"

I gave him a defiant glare. "The only person I belong to is myself."

"Maybe so," Carmichael said, "but he's still laid claim. Sounds to me like this is an elaborate ruse you've created to break free from him and get us to do your dirty work and protect you."

"I've made no secret that I want protection from Skeeter Malcolm, and I suspect an alliance with the other players in town will hold him at bay, but there's more to this situation and you know it, Denny Carmichael. The Sugar Branch Police Department is a prime example."

His eyes narrowed as he studied me, a mocking grin spread across his face. "Touché."

"It won't stop there," I said. "You know Hardshaw's comin' after you first. You're too big of a threat for them to ignore. Wouldn't it be nice to not face it alone?"

His grin faded. "No one rules me. No one."

"No one wants to rule you, but you have to admit there's safety in numbers."

"You're naïve if you think this will work."

I held out my hands. "What do you have to lose by givin' it a try?"

"My business. My reputation. My life."

Dermot gestured to him. "Seems to me you might lose those anyway."

Carmichael clenched his fists. "So I'm supposed to serve the whims of a woman who's not even part of this world?"

"He's right," I said, turning to Dermot. "It's their lives. They should have the final say."

"What are you suggestin'?" Dermot asked.

"They should have a say. They should have a vote." I turned back to face Carmichael. "Like a council. Majority rules."

"Lady is the tiebreaker," Dermot said. "Lady runs the meetings."

Carmichael eyed me closely. Then a smug smile lit up his eyes. "I agree to your terms."

He'd agreed much too quickly and easily to suit me, but to call him out on it would make him lose face, and that was not a skirmish I wanted to invite. Not yet.

"Carmichael has joined us," Jed called out to the others. "Who's with us?"

The majority signed up, and Jed and Dermot told them we'd be in touch to arrange the next meeting setting up the council rules. As they all left, they paraded past us, shaking our hands as a sign of our commitment, but when Carmichael shook my hand, he held it a little too long and he leaned into my ear and whispered, "You still owe me, little girl, and I plan to collect."

He walked away with a shit-eating grin, and I wondered if we'd just been played.

Chapter Thirty-Two

J oe was waiting on the porch when we got back to the farmhouse. I told Jed and Neely Kate to go home. After everything, it felt like I should be the one to allay his concerns.

"You went as the Lady in Black," he said in surprise, and I remembered he hadn't seen me before I left.

"Not Lady," I said with a wry smile. "No hat."

"They all know she's you, so do you need one?"

"Good point."

Conflict flashed in his eyes before he said, "I don't want to know what happened, but I *do* want to know if you're safe now."

I paused. "Not entirely, but I'm safer than I was before the meetin'."

He nodded. "I hope you know what you're doin', Rose."

"I hope so too."

I went upstairs and looked in on Violet. She lay propped up on her pillows, her eyes closed, but her breathing sounded slightly congested, confirming my biggest fear. She was coming down with something.

When I went to bed, I couldn't sleep despite the fact that I was exhausted. I couldn't help feeling like I'd betrayed James, even though he'd turned his back on me first.

Finally, my brain surrendered, and I was sleeping so deeply that I dreamt that James was next to me, his mouth on my neck, skimming up to my lips, his fingers tracing my collarbone.

"James," I breathed out, turning to my side. I wrapped my arm around his back, and something in my head questioned why he was wearing a shirt in bed. He'd never worn clothes in bed before.

My eyes flew open and I gasped at the realization that James was actually in my bed. In my house. Fully clothed and lying next to me.

Moonlight streamed through the windows, illuminating his features.

He pushed me onto my back and his hand wrapped around my throat, resting there lightly. "I could strangle you right now, Rose. They'd be none the wiser that I was here."

My pulse picked up, which I was sure he could feel, but I didn't try to push his hand away. "You won't."

"I could."

"You won't. You love me."

His hand slid down to rest over my breast. "You betrayed me, Rose. You're doin' what I've spent the last year tryin' to accomplish. You're pullin' this county together." His fingertip traced my collarbone. "You're turnin' them against me."

I would have been scared if I'd heard malice in his voice, but I heard only regret.

"You turned them against yourself," I whispered. "I'm only gathering the scattered pieces."

He stared into my eyes and I couldn't read his expression. I had no idea how he'd gotten inside, but I knew he could kill me in an instant, just as I knew he wouldn't. I knew I should tell him off and kick him out, but I needed this time with him. I needed closure.

"You're playin' a dangerous game, Rose. You can't trust most of them." Again, he didn't sound angry. He sounded resigned.

So he knew about the meeting tonight, not that I was surprised. "I know."

"Carmichael will look for the first opportunity to turn on you. He'll watch you build this alliance, standing on the periphery, then he'll try to take it for himself as soon as he thinks it's solid."

I stared into his impassive face. "I already know he's up to somethin'."

"Pay close attention to Martin. If he and Ledger spend too much time together, they start blabbin'."

I had no idea who Martin and Ledger were, but I filed that in the back of my mind for later. Why was he telling me all of this?

"Things are about to become a lot more dangerous. If Hardshaw catches wind of what happened tonight..."

I sat up, feeling wary for the first time. "You're gonna tell them?"

"Not me," he said with a sad smile, lying on his side and staring up at me. "But they'll know."

"Did you try to have me killed?" I asked with a hard edge in my voice.

Hurt filled his eyes, and he pushed up to sit next to me on the bed, his body vibrating with tension. "You think I'm capable of killin' you?"

"That doesn't really answer my question, does it?" When he didn't say anything, I asked, "Did you tell Carter Hale to pay me off to abort our baby?"

Anger filled his eyes. "You can't have this baby, Rose."

I got off the bed, shooting a glare at him. "Unfortunately for you, you have no choice in the matter."

"You have to pick, Rose," he said, anger in his voice. "Me or the baby. You can't have both."

"Are you serious?" I demanded. "And if I decide to keep it? Will you try to force an abortion on me?" My eyes narrowed. "Because fair warning, Skeeter Malcolm, I will never forgive you. *Never.*"

"You actually *want* this baby?" he asked in disbelief. "Were you *plannin'* this?"

"I wouldn't trick a man into havin' a baby with me any more than I would trick a man into staying in a relationship with me."

He shook his head. "And yet you're throwing us away to have this kid?"

"*You're* throwin' us away, because I'm choosing to keep *our* baby. *Your* baby."

"I can't have a kid, Rose," he said through gritted teeth. "So yeah, you're throwin' us away."

My anger surged. "You threw us away before I even *knew* about this baby. You threw us away when you bought the Sugar Branch Police Department. You threw us away when you decided to throw your lot in with Hardshaw. You threw *me* away when you sent those men to that pharmacy knowin' they would kill anyone who saw them."

"I didn't know you were there, Rose."

"So you did condone them killin' an innocent witness?"

His confidence wavered. "Some things are out of my control."

"What's that mean?"

He shook his head. "You don't need to know."

I'd had enough of his deflections. "For once in this pathetic mess we call a relationship, I wish you'd just tell me the truth. Include me in your life. Tell me what in the hell is goin' on! This isn't love, James. Ignoring me and orderin' me to kill our baby isn't love!"

"I don't know how many ways I can tell you this, Rose, but I *do not* want a kid," he said through gritted teeth. "If you do this, you do this without me. You do it alone."

I steeled my shoulders, glaring up at him. "I already know that, James Malcolm. I'm not the complete fool you think I am. Besides, I'm not alone. I have my friends."

He cursed under his breath and stormed toward the window, staring out into the front yard.

I was furious with him, yet I could see he was hurting. Despite everything, that still mattered.

"What are you *doin'*, James?" I pleaded. "Let me help you."

"You're not goin' to that appointment tomorrow, are you?" he asked.

"The abortion appointment?" I asked in surprise. "No. I'm not, but I want nothin' from you. Just leave us be, and we'll do the same."

He turned toward me with a hard glint in his eyes. "I don't call stealin' the loyalty of over half the criminals in this county leavin' me be."

"You've invited the devil into our backyard, Skeeter Malcolm. Don't expect me to sit back and do nothin'."

He took several steps toward me, but his anger had faded and was replaced by acceptance.

"Why in God's name are you workin' with Hardshaw?" I whispered. "What's your endgame, James?"

He lifted his hand to my cheek, his fingertips trailing across my cheekbone. "My endgame was you, Rose, but the baby changed everything. This wasn't part of the plan."

That pissed me off. "Don't you put this on me. How does aligning yourself with Hardshaw play into *me* bein' your endgame?"

He shook his head. "That baby deserves more than my sorry ass could ever give it." Then he brushed past me, reaching for the door.

"James."

He turned back to face me. "From this moment on, we're on opposite sides of a war. Take no prisoners, Rose, because you're a general now."

"Against you?"

"This is bigger than me," he said. "Once I walk out of this room, we have to cease all contact. I mean it, Rose. You can't talk to me again, and you can't be comin' to the pool hall. It's bein' watched. You have to treat me as your enemy, and I'll do the same."

"*No.*"

He released a bitter laugh. "You're the queen of Fenton County now. If you show one iota of concern for me, you'll lose half your army."

He was right, and I knew it. I started to reach for him to force a vision, but he walked out the door without another word.

I considered going after him, but just like Skeeter Malcolm didn't chase after women, I wasn't going to chase after a man who'd pushed me away.

Chapter Thirty-Three

I couldn't sleep after James left, so around dawn, I got up to check on Violet, worried after hearing her congestion the night before. Her body was burning up and sweat drenched her hair and thin nightgown.

"Violet," I said, grabbing her hand as I tried not to panic. "Why didn't you call for me?"

She gave me a weak smile. "I had to make sure you had plenty of time with your man."

I froze. "James? You knew he was here?"

A tiny chuckle shook her body. Then she broke into a coughing fit. When she'd caught her breath, she said, "Who do you think told him to come?"

"I don't understand."

"I won't be here when you have your baby, Rose. I needed to be sure."

"Sure about what? What did you say, Violet?" Had she convinced him to leave me?

"That's between him and me. He made me swear not to tell you, and I assured him I would take it to my grave, which I also assured him would happen in the very near future."

"Vi!"

"I wasn't meddlin', Rose. I swear. I only wanted to know his intentions. That was the one last thing I needed to know."

She broke into another coughing fit, and Carly burst into the room, her eyes wide with panic. "I'll call hospice."

"No," Violet said. "There's nothing to be done. I'm ready for the end."

Carly insisted on calling them anyway while I stayed by Violet's side. Joe came up soon afterward, and we sat on either side of her bed, watching her struggle to breathe. She let me put wet washcloths on her forehead but refused to take anything for the fever.

"The inevitable is comin', Rose," she said, leaning back into her pillows with her eyes closed. "I have no say in my death sentence, at least let me have a say in how it ends."

I walked out of the room to get myself together, and Joe followed, reaching for me. He paused and looked me over with a scrutinizing glance, then pulled me to his chest as I started to cry.

"I can't let her do this, Joe," I said. "I have power of attorney. I can make her accept treatment to fight this off."

"Yeah," he said. "You can, but that's not what she wants, and it won't buy her much more time even if it gives her another few days or weeks. Don't make this a battle, Rose. She's tired. She's said her goodbyes. Let her do this her way."

"I can't just tell her goodbye. Not like this. Not yet."

"It's not your choice, darlin'," he said, looking down at me with a soft smile. "You can't hold on to someone who's ready to go."

My chin trembled as I selfishly thought about James. Had he really been ready to go? I didn't think so, but I couldn't make him stay with me either. He'd chosen his own solitary confinement, but Vi...

Tears pooled in my eyes.

I wouldn't let her die alone.

Once she decided it was time to leave, she didn't last long.

I sat by her side as we watched clouds roll in through the sunroom windows.

"I thought you wanted a sunny day to die," I chided. "Let's wait. I'll get some antibiotics."

"You can't just get antibiotics like they're Tic Tacs," she said with a tiny laugh.

"Try me," I said. "I know a guy."

She smiled, then trained her gaze on the window. "The sun will come out."

"You can't will the sun to come out, Violet Gardner," I said. "Not even *you* can control the weather."

"We'll see," was all she would say. Then she drifted off to sleep, her chest heaving as her lungs made a rattling sound.

People came in and out—Joe, Carly, Neely Kate, and Jed. Jonah stopped by to pray with her, and peace filled her eyes as she thanked him. The hospice nurse stayed close by, checking her vital signs from time to time, but she mostly stayed in the background. But the kids were conspicuously absent. When Violet had moved in, she'd made us all promise not to bring the kids to her deathbed, to spare them the trauma of her death.

Early in the afternoon, I convinced Violet to at least use some oxygen so she didn't have to struggle so much. She hated the nasal canula, saying it irritated her nose, but she kept it in anyway. I lay on the bed next to her, holding her hand as we stared up at the ceiling, and I thought about all the times we'd done this as kids, barely older than Ashley and Mikey. She'd always made me feel so loved, and although she hadn't been able to protect me, she'd ensured I didn't feel alone.

And when it became harder and harder for her to breathe, each breath sounding like she was being dragged through hell, I leaned into her ear and whispered, "I've held you back your entire life, Violet. It's time for you to find your own way now. I'll be okay on my own."

A soft smile spread across her face as she took one last shallow breath and a ray of sun broke through the clouds, filling the sunroom with a golden light.

When I realized she was really gone, I fell on top of her, sobbing. After I felt like I'd poured out my grief for an eternity, Joe gently gathered me in his arms and pulled me away so the hospice nurse could do what she needed to do.

"Maybe you need to lie down, Rose," he said, his face pinched with worry. "I'll sit with you if you like."

I looked up into the face of the man who'd stood by my side in all of this, never asking for anything in return. That was love too.

"No. I need to go outside."

"Do you want me to come with you?"

"Yes."

Bruce Wayne had known what I would need without asking. He'd left a flat of purple chrysanthemums and a spade on the front porch, along with a card that simply said, *I'm so sorry*.

Joe carried the flat to the flower bed at the corner of the house, and I turned to the one thing—other than Violet—that had always given me comfort...communing with the dirt.

❧

VIOLET'S FUNERAL WAS the next Monday afternoon, and it was as though she'd special-ordered the weather—warm and sunny.

After my initial grief, I'd handled Violet's death fairly well, but preparing for the funeral had helped keep me occupied. Carly wasn't handling it well at all, and I realized for the past month Carly's days had been consumed by my sister. She was rudderless now. So we put her in charge of the after-funeral party, and while that had helped, I worried about how she would handle Tuesday.

She was part of our little family now. We'd have to band together to make sure she got through this.

Jed had handled the situation with Wendy. She'd given him scanty details about working for James over the past few months, in exchange for which he'd given her a few hundred dollars and a bus ticket to Memphis. We'd all agreed it was safest for her to leave Fenton County. Neely Kate told me with a smug grin that Wendy had left the house spotless.

Dr. Newton called to offer her condolences, then reminded me I needed to come in for an ultrasound as soon as possible so we could see how far along I was in my pregnancy. Without thinking, I made the appointment for Monday morning. I nearly cancelled it but decided Violet would have insisted I go.

੭੶੶ਓ

MONDAY MORNING, I awoke sad and lonely. I was about to see my baby for the first time, and I didn't want to do it alone. Neely Kate would have come in a heartbeat, and had offered to do so, but I was worried it would hurt her too much.

Mostly, though, I was upset by the thought that my baby would never have a father. Neither of my parents had protected or cherished me, and I wanted more for my baby. I wanted him or her to be loved by two parents. I couldn't shake the thought that Joe would make an amazing father. And the sooner he was part of my baby's memories, the better.

Joe usually went into the sheriff's office early on Mondays, so I hurried downstairs in my pajamas and with morning breath, catching him as he poured coffee into a to-go mug.

"Joe, do you have a moment?"

He must have heard the urgency in my voice because he stopped putting the lid on his mug and turned to face me. "Of course. Is everything okay?"

"Do you have time to sit?"

He checked his watch.

"This will only take a moment."

"Rose," he said, clasping my hand and tugging me to the table. "I was only tryin' to figure out if I needed to call to let them know I'll be late. I'll always have time for you. Talk to me."

I sat at the head of the table while he turned the chair on the side of table toward me.

I took a deep breath, unsure how to broach this.

Worry filled his eyes. "Do you need me to stay home with you this mornin'? I shouldn't have set my meeting before the funeral," he said. "I can just move it to tomorrow."

"No. That's not it." I shook my head. "Or maybe it is." I looked into his warm brown eyes. "I'm havin' an ultrasound this mornin'."

His eyes widened. "Oh."

"About your offer…" I paused. "Are you sure, Joe?"

"About bein' your baby's father?" He leaned forward, determination in his eyes. "I've never been more certain of anything in my life."

"Even if we're not together?" I asked, glancing down at my lap. We'd discussed this before, but it felt right to bring it up again. He needed to be sure. We both did. "I'm in no place to even consider a relationship with anyone, Joe." I forced myself to look up at him. "So if this is an attempt to start something with me…"

"I know we're over, Rose. That's not my goal here." A smile cracked his lips. "I want to be a dad. More than I want to be in a relationship, as weird as that sounds. I've already told you I don't trust my judgment in women, but I want someone to love." His brow furrowed. "Does that sound stupid?"

I placed my hand on my belly. "That doesn't sound stupid at all."

"If you want to do this, I promise I won't up and change my mind. I'm in this for keeps. I won't abandon you. Or the baby."

"You don't feel like I'm usin' you?"

He laughed. "I'm more worried you'll think I'm usin' you. Now what time's the appointment?"

"Ten, but I can move it."

"No way," he said, beaming. "I'll be done with my meeting by then. Is it okay if I meet you there?"

"Of course. Thank you, Joe."

He stood, then leaned over and kissed my forehead. "Oh, Rose. Thank *you*."

కా~

I SHOWED UP A FEW MINUTES before my ten o'clock appointment, and Loretta told me I could go right back.

"Joe's not here," I told the nurse at the open doorway, glancing toward the office entrance. "I don't want to do this without him."

"Not to worry," she said with a warm smile. "When he shows up, we'll bring him right back."

I sent him a text telling him I'd already gone back to the room, but he still hadn't responded by the time I hopped up on the table. Nor by the time the tech lifted my shirt and squirted the cold gel on my abdomen.

"Dr. Newton thinks you're near the end of the first trimester," the tech said, "so we opted to try it this way first. If it looks like it's much earlier, we'll try it vaginally."

"Okay," I said, glancing at the door.

"Don't worry," the tech said good-naturedly as she turned on the machine. "If he doesn't make this one, we'll be doin' another one between eighteen to twenty weeks." She turned to me and winked. "Most daddies prefer that one, truth be told. We'll be able to see more then."

353

Maybe so, but Joe wasn't most daddies. I knew he'd want to be involved in every part.

She placed the wand on my belly and started to push it around. "This might be a bit uncomfortable."

Gray and white splotches filled the screen, but it didn't take long for her to stop and say, "Well, Dr. Newton was right. There's your baby, Rose."

I'd expected to see an abstract blob, but there on the screen, in the middle of a large black space was a head and body, with wisps that faded in and out, suggesting arms and legs.

"See its heart?" she said, pointing to the screen. I saw a fluttering in its chest. Then she turned a knob and a rapid heartbeat filled the room.

"I wish Joe were here," I said, fighting back tears.

"I'm here!" he said breathlessly as he rushed through the door. "Sorry, I got detained." He shook out his hand, and I saw bruises and scrapes on his knuckles.

"What happened?" I asked in alarm. "You need ice on that, Joe."

"It can wait. Nothin' and no one is keepin' me from this."

Then I realized what had kept him—my vision of his fight with Mason had come to fruition. Part of me wanted to chastise him for getting into an altercation, but he needed to claim ownership of this baby, and if that was one of the ways he saw fit to do it, I'd give it to him. This time.

He moved to the top of the table and stared at the screen, sucking in a breath. "There's your baby, Rose."

Tears filled my eyes as I looked up at him. "*Our* baby."

I lifted my hand to hold his and held on tight as we watched our baby moving on the screen.

"Your baby's an active little thing," the tech said with a smile. "It's makin' it hard for me to get measurements." Then she glanced back at me with a huge grin. "But you get more time watching it, so it's a win for you."

The screen kept freezing as she took measurements, and she finally said, "This is only an estimate since you've been havin' spotty periods, but it looks like you're eleven weeks and three days, which puts your due date at May third."

"May," I whispered. It seemed so far away, yet I knew it would arrive before I knew it.

She printed off a photo and handed it to me. "Your baby's first photo."

I took it, relieved that it was an image that captured the shape if its body perfectly, showing a little arm lifted up by its head.

"Can we get one for the baby's daddy too?" I asked.

She grinned. "Of course."

She printed off another picture and Joe took it, beaming.

The tech wiped off my belly, then stood. "I'll give you two a few minutes alone."

She walked out of the room, shutting the door behind her. Joe helped me sit up, then stood in front of me with an anxious look on his face.

"Is everything okay?" I asked. "Is this all too much? You don't have to do this, Joe. I shouldn't have accepted."

"No, Rose," he said in a rush. "No. You have no idea how much I want this." He looked torn, as if he weren't sure how much to say, but his eyes filled with purpose and he continued. "So much so that it's given me pause. *Why* do I want to be part of this? You and I aren't together, and if we don't get back together, it could be very complicated. Sharing custody. Sharing holidays. It could get really messy. Because if we do this, Rose, you can't take it back. You can't tell me I'm part of this baby's life then change your mind." His eyes turned glassy. "I'm gonna be honest with you, Rose. I don't think I could survive that."

Was I doing the right thing? He was right. This was something I couldn't take back. Joe would be part of my life—and my baby's life—forever. But as much as I loved James, he'd told me time and time again he didn't want a family. He didn't want this baby, and my baby deserved to be showered with love. This baby would never doubt that it was loved and wanted. Ever.

Joe could give it that and more.

I slowly shook my head. "I'm not gonna change my mind. And as for our romantic lives and the future...I have no idea what's going to happen. All I know is that you'll be the most amazin' father. We'll figure out the rest as we go along." A lump filled my throat. "For the first time ever, I feel I've got something really *good* in my life. Something that's mine and that no one can take from me, you know?"

He nodded, his eyes filling with tears. "I do."

"But it's something so big and so wonderful, I'm bursting with its goodness, and I don't want to keep it to myself. I want to share it with someone." I gave him a soft smile. "I want to share it with you, Joe."

Joe smiled back. "We've got plenty of time to work out the logistics." He picked up my hand and held it gently in his. "We'll figure out the rest. Together."

I was counting on it.

Bonus Scene
Violet

I knew my death was imminent, but I wasn't ready to go quite yet.

I still had unfinished business.

I needed to speak to Skeeter Malcolm.

I'd made sure the kids were taken care of, and that Rose would be surrounded by the family of her choosing, but her pregnancy both eased my worries and added additional concerns.

I'd suspected her lover was Skeeter Malcolm from the moment she'd told me about the mysterious man she loved. Why would she withhold his name unless she was ashamed of the relationship? Only I was fairly certain she wasn't ashamed of it at all. She was merely secretive to protect them both, but from what? The authorities? His associates? His enemies?

All the same, I'd thought that they were over. She'd spent the last two months moping around the farmhouse, and if she'd made any secretive trips to see him, I suspect I would have noticed. I knew all about secretive trips to see a man. I could have written a book on it.

So imagine my surprise when she told me she was pregnant with Skeeter Malcolm's baby. Maybe the news should have upset me—she wasn't married, after all, and the father was a criminal— but if anyone could handle having a baby in an unconventional way, it was my baby sister. I was proud that Rose had learned to stop caring what other people thought, or at least she'd stopped caring quite so much. Besides, having a baby out of wedlock wasn't the scandal it had been even twenty-five years ago when her birth mother had her. But the father presented a whole new set of problems, and I was determined to stick around until I knew Rose and her baby were safe.

Which meant I needed to take matters into my own hands.

When Carly was downstairs making me homemade chicken noodle soup, a task I'd sent her on to buy me some time alone, I used my cell phone to call the pool hall Skeeter owned. I wasn't surprised when the man who answered told me he wasn't available, but I knew what card to play.

"Tell him I have information about the Murray portfolio."

Rose wasn't the only Gardner with tricks up her sleeve.

"What the hell is that?" the man asked in annoyance.

"Just tell him and let him decide if he wants to talk to me or not."

Twenty seconds later, a deep, angry male voice snarled, "Who the hell is this?"

"I have information," I said in a quiet but firm tone, "but I need to make sure I'm speaking to the right person."

"I don't know anything about a Murray portfolio, so you're barking up the wrong tree." His annoyance rang through loud and clear.

He was lying, not that I was surprised. I hadn't expected him to admit it so readily over the phone. I could be anyone on a fishing expedition. Only I wasn't fishing.

"I know there's two million dollars on the line." I felt the urge to cough, but I held it back as best I could lest he'd think me weak. "You've got a lot riding on it."

He paused so long I thought maybe he'd hung up. "If I had any idea what you were talkin' about, I'd be curious how you'd come by this information."

"I'll tell you everything I know, but you have to come to me. We meet in person. It's safer that way."

He paused again. "Like I said, I'm not sure what you're talking about, but I'm concerned for the well-being of the county. I'll meet you at the Holiday Inn in two hours. I'll text you the room number."

"Sorry," I said, my voice tight and raspy from suppressing the cough. "Like I said, you're gonna have to come to me."

"And where the hell is that?" he barked.

I couldn't stop my small smile. He saw my protest as a sign of defiance. He was a man who liked to control people and situations. How else could he have earned his place in the underworld? What I found surprising was that Rose had shucked the cloak of control our momma had wrapped tight around her only to run into the arms of someone even more domineering, not to mention ruthless. Especially after she'd shied away from Joe for showing those very same traits.

But what really piqued my interest, and another reason for this summons, was why he was so interested in *her*. I loved my sister more than life itself, but I couldn't understand the appeal she'd have for a man like Skeeter Malcolm. She was pretty but not sexy. She had no illegal ventures of her own for him to exploit. The only reason I could come up with was her visions—which she'd readily admitted he was not only aware of but had used for his own purposes.

"I suspect you can find me without any directions," I said, trying not to sound smug. "I'm in Rose's old bedroom."

His previous silences had held a bit of threat to them. This one seemed different, though, which was confirmed when he said my name.

"Violet?" The bite had gone out of his tone.

"You've heard of me?" I asked, and the cough I'd been holding in burst out. It took me several seconds to regain control.

"I'll come see you," he said, his tone quiet. "But it won't be until much later tonight. After midnight."

"After Rose's grand jury testimony?"

He hesitated, then sounded unsure. "Yeah."

"And if I invite you into Rose's home, should I be concerned for her or Joe's safety?"

I'd expected him to mull it over, but his answer was immediate. "No. But you can't tell them I'm comin' either. Especially Rose. This is between you and me."

"Do you want me to tell Carly to leave the back door unlocked?"

"No. I can let myself in."

Did he have a key? Did Joe know?

"Then I'll see you later tonight, James Malcolm," I said, using his proper name like Rose always did. "I'll likely be asleep, but wake me up when you get here."

He merely hung up, not that I was surprised by the lack of pleasantries. I suspected he was a man of few words. Another reason to question what Rose saw in him.

As the day wore on, everyone tried to shield me from the tension over Rose's grand jury testimony, but it hung in the air like one of Muffy's farts. I was relieved when Rose came home and told me she was safe from Mason Deveraux's treachery…the ungrateful bastard.

I'd expected to be anxious as the evening progressed, but everything felt right, like all the threads of my life were weaving their last row. I wasn't worried about my meeting with Skeeter Malcolm. I knew I had the upper hand.

I slept better than I had in days, but there was a heaviness in my chest that assured me I'd been right to call him now. I was sure I didn't have much longer.

Of course, there was a chance he wouldn't show. He was taking a risk slipping into Rose's house in the middle of the night—Joe could easily wake up and shoot him—but Skeeter Malcolm didn't strike me as the kind of guy who'd let a little thing like possible death keep her from what he wanted. Men like Skeeter Malcolm hadn't gotten as far as they had without taking risks.

What I knew about the Murray portfolio definitely made it worth the potential peril.

He didn't say anything to wake me, at least not that I noticed. One minute I was asleep and then I was awake, his large frame silhouetted by the moonlight streaming through the sunporch windows.

"Skeeter Malcolm," I said, my voice raspy. "You're gonna have to help me sit up."

He moved closer, granting me a better look at him. He was tall with broad shoulders and enough muscles to ensure he could enforce his orders, yet he didn't look like a bodybuilder. He was a handsome man and I could understand my sister's attraction to him. While there was a hardness to his face, his eyes softened as he approached me.

"What do you need me to do?" he whispered.

"Wrap your arm around my back. Then plump my pillows behind me."

"Do you want me to turn on a light?" he asked, sounding hesitant.

"No, the moonlight seems appropriate."

He was surprisingly gentle as he lifted me then resettled my pillows. When he finished, he took a step backward, studying me.

"I'm not gonna beat around the bush, Mr. Malcolm," I said, trying to sound direct. "I need to know what your intentions are with my sister."

He didn't look surprised by my question. "If you're askin' if I'm an honorable man, I think my actions speak for themselves."

"That doesn't answer my question," I said. "I asked you about your *intentions*, whether they be devious or loving."

A sly grin spread across his face. "Who's to say I'll be honest?"

"You'd lie to a dyin' woman?"

"I've done a hell of a lot worse." It wasn't a threat and it bore no arrogance. It was merely spoken as truth.

"But you won't lie to me," I said with more confidence than I felt, then went out on a limb. "You love her too much."

Something washed over his face. Leeriness? Regret? I knew how he'd reacted to her pregnancy, but I couldn't help wondering why he'd said those hateful things. His very countenance told me he loved her.

"This needs to stay between us," he said, his tone turning hard. "You can't tell Rose anything I say."

"I'll take it to my grave, which is right around the corner."

Surprise filled his eyes, but it was gone just as quickly. "I'm here about the Murray portfolio," he said, adding a gruffness to his voice. "You know something about it?"

"I do. And what I know is in a sealed file at my attorney's office."

He quirked his brow, his shoulders tensing slightly. "I take it you learned this from your husband?"

"He didn't tell me, if that's what you're implyin', but I was privy to a conversation I wasn't part of."

"You eavesdropped."

I released a tiny laugh. "I'm not ashamed of it. I've spent most of my life eavesdroppin' to protect my sister from the cruelty in this world. Do I need to protect her from you, Skeeter Malcolm?"

He remained still, his expression unreadable.

"Which brings me back to my original question. What are your intentions with Rose?" I paused, wondering if I should tell him the next part, but I suspected he already knew. "She loves you. She's been pinin' for you for two months. And no, she never once told me it was you that she was pinin' over, and no, it wasn't obvious, but I know my sister. I've spent twenty-five years of my life watchin' over her."

"If she didn't tell you, then why am I here?" he grunted.

"Because while I suspected it was you, she confirmed it when she told me that she was pregnant and that you were the father."

"She's tellin' people?" he demanded, his hands fisting at his sides.

"I'm her sister, Skeeter Malcolm, and on my deathbed to boot. Her secret is safe with me." I took a breath, already tiring out. "You told her to get an abortion. Did you tell her that in the heat of the moment?"

"No," he said, his voice tight. "She can't have my baby."

"Well, here's a news flash. She's not changin' her mind."

Some of his edges dulled. "I know."

"So you either need to man up and marry her or you need to let her go."

"You really want *me* to marry your sister?" he asked, sounding incredulous.

"It's not what I want that matters. It's what Rose wants for her and her baby." When he didn't respond, I gave into my curiosity and asked, "Why don't you want the baby?"

Anger flashed in his eyes. "My world is dangerous. I already have to shield Rose from it. How in God's name would I protect a kid? It would never be safe. I'd be forever lookin' over my shoulder to make sure no one was comin' for my family."

"So give it up," I said, my energy fading. "Marry Rose and run away."

"I can't."

"You *can't* or you *won't*?"

"If I run, I'll be hunted down. It will only make it more dangerous for *them*."

"I commend you for realizin' that. Seems to me that a man in your position would be accustomed to takin' what he wants, regardless of the consequences."

"I was that man. Rose changed me. But make no mistake, I'm still mostly selfish. I'm only soft where she's concerned."

"So man up and do what you need to do to make sure your family is safe."

"It's more than that, Violet. I don't want a baby." He must have seen that wasn't argument enough for me because he continued without prompting. "I had a shitty childhood. I don't want that for my kid."

"Rose had a shitty childhood too, but she'll make an amazin' mother, so don't give me that malarkey."

"I don't trust myself to be a father. I don't want my kid to be scared of me, either because of how I treated him or once he found out who I am and what I do. My kid deserves better than that."

"Then be a better man, James Malcolm. Be the man that Rose and your baby deserve."

"That's what I'm tryin' to do, Violet," he said, meeting my gaze and holding it, "which is why I'm pushin' her away."

And suddenly I understood. "By insisting she get an abortion."

"There's no way in hell she'll go through with it, and the harder I push, the more she'll pull away."

"You really do love her," I whispered.

"More than I've ever loved anything in my life. But she deserves better than me. And that baby deserves a daddy, not a criminal who will ruin both of their lives."

"James." I stretched my hand out toward him.

He glanced down at it. For a moment, I thought he was going to ignore the gesture, but then he took my hand in his, holding it as gently as if it were a baby bird.

"Rose is no fool. If she loves you, there's something in you worth lovin'."

He swallowed. "But sometimes it's not enough."

"I wish it were."

"Me too." He dropped my hand and took a step back. "The Murray portfolio... what do you plan to do with the information?"

"I'm usin' it to give Rose full custody of my kids. It will be released upon my death, which is comin' sooner than I'd expected, so get your Ps and Qs in order, Skeeter Malcolm, because the police are gonna be at your doorstep unless you cover your tracks."

"You'd really turn on your husband?"

I lifted my chin and tried to give him a glare, but I just didn't have the energy for it. "He already turned on me."

"So why are you warnin' *me*?"

"Because of Rose."

My eyelids were heavy, and as my energy fled, I sank back into the pillows. "Make yourself worthy of them, even if they never know, James Malcolm."

I closed my eyes and seconds later, I felt lips brush my forehead.

"Have a good death, Violet Beauregard," he said, his voice raspy with emotion. "Your sister will miss you more than you know."

"She'll miss us both," I murmured.

"Yes," he said, so softly I could barely hear him. "She will."

Then he slipped out of the room.

About the Author

*N*ew York Times and *USA Today* bestselling author Denise Grover Swank was born in Kansas City, Missouri and lived in the area until she was nineteen. Then she became a nomadic gypsy, living in five cities, four states and ten houses over the course of ten years before she moved back to her roots. She speaks English and smattering of Spanish and Chinese which she learned through an intensive Nick Jr. immersion period. Her hobbies include witty Facebook comments (in her own mind) and dancing in her kitchen with her children. (Quite badly if you believe her offspring.) Hidden talents include the gift of justification and the ability to drink massive amounts of caffeine and still fall asleep within two minutes. Her lack of the sense of smell allows her to perform many unspeakable tasks. She has six children and hasn't lost her sanity. Or so she leads you to believe.

You can find out more about Denise and her other books at www.denisegroverswank.com

Don't miss out on Denise's newest releases! Join her mailing list: http://denisegroverswank.com/mailing-list/